FALLEN ANGEL

"Please! Don't do that," Hannah said.

"What would you prefer I do? Do white men arouse their women differently? Or do you wish me to pay in white man's coin to lie with you?"

Hannah shoved at his chest, trying to push him away. It was too dark to see his expression but the warmth of his silver eyes and the heat of his body scorched her flesh. "I'm not what you think. I've never lain with a man."

Wind Rider laughed harshly. "Perhaps you've never lain with an Indian but I know you've lain with white men. Do not lie, Hannah McLin, for I know what it means when a woman is called whore. Do not fear, Little Sparrow, I am capable of giving you pleasure if I so desire. Did you receive pleasure from the others or was their coin more important to you than their manhood?"

WIND RIDER

Connie Mason

LEISURE BOOKS **NEW YORK CITY**

To Jerry, you've been my hero for 44 years.
And to our children, Jeri, Michelle, and Mark.
I love you all.

WIND RIDER

Chapter One

December 1864

Hannah's eyes clung with desperate appeal to those of the tall, silver-eyed man before he turned and strode away. He paused to glance at her over his broad shoulder, and in those brief moments of visual contact she was moved by a profound sense of loss. Then Mr. Harley shoved her inside the inn and the stranger was lost from sight.

"Get upstairs, girl," Burton Harley growled as he pushed Hannah through the door into the common room of the inn.

"Hey, Harley," one of the patrons shouted as he nudged Hannah toward the stairs, "you're gonna have to clean her up some if you expect me and the boys to pay good coin to bed her."

Hannah pushed the matted mass of her dishwater-hued hair from her eyes as she resisted the hard pull of Harley's hands. Her dirty brown dress hung like a gunnysack from her bony shoulders, and she wondered how anyone could look at her with desire. The filth that covered her body and clung to her oversized, ragged clothing created a stench she could barely tolerate herself. Yet she welcomed her pitiful state, for it had protected her from unwanted attention until now. Despite her best efforts to appear unnattractive, Mr. Harley had begun eyeing her in a speculative manner. And just today he had suggested that she earn her keep in a way that had shocked and disgusted her.

"I'll see that Hannah smells right pretty for you, Billy," Harley snickered. "It's gonna cost you, though. I wouldn't be surprised if the little Irish slut is a virgin."

Raucous laughter and lewd remarks followed Harley's words, and Hannah turned crimson to the roots of her grimy hair. When she'd indentured herself and sailed to America to become a servant, never in her wildest dreams had she envisioned a master like Burton Harley. She had left Ireland hoping to ease the burden upon her impoverished father, who had seven younger children at home to support. It had seemed a good idea until Harley had bought her articles of indenture and brought her to Denver to work in the inn he had recently purchased.

It wasn't that Hannah minded hard work; far from it. She had worked very hard at home. But when Harley slyly suggested she entertain men in the tiny upstairs room she occupied she had balked.

She had reacted by attempting to run away. Mr. Harley had caught her in front of the inn and severely chastised her before a crowd of curious onlookers, none of whom had come to her defense. Not even the tall, dark man with compelling silver eyes. And now Harley expected her to whore for him.

Praying to the God she thought had abandoned her, Hannah resisted wildly as Harley shoved and pushed her up the stairs. Using her body in such a manner was reprehensible to her. When she had left home she was prepared to devote the next seven years to honest, hard work, but not this, never this. Still a virgin at eighteen, she wasn't prepared to lose her innocence to one of the vile men who quaffed ale in the common room of Harley's inn.

Harley had managed to manhandle Hannah to the top of the stairs now, and she was growing desperate. Just as they reached the landing she turned abruptly, poking him hard in the ribs with a bony elbow. Teetering on the landing, Harley made a desperate grab for the railing, lost his balance, and tumbled backwards down the entire length of the staircase, bouncing to the bottom with a thud.

"Damn bitch!" Harley spat, groaning in pain. His face was white as the sheets Hannah bleached each wash day, and his right leg was bent at an odd angle. "Don't just stand there gawking; send for the doctor!"

Harley's timid wife came running into the common room, saw her husband lying on the floor, and ran upstairs to hide in her room until help came. The poor abused woman was so cowed by her bully of a husband that she was frightened of her own shadow.

When the doctor finally arrived he found that Harley had not only broken a leg but fractured an arm as well, which in all likelihood would immobilize him for the rest of the winter. Hannah's prayers had been answered; not in the way she had expected, but she had certainly gotten a reprieve. With Harley flat on his back for weeks to come, he no longer had the power to force her into prostitution. She had plenty of time now to plan her escape. By the time Mr. Harley was back on his feet the weather would be warm and she could make her way to Cheyenne, where her cousin, Seamus McLin, lived. Once she reached Seamus, she knew he would help her. Absolutely nothing would make her remain in Denver and sell her body to Harley's customers.

Chapter Two

May 1865

Wind Rider loped through the tall prairie grass in long, easy strides, his sturdy brown legs bulging with muscles long accustomed to being pushed beyond the endurance required by most men. His brown shoulders, slick with sweat, gleamed like polished gold beneath the brutal sun on this extremely hot spring day. With only a brief breechclout covering his loins, his strong body was poetry in motion, magnificent in its savage splendor. His feet, clad in moccasins, literally flew over the rough ground. His long dark hair was crowned with an eagle feather and his face and tautly muscled body sported garish black-and-yellow stripes. Sounds of pursuit added wings to his feet as he sprinted toward the wooded hills a short distance away.

While raiding with a war party of Southern Cheyenne and Oglala Sioux, Wind Rider's horse had been shot out from beneath him as he and his companions attacked a stagecoach. They hadn't known the coach would be escorted by troops attached to Fort Lyon and literally had ridden into a trap. After a few wild shots the war party, badly outnumbered, had given up and ridden away. No one had seen Wind Rider's horse fall. Hidden by the tall prairie grass, Wind Rider had scanned the horizon, realizing that his survival depended upon reaching the wooded hills rising majestically above the plains two miles to the north.

With the soldiers hard on his trail, Wind Rider ran like the wind, glancing neither to the right nor the left, placing his life in the hands of the Great Spirit. He thought of his sister, Tears Like Rain, who had taken a white husband and made a life for herself among the white eyes. He had seen her recently in Denver and learned she was to have Zach Mercer's child. He was grateful that she was safe from all the troubles and bloodshed that had erupted on the prairie since the Sand Creek massacre.

Wind Rider had been shocked to learn that Tears Like Rain and Zach had been at Sand Creek during the massacre and had warned their foster father, White Feather, who had escaped safely. Distrustful of white men's false promises, Wind Rider had refused to settle at Sand Creek with his tribe; he rode north, instead, to join the Sioux. Several weeks later, after he had learned about Sand Creek, he had joined thousands of other Indians camped outside Denver to discuss retaliation against the whites who had attacked innocent women and children at Sand Creek.

Many chiefs had smoked the war pipe and now they began a campaign of battle that blazed a bloody path across the prairie. Wind Rider and his friends had been on their way to Powder River country when they spotted the stagecoach, unaware that a column of soldiers followed a short distance behind it. They had been badly outnumbered from the start but had made the most of the raid, striking hard, then running. One of the last to leave the scene of attack, Wind Rider had run out of luck when his valiant pony was shot from beneath him. Now he was fleeing for his life.

The woods loomed before him and Wind Rider pushed himself beyond the stretch of human endurance. His heart pounded furiously within his sun-bronzed breast and the breath exploded from his chest in harsh, panting bursts as he demanded more from himself than he ever had before. Like any good Cheyenne warrior, he was fully prepared to die for his beliefs, but he was not yet ready to meet *Heammawihio*.

One of the soldiers spotted him. "There he is! Shoot the murdering redskin."

17

The stark planes of his face displayed little emotion as Wind Rider raced toward the woods and the hills beyond. The hot breath of the soldiers' horses seared his neck as they ran him down like a wild animal. With a speed born of desperation he avoided their bullets, shifting and dodging with a cunning only an Indian, or one raised as an Indian, could possess.

Unfortunately, luck deserted him just as he plunged into the cool darkness of the forest. A bullet from a trooper's gun tore into his thigh and he cried out in pain. But it neither slowed nor stopped him. He gritted his teeth against the searing pain and maintained his grueling pace.

Demanding more of himself than was humanly possible, Wind Rider burst through the woods and sprinted up the hill, losing the soldiers easily among the tall pines, stately willows, and cottonwood trees. High up on a hillside he ducked into a cave to wait out the soldiers' passage. He knew the bluecoats wouldn't search forever for a lone Indian, and once they gave up the search he'd make his way to the camp, where he hoped his companions awaited him. His leg needed tending, but necessity demanded that he wait until the danger was past.

Night covered the plains like a blanket, blotting out the sun and awakening the moon. Wind Rider could feel the fever rising in his body and forcibly shook off the lethargy making him groggy and inattentive. He had abandoned the cave shortly after dark, stopping briefly to cleanse his wound in a sluggish brook and to pack it with wet leaves to stem the flow of blood. To keep from dwelling on the pain, he turned his thoughts to his sister, recalling how well and happy she had appeared when he had seen her in Denver. Wind Rider seriously doubted he'd ever find that kind of happiness himself.

Then, unaccountably, a vision of vivid green eyes passed through his mind. Searching his memory, he recalled the indentured servant he had seen in Denver, remembering how she had fought off her master's heavy hand and how she had searched for help among the onlookers without finding it.

Despite her youth, Wind Rider knew she was a whore. His memory conjured up a small, nondescript woman with plain features, matted hair the color of dun, and bones protruding from beneath her skin. She had been dirty beyond imagination, but her one memorable feature had been her compelling green eyes. Why he should think of her now was beyond his comprehension, but think of her he did, even though she had lain with many men and was unworthy of his consideration. Cheyenne men respected virtue and modesty in a woman. They practiced restraint in all their dealings with Cheyenne maidens and were accustomed to long periods of celibacy. Loose women were scorned and shunned among his people.

The moon was high in the sky when Wind Rider neared the place where his friends had made their camp. By now his pain was excruciating, but he forced himself to keep going, ignoring the agony in his wounded leg. The Sioux camp wasn't far, and if he hurried, he could reach it before his comrades left. But the farther he walked, the more unbearable the pain became. His swollen leg barely supported his weight and he was close to collapse. Dawn had just painted the sky with streaks of gray and mauve when he stumbled upon a woman sleeping beneath a tree, wrapped in the filthy remnants of her tattered dress.

Hannah shifted uncomfortably on the hard ground, wishing she'd had the foresight to bring a blanket with her. She had no idea how long it would take to reach a road where she could hail a stagecoach to Cheyenne but prayed it would be soon. She'd made good time the first day and hoped to do better today. Her eyes were still tightly closed as she stretched the kinks out of her body and wished for a cup of hot coffee.

Wind Rider's narrow-eyed gaze settled disconcertingly on the woman curled up on the hard ground. He recognized her immediately. Dimly, he wondered what she was doing so far from Denver. He thought it a strange coincidence that he had been thinking of this very woman just a short time ago, reviling her for being the kind of woman he could never respect. Where was her master? he wondered curiously. What was he thinking to let her roam at will in the woods where danger existed?

Wind Rider's lip curled derisively when he saw her stretch. She was so thin, one had to look closely to tell that she was a woman. Her hair was tangled and covered with dirt and leaves; she could have harbored an entire family of mice in the filthy mass.

Slowly, Hannah opened her eyes. She blinked repeatedly, and when the apparition did not go away she cried out in dismay. Some devil inside Wind Rider made him nudge her with his toe.

Hannah stared at him in fear and awe, hoping she was dreaming and fearing she wasn't. She had never seen an Indian up close before, and this one was truly frightening, with his painted body and fierce expression. Nearly naked, his muscular frame was sleek and golden. He was tall and straight, the corded muscles of his chest and shoulders rippling beneath his smooth flesh. His powerful physique blotted out the rising sun, and just the sight of him set her blood pounding in fear and wonder. His nose wrinkled and his silver eyes glittered as if he could smell her fear.

Silver? Her brow furrowed in concentration. Where had she seen eyes like that before? She wasn't aware that Indians had eyes any color but brown. Yet there was no mistaking this steely-eyed savage for anything but a fierce Indian warrior. When he nudged her with his toe she gasped and scooted out of his reach.

"Go away!" Her voice trembled with fear. When the Indian stared at her as if he had no idea what she was saying, Hannah assumed he couldn't understand English. "Go," she repeated, making a swishing motion with her hands. "Leave me alone."

Reaching down, Wind Rider grasped her shoulders and hauled her to her feet. The green pools of her eyes were so entrancing, he felt an inexplicable urge to plunge into them and never come up for air. Hannah resisted, convinced he meant to kill her.

"Don't hurt me, please," she whimpered, cringing beneath the hard grip of his hands.

Wind Rider's nose twitched, as if he had just sniffed something offensive. "Phew, you stink."

Hannah blinked. "Wh-what? You speak English."

"I speak the white man's tongue but do not like it."

"Let me go, please," Hannah pleaded. "I'm no threat to you."

"Everyone with white skin is a threat to my people. Your great numbers are depriving us of our lands and livelihood."

"What are you going to do with me?" Hannah shuddered, recalling the lurid tales she'd heard at the inn about Indians and what they did to their captives.

Wind Rider's eyes glittered unnaturally as fever raged through his body. He knew he was strong and fit, but he wasn't so naive as to think he was invincible. It was obvious his wound was festering, and he wasn't certain how much longer he could continue without help. Finding the woman was a stroke of luck.

"There is a bullet in my leg; you must remove it."

Hannah's gaze flew to Wind Rider's thigh, her eyes widening when she saw angry red flesh surrounding the crude bandage of leaves. Her mouth worked wordlessly, realizing that he must be in terrible pain despite his stoic reserve. She recoiled in revulsion. How could she touch that bronze flesh without fainting dead away?

"I cannot. I-I've never done it before."

Desperate, Wind Rider whipped out his knife, pressing it against the tender curve of her neck. "You will."

Hannah gulped and stared at him, not trusting her voice. Would he kill her if she refused? "Will you let me go afterward?" she dared to ask.

"I will think about it," Wind Rider promised. "Is there water nearby?"

"There's a stream a short distance away. Can you walk?"

"You will help me," Wind Rider said, clutching her thin shoulders. Her bones felt so fragile beneath his huge hands, he could easily crush them with his fingers. He wasn't certain her slight weight could support him, but it did, giving him the impression that she was stronger than she appeared. He allowed her to pick up her sack, and they started off toward the stream.

Wind Rider sat gingerly on the bank of the stream while Hannah stared at his thigh in utter fascination. She had never seen so much of a man's body before, except for her younger brothers, and they didn't count. She grudgingly admitted his body was magnificent, though his proud, handsome features were as fierce as any she'd ever seen. Stark and noble, savage, yet somehow different from what she had expected Indians to look like. Stranger still were his silver eyes. Could he be a half-breed? she wondered, regarding him from the corner of her eye. If he was, he certainly gave no indication that he possessed a drop of white blood.

"I will soak my leg in the river while you gather wood to start a fire," Wind Rider told her. "Once the bullet is removed you will need to cauterize the wound. Do not attempt to run away," he cautioned when her expression turned speculative. "Even wounded I can run faster than you."

Hannah didn't doubt him for a moment. It didn't take long to gather sticks of wood and dried grass. When she set the pile before Wind Rider he removed his flint from the parfleche he carried at his waist and struck a spark that caught immediately. "Wash your hands in the stream," he said, thrusting his knife directly into the fire. "Cheyenne maidens have more pride than to abuse their bodies with filth. Do you never bathe?"

Hannah's lips thinned resentfully. "You know nothing about me and certainly have no right to judge me." Nevertheless, she knelt beside the stream and washed the grime from her hands. When she returned to Wind Rider's side he handed her the knife, staring at her strangely.

The woman didn't recognize him, Wind Rider thought as he pulled the crude bandage of leaves from his wound. But he remembered her. No man could look into those compelling green eyes and forget her. He knew she was an indentured servant and a whore, that she sold her body to men for money and, from what he had observed in Denver, was abused by her master. She was skinny and plain, and no decent Cheyenne warrior would look on her with desire or wish to lie with her.

"The bullet," Wind Rider said, gripping her arm as she accepted the knife with marked reluctance. "And do not make the mistake of thinking I am incapable of swift retaliation should you decide to attempt something foolish."

Hannah tore her gaze from the icy menace in the Indian's cold eyes, thinking him perfectly capable of reacting swiftly and cruelly. She gazed down at the swollen flesh surrounding the wound and shivered. She had no idea how to go about removing the bullet; it seemed almost a sacrilege to mar that smooth bronze flesh more than it already was.

"Do it!" Wind Rider gritted from between clenched teeth. His brutal grip on her arm tightened.

Wincing in pain, Hannah uttered a silent prayer and pierced his flesh with the tip of the knife. Hannah gagged and turned away, but the pressure on her arm increased until she was forced to return to her loathsome task. She spared a fleeting glance at Wind Rider, amazed that he could bear the pain without uttering a sound or passing out. He held his leg absolutely still beneath her unskilled probing.

White beneath the bronze planes of his face, his expression gave away nothing of the agony he was suffering. All the while she worked over him, he watched through slitted eyes, fully prepared to intervene should she attempt something reckless.

"I feel the bullet!" Hannah cried triumphantly as she probed deeper. The groan that slipped from Wind Rider's lips was scarcely audible as Hannah carefully pried the bullet from the gaping wound. "There; it's out!" Relief swept through her like a tidal wave. Had she been required to dig into his flesh a moment longer she couldn't have borne it.

A lesser man would have passed out long ago, Hannah thought, amazed at the Indian's fortitude. She wondered what his name was, and if he was, indeed, a half-breed, or merely a strange breed of Indian with silver eyes.

"You must cauterize the wound," Wind Rider said, his voice a raspy whisper. His eyes were dilated, his skin ashen, but he was still watchful, still aware of what needed to be done to save his life. "Place the knife in the fire and when it is red-hot hold it against the wound."

Hannah's eyes widened and she gasped in horror. "I cannot. How will you stand it?"

"I have gone through it before," he said stoically.

Her eyes traveled up the virile length of his body, noticing for the first time the wound just below his ribs. The scar had healed but was still red and puckered.

Following his instructions, Hannah heated the knife in the fire. When it was red-hot she removed it, pausing a scant moment to search his face. Impressed by his courage, she felt a grudging admiration for him and his ability to withstand intense pain, despite the fact that he was a savage heathen. When she placed the red-hot blade against his flesh his body jerked convulsively, and a great shudder passed through him. But his eyes never left hers. They clung to her as if to a lifeline, impaling her with silver shards, hard, relentless, probing . . . desperate.

Abruptly, Wind Rider released her arm, and she shot to her feet, sickened by the stench of burned flesh. With a cry of dismay she tossed the knife to the ground.

Pain. Relentless. Stabbing. Intense. It tore into him, savaged him, gnawing at his flesh like a ravening beast.

Feeling himself spinning into a black abyss, Wind Rider focused on the young woman leaning over him, her vivid green eyes all that kept him from sinking into oblivion. How could he have thought her plain? he wondered dimly, with those eyes that ate into a man's soul. He must be hallucinating, he thought, to find anything attractive in the plain brown sparrow.

"Are you all right?" Hannah asked hesitantly. She hated to show concern for an Indian, but she couldn't help herself. Her mother had always said she was too tenderhearted for her own good. Besides, he hadn't harmed her, and she hoped he'd let her go now that she'd helped him.

Wind Rider found it difficult to think, let alone speak, so he nodded his head.

"What is your name?" she asked suddenly. For some reason it seemed important to know the name of the man whose life she might have saved.

Breathing deeply, Wind Rider fought to control the pain, and little by little he succeeded. "I am called Wind Rider."

"My name is Hannah. Hannah McLin," Hannah offered shyly. "May I leave now?"

Wind Rider thought her voice lovely—soft and lilting. The melodious rhythm intrigued him. He'd never heard anything like it before. Except for her eyes and voice, he thought ungraciously, nothing about her was attractive.

"Where will you go if I let you leave?" he asked, finally finding the strength to form the words. He had no idea why he should care, except that she had helped him when she could just as easily have plunged the knife into his heart. Lord knows he had been at her mercy. Though he had endeavored to frighten her into compliance, he was as weak as a babe, and she had to know it. Something told Wind Rider that fear wasn't the reason this woman had helped him. He recognized goodness when he saw it, and whore or no, Hannah McLin had a tender heart.

"To Cheyenne. As far away from Mr. Harley as I can get," Hannah said at length.

"Who is Mr. Harley?"

"He's the man to whom I'm indentured. By law I'm required to work for him for seven years."

Still groggy from pain, Wind Rider couldn't comprehend the need for someone to sell herself into bondage. Did white society have other laws equally as repugnant? he wondered dully. "The Cheyenne do not sell themselves," he said, sending her a glance that spoke eloquently of his contempt for someone who would do such a thing. "Have white eyes no pride?"

Hannah bristled angrily, her eyes flashing green fire. "I did what I had to do to survive; you have no right to judge me. You, a savage, who raids, kills, and rapes innocent people, have no right to condemn others. As long as Indians roam the plains, no decent folk are safe."

"We do what we must to survive," Wind Rider said, throwing her words back at her. His silver eyes turned icy with hostility. "Have you not heard of Sand Creek, where hundreds of innocent women and children were killed by white soldiers?"

Hannah nodded; she had been aware of the gossip but wasn't certain there was any truth to the stories. Many versions had circulated, and she hardly knew what to believe. She'd heard just recently that the president had appointed a commission to investigate the rumors concerning a massacre. But, truth to tell, she had been too preoccupied with her own survival to pay much heed to politics and such.

"I know little about such things." She hesitated a moment, then said, " 'Tis time I left. I dare not linger in the area too long. Knowing Mr. Harley, he's sent the authorities to search for me."

"There are Indian war parties roaming the area," Wind Rider warned. "The Crow are particularly brutal to women captives."

Hannah blanched. "I won't let you frighten me. Death at the hands of Indians is no worse than . . ." She faltered and glanced off into the distance. "I won't return to Mr. Harley, no matter what. I thought I would be free to go if I helped you."

Wind Rider struggled to his feet. Grinding pain tore through him, and he gritted his teeth against the vicious onslaught as he gasped out the words. "If-you wish-to leave-you-are free-to go."

"Should you be on your feet?" Hannah asked, awed by Wind Rider's stamina and seeming immunity to pain.

Wind Rider's grimace was a parody of a smile. It amused him that this plain-faced woman felt concern for him. Except for his sister's husband he hated all white eyes. And if he ever learned that Zach Mercer had mistreated Tears Like Rain, he'd kill him without regret. He was Cheyenne by choice and would always be Cheyenne. He couldn't love White Feather more if he had been his real father. Bluecoats had killed his people and forced them from their ancestral lands, and he'd made a solemn vow to fight to the death to restore the plains to their rightful owners.

"The pain is nothing," Wind Rider said simply. "I must find my Sioux friends and return to Powder River country." He tested his leg by putting his weight on it, bearing the resulting pain with tight-lipped fortitude. "Good-bye, Hannah McLin. It is unlikely we will meet again."

"Good-bye, Wind Rider," Hannah said, strangely reluctant to leave.

The handsome Indian was unlike any man she'd ever met, and she'd met many during the time she'd worked at Harley's inn. Experience had taught her that men were crude and brutal and couldn't be trusted. They thought only of their creature comforts and treated women like chattel, placed on earth to give them pleasure. If women were not submissive enough, men gained perverse enjoyment from subduing them with their superior strength. Except for her father and brothers and her cousin Seamus, Hannah feared and hated all men equally.

Wind Rider regarded Hannah with a touch of awe, annoyed that this ragged scrap of humanity covered with grime had somehow managed to reach a place in him he hadn't known existed. He didn't like the feeling; he had lived too long with the Cheyenne to trust white eyes. Black Kettle had trusted them, and his people had suffered for it.

Hannah picked up her sack and walked away without looking back, fearing Wind Rider would try to stop her. She hadn't walked twenty paces when a group of riders came bursting through the trees, cutting off her escape. She reared back in fright as she counted a dozen armed savages, many brandishing spears decorated with bloody scalps. They greeted Wind Rider with exuberant shouts of welcome. Hannah stood frozen with fear as they spoke to Wind Rider in guttural tones.

"Ho, my friend; it is good to find you alive." The warrior who spoke was tall and well-formed, with a large nose and a thin mouth that gave him a cruel look. Like Wind Rider, he wore only a breechclout, and Hannah could see that his body was a much deeper shade of bronze than Wind Rider's.

"I am equally glad to see you, Runs-Like-A-Deer."

"What happened to you?" a short, ugly man with a scarred face asked. He was called Cut Nose because of the way a scar bisected his nose.

"My horse was shot from beneath me and an enemy bullet found my flesh," Wind Rider told Cut Nose.

While they spoke Hannah slowly edged backward, hoping to escape unnoticed. But Cut Nose's sharp eyes caught the movement, and he reined his horse to cut off her retreat.

"I see your wound didn't stop you from taking a captive." He sent Hannah a contemptuous look. "The woman is ugly; hardly worth the trouble of taking her back to camp. I say we kill her now. Or," he added crudely, "perhaps you like a woman with no flesh, and bones sharp enough to give pain when you lie upon her. Her scrawny body will provide scant warmth and little comfort beneath your blankets if you plan on scewering her upon your mighty lance, my Cheyenne brother. Our Sioux maidens will give you much more pleasure." He turned to his companions. "Driving my knife through the white captive's heart will give me great pleasure."

"What are they saying?" Hannah asked fearfully.

Wind Rider spared her a worried glance but ignored her question. He dare not free her now, for his friends would think him weak and cowardly and probably kill her despite his protest. For some reason he couldn't allow them to kill her; he didn't wish to see Hannah McLin dead. "The woman is my captive; I will decide what is to be done with her."

"She will slow us down," Runs-Like-A-Deer said. His lip curled downward into a scowl. "We are short of horses. Cut Nose is right; killing the woman is the sensible thing to do."

"Take her now upon the ground, Wind Rider, if you've a mind to," Cut Nose chided, "if you can stand the stench. If your enjoyment of her is great, perhaps I will change my mind and take her myself before I end her miserable life."

"I am in no shape to bed anyone," Wind Rider argued. "I say she comes with us. She is my captive. It is our way. She belongs to me, and I have need of a slave. I have no wife to cook for me or see to my needs. I have no desire to bed her—she is far too ugly for my taste—but she can be taught to work hard. I will beat her if she does not please me."

"The Cheyenne are a strange lot," Cut Nose said, shaking his head. "You fight bravely, Wind Rider, but your lack of judgment is appalling. Anyone can see the woman is worthless as a slave. If I didn't know you for a fierce fighter and a bitter enemy of all white eyes, I'd say your white blood was making you weak."

Wind Rider's eyes narrowed dangerously. He had never gotten along with Cut Nose, and if he hadn't been wounded and in pain, he would have challenged him. Cut Nose seemed to enjoy questioning his loyalty and reminding him of his lack of Indian blood, despite the fact that they raided side by side with equal zeal.

Sensing a confrontation they could ill afford, Runs-Like-A-Deer stepped between the two antagonists. "It is as Wind Rider says: The captive is his to do with as he pleases. We will take her with us to Powder River country. Standing

Bear can ride with me; he is the smallest. Wind Rider can share Standing Bear's horse with the woman until we can steal mounts for them."

Since Runs-Like-A-Deer was the undisputed leader of the Sioux raiding party no one questioned his authority. Standing Bear leaped off his horse and handed the reins to Wind Rider. Wind Rider accepted them with a nod and turned to Hannah.

"Am I free to go now?" Hannah asked hopefully.

"You are my captive," Wind Rider replied gruffly. The harsh tone of his voice startled Hannah. His manner had changed so abruptly, her eyes showed her confusion. A few minutes ago he had been willing to let her go in peace. What did it all mean?

"Your captive? I-I don't understand. Let me go. You promised."

His answer was to grab her roughly and toss her upon the horse's back. He knew many of the Sioux understood the white man's tongue and he didn't want to give them the impression that he was coddling his captive because she was white, like he was. In order to keep her alive he had to treat her with the contempt due any other white captive. And in this instance, because Cut Nose had questioned his loyalty to his people, he must dispel their doubts and show them that he could be as cruel as they when dealing with captives.

"I said I'd think about it," he said, refusing to look Hannah in the eye.

Chapter Three

"I cannot abide your stench," Wind Rider said after they had ridden a good distance.

Seated behind him on the horse, Hannah clung to his narrow waist with fierce desperation. She'd ridden docile farm animals in Ireland but never anything like this swift Indian pony. Despite her reluctance to touch Wind Rider's smooth dark skin she was forced to press herself against him so tightly, she could feel the scalding heat of his bare flesh through her rough clothing, providing mute evidence of the fever raging within him.

"Let me go and you can be rid of me," Hannah said hopefully. "I don't wish to offend you."

"You will bathe," Wind Rider decided. "You will wash your body and hair at the next stream we come to."

"No!" Though Hannah hated being unclean, she appreciated the fact that it protected her from unwanted attention. She had deliberately become the disgustingly filthy creature Wind Rider thought her when she realized that the sight of her unwashed flesh and matted hair kept Mr. Harley's customers away from her. It was a small sacrifice to keep her virginity intact. She could not bear the disgrace if she was forced to become one of those poor creatures who sold their bodies for a living.

"I do not understand white women," Wind Rider snorted, wrinkling his nose in disgust. "If you are to prepare my food, you will be clean."

"Prepare your own food," Hannah remarked sullenly. "I don't want to be your slave. Had I enjoyed slavery I could have remained with Mr. Harley."

"Would you rather be dead? Cut Nose was all for killing you outright, and Runs-Like-A-Deer thought it a good idea. You are alive only through my intervention. If you wish to live, you will be my slave and do as I say."

Wind Rider kneed his mount, and all conversation ceased as Hannah clutched his middle to keep from falling.

They rode without respite until nightfall, when the war party made camp beside a stream swollen by spring rains. Wind Rider slid off his mount, favoring his wounded leg. He grunted in pain, then turned and pulled Hannah none too gently to the ground.

"Gather firewood," he ordered Hannah as several men went off into the woods to hunt. "Do not try to escape; it will only make the others angry." He dropped to the ground so heavily, Hannah realized he must be exhausted after suffering so grave a wound and losing so much blood.

Fearing the other Indians, Hannah stayed within sight of Wind Rider as she gathered driftwood for the fire. She returned with an armful of sticks and dropped them at Wind Rider's feet. In a very short time he had built a fire to cook the game his companions provided for their supper.

That night they feasted on squirrel and rabbit, roasted wild onions, and clear, cool water. Wind Rider gave Hannah a small portion of the meat, and when she gobbled it down as if she were starving—which, in truth, she was— he offered her more, despite Cut Nose's snide remark about wasting good food on a woman too ugly to warm a man's blankets.

As she ate, Hannah noted Wind Rider's listlessness, his flushed skin, the way he favored his wounded leg, and she realized his fever must be rising, as fevers so often did at night. Many times in Ireland she had helped her mother nurse her brothers and sisters through illnesses, and she recognized the signs. She wondered how he expected to keep up with the others tomorrow, ailing as he was. She was nodding over the remnants of her meal when Wind Rider nudged her awake.

"Lie down and I will tie your hands and feet."

Hannah paled. "Must you bind me? I promise not to run away."

"If I do not, the others will think I have grown soft. I will not tie you tightly."

Once she was bound it was difficult for Hannah to find a comfortable position, but tired as she was she eventually fell asleep. She didn't awaken until she heard voices and realized it was daylight. She had slept through the entire night without awakening. Runs-Like-A-Deer was speaking to Wind Rider. She had no idea what was being said, but she knew from the tone of voice that something was wrong.

"You look ill, Wind Rider," Runs-Like-A-Deer said. "Is your wound troubling you?"

Hannah gazed intently at Wind Rider, thinking how unwell he looked. His face was flushed beneath his tan, and his eyes glittered brightly from fever. He had to clutch his hands at his sides to keep them from trembling.

"It will take more than a simple wound to stop me," Wind Rider replied.

"Perhaps you should rest today," Runs-Like-A-Deer suggested. "We will linger here until you are well enough to continue."

"There are twelve of us and only one of him," Cut Nose contended. "I say we go on. We still have a long way to go, and the bluecoats are looking for us. It is dangerous for us to linger here longer than necessary. If Wind Rider tries to ride in his condition he will slow us down." He sent Hannah a hard-eyed look. "Let Wind

Rider's slave nurse him until he is ready to ride."

Wind Rider stared at the Sioux warriors with whom he had made his home these past few months. They had welcomed him into their tribe and, despite the fact that he was Southern Cheyenne, had treated him as one of their own. He must think of their welfare. Cut Nose spoke the truth. It was not Wind Rider's wish to slow them down, nor should he expect them to delay their journey until he was well enough to travel.

"Cut Nose speaks the truth, Runs-Like-A-Deer. If I try to ride while fever rages through my body I will slow you down. It is best that I remain behind with my captive and ride when I am well. We will meet again at Red Cloud's encampment in Powder River country."

"I will stay with you." Another Cheyenne warrior who had joined the Sioux stepped forward. He was not of Wind Rider's tribe, but he and Wind Rider had become good friends.

"No, Coyote, you must go with the others," Wind Rider said. "I am not so ill that I am helpless."

Coyote squatted down beside Wind Rider and placed a pouch in his hand. Among the Cheyenne he was known as a medicine man, one knowledgeable in herbs and healing. "Boil these herbs in water and drink them, they will take the fever from your body."

"Thank you," Wind Rider said sincerely. "I will do as you say."

"Perhaps we should take your captive off your hands," Cut Nose suggested slyly. "We will clean her up in the stream and use her for our whore. We have been many suns without a woman. True, the woman is ugly, but she need not be pleasing to look at to appease our lust. Unlike our Cheyenne brothers," he said disparagingly, "Sioux men are not accustomed to long periods of celibacy."

"The woman is mine," Wind Rider insisted. It annoyed him that he was too weak to offer more than token protest if they ruled against him. "I have need of my slave. It is my right."

Cut Nose tried not to display his disappointment, realizing that Runs-Like-A-Deer would probably decide in Wind Rider's favor. It surprised him that he wanted the woman; she was dirty and plain and thin as a stick. But something about her made her desirable to him in a way he could not explain.

Before the other warriors departed they went through their belongings and generously offered Wind Rider what they did not need. Wind Rider had lost his horse and other items necessary to survival, and he was grateful for the water pouch, cooking kettle, gourd cup, leggings, moccasins, shirt, and small supply of pemmican and parched corn. Someone even added a parfleche in which to carry everything. Fortunately, Wind Rider still carried his medicine bag around his neck, with his personal talisman and good-luck items, his knife and his rifle.

Hannah sagged in relief when the warriors rode off in a cloud of dust. Cut Nose frightened her. She'd take her chances with the devil she knew rather than with the group of bloodthirsty Sioux she didn't. Once they were out of sight Wind Rider untied Hannah. Weaving from side to side, he stared at her through fever-shot eyes.

"Find more wood," he ordered as he dropped down beside the fire. "I will drink Coyote's remedy."

Hannah's eyes brightened with speculation. Wind Rider was ailing; it wouldn't be difficult to escape. But escape to where? she wondered dully. She had no idea where she was. Wind Rider had spoken of Powder River country, wherever that was, and the fact that it was inhabited by many, many Indians. Was she already in the middle of Indian country? Would she be safer striking off on her own into unknown territory or remaining with Wind Rider?

"If you're thinking about escaping," Wind Rider said, reading her mind, "it would be most foolish of you. After the massacre at Sand Creek most Indians would kill you on sight, or torture you in the most horrible way imaginable."

If he had intended to frighten her he had succeeded. Hannah's face turned white beneath the dirt. "Does that include you? Are you taking me to Powder River country to torture and kill me? If you are, kill me now. I cannot stand the waiting."

Wind Rider frowned. What *did* he intend to do with the woman? In the village she would be treated with the utmost contempt, tortured by the women of the tribe; starved, maybe, or hurt when he wasn't around to protect her. That thought led to another: Why did he even care? Except for her vibrant green eyes and lilting voice there was nothing outstanding about Hannah McLin. Small, plain, and colorless, he compared her to a little brown sparrow. She wasn't even fit to serve as whore to the tribe. White men had strange tastes, indeed, if they would pay to bed so lackluster a creature. Yet a whore was exactly what the woman was, for he had heard her master label her as such when he had been in Denver, posing as a white man.

"I will not kill you . . . yet," Wind Rider said in a menacing manner. "I have need of you. Fetch the wood, but stay where I can see you. When you return bring me water so that I can boil the herbs Coyote gave me."

Hannah thought about turning and fleeing, but the flash of cold steel in Wind Rider's eyes changed her mind. He might be feverish and unable to keep up with the furious pace set by his friends, but he was far from helpless. And like it or not, he was the best protection she had at the moment. For some obscure reason he had defended her against Cut Nose, and since she was far too young to lose her life she obeyed Wind Rider. But just because she preferred to remain with Wind Rider for the time being didn't mean she had lost her fear of the fierce, silver-eyed renegade. Far from it. When he turned his cold, piercing gaze on her the experience left her shaken.

Wind Rider's eyes were glazed and his hand unsteady when Hannah handed him the gourd containing the herbal drink she had prepared. She reached out to help him, tipping the gourd to his mouth, momentarily forgetting that she was the captive and he the enemy. She saw only someone who needed help.

Wind Rider fought to remain conscious. The ride had been a grueling one. He had lost a lot of blood and his strength had slowly drained from his body. If Hannah hadn't had the courage to remove the bullet and cauterize the wound he might have bled to death. Superbly fit as he was, he knew he would mend swiftly, and within a day or two he would be ready to ride again. His head nodded; his eyes grew heavy. Previous experience had taught him that healing sleep was better than any medicine. Dimly, he wondered if Hannah would still be here when he awoke.

Hannah watched Wind Rider drift off to sleep. When his body was totally relaxed and she was certain he slept she knelt beside him, looking her fill, something she had wanted to do since the first moment she had seen him. Her gaze roamed the length of his scantily clad body, pausing in her journey to look closely at the blackened wound marring his thigh. It wasn't pretty to look at, but she supposed in time the scar would blend in with the rest of his golden flesh.

It amazed Hannah that a man could be so handsome, so perfectly formed. His hard body was so beautiful, it gave her a fluttery feeling in the pit of her stomach. Smooth and blemish-free except for a few scattered scars from previous wounds, his flesh flowed over his bones like molten gold. She had noticed immediately that his skin wasn't as dark as that of his companions, but his long, flowing hair was the same midnight black.

His chest rippled with corded tendons; his legs were strong and muscular. His breech-clout barely covered the taut twin mounds of his buttocks and the bold thrust of his manhood. Even at rest the outline of his male appendage beneath the scrap of deer hide was awesome. Her face turned beet red and she turned away, embarrassed at the perilous journey upon which her eyes had embarked. Her thoughts still consumed with the handsome Indian, she busied herself with the fire. Hunger gnawed at her, and she sat down on a stump and ate the remains of last night's meal, left for them by the Sioux war party.

Wind Rider slept though the day and into the night. When it grew dark Hannah placed the blanket over him and once again considered escape. It would be so easy, she reflected, to quietly disappear into the woods. She could take Wind Rider's horse, though she wasn't an experienced rider. There was a world of difference between the plodding farm horse she had ridden back home in Ireland and the wild Indian pony that had carried both her and Wind Rider. Still, it was worth a try, she decided as she moved stealthily from the firelit perimeter of their small camp.

"You would be foolish to run." The deep resonance of his voice held a note of warning, sending a tremor of apprehension down her spine.

Perched on the horns of a dilemma, Hannah paused, regarding Wind Rider speculatively. He rested on his elbows, peering at her through the darkness. She shivered, wondering if his silver eyes had the ability to see through the dark. "You're awake."

"I haven't been sleeping for some time."

Hannah felt herself flush all over. Had he been awake when she had perused him so thoroughly? "You are in no condition to stop me." She took two steps to test him.

"Try me." The challenge in his voice was unmistakable. It made her regret having helped him. He was a savage, for heaven's sake, capable of all sorts of depravity.

"Come here." The authority in his voice was unmistakable.

Slowly, Hannah approached Wind Rider, her expression wary. "What do you want?"

"Sit down beside me."

Hannah stopped in her tracks. Did he intend to attack her? Had she kept her virginity only to be raped by a heathen Indian? "What are you going to do? If you intend to rape me, I'll fight to the bitter end."

Wind Rider looked astonished. "Rape you! Ha!" The air exploded from his chest in a harsh burst of laughter. "Only a blind or desperate man would rape a woman as ugly and undesirable as you, and I am neither. I merely want to tie you so you can't escape."

His words were like a punch to the gut. She had deliberately tried to make herself as unattractive as possible, but for an Indian to tell her she was ugly and undesirable was a blow to her pride. "If I displease you so much, why not let me go?"

The answer was as much a mystery to Wind Rider as it was to Hannah. Releasing her would be a simple matter, and probably best for both of them. He had no idea why he resisted the idea, except that he had convinced himself that he truly needed a slave. He had carefully avoided the Sioux maidens who would have gladly joined with him. Under Sioux law he was allowed more than one wife, but he preferred none. Times were too precarious for him to take wives and raise a family. He had no idea if he'd be alive a day, a month, or a year from now. If he had a family, who would see to their welfare if he was killed in a raid? And living on a reservation like the white eyes wished wasn't an option.

"Could you survive in the wilds by yourself?" Wind Rider asked bluntly. "This is Indian country. You could encounter someone who isn't as disposed to keep you alive as I am. You are far too scrawny and weak to be of much use as a slave. Most Indian men have wives to see to their needs, so your life will be of little value to them. It might be different if you were beautiful, but you are not." He sent her an inscrutable look. "But if you truly wish to leave, you are free to go."

Hannah gave him a startled look. "Do you mean it?"

"I have said so."

Hannah didn't know what to make of Wind Rider's words. He sounded sincere, but how far could one trust an Indian? "Thank you," she said, deciding to take him at his word.

Narrow-eyed, Wind Rider watched Hannah slip into the woods. He had thought her too intelligent to believe she could survive on her own, but obviously she was so anxious to escape that she gave little consideration to his warning. After she had disappeared he continued to stare at the place where he had last seen her, a grim smile stretching his lips.

Hannah wanted to run like the wind but bowed to caution as she slipped from tree to tree, following a moonlit path through the woods. She had no idea what or whom she might run into, and crashing heedlessly through the underbrush might alert some unknown enemy. She recalled Wind Rider's warning and wondered if she had, indeed, been foolish to leave the protection he had offered, such as it was. But she couldn't help thinking the handsome savage had some ulterior motive where she was concerned. She had never heard of an Indian kindly disposed toward whites, and Wind Rider's companions had been all for killing her.

Cautiously, Hannah made her way through the woods, wondering if she'd ever find a trail she could follow to a town. She stopped to rest twice, the last time falling asleep for several hours. She awoke at dawn, disgusted with herself for sleeping when she needed to put distance between herself and the silver-eyed savage. When she heard the rush of water she grew excited. Elated, she raced toward the sound and found a stream, realizing that if she followed it long enough it would eventually lead her to a town.

Bursting from the trees, Hannah slid to an abrupt halt. She had, indeed, found water, and Wind Rider was calmly bathing in it. A small cry of dismay escaped her lips. Wind Rider heard the sound and turned in her direction, his lips curving into a mirthless smile.

"What took you so long?"

Beyond speech, Hannah lost the ability to move. Had she traveled in circles the entire night? Her glance took in the fire for which she had gathered wood and the place where Wind Rider had spent the night. The indentation of his body was still imprinted upon the soft grass.

"I-I don't understand."

"An Indian child knows more about the wilderness than you do. You traveled in circles, just as I knew you would."

Hannah plopped down on the ground, her expression mutinous. "You never intended to let me go."

"I wanted to teach you how little you knew about the wilderness and survival."

Hannah mulled over his words then said, "You are cruel. You torment me with freedom, then take it from me." She stared at him sullenly, resentful that he appeared quite hale, all signs of fever gone.

"Perhaps," Wind Rider allowed. "Why don't you join me? If we are to ride double, I'd prefer to do so without your stench offending me."

"I'm perfectly happy the way I am." She regarded him warily and scooted backward when he walked slowly toward her through the water.

The breath caught painfully in Hannah's throat as the sun chose that moment to break through the gray dawn, revealing Wind Rider's nude body to her startled gaze. She tried to look away, but the magnificence of his masculine beauty utterly defeated her. Washed clean of the hideous paint, his face held surprisingly few Indian characteristics. She had thought him impressive with his breechclout firmly in place, but without it he was truly breathtaking.

Wind Rider was surprised that the sight of his nude body turned Hannah's face a bright red. Even more amazing was the way he hardened

Connie Mason

beneath the plain little sparrow's bold perusal. One would think she'd never seen a man's naked body before. Wind Rider thought her a good actress for he knew she was a whore who sold her body for white man's coin.

Hannah was so enthralled with him that she wasn't aware of his intention until he picked her up and lunged toward the water. She squawked in protest when he flung her into the deepest part of the stream.

Unable to swim, Hannah clawed her way to the surface, spewing forth a stream of water. "I-I can't swim," she sputtered before sinking beneath the weight of her clothes. She was certain now that Wind Rider meant to drown her. Unwilling to die without a fight, she bobbed to the surface again. Wind Rider was nowhere in sight. She went under again, swallowing a mouthful of water in the process. Just when she stared death in the face she felt a tug on her hair and broke the surface, coughing and gagging.

Wind Rider dragged Hannah to shallow water, shaking his head in disgust. "Can you do nothing right, woman? You can't ride and you can't swim. My sister learned to swim at an early age, like most Indian maidens."

"I'm no Indian," Hannah said, gasping and choking. "Were you trying to drown me?"

"If I was smart, I would let you drown."

She started to rise, but he pushed her back down hard. "Take off your clothes."

She glared at him mutinously. "No."

52

He grasped a handful of material and was startled when her dress literally disintegrated in his huge hands. Snorting in disgust, he pulled her free of the dress and tossed it aside. She cried out in alarm when it floated downstream. She wore nothing underneath it but a shift so threadbare that it ripped apart beneath Wind Rider's hands as he tore it from her body and flung it after the dress.

"What are you doing?" She huddled in the water, her arms crossed over her bare breasts and her legs pulled close to her body. She looked pale, thin, and frightened, and as vulnerable as a newborn babe.

"Trying to get you clean." Scooping up a handful of sand, he attacked her skin with a vengeance. The layers of dirt literally floated off her back, arms, and neck. When Wind Rider pulled her to her feet so he could scrub the rest of her body, she cringed and pulled away.

"No, don't touch me."

Wind Rider stepped back, suddenly, shockingly aware of her tender white flesh, small, firm breasts, and long, slender legs. How could anyone be so appallingly thin and still appear womanly? he wondered dully. Her nipples were pink and elongated, her breasts like small, round apples, so tempting he wanted to taste them. The woman's hair between her legs was not dull brown like that on her head but a rich, vibrant auburn. It glittered in the awakening sun like gleaming copper. The sight brought a painful jolt to his loins and he quickly looked away. In that instant he'd had a brief glimpse of why men were willing to pay for the use of her body. Even more startling was the fact that, cleansed of dirt and grime, her face wasn't nearly as unattractive as he had first thought.

All he could think to say was, "Finish your bath and wash your hair." The filthy mass of hair streamed down her back in a tangled, knotted mess. Immediately, she ducked her head beneath the waist-deep water, embarrassed to the point of tears. No man had ever seen her naked before, and it angered her that an Indian had been the first.

Wind Rider stood at the water's edge, a nude statue that rivaled the finest works of art. He watched Hannah through slitted lids, his expression devoid of all emotion, the planes of his face stark against the brilliance of the sunlight. He could not turn his eyes away as Hannah ducked her head beneath the water and scrubbed it with sand. Within minutes the vibrant hues of rich auburn interspersed with streaks of gold emerged, and against his will he recalled the copper curls crowning her woman's mound. His body reacted swiftly and unexpectedly.

Despite Hannah's hollow cheeks, long, thin neck, bony collarbone, concave stomach, and prominent ribs, a jolt of raw desire exploded through him. His man's part rose high and hard, filled with the blood of sudden, inexplicable need. Perhaps Cut Nose had been right, he thought dimly. The woman was a whore;

he should use her like one. But when she
turned and looked at him the sight of her
small, vulnerable body and the mute appeal
in her green eyes made a profound impact
upon him. He snorted in disgust. What kind
of Cheyenne warrior was he that he couldn't
restrain his manly urges?

He should feel contempt, loathing, and utter
disregard for a white captive. Instead, this
small, insignificant woman had found a place
inside him he hadn't known existed. Cut Nose
hadn't been too far from the truth when he
had accused him of coddling his captive, Wind
Rider thought derisively. White men had killed
his people, stolen their lands, and tried to
wipe them from the face of the earth. How
could he feel anything but hatred for this
pale-faced, worthless creature? He should kill
her and be done with it, since he no longer
needed her.

Hannah dared a glance at Wind Rider, startled to find him staring at her in a curious
manner. Was it loathing? What had she done to
cause him to hate her so much? she wondered.
She slid her gaze down his body, gasping when
she saw his engorged sex. His violent reaction
shocked her. How could he react in such a
blatantly sexual manner when he thought her
ugly? She was aware of how thin and unattractive she appeared to men and until now
had been proud of her ability to make herself
homely. What did this Indian see that no other
men had?

"I have nothing to wear," Hannah called out when she had rinsed every last grain of sand from her hair.

Wind Rider turned and found the buckskin shirt one of his friends had left for him. He held it aloft, waiting for her to come out of the water and claim it.

She swallowed convulsively. "I-I'm not decent."

Wind Rider sent her a chilling smile. "You may ride naked if you prefer, but your white skin will burn beneath the prairie sun." He turned away.

"Wait! I'll wear the shirt. Place it on the ground and turn around."

Wind Rider laughed harshly. "I did not think whores were so modest. Do not pretend with me, woman, for I know what you are. I have nothing but contempt for women who sell their bodies to men. Perhaps I will give you to the village men to use for their pleasure as Cut Nose suggested. Now that you are cleaned up, perhaps they can overlook your ugliness and white skin."

Hannah gasped in dismay. Where did Wind Rider get the idea that she was a whore? Didn't he know she had run away because Mr. Harley wanted her to sell her favors for his personal gain? No, of course not, she answered her own question. How could he know?

"I'm not what you think," she denied vehemently. "Will you turn around so I can leave the water?"

Crossing his arms over his bronze chest, Wind Rider refused to budge. "Your body does not tempt me, woman."

Hannah flushed, vividly recalling the rampant state of his sex only moments before. She kept her eyes on his face, fearing to glance down to see if he was still aroused. Raising her chin to a defiant angle, she rose to her feet and walked slowly ashore.

Wind Rider tensed, wondering why he was putting himself through such agony. He must be desperate for a woman to become aroused by a skinny white woman who until a few moments ago had appeared utterly repulsive to him. But there was nothing repulsive about her now. Water streamed off the elongated tips of her breasts and puddled in the glorious copper hairs adorning her woman's mound. The sight was so stirring, Wind Rider turned abruptly and walked away, blaming his white blood for making him desire the kind of woman he had always despised.

A white woman.

Chapter Four

Hannah tried valiantly to preserve her dignity, but it was difficult while sitting astride Wind Rider's pony, locked in the cradle of his loins with her legs exposed and the buckskin shirt he had given her hiked up to her thighs. When he saw she had difficulty keeping her seat behind him he had insisted that she ride before him, straddling the horse's withers. With his arms surrounding her and his body heat making her giddy, Hannah sensed a danger that had nothing to do with the obvious one she would expect from being held captive by an Indian. No, it was much more complex.

Wind Rider rode steadily north, aware in the most basic way of the woman fitted snugly between his thighs. It wasn't as if taking a captive was unique; far from it. Since

Sand Creek dozens of settlers had been killed in widely spread raids across the Cheyenne plains, and women and children had been seized and dragged away as captives. The Cheyenne trail of looting, burning, and murder had moved north, heading for the safety of the Powder River country, where the Sioux were camped. Wind Rider had joined them in the winter of 1864, raiding with them for weeks at a time before returning to the village.

Hannah heaved a sigh of relief when Wind Rider stopped beside a stream late that day. They had ridden without respite, munching on pemmican when hunger could be staved off no longer. She slid from the horse's withers, hanging on a moment until her rubbery legs stabilized. Wind Rider had already leaped to the ground, favoring his wounded leg only slightly. Hannah watched him disappear into the woods. Her bladder near to bursting, she chose a path in the opposite direction. She was washing her hands in the stream when Wind Rider reappeared.

"Gather wood," he ordered brusquely. "Do not stray too far or you will become lost."

Hannah bristled with impotent rage. Was it her lot in life to be ordered about by men? First Mr. Harley and now Wind Rider. It was demeaning. One day, she vowed, she'd not be beholden to any man. Meanwhile, she had no choice but to do as Wind Rider directed. A short time later, when she heard rifle shots reverberate across the plains, she started violently, until she recalled Wind Rider's intention to hunt for their supper. When she returned with the wood he was gutting and skinning a fat rabbit. She sat down on a log to watch him as he finished with that rabbit and started on another.

"You speak English amazingly well," she said idly, fascinated by the movement of his strong hands and nimble fingers.

He sent her an austere look. "The white man's tongue is not difficult to master."

Hannah stared at him. "Is your mother white? Did you inherit your silver eyes from her? Did she teach you to speak English?"

Annoyed by her infernal questions, Wind Rider slashed his hand in the air. "Quiet! Are all white women so nosy? A Cheyenne would never inquire into another's past. I am Cheyenne; that is all you need to know."

"But you don't look . . ."

"You are brave, Hannah McLin. I could kill you without remorse. I have killed before and would not hesitate to do so again."

What Wind Rider didn't say was that he'd never in his life killed or harmed a woman or child. Killing pony soldiers who had attacked his people was one thing, but he had yet to participate in an attack on settlers. His own sister and her husband, Zach Mercer, were settlers who lived not far from Denver.

Fear shuddered through Hannah. She did not doubt that Wind Rider was capable of performing every vile atrocity attributed to Indians. His words made her think seriously of escape. Lowering her lashes to shutter her thoughts, she desperately searched for a plan. Obviously, she needed more information.

"When will we reach your village?" Hannah asked after Wind Rider had spitted the rabbits and set them over the fire to cook.

"If we encounter no delays, we will reach Red Cloud's camp tomorrow."

"Who is Red Cloud?"

"He is a great Sioux chief."

Hannah fell silent, realizing that she wasn't going to get much from Wind Rider in the way of conversation.

Wind Rider watched Hannah warily. She was too nosy by far, he decided. He should either kill her or let her go, but unfortunately he could do neither. Killing her definitely didn't appeal to him, and letting her go would be tantamount to a death sentence, for she was ill-prepared to survive on her own. Besides, she'd likely be captured by someone who would delight in torturing and killing her after using her body to satisfy his blood lust for white flesh.

Wind Rider tested the rabbits, found them done to a turn, and ripped one into pieces. He offered Hannah a share, which she accepted with alacrity and tore into with relish. Juice ran down her chin, but she didn't stop to wipe it away until the last morsel had been chewed and swallowed. She looked at the remaining rabbit with such longing, Wind Rider offered her a share of that one, too. He had hoped to save it for their morning meal, but Hannah's ravenous appetite changed his mind. He felt scathing contempt for the girl's master, who obviously had starved her and worked her excessively. White men puzzled him. He didn't understand why whites were allowed to mistreat one of their own so severely.

Kneeling beside the stream, Hannah washed her hands and face, then searched for a place to bed down. Wind Rider placed a blanket beneath a tree and walked to the water's edge. Wading into waist-deep water, he submerged himself briefly, then rose like a golden statue and, ignoring Hannah, walked into the nearby willows for a moment of privacy. When he returned Hannah was sitting on a log beside the fire.

"Lie down," Wind Rider said gruffly. He jerked his head toward the blanket. Hannah ignored him. "I am tired. I wish to sleep."

"Go ahead," Hannah said carelessly.

Wind Rider's eyes glittered dangerously. "Do not defy me, woman. I do not trust you. Lie down." His tone brooked no argument. Rising slowly, Hannah walked to the blanket and stretched out.

"What are you going to do?"

Using the rope that had been rolled up in the blanket, Wind Rider bound both of Hannah's wrists and attached the end of the rope to his waist, leaving a two-foot slack to allow her freedom to turn in her sleep. The short tether would bring their bodies too closely together for his peace of mind, but there was no help for it. The buckskin shirt barely reached her knees, and the knowledge that she wore nothing underneath it was distracting. The sight of her slim but shapely legs made him forget that he had once thought her scrawny and plain.

Hannah hated being confined at Wind Rider's side, so close she could feel the heat of him against her own cool flesh. The only concession he had made to his state of nudity was donning the leggings provided by one of his Sioux friends. Since she wore his only shirt nothing else was available to him. But he seemed unaware of the chill in the air as he lay down, forcing Hannah to conform to the curve of his body. Scooting as far from him as the rope allowed, Hannah's tense body refused to relax until she heard the even cadence of Wind Rider's breath and knew he was sleeping.

Wind Rider awoke in the dead of night, astounded to find Hannah snuggled against him. During the night she had sought his warmth, and his arms had welcomed her without conscious thought. A firm little breast filled his hand; his fingers rested on an elongated nipple. Two slim legs lay intimately entwined with his strong ones, and the sweet mounds of her buttocks pressed snugly against his loins.

Her silky hair tickled his nose and he brushed it away, amazed at the softness and texture. A few days ago it had been so filthy he wouldn't have dared touch it for fear of encountering vermin.

Of its own volition his hand left her breast and slid down the curve of her hip. When he met bare flesh he inserted his hand beneath the fringed hem and inched the shirt upward, seeking the warmth of her inner thighs. The smoothness and heat of her flesh startled him, and he groaned as if in physical pain. If anyone had told him a month ago that he'd desire a white woman with such intense longing, he would have laughed. It had never occurred to him that he'd find Hannah desirable.

His hand slid higher, gravitating toward a beckoning heat, recalling how astounded he'd been when he'd first seen the glorious, fiery crown of her woman's mound. Exhausted, Hannah groaned but did not awaken when Wind Rider slid a finger into the tender cleft between her legs. Moistness flowed from her honeyed depths and Wind Rider wondered how many men had feasted upon her tainted flesh. But tainted or not, the compelling need to join the ranks of those nameless men who had lain with her existed deep inside him.

Feeling vaguely uncomfortable, Hannah groaned and jerked awake, startled to find Wind Rider bending over her, his hands doing indecent things to her. Things that made her tingle and burn between her legs. "What are you doing? Don't touch me!" A forbidden heat welled up from her loins.

Wind Rider's generous mouth stretched into a mirthless grin. "You are wet and hot for a man."

"I-I don't know what you're talking about."

He slipped a finger inside her and her body lurched upward. "Please! Don't do that."

"What would you prefer I do? Do white men arouse their women differently? Or do you wish me to pay in white man's coin to lie with you?"

Hannah shoved at his chest, trying to push him away. It was too dark to see his expression, but the warmth of his silver eyes and the heat of his body scorched her flesh. "I'm not what you think. I've never lain with a man."

Wind Rider laughed harshly. "Perhaps you've never lain with an Indian, but I know you've lain with white men. Do not lie, Hannah McLin, for I know what it means when a woman is called whore." His finger slid deeper and Hannah gasped, squirming to accommodate the foreign object into her narrow passage. "Do not fear, Little Sparrow; I am capable of giving you pleasure if I so desire. Did you receive pleasure from the others, or was their coin more important to you than their manhood?"

Hannah paled. "No, please . . . I'm not a whore. Where did you hear that? Don't do this to me. I'll be your slave, I'll work hard, but don't rape me."

If Hannah did not remember him, he wasn't going to tell her that he'd seen her in Denver many moons ago. "A slave is less than dirt," Wind Rider spat, so desperate to thrust himself inside her that his heart was thumping wildly against his ribs. "I can use you in any way I desire. If you do not please me, I can kill you."

"I'd prefer you killed me," Hannah said softly. Abruptly, the building pressure inside her eased as Wind Rider removed his finger.

"You'd prefer death to me? Is lying with an Indian so repulsive to you?"

Hannah swallowed convulsively, searching her heart for an answer. Truth be known, Wind Rider wasn't repulsive at all. It frightened her to think she'd even consider bedding with the heathen savage. She'd always assumed that one day she'd marry; lacking worldly goods, she intended to give the gift of her virginity to her bridegroom. After her period of indenture she'd be free to live her own life, find a mate, and settle down to raise a family. Maybe in time she could bring some of her younger brothers and sisters to America. What she hadn't counted on was a vicious master like Mr. Harley, or being taken captive by Indians.

"Answer me," Wind Rider repeated. "Is death preferable to bedding an Indian?"

"Yes!" Hannah shouted recklessly. "If you rape me, I'll find a way to kill you and then myself." They were fearless words, spoken in the heat of passion.

Wind Rider went still. It seemed inconceivable that a whore would prefer death to lying with a man, Indian or no. He was sorely tempted to grant her wish. His hand curled around the hilt of his hunting knife and he slowly drew it forth. Hannah had no idea what he intended until the sharp point pricked the skin at the base of her neck and she felt the warm trickle of blood.

"Go ahead," she taunted, tossing caution to the wind. Wouldn't death be preferable to enforced slavery? Having to answer to a master like Wind Rider would test her sorely. She must never let down her guard and forget that her captor was a vicious savage. Wind Rider had already threatened to give her to his friends if she didn't please him.

Impressed by her courage, Wind Rider's grip on the blade eased. How could a little brown sparrow possess such amazing fortitude? he wondered. She had goaded him beyond restraint and still he wanted her. And, *Heammawihio* willing, he'd have her. Only it wouldn't be rape. He would slowly destroy her will until she willingly—nay, eagerly—spread her legs for him, submitting to him just as she had submitted to the white men she had welcomed into her bed. He would bring her to passion slowly, with great expertise, until she panted for want of him. And after he'd had her he'd give her to his friends to use for their pleasure. He must never forget that Hannah belonged to a race he hated passionately.

Wind Rider smiled, pleased with the picture he'd just painted in his mind. Deep in his heart he knew something was flawed with the image, but he buried it deep inside him, intending to face the problem when the need arose. The knife slipped from his fingers to the ground.

Hannah knew the moment Wind Rider decided to spare her life. The pressure on her neck eased and she could feel the tenseness leave his body. "I will have you, Little Sparrow," Wind Rider vowed. "When it pleases me. Right now you do not tempt me. Your bones are so sharp, they will likely puncture my flesh."

Wind Rider smiled at his cleverness. He thought Little Sparrow a fitting name for such a scrawny little bird as Hannah McLin.

"Go to sleep," he ordered curtly. "Tomorrow we ride hard to reach Red Cloud's village." He turned his back on her.

Hannah sought to control her erratic breathing as Wind Rider drifted toward sleep. It seemed forever before his body relaxed. Rising to her elbow, careful not to disturb the sleeping man at her side, she held her breath and reached across his body for the knife he had dropped after deciding not to kill her. There was just enough moonlight for her to see the gleaming outline of the blade. Her fingers curled around the hilt and she hugged it close to her body.

After making certain Wind Rider still slept, she sawed at the length of rope connecting their bodies. Plunging the knife into Wind Rider never entered her mind, for she doubted she could strike a killing blow, and anything less would spell her doom. Escape from the heathen devil was a driving force inside her as she felt the rope slacken and separate. In seconds her hands were free, and she knotted the rope around her waist and thrust the blade inside.

She slipped away in the early hours before dawn, determined not to walk in circles again. Instinct told her to follow the stream and she did, walking in shallow water so as to leave no tracks. Her shoes had been ruined when Wind Rider tossed her into the river the day before, and now she carefully avoided sharp rocks and stones. Later, when she was sure she wasn't being followed, she'd gather leaves and tie them to her feet to protect the tender soles of her feet. For now, walking on the sandy stream bottom was protection enough.

Hannah trudged through the murky dawn into a dull morning dominated by dark skies and distant thunder. The roiling clouds overhead looked ominous, and she hoped the storm would hold off until she found adequate shelter. To her chagrin, a slow rain began falling immediately, turning into a downpour within minutes. Lightning danced across the sky and thunder rattled the heavens. When a bolt of fire struck a few feet away she scrambled from the stream, frantically searching for a safe haven. All she found was a small indentation carved out of the bank by high water. It appeared just big enough for her to scoot beneath.

The rain continued without respite. Rivulets of muddy water cascaded down the bank and into her shelter, dirtying her skin and matting her hair. When the storm abated an hour later she crawled from her crude shelter, so splattered with mud and filth, her own mother wouldn't have known her. Unfortunately, Wind Rider had no difficulty recognizing her. Her untimely exit from beneath the overhang occurred at the exact moment Wind Rider passed by her hiding place. He had been searching for her since he had awoken and found her gone.

"Foolish girl," he chided derisively. His hooded eyes made a slow perusal of her filthy state, satisfied that she hadn't been harmed, although she was soaked to the skin and shivering. He tried not to notice the way the buckskin shirt clung to her wet skin but failed miserably. "Don't you know by now you cannot escape from me?"

Hannah turned to run, but he was upon her in seconds as he slid from his mount and sprinted after her. Pinning her to the ground, he slid a length of rope around her neck and tugged her to her feet. "I warned you about trying to escape."

Impetuous by nature, she knew it had been foolish to flee into hostile territory, but desperate times called for desperate measures. "What are you going to do?"

"You shall see." He tied the other end of the rope to his waist and remounted. Hannah expected to be lifted up to ride before him, but he merely jerked the rope, forcing her to walk beside his horse.

"This is how we treat captives. Learn from it, Little Sparrow." The name came easily to his lips, as if it was meant to be. "Next time you try to escape I will not be so tolerant."

"Tolerant! How far must I walk? I have no shoes; my feet will be cut to ribbons."

Frowning, Wind Rider had forgotten that Hannah's shoes had been ruined, not that they were all that good to begin with. He reined his horse to a halt, rummaged in his parfleche, and found the moccasins one of his friends had given to him. He tossed them to Hannah. "Put them on."

Grateful for the small consideration, Hannah pulled on the moccasins, tying the thongs securely to hold them on her small feet. She barely had time to straighten up when Wind Rider yanked on the rope and jerked her forward. "Do not dawdle; I wish to reach camp before nightfall."

Stumbling along beside Wind Rider, Hannah wasn't aware that he deliberately kept the pace slow and easy to accommodate her slow progress. Nor did she know that the village was no great distance away. Had he really intended to punish her, he would have forced her to run to keep up with him. But he didn't want her hurt excessively. He merely wished to teach her a lesson, for once they reached the village she would be severely punished if she repeatedly tried to escape. White slaves were usually treated worse than dogs. Only children, and white women who were taken as wives by warriors were integrated into the tribe.

Hannah's legs trembled beneath her as she tried to keep up with the pace set by Wind Rider. Placing one foot before the other, she concentrated on staying on her feet, fearing that Wind Rider would drag her along the ground if she fell. Her concentration was such that she had no idea they were near the village until the barking of dogs announced their arrival. She came to an abrupt standstill, until the tug of the rope reminded her that she was at the mercy of a vicious savage. Demeaning as it was, she staggered into the Indian camp at the end of a rope.

Skin splattered with dried mud, her hair a rat's nest of filthy snarls, Hannah presented much entertainment as Wind Rider led her through the village. Children followed, shouting, pointing, laughing. Some jabbed her with pointed sticks until Wind Rider sent them fleeing with a few sharp words. The women weren't so easily dismissed. A few pelted her with dung while others tugged at her hair, obviously making fun of her pathetic state.

Hannah ducked the dung as best she could but wasn't entirely successful. Before long her hair and skin were splattered with filth. The people following behind her and Wind Rider had grown into a small crowd. Wind Rider reined in abruptly, and she plowed into the side of his mount, staggered, and sat down hard on the muddy ground. Derisive laughter turned her cheeks fiery red and her Irish temper exploded. Picking herself off the ground, she glared defiantly at the Indians, who were pointing and holding their noses, as if offended by her stench.

"Aiyee! Our Cheyenne brother has returned with his slave. I'm surprised you spared her life; she smells worse than the village dogs. There is no accounting for some men's tastes." The crowd cleared a path for Cut Nose.

Hannah glared sullenly at the ugly Sioux, aware that he was making fun of her. While he and Wind Rider greeted one another, Hannah looked curiously about her. The village appeared to be quite large, with more tepees than she could count spread over a flat plain. She could see hills in the distance, and a river winding through them. Dogs ran helter-skelter, barking and fighting with one another for scraps of food. The sound of raised voices brought her attention back to Wind Rider and Cut Nose. She wished she knew what they were arguing about.

"You are a courageous man, Wind Rider, to bring this wretched creature to our village. If you wish to be rid of her, I will buy her from you." He leered at Hannah, looking through the dirt and grime to some perceived worth. He'd always hungered to taste white flesh but had never had the opportunity. "Take your pick of any of my finest horses."

"She isn't for sale." Wind Rider's harsh voice brought a sneer to Cut Nose's ugly face.

"Can it be that you have already mounted her despite her stench? Obviously you have derived some pleasure from her or you wouldn't turn down my offer. No man has finer horses than I, and you have so few."

A slow flush crept up Wind Rider's neck. He didn't like to be reminded that he had lost his fine herd when he had left his tribe at Sand Creek and ridden north to join the Sioux. Had he wanted a wife, he couldn't have paid the bride's price.

"The woman is my slave; she is not for sale," Wind Rider repeated with ominous portent. "No one is to touch her; is that clear?"

Runs-Like-A-Deer chose that moment to appear, obviously pleased to see Wind Rider looking so hale and hardy. "No one is questioning your right to the white woman, my Cheyenne brother," he said, sending Cut Nose a stern look. Runs-Like-A-Deer was a respected chieftain whose word was rarely disputed. Though not as important as Red Cloud, he was nevertheless a wise and courageous warrior. He belonged to the mighty War Dog society, as did Cut Nose and Wind Rider. "I do not think even

Red Cloud would dispute your right. Unless," he added idly, "he wishes to ransom her to the white eyes for one of our own."

Wind Rider relaxed and slid from his mount. "Little Sparrow is worthless to the white eyes," he said disparagingly. Not entirely true, Wind Rider thought but did not say. If Little Sparrow could be believed, her owner might be searching for her at this very moment. "I'm sure there are other more important hostages to offer to the white eyes. This one I will keep."

Runs-Like-A-Deer noted Wind Rider's look of fierce possession and the fact that he had given the woman an Indian name, and wondered at it. But it was none of his business; he did not inquire into Wind Rider's motives, although he knew Cut Nose had taken a liking to the frail captive and would do his utmost to claim her for himself. Runs-Like-A-Deer couldn't imagine what either man saw in the plain little sparrow, but that was their affair. For himself, he preferred his two plump wives, whose well-rounded flesh warmed his blankets on cold nights.

When both Cut Nose and Runs-Like-A-Deer turned and walked away Hannah steeled herself for what was to come next. She didn't have long to wait. Wind Rider barked an order, and one of the children ran off. He returned a few minutes later with a pole about three feet long and a length of rope. Wind Rider pounded the pole deeply into the ground with a rock and fastened the end of her tether to it. He tied her hands, then stood back to inspect his handi-work.

"No, don't leave me like this!" Hannah tugged at the rope with her bound hands.

Hardening his heart, Wind Rider turned and entered his tepee. The flap came down into place with a jarring thud. The women and children who had been watching with much amusement decided Wind Rider's exit gave them license to do as they wished with the captive. Whooping with joy, the children found sharp sticks and formed a circle around her, taunting and jabbing her cruelly. Refusing to cry out, Hannah glared at them defiantly. But when the women joined in the enter-tainment she could not suppress a yelp of pain when a particularly vicious blow bruised her ribs.

Wind Rider tried to close his ears to the cries of his captive as the women and children taunted her. Many of the women had lost chil-dren and husbands to the white eyes and they deserved their fun, as long as it didn't get out of hand. But when Hannah let out a wail of agony he reacted instinctively. He thrust aside the tent flap and burst through the opening. Legs spread wide apart, he stood over Hannah, glaring fiercely.

"Be gone!" he ordered harshly. "I will pun-ish my slave as I see fit." His words were met with sullen looks, but were obeyed neverthe-less. When they were alone he nudged Hannah with his toe. "Are you hurt?"

Hannah glowered at him. "Why should you care? I never saw such vicious women. Will they be back?"

"They will not return. You didn't answer me. Where are you hurt?"

"I—my ribs. The women derived great pleasure from jabbing me with sharp sticks."

"They will not hurt you again." He turned to reenter his tepee. He was filthy and wished to go down to the river and bathe. And he was so hungry his ribs were touching his backbone.

"Wind Rider! My brother told me you had returned. Are you recovered from your wound?" The woman who spoke carried a kettle and offered it to Wind Rider. "I thought you might be hungry after your long journey."

Wind Rider turned, saw Spotted Doe approaching, and smiled. Though not as modest and retiring as Cheyenne maidens, Spotted Doe, an exceptionally pretty young Sioux woman, gave every indication that she favored him above other men. She was sister to Cut Nose.

"I am well, Spotted Doe. Thank you for the food. I am indeed hungry."

"You should have a woman to care for you and cook your meals," she hinted slyly. Her bold smile indicated that she should be that woman. "If you'd like I'll tend to your wound."

"Perhaps later, Spotted Doe, after I bathe and eat. But I assure you it is fine." Wind Rider couldn't get over the difference between shy Cheyenne maidens, who cherished their virginity, and bold Sioux women, who found no reason to abstain from sex if they found a man who pleased them. And if they were displeased with their man after marriage, they simply divorced him. All they need do was leave their mate's tepee.

Spotted Doe smiled enticingly. "I will return later." Suddenly she spied Hannah, huddled against the pole to which she was bound. "So this is your slave." She placed a finger to her nose. "She stinks. Cut Nose said she was an ugly, pitiable creature and my brother did not lie. What are you going to do with her?"

Hannah stared at the beautiful Indian maiden, aware of her contempt and loathing. The woman's large, doelike eyes held no hint of compassion, no spark of kindness. The only time they softened was when she looked at Wind Rider. Was she Wind Rider's woman? Hannah wondered dimly.

"She is my slave and will do whatever I tell her," Wind Rider said. "Women's work is difficult; she will not be idle."

Spotted Doe's eyes narrowed. "I am glad she is ugly. If she was beautiful, you might be tempted to take her to your blankets."

"The woman is a whore, accustomed to bedding many men. But fear not, Spotted Doe, I have no intention of bedding my slave. Little Sparrow does not appeal to me."

Wind Rider had no reason to believe he would soon wish back his words.

Chapter Five

Hannah sagged against the pole to which she was bound, glad to see the last of the lovely Sioux maiden. The girl's dark, glowering looks gave mute evidence to the scathing contempt she felt for the white female slave Wind Rider had captured. Had the maiden considered Hannah a threat for the affection of Wind Rider, Hannah had no doubt she would have found a way to eliminate the threat. Hannah thanked God the maiden considered her unworthy of the attention of a mighty warrior like Wind Rider.

Wind Rider watched the seductive sway of Spotted Doe's hips as she walked away. He hadn't had a woman in a long time, and he wondered if the Sioux maiden would lie with him. He briefly considered visiting one of the camp whores, or a widow known to accommodate young warriors, but somehow the idea did not appeal to him. He glanced at Hannah, recalling how she had looked with her body free of filth and her hair gloriously clean and shining. His body hardened, envisioning the copper-hued forest cresting her woman's mound. He wondered how it would feel to thrust his mighty rod into the tight warmth of her sheath. He scowled fiercely, sickened by the thought of the countless men who had used her body in such a manner.

Hannah wondered what Wind Rider was thinking. He was staring at her so intently and frowning so sternly, she feared that he meant to do her bodily harm. A roll of thunder called her attention to the drenching rain that had plagued them off and on all day. Would Wind Rider leave her out in a raging storm all night?

Wind Rider heard the thunder and wondered the same thing. If he left his captive to the mercy of the elements, she might become ill and die. Yet she stank so badly he didn't dare allow her inside his tepee. Another roll of thunder made up his mind. Turning abruptly, he disappeared into the tepee, emerging a few minutes later stripped to his breechclout and carrying a bundle under his arm. Then he bent and untied the end of the rope binding Hannah to the pole. He tugged her to her feet.

"Where are you taking me?"

Disdaining an answer, Wind Rider jerked on the rope. Hannah stumbled after him, the pressure on her tender neck propelling her forward. He took her to the river, untied her hands, and removed the rope from her neck. He frowned when he saw the ugly raw burns marring her flesh. He had had no idea her skin would be so sensitive. Once she was free of her fetters he pushed her toward the river. When she balked he removed something from the bundle he had brought along, swept her into his arms, and walked into the water. When the water surged up to his waist he set her on her feet and shoved some leaves into her hand.

"Soap plant," he said. "Use it to wash away your stink. Take off the shirt; it smells of dung."

Hannah blanched. "No."

His mouth thinned. Before she knew what was happening Wind Rider grasped the hem of the shirt and pulled it over her head. Then he pushed her beneath the water. She came up sputtering, her green eyes flashing. Wind Rider smiled grimly. A clap of thunder, closer this time, reminded him of the approaching storm. With a flip of his wrist he removed his breechclout and tossed it onto the shore. Then he calmly began scrubbing his body with soap plant. When he finished he turned to Hannah, annoyed that she had made no move to bathe.

"If you are to sleep inside my tepee tonight, you must bathe."

Hannah looked stunned. "Inside your tepee?" She touched her throat, still raw from the rope.

Though she had no desire to be tethered again to the pole, spending the night in Wind Rider's tepee was even more frightening. He was too male, too powerful, too intimidating—too handsome by far. He did things to her that made her body yearn for something too outrageous to contemplate.

"Are you going to bathe, or must I do it for you?"

Staring at the soap plant in her hand, she slowly began to rub her skin, working up a lather. She tried not to look at Wind Rider, aware that he was staring at her in a most disconcerting manner. When she felt his hands on her back she stiffened. She relaxed when she realized he was merely washing where she could not reach. When his hands slid around to her breasts, she grasped his wrists.

"Don't."

He freed himself easily, sliding his hands to her back again, then down her spine to her buttocks. Hannah cried out when he boldly inserted a hand between her thighs and stroked.

"Do you like that, Little Sparrow?" he whispered into her ear. His fingers grew daring as they teased the portals of her womanhood.

She felt the thrust of his arousal against her buttocks and tried to whirl away. The resistance of water against her body made her sluggish, and Wind Rider easily captured her, pulling her hard against him. "No, please, don't touch me like that."

"You have been without a man's touch a long time, Little Sparrow. Do you ache inside? Do you have a need to be ridden? If I recall, you are almost presentable when your body is free of dirt and grime." He turned her in his arms, dragging her against him from breast to groin. "Your heart is fluttering like a captive mare, Little Sparrow. I will be your stallion."

"Why do you call me that? My name is Hannah, and I have no great need. Not the kind you're talking about." She pounded on his chest. "Let me go, you heathen savage!"

The stark planes of Wind Rider's face hardened, and he pushed her away. "I would rather bed a rattlesnake than a whore who thinks herself too good to lie beneath an Indian."

"I'm not a whore! Why do you call me that when you know nothing about me?"

Glaring at her, Wind Rider shoved her beneath the water. When she bobbed to the surface he attacked her head with the soap plant. Not until he had worked up a rich lather did he answer her question.

"I saw you before, but you do not remember. Many moons ago in Denver. You were outside an inn; it was wintertime. Your master was beating you for running away. He called you a whore and spoke of selling your body to his customers."

Hannah stared at him, searching her memory. Her mind traveled back in time, instantly conjuring up a tall man who had briefly joined the crowd that had gathered to watch Mr. Harley punish her for running away. Her memory was clear as a mountain brook; that man was no Indian. He was as white as she, with silver eyes that hinted at compassion. This steely-eyed Indian had no compassion in his soul. She remembered how their eyes had met briefly before he turned and walked away. Suddenly comprehension dawned. Could that man have been Wind Rider? The answer left her breathless. It had to be, or else how could he describe the scene so accurately? When the truth dawned on her she looked physically ill.

"I see you remember." He smiled mirthlessly. "I recognized you immediately. That is how I knew you were a woman of easy virtue."

"I-I don't understand. There were many men watching that day, but they were white. I'd swear to it. I saw no Indian in the crowd."

Wind Rider neither denied nor affirmed her claim. "Finish your bath. Rain will fall soon and I am hungry." He turned and walked away.

The breath caught in Hannah's throat. The extraordinary sight of his nude body rising slowly from the water transfixed her. The fading light revealed a body golden all over; a true vision of masculine virility, with rippling muscles and corded tendons. The notion that he might be white was more than she could comprehend. Logic told her that he was a half-breed, which seemed entirely possible. She continued to stare at him until he had fastened his breechclout about his slim hips.

Wind Rider retrieved the blanket he had brought with him and beckoned to Hannah. "Come." He held the blanket aloft.

Averting her gaze, Hannah walked from the water, aware of the scorching heat emanating from Wind Rider's narrowed eyes. Shielding her body with her hands, she walked directly into the blanket stretched between his arms. His arms closed around her, bringing the ends of the blanket together. Then he slowly rubbed her body dry.

"I-I can do that," Hannah gasped, stunned by her body's reaction to his touch.

"You have gained weight," Wind Rider observed.

The brief glance he'd had of her nude body showed him the result of the satisfying meals he had provided for her since her captivity. A few more weeks of regular meals and he'd dare anyone to call her scrawny. And as for her being plain, nothing was further from the truth. A cloud of rich auburn hair framed a face as delicate as a lacy web with dew clinging to its silken threads. She'd never be as strong as an Indian maiden, but she had enough grit and determination to make up for it. And her lilting voice sounded like the sweet music of the gods.

Annoyed at the direction his thoughts were taking, Wind Rider's voice was harsher than he had intended. "If you give me no trouble, I will not place the rope around your neck."

"What trouble can I cause in a camp filled with Indians?" she replied sullenly.

Wind Rider nodded. "Come. My ribs are touching my backbone. I am anxious to taste Spotted Doe's stew."

"I suspect she'd like you to taste more than her stew," Hannah muttered crossly.

"What did you say?"

Hannah started violently. What in the devil was she thinking? She didn't care if the big buck bedded every Indian maiden in the village. "Nothing."

"Hurry; it's starting to rain."

Sure enough, raindrops pelted them just as they reached the edge of the village. Holding up the blanket so she wouldn't trip, Hannah hurried along beside Wind Rider. She ducked into the tepee just as the sky opened, grateful that he hadn't insisted upon tying her to the stake outside. Spotted Doe was waiting for them, her face a mask of fury.

"I've been waiting for you," she said, sidling up beside Wind Rider. "I have built a fire to warm the stew I prepared. When you are finished I will tend your leg." She sent Hannah a venomous look when she noted that Wind Rider's slave no longer resembled the pathetic creature she'd first seen tied to the stake. Though the light was dim, she could tell that the slave was young and beautiful—too beautiful. "What is she doing here? Why have you brought her inside your lodge?"

Annoyed at Spotted Doe's possessive manner, Wind Rider merely shrugged. "It is storming outside. She will be no use to me if she falls ill."

"Where are her clothes? She looks different somehow."

"Her clothes were filthy. I could not abide her stench so I took her to the river to bathe. I hoped you might have a garment she could wear. It needn't be new. Anything serviceable will do."

As much as Spotted Doe wanted to deny Wind Rider's request, she could not. She wanted him to look upon her with favor. He needed a wife and she was much taken with him. Other warriors paled in comparison to the big Cheyenne buck. She had heard that Wind Rider was white, but he exhibited no signs of white blood. He rode with Cut Nose and raided with equal ferocity. He was a War Dog soldier who had proven his courage many times over.

"If you wish it, I will find something for your slave to wear. Now I will tend your wound."

"There is no need, Spotted Doe."

"It pleases me to do it. Coyote gave me a healing salve to apply to your wound."

Wind Rider sat beside the fire while Spotted Doe knelt at his side, spreading the salve over his wound with gentle hands. She lingered as long as she dared, until Wind Rider grew restive; then she rose and prepared to leave. "I will return with the tunic for your slave."

"It is raining and she has no need of it tonight, Spotted Doe. Bring it tomorrow."

Spotted Doe glared at Hannah, unwilling to leave her alone with Wind Rider but knowing she had no choice. "I will do as you say. Enjoy your meal, Wind Rider."

A sigh of relief trembled past Hannah's lips. "Spotted Doe hates me."

Wind Rider sent her a scathing look. "Why do you find that strange? Your people have taken our lands, killed our women and children, and destroyed the buffalo that feeds us. Is it any wonder that my people hate you?"

"How can you blame me for any of that? My home is across the sea in a country called Ireland. My family has never even seen an Indian, let alone killed one."

"You are white," Wind Rider said with finality. "My people see nothing but your white skin." He bent and removed the kettle of stew from the fire. From a parfleche he found bowls and spoons, then carefully divided the stew between the two bowls. He handed one to Hannah. "Sit and eat."

Hugging the blanket to her chest with one hand and holding the bowl with the other, Hannah sat awkwardly. Then she devoured the stew with gusto, finding it surprisingly good despite the fact that it had been prepared by Spotted Doe. When every last morsel had been consumed she sat back and sighed, so exhausted she could barely keep her eyes open.

Replete, Wind Rider rose and stretched. Then he pulled a thick mat of furs from a corner of the lodge and placed it close to the fire, indicating that Hannah should lie down upon it.

Hannah licked her suddenly dry lips. "Where are you going to sleep?"

"I have no other mat. We will share this one."

"I'll sleep on the ground."

His expression hardened. "Why are you afraid? We have shared a mat before."

That's why I'm afraid, Hannah thought but did not say.

Her arguments were ineffectual as Wind Rider shoved her down upon his mat. Before she could rise he whipped off his breechclout and joined her. Grateful for the protective covering, Hannah pulled the blanket tightly around her and tried to relax.

Wind Rider cursed himself for a thousand fools. How could he desire this white woman when those of her race were slowly destroying his people? He trusted no one with white skin. He had lived his life for the past fifteen years as a Cheyenne and had no desire to change now. Turning his back on Hannah, he forced his body to relax, convinced that she was a wicked spirit who used strong medicine to make him want her. The storm raging outside was not nearly as fierce as the one raging inside Wind Rider.

Spotted Doe arrived early the next morning. Wind Rider had already arisen and nudged

Hannah out of the blankets. When Spotted Doe rattled the bones at the entrance of the lodge Wind Rider bade her enter. She ducked beneath the flap, her gaze settling on the single mat that Wind Rider and Hannah had shared. She sent Hannah a malevolent glare.

"I have brought a tunic and moccasins for your slave," she said, tossing a bundle at Hannah's feet. "They are old but good enough for a slave."

Hannah retrieved the bundle and held it to her chest. No matter how old the clothing, they were better than the blanket she clutched around her shoulders. She wanted to dress immediately, but not with Wind Rider and Spotted Doe watching. Wind Rider sensed her dilemma and reacted to her mute appeal with uncharacteristic kindness as he ushered Spotted Doe toward the tepee entrance, holding the flap open so she could leave.

"I must speak with Red Cloud," he said, hoping to speed Spotted Doe on her way.

"Red Cloud is not here," Spotted Doe informed him. "He has gone to a great council called by the army at Fort Laramie. Many Sioux leaders will be there to negotiate peace with the white eyes."

"Peace, bah! Have the Sioux learned nothing from Sand Creek? They should ask the Cheyenne about promises made by white eyes."

Modestly dressed in the threadbare tunic that covered her down to her ankle-high moccasins, Hannah chose that moment to step out into the brilliant light of the morning sun. When Spotted Doe saw her, her eyes widened in disbelief. Inside the dark tepee she'd noticed the change in Hannah but had no idea it would be so dramatic. But now, in the light of day, the change in the slave was utterly astounding.

There was no disguising her slimness, but now it was enhanced by a cloud of copper-hued hair that framed delicate features and absolutely stunning green eyes. Washed clean of dirt and grime, her skin was as white and smooth as that of a newborn babe. Her lips were full, red, and lush. Long feathery eyelashes the color of rich copper made her green eyes appear even more dramatic.

"What have you done to her?" Spotted Doe gasped. "This is not the same woman you brought here yesterday."

"I have no other slave," Wind Rider said, transfixed by Hannah's complete metamorphosis.

"What is she saying?" Hannah asked as Spotted Doe continued to stare at her as if she were something offensive.

"Nothing," Wind Rider barked harshly. "Gather wood; I am hungry. I will ask one of the older women to teach you to cook the food I provide. If you do not do as she says, she will beat you."

"Aren't you afraid I'll run away?"

A grim smile stretched across Wind Rider's generous lips. "You are not stupid. You will not run away."

Seething with anger, Hannah realized that Wind Rider spoke the truth. There were no white settlements nearby, and she greatly feared Indian methods of punishment should she be recaptured. She turned abruptly and walked toward the river, where many trees grew along the bank. Wind Rider watched until she was out of sight, wondering if he should follow.

Wind Rider wasn't the only one watching Hannah's progress through the village. Every young buck lucky enough to be out and about turned to stare after her, including Cut Nose. The ugly warrior's eyes bulged grotesquely and the air left his chest in an explosion of disbelief when he recognized Wind Rider's slave. He had been willing to buy her before this miraculous transformation, but now he was more determined than ever to have her in his blankets. From the very beginning he had looked below the dirt and grime and seen something no one else had seen, but never in his wildest imagination did he expect anything so spectacular. When he saw Hannah walk in the direction of the river he followed, taking a different route so as not to arouse suspicion.

Hannah walked a short distance along the river bank, gathering sticks and driftwood along the way. When she had an armful she turned back toward camp. Fear twisted her gut when she saw Cut Nose step from behind a tree. The wood fell from her arms.

"Stay away from me!" She wasn't certain he could understand English, but he certainly had to know what she was saying from her tone of voice.

Cut Nose laughed harshly. He understood the white man's tongue well enough. Like most Plains Indians, he had picked up the language from traders, mountainmen, and Indian agents. "A slave has no rights." His words were slow and stilted but understandable.

"I belong to Wind Rider," Hannah felt compelled to say. The crafty look in Cut Nose's eyes told her exactly what he wanted from her.

"He will not mind. Did you not know you will become the village whore when he tires of you? It is our way. You will be sent to live in a lodge at the edge of the village, where our warriors can visit you at will."

"No!" Hannah denied vehemently. "Wind Rider would not do that."

"It is the custom. But I have decided I cannot wait. I will mount you now, while you are still young and desirable and before the others ruin you. My friends are not always gentle, and since you are white they will not care if they hurt you."

Without warning he lunged at her. She whirled, attempting to flee, but she wasn't fast enough. Cut Nose was upon her in seconds, bearing her to the ground. He fell atop her heavily, forcing the breath from her lungs. When his hard hands skimmed her thighs and raised her tunic above her waist she struggled valiantly but to no avail. Inserting his hand between their bodies, he tore his breechclout aside and shoved her legs apart. When she pounded against his chest, he seized her hands and held them above her head, leering at her with evil purpose.

Hannah let out a shrill screech, steeling herself for Cut Nose's invasion. "Quiet!" Cut Nose barked. Releasing one of her hands, he clouted her alongside the face to make her more tractable. Finding one hand free, Hannah retaliated by digging her sharp nails down his cheek. Cut Nose spit out a guttural curse, drew his hand back, and prepared to deliver another blow. Hannah closed her eyes and waited, hoping he'd strike her hard enough to render her unconscious. But the blow never fell.

The pressure of Cut Nose's body eased and then was gone. Hannah opened her eyes, surprised to see Wind Rider standing over her, his expression fierce. He had kicked Cut Nose from atop her and stood with his fists clenched, his magnificent body tense, ready to strike again as Cut Nose picked himself up from the ground. Though Hannah had no idea what they were saying, their harsh tones and loud voices led her to believe the situation was explosive.

"The slave is my property. I have said no one is to touch her," Wind Rider challenged.

"And I have offered to buy her from you," Cut Nose returned. "I will give you three horses instead of the one I offered before. I am being most generous to my Cheyenne brother. Besides," he added slyly, "the slave wanted me. She enticed me here and offered herself to me."

"You lie!" Wind Rider denied vehemently. "The blood on your face tells me she was not willing. For the last time, Cut Nose, Little Sparrow is not for sale."

Cut Nose's eyes narrowed. He wasn't about to give up so easily. "She must be very good between the blankets for you to turn down three horses. I will give you five horses, but no more."

"I don't want your horses."

"And," Cut Nose offered as an added inducement, "you may have my sister. She will make you a good wife. She has already told me she favors you. Many good braves have offered for her."

"You are more than generous," Wind Rider said with a hint of sarcasm, "but I do not want a wife."

By now Hannah had staggered to her feet, nursing her aching jaw. It was already turning black-and-blue from Cut Nose's blow. Wind Rider saw it and sent Cut Nose a threatening glare. Then he reached out a protective arm and pulled Hannah beside him.

Cut Nose sneered derisively. "You are a white eyes masquerading as a Cheyenne. How long will it be before you turn traitor to our people? I will ask the council to banish you from our tribe; then I will claim the slave as my own."

Wind Rider laughed harshly. "You may try, but they will not listen to you. I have fought bravely beside my Sioux brothers. I have raided army supply wagons and counted coup upon the enemy many times. I challenge any man to question my courage or loyalty."

Cut Nose sent a leering glance at Hannah, who was plastered against Wind Rider's side. "Perhaps I will challenge you, my white Cheyenne brother, if the council does not vote to banish you from the tribe. You have refused to join with my sister and shamed my family." Whirling on his heel, he strode away.

Hannah allowed herself to breathe again. "He wanted to rape me," she said shakily.

Wind Rider grasped her chin and turned her face toward him. The bruise on her cheek glowed an ugly purple against her white skin. "Did he hurt you?"

The question angered Hannah. Why should Wind Rider care if Cut Nose hurt her when he hadn't treated her with any degree of kindness since he'd captured her? "Do you care? I'm surprised you stopped him from raping me. You Indians are all savages."

Wind Rider's jaw stiffened. "You belong to me. No man has a right to touch you unless I allow it. Did you invite his attention? Did you entice him as he said?"

Hannah paled. "I did no such thing! Cut Nose said you'd make me the village whore when you tired of me. He said it was the custom."

"Cut Nose is right, it is the custom, but it is my decision whether or not that happens. We will speak of this later. Gather the wood; I am hungry."

Her mind in a turmoil, Hannah did as she was told, aware that her future—or lack of one—depended on this fierce Indian, who did not look at all like an Indian.

Wind Rider did not let Hannah out of his sight as he followed her back to camp. "I will build a fire this once, but in the future the chore will be yours. You must not forget that you are my slave."

Hannah already knew how to build a fire; she had done it when she traveled west with the Harleys. They had joined a wagon train at Independence, and all the difficult chores had fallen to her.

Hannah was wondering what Wind Rider expected her to cook when an old woman hobbled over and placed a skillet on the fire to heat. Then she took some ground grain from a parfleche she had brought with her and mixed it with water, placing it in the sizzling skillet. The aroma was delicious, and Hannah's mouth began to water. When the old woman spoke to Hannah in guttural Sioux, Hannah looked at her dumbly. Angered by Hannah's inability to understand, the old woman picked up a thin stick and began beating her about the shoulders and back.

"She wants you to get the bowls and honey."

"I don't know where to look."

"Inside the tepee. There is a deerskin pouch hanging on one of the back poles. Inside you'll find bowls and a small amount of honey for the frybread."

Hannah hurried inside the tepee, and the old woman smiled broadly and nodded. When Hannah returned the woman was gone. Spotted Doe had taken her place. The Indian maiden's dark eyes rested on Hannah, so filled with malice, Hannah stopped abruptly in her tracks. Hannah listened intently to the conversation between Wind Rider and Spotted Doe and didn't need an interpreter to know that the woman was angry.

"Cut Nose told me how you shamed our family," Spotted Doe said sourly. "Am I not good enough for you? Is there some other maiden you wish to join with? Perhaps you prefer a Cheyenne maiden. If you wish it, I will become your second wife."

"How could I take a second wife when I have no first wife? I have no plans to take a wife at this time."

"What about her?" Spotted Doe asked, gesturing toward Hannah. "Will your slave warm your blankets?"

"If I wish it."

Rage seethed through Spotted Doe. "Is it because she has white skin like yours?"

Wind Rider tensed. Never in all his years with the Cheyenne had his loyalty been questioned. "I am Cheyenne, brother to the Sioux. White men have destroyed my hunting grounds. They killed my mother, Gray Dove, and sent my tribe fleeing for their lives."

Spotted Doe flushed and lowered her head, aware that she had spoken rashly. "I did not mean to anger you. But I must warn you, Cut Nose is a vindictive man. For some reason he wants your slave. He has gone to the council to request that you be banished from the tribe. But if you join with one of our women, they will be more favorable toward you."

"I am not afraid to appear before the council. I have friends who will speak for me. No one can doubt my loyalty after fighting beside me in battle."

Spotted Doe smiled at him and placed a small hand on his arm. "I hope you are right. But if they decide they need further proof, joining with one of our women will convince them of your loyalty. My family is willing for me to join with you, and since you have no horses to offer as a bride price, Cut Nose will gladly accept your slave."

Chapter Six

Hannah knew by the fierce scowl on Wind Rider's face that Spotted Doe had angered him. But she didn't have time to question him because Coyote arrived, dismissing Spotted Doe with a wave of his hand. Hannah squatted beside the fire, wishing she could understand.

"I have just come from the council," Coyote told Wind Rider. "They will meet to consider Cut Nose's allegations concerning your loyalty. Cut Nose fears you will betray us because you are white, but I know better, my brother. Your heart is pure Cheyenne."

"Thank you, Coyote. When is the council to meet?"

"They will meet tomorrow when the sun is at its highest. They will hear Cut Nose first, and then you will be called upon to defend yourself. I think Cut Nose is jealous of you. He wants your slave," Coyote confided, casting a surreptitious glance at Hannah. "He is telling everyone that his family has suffered great embarrassment because you refused to join with his sister."

"I do not wish to take a wife."

"It would be wise if you reconsidered," Coyote advised. "Cut Nose is willing to accept your slave in lieu of a bride price."

"The council has no reason to question my loyalty," Wind Rider repeated. He cast a sidelong glance at Hannah. "I will not give up my slave. The council may question me all they like; I have nothing to hide. I have never given them any cause for doubt. I am the son of White Feather, respected chieftain of the Southern Cheyenne."

"I agree, my brother, and so will the council if they are wise. Runs-Like-A-Deer and I will speak in your defense. So will others of the council."

"Thank you, my friend."

Hannah watched Coyote walk away, wondering what their conversation had been about. It sounded serious. She jumped when Wind Rider said, "Come inside the tepee. I wish to speak to you in private."

Hannah scooted inside, wondering what Wind Rider wanted to talk about. Wind Rider closed the tent flap and stared at her with such absorption, she retreated a step, seared by the silver intensity of his eyes.

"Cut Nose wants you. He offered me his sister and is willing to accept you as the bride price since I have few horses."

Hannah blanched. She'd die before she'd allow Cut Nose to touch her. "Did you accept his offer?" She was trembling so badly, the words tumbled one after another from her white lips. "Spotted Doe is very beautiful." She sucked in her breath and held it, waiting for Wind Rider's answer.

Not as beautiful as you, he thought. "I do not need a wife," Wind Rider said harshly. "Nor am I willing to trade you to Cut Nose."

His answer gave Hannah the courage to breathe again. What would she have done if he had agreed to Cut Nose's proposal? When her knees started to buckle Wind Rider reached out to steady her. His eyes widened when he felt a shock travel up the length of his arm. Had Little Sparrow felt it, too? he wondered.

"I do not wish to be traded to Cut Nose," Hannah whispered shakily. "If I must have a master I prefer it to be you." Hannah couldn't imagine what possessed her to say such a thing. She wanted no master, especially not an Indian master. But Wind Rider was such a contradiction, she didn't understand her own feelings where he was concerned.

She feared him, that was true, yet he hadn't really hurt her. And sometimes he treated her with more kindness and consideration than Mr. Harley had. There were times, like now, when she could have sworn he possessed not one Indian trait or characteristic. But when he was painted with hideous stripes, his hair hanging loose about his wide shoulders, carrying tomahawk and bow, he looked every bit as savage as his companions.

Wind Rider's eyes narrowed. "What kind of whore's trick are you playing? False words do not impress me."

That word again! Hannah's temper flared. "I am no whore!"

"Perhaps I will find out for myself." He reached for her, dragging her against his hard length. Her lips were red and lush, and he ran his tongue over their full contours, sampling their ripeness. She tasted so sweet, he hungered for more.

In a saloon in Denver he had seen white men press their mouths against those women who sold their bodies for coin. They seemed to enjoy it, and as he licked Hannah's lips he was tempted to try it himself. Cheyenne did not press mouths like white eyes. They licked their lovers' faces, and sometimes their bodies, and pressed their cheeks together or rubbed noses. But this, he decided, as he covered Hannah's mouth with his, was so pleasant, he could easily become addicted.

Stunned by her reaction to Wind Rider's kiss, Hannah melted into the hard wall of his chest. It was Hannah's first kiss, and her mouth opened in surprise. She had no idea it would make her tingle all over or ache in places she had never ached before.

Instinct guided Wind Rider as he thrust his tongue inside Hannah's sweet mouth. Her taste was utterly captivating, and he pressed her closer, until he felt the hard peaks of her breasts stab into his chest. A groan of sheer agony slipped from his throat. His big hands splayed over her slim back, sliding downward along her spine, cupping the sweet mounds of her buttocks into his groin. His manhood throbbed strong and hard between them, prodding the tender curve of her stomach.

Hannah felt his hips rock against her and came abruptly to her senses. How could she respond so fiercely to this savage? It was the first time she had ever felt desire for a man. But she feared and distrusted all men. What made Wind Rider different from any other man, to make her feel the kind of things she was experiencing in his arms? She fought to regain her sanity, struggling desperately to free herself from the lure of his strong arms. "No!"

He held her captive, mesmerized by the rapid flutter of her heart against his breast. "You are my slave. You will do as I say." He fell to his knees, dragging her down with him. "Take off your tunic." Wind Rider had no idea what possessed him, but if he didn't have Little Sparrow now he would surely perish. It must be his cursed white blood clamoring within him, he thought disgustedly.

Hannah's eyes darted toward the entrance, visually measuring the distance. "You can't escape; don't even think it." His fingers grasped the ties holding her tunic together at the shoulders. He wanted her so badly, he would have ripped it from her body if someone hadn't rattled the buffalo bones outside the lodge. Frustration seethed through Wind Rider as he glanced at the closed flap, tempted beyond redemption to ignore the summons.

"Wind Rider, it is Runs-Like-A-Deer. I must speak with you."

Wind Rider spat out a curse as he rose to his feet, adjusted his breechclout, and flung open the flap. He didn't invite Runs-Like-A-Deer inside but stepped out instead.

Hannah slumped in relief. If someone hadn't arrived to speak to Wind Rider, he would have taken her. *And she probably would have helped him.* How could she act so wantonly? She was still shaking, wondering how long her reprieve would last. When Wind Rider's visitor left would he finish what he had started? She touched her flushed cheeks, not surprised to find them burning. If she had been home in Ireland, she would have rushed to the church and confessed her sins to the priest, for she had actually felt desire for a savage heathen. For a fleeting instant she had wanted to lie beneath his big golden body, yearned for the touch of his hands on her bare flesh, wished to experience the forbidden mysteries that would have made her a woman.

When Wind Rider ducked back inside the tent and scowled fiercely at her Hannah's thoughts scattered.

"I go now to the purification hut. Tonight the council will decide who will be your owner," he told her gruffly. His body still wanted Hannah so badly, the physical pain was nearly unbearable. "Runs-Like-A-Deer will accompany me."

"Wh-what about me?" She feared Cut Nose would try something, with Wind Rider gone. "I'll be alone."

"Woman-Who-Waddles will stay with you. Do not worry about Cut Nose; he goes also to pray and fast with his friends."

Hannah relaxed visibly, though her face was still pale. "What if the council decides against you?"

"They will not." He said it with such conviction, Hannah felt reassured—but not completely.

"But what if they do?"

He sent her an inscrutable look. "I will leave and you will belong to Cut Nose." He did not tell her that if such an incredible thing were to happen he would not leave her to the mercy of Cut Nose. Somehow, some way, he would take her with him.

"Oh, God."

A few minutes later the old woman who had showed her how to make frybread arrived with her mat rolled up under her arm. She spoke briefly to Wind Rider, placed her mat in a corner, and went outside, where she busied herself at the fire.

"I will not be far away," Wind Rider told her. "Do not try to escape." Then he ducked through the flap and was gone.

The council convened promptly at noon the following day. Hannah lingered outside the tepee with Woman-Who-Waddles, watching closely as Cut Nose addressed the circle of men who were to decide for or against Wind Rider. It seemed to Hannah that Cut Nose spoke most eloquently, gesturing wildly to make a point. So much depended on the outcome of the council that Hannah could think of nothing but what would happen if Wind Rider was banished from the tribe.

After what seemed like hours Wind Rider joined the council. Hannah thought he appeared strong and confident as he spoke to the group. She could hear nothing of what was being said and couldn't glean a thing from their stoic expressions.

Wind Rider noted many friends among the council members, including Runs-Like-A-Deer and Coyote. He knew Cut Nose had stated his case quite persuasively but nevertheless felt optimistic about the outcome. No viable reason to dispute his loyalty to the People existed.

A chieftain named Iron Fist was the first to question Wind Rider. "Cut Nose has brought serious charges against you, my Cheyenne brother. It is a well-known fact that you are white, and Cut Nose fears you will betray our people to the white eyes."

"You know me, Iron Fist. We have fought side by side in battle. Have I ever given you cause to suspect my loyalty? My heart is Cheyenne. My father is White Feather. I have counted coup against our common enemy the Crow and Pawnee and killed pony soldiers who want to take our land away."

"It is as Wind Rider says," Coyote agreed, nodding sagely. "I would trust Wind Rider with my life. His chest bears scars from the Sun Dance and his body carries wounds suffered in battle with white eyes. What further proof do we need?"

The men of the council nodded in agreement, but Iron Fist, a friend of Cut Nose, was not entirely convinced. "Cut Nose has suggested that you marry one of our women to prove your loyalty." Once again the men of the council nodded, thinking the idea a good one.

"I do not have the bride price."

"Cut Nose says his sister is eager to join with you. His parents are willing, and it is a good match. He will forfeit the bride price in exchange for your white slave."

Wind Rider sent Cut Nose a fulminating glance. "Cut Nose speaks out of jealousy. The slave is mine to do with as I please. It is the law of our people."

"I agree with Wind Rider," Runs-Like-A-Deer interjected. "He found the slave. It is his choice whether he wishes to trade her."

"I generously offered to trade five of my best horses for Wind Rider's slave," Cut Nose charged, jumping into the fray. "It is more than she is worth. Then I offered to give him my sister and he refused, thereby insulting my family."

Wind Rider sneered. "Am I here to defend my loyalty or my right to marry when and whom I please?"

Iron Fist nodded, then grew thoughtful. His words went right to the heart of the problem. "It seems to me the whole issue revolves around one insignificant female slave. The dissension troubles me. The simple solution is to kill her. I have seen the woman, and she does not appear strong enough to be of any use as a slave." Many nodded in agreement. The death of a female slave seemed a small sacrifice to restore peace among two of their bravest warriors.

Wind Rider felt as if he had been gut-punched. He would flee with Little Sparrow before he'd allow her to be tortured or killed.

Cut Nose smirked slyly. If he couldn't have the woman, neither should Wind Rider. "It is a wise decision, Iron Fist."

"But it is not the decision of the entire council," Coyote cautioned. "We will smoke and give the matter more thought."

Suddenly Wind Rider leaped to his feet, his face stark as he glared at each of the council members in turn. "I will join with the slave.

Once she is my wife none can dispute my legal right to her. It is not uncommon for a brave to join with a white captive. She will give me strong sons and daughters. As my mate she will be integrated into the tribe and become one of us."

Wind Rider heard his voice and couldn't believe the words were coming from his mouth. Taking a wife was the last thing in the world he wanted to do, especially a wife so frail a good wind would blow her over. She'd probably be too weak to do all the hard work that needed to be done or bear him strong children. In the past, when he had pictured himself with a mate, she never had soft white skin or hair that rivaled the sunrise.

"You wish to join with her?" Iron Fist repeated. Wind Rider nodded. "It is not unheard of among the People, but I would advise you against it."

"If Wind Rider joins with the white captive, it will add insult to injury after refusing my sister," shouted Cut Nose, leaping to his feet and glaring at Wind Rider.

"I will have Little Sparrow," Wind Rider insisted. "I would prefer to have the council's approval, but if I do not it will not stop me. I will leave the tribe. There are many tribes scattered throughout the Black Hills and the Badlands in need of a strong warrior to fight the white eyes."

Iron Fist conferred briefly with the council members while Wind Rider and Cut Nose glared at one another, awaiting their decision. Wind Rider listened closely, smiling when he became aware that the members were voting in his favor.

"It is the council's decision that Wind Rider should be allowed to remain with the People. We have all seen proof of his courage in battle. Red Cloud himself trusted him enough to send him to Denver to pose as a white man and seek information after the attack at Sand Creek.

"Therefore, we find no cause to question his loyalty or banish him from our tribe. And he may join with whomever he pleases. The white slave is his property. Though Cut Nose has offered in good faith to buy her, it is Wind Rider's choice, and he has chosen to keep her. Perhaps Wind Rider will take Spotted Doe as a second wife to appease Cut Nose's family."

"I will think on it," Wind Rider said, though in truth he had no intention of taking a second wife. And perhaps not even a first. If he was lucky, he could put off joining with Little Sparrow until the council forgot about it.

Iron Fist quickly laid that hope to rest. "Tonight we will have a celebration in honor of your joining. All the tribe will gather to dance and feast. Since your wife has no relatives among us, Woman-Who-Waddles will act as her family and help her prepare for the celebration."

Iron Fist dismissed the council with a wave of his hand, and one by one the members drifted away, carrying word of the celebration. Some men went out immediately to hunt, and Wind Rider expressed his desire to join them, but first he had to speak to Hannah. He suspected she'd fight the council's decision to the bitter end. Cut Nose was so angry, he stomped away in a high rage.

Hannah was a nervous wreck by the time the council members had drifted away. Wind Rider's stoic expression gave nothing away of the council's decision. He turned to stare at her, his face dark and unreadable. When he started toward her Woman-Who-Waddles melted away, leaving her alone to face Wind Rider and whatever it was that was making him so angry. Had he been banished from the tribe? she wondered fearfully. She'd run away or die trying before she'd allow Cut Nose to touch her.

Reaching her side, Wind Rider grasped her arm and pulled her inside the lodge. "What is it? What has the council decided? I won't go to Cut Nose!"

"There is no need. The council has decided in my favor."

A trembling began in Hannah's knees. She had been so frightened . . . "Why are you so angry if the council decided in your favor?"

"Some of the council members wanted to kill you."

Hannah clutched her throat and her eyes grew round. "Kill me? Am I to die?" She prayed it wouldn't be by Wind Rider's hand.

"Perhaps you will prefer death," he said cryptically. "Tonight we are to join."

Hannah stared at him. Did that mean what she thought it meant? "I don't understand."

"Tonight you will become my wife. After we are joined no one will dare question your place in the tribe."

"Your wife! How can that be? I don't want to marry a savage. Besides, there is no priest to perform the ceremony."

Wind Rider snorted in disgust. "No holy man is necessary. According to tribal laws and tradition, once the bride enters her husband's lodge they are wed." He didn't say that divorce was accomplished just as easily. All a woman had to do was leave her husband's lodge and they were considered divorced.

"I won't do it," Hannah insisted stubbornly. "It won't be legal."

"Would you prefer death? Or perhaps," he added with a hint of malice, "you would prefer Cut Nose. It wasn't my wish to join with you, but it was either that or watch them kill you."

Hannah thought neither of those choices particularly palatable. Obviously Wind Rider expected no argument; he went to the back of the tepee and found his bow and quiver of arrows, then ducked beneath the flap. Hannah followed him outside. "Where are you going?"

"Hunting. Woman-Who-Waddles will bring you appropriate clothing for tonight and help you erect our honeymoon lodge."

"H-honeymoon lodge?"

"It is the custom for the bride to erect a lodge out of sight of the village where the bride and groom can be alone to get to know one another. They are expected to remain there seven suns or, in your tongue, one week."

"A week?" Hannah squeaked in disbelief. "Whatever do they do for an entire week?"

Wind Rider's lips quirked upward. "For a whore you are incredibly stupid. I hope you can remember all the ways in which you pleased your white lovers. It will be interesting to learn if white women act differently between the blankets than Indian maidens."

Hannah's mouth dropped open, shocked by Wind Rider's words. It hit her with stunning impact that tonight she would be expected to lie with the handsome savage. His hands would be all over her body; he'd touch her with his lips, his mouth, and he'd force his way into her body. He'd learn the truth, and never again would he call her whore. Just the thought of what tonight would bring sent a shiver of anticipation down her spine. Tongue-tied, she watched him stalk off to join his friends, who were already mounted and waiting for him.

Woman-Who-Waddles appeared the moment Wind Rider left. She giggled and rolled her eyes as she pulled Hannah through the woods to a remote site close to the river. Two women were already there, struggling with a large tepee. They pulled Hannah into their midst, showing her how to place the tent poles and stretch the buffalo skins around the exterior. Within an amazingly short time the honeymoon lodge was ready for occupancy. The two women left and returned shortly with an armful of soft skins and furs for the bed.

Grasping her hand, Woman-Who-Waddles and the others pulled Hannah toward the river. In short order they stripped her of the worn doeskin tunic given to her by Spotted Doe and ducked her beneath the placid surface of the water. Then they literally attacked her with soap plant, scrubbing until her hair and skin was sparkling clean. Wrapping her in a soft blanket, they led her back to Wind Rider's tepee.

The next hours were spent grooming Hannah's hair and dressing her in a pure white doeskin tunic richly embroidered with beads and lavishly fringed. Hannah exclaimed over it with delight, which seemed to please Woman-Who-Waddles. Sometime during the long afternoon Hannah heard the hunters return, but since none of the women understood English she could not question them about tonight's ceremony. The drums began beating at dusk, and Hannah was more frightened than she had ever been in her life.

The women left her then, all but Woman-Who-Waddles, who hovered over Hannah like a mother hen. Suddenly the tent flap opened, and Spotted Doe ducked inside. She faced Hannah squarely, her face dark with hatred.

"It should be I joining with Wind Rider today."

"You speak English," Hannah gasped, astounded.

"Do you think we are all stupid? I learned the white man's tongue from the traders and trappers who visit the tribe regularly. And when the Indian agent comes I listen closely to learn more. Wind Rider is too good for you. The council should have demanded that he join with one of the People and given you to Cut Nose. You are a slave. Cut Nose would treat you as you deserve instead of pampering you."

"It wasn't my decision to join with Wind Rider," Hannah argued defensively. "I didn't ask to be captured."

Spotted Doe's eyes flared in sudden malice. Without warning, she reached for the knife in her belt and advanced toward Hannah. Woman-Who-Waddles saw what was happening and rushed to Hannah's defense. Blocking Spotted Doe, she berated her roundly and pushed her out the door.

"Thank you," Hannah whispered shakily.

Woman-Who-Waddles patted her shoulder consolingly, then took her hand and led her outside. The night was fragrant with the scent of spring. The air was soft and mild. A huge fire blazed in the center of the camp, and the beating drums and foreign words that floated around her gave the scene a dreamlike quality. This can't be real, Hannah thought despairingly. None of this is happening to me.

The wild tempo of the drums increased, and Hannah could see the dancers, circling around the fire to the beat of the heathen music. Most of the dancers were men, joined occasionally by some of the bolder women. Hannah noted that several of the men seated around the fire tipped up bottles and drank deeply of the liquor Hannah assumed was whiskey, provided by unscrupulous traders. Dragging her feet, Hannah would have turned and fled back to the tepee if Woman-Who-Waddles hadn't tugged her forward with amazing strength considering her advanced age.

Hannah had no idea what to expect. Her eyes were frantic as they searched the crowded area. And then she saw him. He stood head and shoulders above the other braves. Dressed in supple doeskin the shade of pale butter, his tunic and leggings were elaborately decorated with feathers and beads. Fringes hung from both sleeves and down the sides of his leggings. His moccasins were also beaded and laced nearly to his knees. He was magnificent, every golden inch of him. His black hair hung loose, held in place by a rawhide thong sporting a white eagle feather.

Wind Rider sensed Hannah's presence before he saw her. Turning to look beyond the dancers, he saw her approaching, escorted by Woman-Who-Waddles. She was dressed in white, he thought ironically, the color of purity. Looking at her angelic features, one would never guess she was a whore. His sanity must have deserted him to join with a woman of easy virtue.

In the short time she had been his captive her flesh had filled out. Though she'd never be plump, she could no longer be classified as scrawny. She was perfect, from the top of her burnished head to the tips of her small feet.

He watched her approach, his loins heavy, his manhood stirring restlessly beneath his breechclout, and he knew a need such as he'd never experienced before. In all his years with the Cheyenne he'd never felt such a wild clamoring in his blood or been driven by an almost painful desire to thrust himself into a woman's body. Not just any woman. His woman. Little Sparrow.

It was the first time in his recent memory that he could recall not cursing the white blood that ran through his veins, for it was the same blood that ran through the veins of Hannah McLin.

She stood before him now, searching his face with frightened green eyes. He took her hand, led her to a place in the circle, and pulled her down beside him. Almost immediately a bowl was placed in her hands, but she could not eat. Neither could Wind Rider, it seemed, for he barely tasted his food before setting down the plate.

"You are very beautiful tonight," he whispered into her ear. "I did not want to take a wife, but tonight I find little to complain about, unless it is the knowledge that I won't be getting a woman known for her virtue. Cheyenne men admire purity in a woman, and Cheyenne women guard their virtue zealously. It is a gift they give their husbands upon their marriage.

Tonight I will try not to think about the other men you have lain with."

Hannah blinked but said nothing. What good would it do? If this was indeed going to be her wedding night, Wind Rider would find out soon enough that she was as virtuous as the purest Cheyenne maiden. Certainly more virtuous than some of the Sioux women she'd seen since her captivity, especially if they were all like Spotted Doe.

The dancing continued, growing more frenzied as the night progressed. Wind Rider grew impatient, and some of his friends realized it. They began taunting him with ribald remarks, as friends were inclined to do to bridegrooms, causing some of the women to cover their ears and giggle. Suddenly Wind Rider had had enough. Without warning he rose to his feet, jerking Hannah with him.

"What is it?" Fear skittered through her. The moment she had dreaded all evening had arrived.

"It is time to go."

"What about the wedding? I thought there was to be a ceremony. Have you changed your mind about marrying me?"

"The moment we walk inside the honeymoon lodge we are wed," Wind Rider told her. "No special ceremony exists. According to tribal customs, once we declare our intention to join we are considered wed. Come." He took her hand, leading her away from the campfire and the celebration.

Dragging her feet, Hannah shook her head in vigorous denial. "It-it's immoral! It's sinful. It's not the way it's done in white society."

"Forget about white society. You are the wife of an Indian now. In this village Indian law prevails. Believe me, Little Sparrow, we are wed. And when your soft white belly swells with my child there will be no room for doubt."

"Oh, my God."

Her knees buckled beneath her. She would have fallen if Wind Rider hadn't scooped her up into his arms. When she saw the honeymoon lodge looming before them in the moonlit darkness she repeated softly, "Oh, my God."

Chapter Seven

Someone had thoughtfully lit a fire inside the lodge and sprinkled it liberally with sweetgrass and sage. It flickered invitingly against the walls. Furs were laid out to form a soft nest and fresh pine boughs scattered about to produce a pleasant scent. But Hannah was aware of nothing except the implied promise of Wind Rider's hard body as he carried her inside and set her down on her feet.

Refusing to look at the bed, she stared at the small patch of sky visible through the smokehole, seeing the stars gliding lazily by and wishing she could join them. Wind Rider noted the direction of her gaze and said, "The fragrant smoke from the fire carries the prayers of the People to the spirits above through the smokehole. There is much for you to learn. I will teach you."

He reached for her, his fingers strong and steady as he began to unlace the front of her tunic.

"Tell me more," Hannah said breathlessly, wanting to put off the inevitable. The movement of his fingers against her flesh sent her senses reeling.

Wind Rider prayed for patience, struggling to still the blood clamoring through his veins. "The floor of the lodge represents the earth, the walls the sky; the tepee poles are the trails leading from the earth to the Spirit World. The tepee has a special place in our lives. When the flap is closed a visitor is required to announce himself and await permission to enter. Men usually go to the right when entering and a woman enters behind her husband and goes to the left. Passing between the fire and anyone else in the lodge is bad etiquette."

Hannah half listened, all too aware of the way Wind Rider's eyes were caressing her body. Her breath caught in her throat and held as his words came to a halt and his hands spread the unlaced opening of her tunic apart, baring the rounded curves of her breasts. His body was taut. A muscle in his jaw jerked. His silver eyes were slumberous, his nostrils flared.

Hannah felt a thrill of apprehension. When Wind Rider slipped the tunic from her shoulders she had to breathe or die. She chose to breathe. When the tunic caught on the upward tilt of her breasts Wind Rider tugged impatiently. Hannah grasped his hands in an effort to stop him.

"Wait! The dress is too beautiful to tear. I will do it."

Wind Rider nodded. His eyes shimmered like liquid silver. "Woman-Who-Waddles will be pleased to know that you like the dress. She made it for her daughter, who was to marry Coyote."

Hannah shoved the tunic past her breasts, where it caught on her slim hips. "What happened to her daughter? Why didn't she wear the dress?"

Wind Rider licked his lips, staring at the pink nipples crowning her pert breasts. He thought them small but perfectly formed, and longed to sample their sweetness. "She died of the spotted sickness. Woman-Who-Waddles is happy to have you wear her daughter's dress."

"Thank her for me."

Wind Rider did not answer. He was too aroused to reply. The breath grated harshly from his lungs and he reached out to stroke her right breast. Her skin was soft and warm, and he rubbed the pad of his finger across her nipple, watching it tauten into a hard bud.

Hannah trembled at the staggering need this man aroused in her. She didn't understand how she could feel so intensely about a savage who had made her his slave. And she certainly did not feel married. The heathen ceremony was far removed from a proper church wedding officiated by a priest. But Wind Rider's expression left little doubt in her mind that he considered the wedding legal and binding and expected to bed her this very night.

The air between them was charged as they stared at one another, the tension thick enough to slice as Wind Rider placed his hands on her slim hips and pushed downward, shoving the tunic free. It slid down her legs and pooled around her ankles. Wind Rider lifted her effortlessly and kicked it aside; then he bent and removed her moccasins. He could barely find his breath when he slid his eyes upward along her body.

Her flesh was smooth and white, her breasts as firm as plump apples. Her waist was narrow, her hips slightly flared, her legs long and shapely. His gaze fastened on the fiery triangle between her legs, hiding a treasure that would soon be his. He didn't touch her; he didn't dare. Not yet, not with his blood pumping furiously through his veins, clamoring for fulfillment. Only a savage would throw his woman down and thrust into her again and again without a care for her needs, and he was no savage. With great difficulty he forced a calm he didn't feel, his eyes never leaving hers as he tore off his clothing.

His shirt hit the ground with a thud, followed closely by his leggings. Hannah swallowed convulsively as his body emerged, golden and virile and utterly magnificent. With a flick of his wrist he released his breechclout, and her eyes widened. Thick and pulsing with a life of its own, his manhood thrust out from his body like a velvet-covered pillar of steel. Terror brought a gasp to her lips. She could never take all of him. Before this night was over he'd surely kill her.

Wind Rider's silver eyes glittered with pleasure when he saw Hannah stare at his erection. "Do I compare favorably with your lovers? Is my sword mighty enough to satisfy you? Tell me, Little Sparrow, tell me you find me pleasing." He grasped her shoulders, bringing her against him with jarring impact. The washboard ridges of his belly jerked in violent response.

"I've had no other lovers."

He laughed harshly, rocking against her to demonstrate his need. The sensation of his smooth, hot flesh pressed against every inch of her breasts, belly, and legs was so exquisite, it was almost unbearable. "There is no need to lie. Your past does not matter. But if you give me reason to doubt your faithfulness in the future, I will kill you."

Hannah blanched. He sounded so fierce, she was inclined to believe him.

"Give me your mouth, Little Sparrow. I long to taste it as I did before."

"It's called a kiss," Hannah offered without thinking. "It is common practice in white culture. Most men find it enjoyable."

"And women?" Wind Rider probed. "Do women find it enjoyable?"

Hannah had only that one kiss from Wind Rider with which to judge, but she could definitely say it had been a pleasant experience. "Yes, women find it enjoyable."

"Then we will kiss." His mouth came down on hers, stealing her breath and forcing her lips open. Then he tasted her, as he had longed to do, using his tongue to thrust and withdraw, savoring the sweet heat of her mouth. He groaned as if in pain and carried her down with him to the bed of furs at their feet.

Hannah shivered, but not from cold. "Wind Rider."

His name on her lips was sweet music to his ears. "I am here, Little Sparrow. Forget the other men who have gone before me. Tonight we will find paradise together."

"There were no others . . . oh . . ." The words died in her throat as Wind Rider's lips slid down her neck to feed at her breasts. Sucking and licking, he moved from one to the other, nipping with his teeth, then soothing with the wet roughness of his tongue.

"Do you like that, Little Sparrow?"

He didn't wait for an answer as his lips slid downward across the flat planes of her belly, stopping to gently tongue her navel while his hands sought the warmth between her legs that he craved with every fiber of his being. Parting the silken forest at the base of her thighs, his fingers slid into the moist crevice, the incredible heat of her tender flesh scorching him. With unerring expertise he found the swollen bud of her womanhood and massaged slowly, using the callused pad of his fingertip to arouse her.

Hannah cried out, stunned by a passion she never knew she possessed. She clutched at him in mute desperation, unable to prevent her hands from exploring the smooth golden flesh of his back and shoulders. The rippling sinews and suppressed strength of his big body raised her level of excitement to panting rapture. Her hands strayed lower, finding the taut mounds of his buttocks, wondering how something so hard could feel so smooth and supple. He moved between her legs, spreading them wide. Hannah steeled herself for the pain of his entry, but instead felt the slippery thrust of his finger inside her.

"You're so hot and wet inside." His voice whispered against her ear, low and intense, and so full of need she trembled anew.

Hannah twisted restlessly, adjusting to the discomfort of a foreign object inside her body. The movement succeeded in driving his finger deeper, and the discomfort turned to pleasure, a kind of pleasure she'd never known before. His gentle thrusts sent her senses soaring as her body began to tingle and burn, seeking a mysterious goal she had never before achieved. Wind Rider's assault continued, allowing Hannah no respite as her body tingled and vibrated to the tune of his talented hands. When his mouth took hers, adding another dimension to her torment, the tingling became so intense, she felt herself starting to disintegrate.

Suddenly the pressure eased and Hannah felt as if she would die if she didn't find what she was looking for. "Wind Rider, please."

"Please, what?" His voice was as strained as hers, his need as great.

"I want . . ."

"What do you want, Little Sparrow?"

"I-don't know. Please . . ."

"Spread your legs. I will not withhold what you seek."

His manhood prodded against her belly, huge and throbbing and frightening. She stared at it, fearing he would break her in two if he tried to put it inside her. He placed the swollen tip against the slick portals of her womanhood and she began to shake.

"No! I can't! You're too big!"

"I am no different from any other man," Wind Rider said, proud of his size and strength despite his modest words.

"Don't do this."

"You are my wife, Little Sparrow. Besides, it is too late."

And it was too late. She felt herself stretching to accommodate him, felt the discomfort of his entry as he pushed forward.

"You're incredibly tight," he said, perplexed at the resistance of her narrow passage.

Hannah whimpered, passion dying as quickly as it had been born. Then her whimper turned to a startled cry of agony as Wind Rider thrust his hips and broke through her maidenhead. He stilled, waiting for her body to adjust to him, then he moved slowly and deliberately, trying to reconcile himself to the startling revelation that Hannah was a maiden who had never lain with a man. He had not expected it, would not have believed it if he hadn't felt the barrier of her virginity himself.

"It won't hurt for long, Little Sparrow, I promise. I will finish quickly to ease your pain."

He was so close to the edge, it took little effort to stroke himself to a shuddering climax. A sigh of blessed relief issued from Hannah's lips when he withdrew and settled beside her on the mat.

"Did I hurt you badly?" he asked once his breathing slowed to a normal pace.

"Yes." Her sullen reply was not just the result of the pain, but also of disappointment. For some reason she felt let down, as if there should have been more.

"Next time will be easier, and you will feel pleasure."

"Does there have to be a next time?"

"You will wish it as much as I."

Hannah watched warily as he rose and found his breechclout, which he wet thoroughly, using a pitcher of water sitting in a corner. He returned and knelt beside her; spreading her legs and washing her as gently as he would a babe. Hannah's face turned crimson. It never occurred to her that a man would perform such an intimate task. When he finished he lay back down beside her. Then, with slow deliberation, he aroused her anew, using his mouth, hands, and tongue to bring her to the peak of passion.

When at length the hot tip of his tongue touched the throbbing bud nestled at the juncture of her thighs, shock turned her rigid and she cried out in protest. "What are you doing?"

"I will not hurt you," Wind Rider said, pressing against her belly with the palm of his hand to hold her still. "I wish to bring you pleasure."

He bent his head, laving her tender, swollen flesh with his tongue. Her body jerked reflexively, and the burning began, deep inside her most secret passages. She felt on the verge of explosion. His tongue pursued her relentlessly, and when he thrust his finger inside her she went up in flames, shattering into so many pieces, she doubted she'd ever be whole again. Lifting his head, Wind Rider watched her climax, his expression that of a hungry wolf.

Hannah could not suppress the shudders traveling the length of her body, nor understand the unbelievable ecstasy pouring over her. Then she knew no more. When she came to her senses, Wind Rider was leaning over her, regarding her with wonder.

"I did not want to cheat you this time."

"You didn't. I've never . . . I didn't know . . ."

A mysterious smile stretched the corners of his mouth. He couldn't ever recall being so pleased at anything. "Sleep, Little Sparrow. We have plenty of time to get to know one another. In seven suns I will know every inch of your white body, and you will know every inch of mine."

Hannah smiled and stretched her hand across the mat, expecting to encounter warm, vibrant flesh. Sunlight filtering through the open smokehole stabbed relentlessly at her face, bringing her abruptly awake from a most pleasant dream. Her body ached in places she never knew existed, and movement brought a small groan from her lips. Her face glowed hotly when she recalled what had taken place last night and once during early morning, when Wind Rider had awoken her with nibbling kisses against her breasts and stomach. Abruptly she became aware that she was alone on the mat. Her hands touched the place where he had lain, still warm from his body, and she sat up, calling his name.

There was no answering response. Panic seized her, and she crawled to the open flap. Had Wind Rider abandoned her already? Had she done something to displease him? Then she saw him, and the breath slammed from her lungs. He was standing in the river, bathing, his golden body glistening in the morning sun. He sensed her eyes on him and turned slowly, a wide smile stretching his lips.

"Come and join me," he invited, holding out a sun-bronzed hand.

Realizing she was naked, Hannah turned back to don her tunic but changed her mind. The beautiful white dress was the only one she had, and she didn't want to ruin it in the water. Besides, Wind Rider had seen every part of her; she had nothing more to hide from him. Ducking through the entrance, she walked toward the river, her face flaming when she noted the intensity of Wind Rider's silver gaze on her naked form.

The water was cold but not unbearable. In fact, it felt wonderfully refreshing as she washed the scent of Wind Rider's lovemaking from her body. When she reached Wind Rider's side he slowly, gently, began washing her with soap plant.

"Did I hurt you last night?" His question took her by surprise. She'd had no idea he would even care.

"A little," she admitted, blushing.

"Finding you a maiden was something I never expected. But it pleases me to know my wife gave me the gift of her virtue."

"If you'd listened to me, you would have known." Her back tingled where his hands plied the soap plant. He turned her around and stroked soap over her breasts and stomach.

"I'm listening now. Why did your master call you a whore?"

Hannah sighed, the slow movement of his hands so arousing, she could barely concentrate. When his hands dipped down between her legs her thoughts scattered like leaves before the wind. "I-I . . ."

"Never mind; you can tell me later," Wind Rider said as desire spilled through his veins like thick, sweet honey. He slipped a finger inside her, and Hannah cried out, grasping his shoulders to keep from falling.

"What are you doing?"

"I want you again, Little Sparrow. You make me forget the restraint practiced by my people. When I am near you I cannot control myself. You make me crazy with the need to thrust myself into you again and again."

His words acted like an aphrodisiac to her senses as Hannah felt herself grow hot. An ache began in her loins, and she pushed against him, loving the feel of her soft breasts against the hardness of his chest. She knew she was acting in a brazen manner but couldn't seem to help herself. Wind Rider was turning her into a savage, just like he was. Or was he a savage? Intuition told her that no Indian blood flowed through his veins. It wasn't something anyone had said but rather a gut feeling she could not shake.

Grasping her buttocks, Wind Rider pulled her into the cradle of his loins, his manhood rising hard and heavy between them as he rubbed against her, letting her feel what she did to him.

"Wrap your legs around my waist," he said in a strained voice.

Hannah obeyed without hesitation, unaware of what he intended but trusting him implicitly. He raised her slightly, then thrust into her, filling her so completely, Hannah felt his hardness stretching her and feared she would burst.

There was no pain, only a full sensation that was not unpleasant. When he licked and sucked her breasts the rapture was so great she moaned in response.

Moving her up and down the extended length of his staff, Wind Rider felt her tightness surround and squeeze him and nearly exploded. He couldn't believe his reaction to Hannah, for he'd never before lost control with a woman. Cool and detached, he'd always made certain the woman felt pleasure, but he'd never immersed himself to the extent of letting his need rule his mind or body. But with Hannah he was like a rutting animal who could not get enough.

Hannah felt the tremors begin deep in her loins as wave after wave of ecstasy pounded through her. Her cries triggered Wind Rider's climax and he shuddered violently, releasing his seed in a gushing torrent. Afterward they washed again in the river and returned to the lodge. Hannah was surprised to find that someone had left food for them while they cavorted in the water. They ate ravenously, then sat outside in the sun to rest and renew themselves. Hannah had donned her dress, but Wind Rider wore only a brief breechclout.

"I want you to tell me how you came to be owned by the white eyes," Wind Rider said lazily. "You said you came from a country that lies across a huge sea."

"The country is called Ireland. I come from a poor family and have many brothers and sisters. The potato famine left thousands of people starving, my family among them. I left home so my father would have one less mouth to feed."

Wind Rider's brow wrinkled. "So you sold yourself to another? It doesn't make sense."

"That's not exactly right. I sold my services for seven years to pay for my passage to America. It's called indenture. Upon arrival in Boston, the ship's captain sold my indenture to Mr. Harley. We left immediately for Independence and joined a wagon train. We left the Oregon Trail at Julesburg and traveled south to Denver, where Mr. Harley intended to open an inn."

Wind Rider digested all this thoughtfully. "White people are strange. Why did your master call you a whore?"

"Mr. Harley is a cruel man," Hannah said bitterly. "He wanted me to bed the men who came to the inn, but I refused. When he insisted I ran away. The law will punish me if I'm caught and return me to Mr. Harley to serve out my indenture."

"What happens after your indenture is served?"

"Then I am free to pursue my own life. I hoped to save enough money to send for some of my brothers and sisters. But Mr. Harley has made that impossible."

"You looked so pitiful the first time I saw you. I knew the man must have starved you, beaten you, and worked you excessively. I will kill him if I ever see him." His words were spoken with such utter lack of emotion that

Hannah believed he could kill Harley without a shred of remorse.

"My appearance was partly my doing," Hannah admitted. "I tried to make myself as unattractive as possible so as not to attract attention. But it didn't work. Mr. Harley decided to clean me up and offer me to his customers despite my lack of appeal. That's why I ran away. Most likely he has notified the authorities and they are looking for me right now."

"He cannot have you." Wind Rider spoke with such heat and conviction; Hannah was amazed that he cared so much.

"Tell me about yourself," Hannah said quietly. "Was your mother white?"

Wind Rider hesitated so long, Hannah thought he hadn't heard. She was about to repeat her question when he said, "My father is White Feather. My mother, Gray Dove, was killed by white soldiers from Fort Lyon."

Hannah stared at him. His silver eyes and white features disputed his claim. "Why won't you tell me the truth?"

Wind Rider remained silent, considering his answer. Sooner or later Hannah would hear the truth from someone. Many Sioux spoke the white man's tongue.

Hannah tried another approach. "You mentioned a sister. Is she still with the Cheyenne?"

Wind Rider's features softened. "Tears Like Rain lives near Denver with her husband, Zach Mercer. He is white, but I believe he loves her.

He calls her Abby. It was her name before . . ."

Hannah's attention sharpened. "Before what?"

Wind Rider let out a harsh breath. "Before White Feather adopted us."

"I was right; you are white!" Hannah crowed delightedly.

Wind Rider stiffened. "I am Cheyenne. Never forget it, Little Sparrow. I do not belong to the white world. Since the age of ten I have lived with the Cheyenne. Their world became mine; I adopted their customs. I know nothing about white society. White eyes drive us from our land and kill our people. They slaughter innocent women and children and try to force us to live on reservations, where the land is poor and no buffalo remain."

"How do you know you can't live in white society? Obviously your sister made the transition successfully."

"It was not easy for Tears Like Rain. She fought against our father's decision to return her to the white world. If I know my sister, she fought Zach Mercer every step of the way."

"Is she happy now?"

Wind Rider smiled, recalling how happy Tears Like Rain had looked when she told him about the child she was expecting. "I believe she has accepted what cannot be changed. She has a white husband whom she loves, and is expecting his child soon."

"You have a white wife," Hannah reminded him. "It would be so easy for you to return to the white world. I'm sure your sister would help you adjust."

"Never!" He said it with such fierce conviction, Hannah was utterly convinced he meant it.

"I can't ever go back to Denver because of Mr. Harley, but there are other cities in which we could live. You could find a job and—"

"A job?" Wind Rider snorted derisively. "I have a job. It is chasing white eyes from our land."

"You can't succeed, you know. You have no idea how many people are leaving the East to settle in the West. They are so numerous that soon there will be large cities springing up across the plains. I saw them, Wind Rider. In Boston there are so many people, the streets were teeming with them. Other eastern cities are probably just as crowded. In Independence, wagon trains stretched out in mile-long lines, waiting to begin the journey West.

"Tracks are being laid to carry trains bringing more people across the prairie. In Denver they call it progress. People say that one day no Indians will roam free. Leave now, Wind Rider, leave while there is still time to make a new life for yourself. Raiding and fighting can only lead to your death."

"You are wise for one so young," Wind Rider said, astounded by her perception. He had already come to the same conclusion many moons ago, but he had vowed to fight to the bitter end. "As for my death, it is inevitable.

When I left Sand Creek I knew I traveled a path that led to the spirit world."

"But there is no need!" Hannah cried. "You're white. I-I don't want you to die."

He regarded her curiously, his face softening. "Why? I have not been kind to you."

"You have not hurt me. You saved my life. If I had not met you, I would have died long before I reached Cheyenne. I was so naive. I had no idea how dangerous it was to leave Denver as I did to try to reach Cheyenne on my own. I was ignorant of the distance I would have to travel alone. But I was so determined not to sell my body for Mr. Harley's benefit that I could think of nothing but escape, no matter what the cost."

"You are a remarkable woman, Hannah McLin. You are small and delicate but have the courage of a warrior. And you are very young and naive. There is no returning for me.

"Besides, you talk too much, Little Sparrow." He grasped her hand, pulling her to her feet. "Come, I will show you where to gather the soap plant we used for our bath. When we return we will lie on the river bank and make love with Grandfather sun shining down upon us."

Chapter Eight

"What are these scars?" Hannah asked curiously. She ran her fingers lightly over the faded ridges on either side of Wind Rider's broad chest. She hadn't noticed them before, probably because they were old and barely discernible.

"When I was fifteen winters I participated in the Sun Dance."

"Sun Dance? What is that?" Her fingers stilled on the scars, savoring the warmth of his flesh, amazed at her boldness and the sense of rightness she felt lying in this man's arms. They had made love so many times during the past days, she had lost count. And each time had been better than the last. Knowing that he was white eased her conscience somewhat, for it was incomprehensible to her that an Indian could captivate her so utterly.

"The Sun Dance is many things to different tribes. But to the Cheyenne it is world renewal. A warrior makes a vow before participating in the Sun Dance, not so much for himself but for the whole tribe. Attending upon his vow and its fulfillment is an abundance of good water and good breath of the wind. As the ceremony progresses, a lodge is erected and a fire built, which represents the heat of the sun. The lodge is built facing the east so that the heavenly bodies may pass over it and fertilize it."

"It sounds complicated," Hannah said, placing a kiss over each scar. "You still haven't explained how you got the scars."

"I will explain." The touch of her lips against his flesh sent a quiver of anticipation down his spine. "The Sun Dance requires eight days to complete. The first four days are given over to building the dance lodge and to secret rites, which you would not understand. The last four days are devoted to the public dance in the Sun Dance lodge. The dancer is called 'The Reproducer' because through his act the tribe is reborn and increases in number.

"Self-sacrifice, in which many but not all men indulge, takes place outside the Sun Dance lodge. You might think it barbaric. We call it 'hanging from the center pole.' One who has vowed to do this asks the medicine man to help him. The medicine man fastens the end of two ropes to the crotch of a pole erected outside, adjusting them so that they will reach just to the breast height of a standing man. He next punches or cuts two holes in the skin just above each nipple and pushes a small skewer through each pair of holes so that a narrow strip of skin laps over it and holds it against the breast."

"Oh, no," Hannah gasped, horrified. "It must have hurt dreadfully.

"It is not so bad." Wind Rider shrugged, proud of the ordeal he had undergone. "The free ends of the rope are fastened about the skewers so that the sacrificer may dance fastened to the pole all night. If by morning he has not succeeded in tearing the skin loose to free himself, the medicine man cuts the skin off and his ordeal is ended. To help overcome the pain, the sacrificer blows a whistle, invoking the help of the spirits to ease his suffering."

"You're right, I don't understand," Hannah agreed, unable to comprehend the type of self-torture practiced by Indians. "Why would any man do such a thing?"

"For many reasons," Wind Rider said. "Most often it is a vow pledged as a means to gain the spirits' pity and thereby obtain good fortune. It is also an act of courage that brings great public approval from the People, and it gains one much prestige."

"Why did you do it?" She was trying hard to understand what drove Wind Rider, but it was difficult.

"I did it because I wanted to prove I was Cheyenne despite my white blood. I wanted to show I did not lack courage. When I reached fifteen summers I sought my vision and among other things I saw myself participating in the Sun Dance, earning praise and respect from the People. Once I had participated none could doubt that I was truly Cheyenne."

Hannah's hands roamed freely over his chest and shoulders, marveling at the smoothness of his golden skin, the firmness of the underlying muscle. She had no idea what would happen at the end of these seven days, but she intended to make the most of them. She knew Wind Rider hadn't married her because he loved her, and she worried that he would give her to Cut Nose when he tired of her. Undoubtedly Wind Rider would raid again one day soon, and she feared he wouldn't return. She couldn't bear the thought of being left to the mercies of the Indians without Wind Rider to protect her.

"How did you seek your vision?" she asked idly.

With Hannah's hands on his flesh he could barely think, let alone answer her question. He had never felt this way about a woman before and he had no time to explore the strange emotion that made him desire this woman above all others. His eyes glowed like liquid silver as he felt his body harden.

"I will tell you about my vision . . . later."

He rolled her over on her back, seizing her lips to still her words. It didn't take long for him to decide that he thoroughly enjoyed kissing. He kissed her ravenously, until her lips opened beneath his, inviting his tongue. He obliged eagerly, thrusting into the sweet cavern of her mouth until she lost her breath and grew dizzy. With blackness swiftly approaching, he released her mouth and kissed her eyes, her cheeks, her nose, sweet butterfly kisses that sent heat rushing through her veins while his hands played with her breasts and teased her nipples into painful erectness.

His hands moved over her body with amazing gentleness; her soft sighs and moans made him long to thrust into her and stroke himself to completion. Mastering his powerful need with incredible restraint, he continued to arouse Hannah to a fever pitch, savoring the way her body responded to his touch. His hand slipped between her legs, finding her wet and ready, but for some reason he wanted to bring her more pleasure than she had ever known.

"Wind Rider, please . . ."

He knew what she was asking but was not ready to appease her hunger. "Soon, Little Sparrow, very soon." His face was stark with passion, hard and greedy, ravenous, his muscles tense. No part of her body was sacrosanct as his lips and hands worked their magic on her. By the time he grasped her waist and set her astride him she was reduced to begging, so great was her need. "Now, Little Sparrow, now."

He raised her body and shoved her down hard on his erection. He pierced her deeply, so deeply she arched her back, threw back her head, and screamed.

"Ride me, Little Sparrow," Wind Rider urged. He grasped her buttocks, sliding her up and down his great length, teaching her the rhythm. "Ride me, sweet one. Let me be your wild stallion and I will take you on a wondrous journey."

"Yes, oh, yes," Hannah gasped, twisting her body in wild abandon. Nothing in her limited experience had prepared her for this man. No matter what happened in the future, she would have these seven days to remember and savor all of her life.

A fine sheen of sweat turned Wind Rider's skin to molten gold. His finely honed muscles rippled, and the tendons in his neck bulged as he strained to contain his climax until Hannah had reached hers. When he felt the tremors signaling the beginning of rapture, he feared he would leave her behind. Inserting a hand between their bodies, he found the tiny bud of sensation located at the juncture of her thighs and massaged gently with the pad of his finger. When his mouth closed over a swollen nipple, sucking vigorously, she reacted instantly and violently.

"Wind Rider!"

"Come with me, Little Sparrow," he urged raggedly. "Come."

She did. Wantonly. With utter abandon. Every delicious contraction was intensified by the circular motion of his fingertip. She held nothing back, offering herself upon the altar of his masculinity, demanding that he return her offering in kind.

Lost in the throes of ecstasy, his seed spewed forth in a hot stream of liquid fire. Without his knowledge he cried out her name at the moment of climax. When she had nothing more to give she collapsed against his chest, unable to move, incapable of speaking, unwilling to think.

Wind Rider lay unmoving beneath her, utterly stunned by the turbulence of their lovemaking. If he died tomorrow, as indeed he might, given the precarious nature of his existence, he'd go to his death knowing he'd experienced the greatest joy known to man. To his knowledge, few mortals were granted that privilege.

He frowned, staring at Hannah as if seeing her for the first time. Carefully, he lifted her off him and lay her down beside him. He suddenly understood something that had previously escaped him. Somehow, in some way, this woman was a threat to his very existence.

He was Cheyenne; Hannah was white. He could not allow himself to feel so deeply for a white woman. Already she had tried to convince him to leave the People. If he allowed her to conquer his heart, he would lose his identity, and that would be disastrous. He could not exist in the white world, nor would he abandon his people for a woman. Self-preservation demanded that he harden his heart against her, that he enjoy her body while he was able, but, when the time came, that he must forget she ever existed. It would not be easy, but if he was to save himself he must force himself to resist the magical allure of Hannah McLin.

"Why are you looking at me so strangely?" Hannah asked. A shiver of apprehension slid down her spine. Something had changed, but she knew not what. "What have I done?"

"You have done nothing. *Heammawihio* has opened my eyes."

"What does that mean?"

"*Heammawihio* is the great spirit above who guides our lives. I had nearly forgotten why I rode north to join the Sioux, but in his wisdom *Heammawihio* reminded me. Our time in the honeymoon lodge grows short. Tomorrow we must return to the village."

"Then what?"

"Then you will do what every Indian wife does and I will do what I must to drive the white eyes from our land. Perhaps," he taunted, not really meaning it, "I will take a second wife as the council suggested, to help with the chores." He watched her closely to see if his words had the desired effect. He couldn't let her think she had become so important to him that he would forget his duty to his people.

The effect upon Hannah was devastating. During the past few days she had never been so happy or carefree. Wind Rider had given her his undivided attention, making her feel special and beautiful, though she knew she wasn't. Their honeymoon had given her hope that one day he would listen to her pleas and return to his white heritage. But now his words had demonstrated just how cold-blooded he could be, how heartless. He had taken her body in lust, used her, taught her to need him, then cruelly shattered her hopes and dreams by withdrawing everything of himself he had given. Had it been a game with him? She did not think he could be so cruel.

"Perhaps you should take a second wife," she retorted. She knew it was her pride speaking, but she couldn't stop herself. "You are beginning to bore me anyway." She almost choked on the words, recalling how moments ago he had taken her on a journey she would remember for the rest of her life.

Their last night in the honeymoon lodge was a bittersweet one for Hannah. Wind Rider made love to her with practiced detachment, as if trying to distance himself now that their time alone was at an end and his duty to the tribe took precedence. When he finished he lay back and stared at the stars through the smokehole, trying to come to terms with his emotions.

"My vision did not tell me I would meet someone like you."

His voice was so low, Hannah had to strain to hear him. "What kind of vision are you talking about? You mentioned something about a vision before."

"When an Indian youth reaches a certain age he goes off by himself to pray and fast.

He remains many days, until a vision comes to him. Often a vision will give him the name that he will bear the rest of his life. Sometimes it foretells the future. When a time of decision comes in a warrior's life he goes on a vision quest, seeking guidance."

"What did your vision tell you?" Hannah asked curiously.

"The medicine man interpreted it shortly after I returned from my quest, but he said some things would be made known only to me by the Great Spirit. I saw myself astride a great stallion, riding away from the village on a gust of wind. Thus my name, Wind Rider. A small brown bird perched on my shoulder. Then I saw myself slowly disappearing into thin air as I rode away. As I faded from sight I saw that I was wearing white man's clothing. The medicine man said the small bird was my personal talisman and that I should protect it at all times."

"What do you think it meant?" Hannah asked curiously. She found the idea of the vision fascinating, whether or not it meant anything.

Wind Rider did not answer immediately. When he finally spoke his voice was flat, utterly devoid of emotion. "I believe I foresaw my own death. When I disappeared into thin air it meant I would walk the Spirit Path before my time."

Hannah gasped in dismay. "No! It was only a dream. You have no idea what it meant."

Imagining Wind Rider's death was too painful to contemplate.

"It was no dream, Little Sparrow. Visions do not lie. The life I lead is a dangerous one. Each time I ride against the white eyes I wonder if it will be my last. But the meaning of the brown bird on my shoulder has suddenly become clear." He stared at her, as if seeing her for the first time. "You are my little brown bird, my personal talisman. Perhaps you will bring me powerful medicine."

"I certainly hope so," Hannah said fervently. "You don't have to raid," she reminded him. "You're white, for God's sake! You can leave; there is nothing holding you back."

Wind Rider turned away from her. "How can I turn my back on the only life I can remember? White Feather taught me everything I know. He rescued me and my sister from the Crow after they killed our parents and adopted us. Since then I've learned that my own kind are the savages. They kill the People and drive them from their lands because they are greedy. They are not content to share the land with the People; they want it all. They want to herd us onto reservations like animals."

Hannah had no reply. From what she'd heard, Wind Rider's assessment of the situation between Indians and whites was correct. But not all white men were necessarily like the ones Wind Rider had described. She mentioned that fact to Wind Rider.

"Perhaps not," he concurred, thinking of Zach Mercer, who had fallen in love with his sister. Zach had also fought beside the Cheyenne when the Crow had invaded their village. "But what you ask is impossible. We will speak no more about it."

The moon rode high in the sky. Wind Rider shifted positions on his pallet of furs, uncomfortably aware of Hannah's warm body curled beside him. Once he had recognized the fact that Hannah was becoming essential to his well-being, he had vowed to disengage his emotions from the white wife he hadn't really wanted. He didn't need her as desperately as he imagined, he told himself even as his arm crept around her slim waist with a will of its own. A good Cheyenne warrior practiced restraint, learned to quell his body's urges, and didn't allow his need for a woman to blind him to his duty. He had already made love to Hannah more than once tonight, and that should be enough for any man.

But no amount of denial could refute his need for the small bundle of warm flesh sleeping at his side. Perhaps it was his white blood, or something in his ancestry that made him want Hannah McLin so desperately. The hot blood clamoring in his veins had to come from his white heritage, he decided grumpily as his hand shifted upward from Hannah's waist to settle on a plump white breast. With a groan of dismay, he shoved his thoughts to the back of his mind and covered Hannah's body with his, awakening her with a deep kiss.

Convincing himself that needing Hannah didn't necessarily mean he was obsessed to the point of forgetting all else, he rolled on top of her, spread her legs, and joined their bodies. If he divorced himself from his emotions, he saw no reason why he shouldn't avail himself of his wife's body.

Hannah awoke with a start, the soft warmth of Wind Rider's lips coaxing her from a dream world into reality. This time there were no flowery words as he joined their bodies, no promises, no aching tenderness. There was only passion, hunger, and brutal need. Hannah sensed his confusion, felt the forces tearing him apart, and her heart nearly shattered from an emotion she didn't want to acknowledge.

Straining over Hannah, Wind Rider denied that she meant more to him than a warm body to assuage his needs. To acknowledge his feelings would betray his Cheyenne heart. Yet despite his forced emotional detachment from the woman in his arms, Wind Rider wanted to give Hannah pleasure. Deliberately gentling his strokes, he slowly brought her to passion, waiting until she cried out and shuddered in climax before seeking his own fulfillment.

Hannah awoke late, aware of an emptiness, not just in her bed but in her heart. She knew without being told that Wind Rider was gone. Her body ached, feeling his loss keenly, wondering what would happen when she returned to his lodge in the village. Voices outside the lodge brought her to her feet. Dressing quickly, she stepped outside into the bright sunshine. Woman-Who-Waddles stood nearby, accompanied by the same two women who had helped her erect the honeymoon lodge. They had brought a horse and a travois, which she supposed was to be used to transport the tepee back to the village.

Woman-Who-Waddles greeted her effusively; then she and the other women set to work. Within a very short time the tepee was dismantled and loaded on the travois. Hannah followed behind to the village. When they reached Wind Rider's tepee Woman-Who-Waddles indicated that Hannah was to go inside. She gave Hannah a look that could only be interpreted as pity, but the look was so fleeting Hannah quickly dismissed it. Instead, she searched for Wind Rider, wondering why he wasn't on hand to greet her. Hurt and dismayed, she turned and entered the tepee.

A prickling sensation at the nape of her neck told Hannah she wasn't alone. Disappointment made her shoulders slump when she saw a woman tending a small fire in the center of the tepee. Had Wind Rider sent someone to help her? Her question was answered when the woman rose to greet her.

"Spotted Doe, what are you doing here?" Spotted Doe was the last person Hannah would expect to pay a visit so soon after returning from the honeymoon lodge.

"Has Wind Rider not told you?" The malice in her voice did not bode well for Hannah.

"Told me what?"

"While you were away the council decided that he should take a second wife. He was told when he returned from the honeymoon lodge, and he approached my brother early this morning. Naturally, Cut Nose agreed to our joining."

Hannah blanched. No, it couldn't be true! Wind Rider wouldn't do such a terrible thing to her, no matter what the council's decision. "Why would the council demand that Wind Rider take a second wife?"

Spotted Doe didn't say that Cut Nose had complained so loudly about his family's embarrassment over Wind Rider's refusal to join with his sister that the council had reconsidered and decided that Wind Rider should appease the family by taking Spotted Doe as a second wife. "I do not know. If you do not like it, you may divorce him."

"Little Sparrow will not leave my lodge," Wind Rider thundered fiercely. He had ducked into the tepee in time to hear Spotted Doe's words.

Hannah whirled, struck anew by the magnificence of his golden physique, blatantly exposed by the brief breechclout.

"She may divorce you if she wishes," Spotted Doe replied sullenly. "It is the custom."

"Leave us," Wind Rider ordered brusquely. "I wish to speak in private to Little Sparrow."

"There is no need," Hannah said stubbornly. "I will take my things and leave."

Spotted Doe sent Hannah a baleful look and refused to budge.

"Go!" The stern tone of Wind Rider's voice left no room for argument, and Spotted Doe turned and ran from the lodge, but not before sending Hannah another murderous glare.

"Why?" No matter how hard she tried, Hannah could not keep the hurt from her voice. Though she was Wind Rider's wife against her will, she felt the wrenching ache of betrayal. Somehow this fierce white Indian had stolen her heart, and she didn't know what to do about it.

"There is nothing wrong with taking a second wife," Wind Rider said, making it sound as if it was something he had intended to do all along. "I was not aware of how much I embarrassed Cut Nose's family when I refused to join with Spotted Doe. Making her my second wife will appease her family and satisfy the council."

"What about me? You didn't have to marry me."

"No," Wind Rider agreed evenly. "I could have let Cut Nose have you."

"Is what Spotted Doe said true? Can I divorce you simply by leaving your lodge?"

Wind Rider scowled. "You can try, but I wouldn't advise it. I suspect it is what Cut Nose wants. I know him. He is counting on his sister distracting me, to make me forget I have a first wife. If you divorce me, you will fall in with his plans."

Hannah slumped in defeat. Was there no escape from the overwhelming power this man held over her? How could she pretend not to see or hear when he coupled with Spotted Doe, doing with her all those arousing things he had done with Hannah? "I wish I had never met you."

Wind Rider wished the same thing. Finding Hannah in the woods that day had been a most disastrous meeting. During the brief time he had known her, she had succeeded in making him aware as never before that he was white. She had forced him to face things he neither liked nor accepted. He wanted to tell Hannah that joining with Spotted Doe wasn't his choice, that he had done so to keep peace in the tribe. Truth be known, he wanted no other woman. But neither did he wish to leave Red Cloud's village. Raiding with the fearless Sioux suited him.

"You will try to get along with Spotted Doe," he said finally. "I will have peace in my lodge."

"Tell that to Spotted Doe," Hannah snorted belligerently.

Wind Rider stared at her but did not reply. She looked so adorable with her green eyes flashing and her cheeks burning that he wanted to throw her down on the mat and make violent love to her, thrusting into her again and again until there was no more talk of her leaving his lodge. Shaking his head to clear it of such disturbing thoughts, he turned and ducked through the opening.

"What did you say to make him so angry?" Spotted Doe entered the tepee the moment Wind Rider left, confronting Hannah angrily.

"Nothing."

"Are you going to divorce him? What does a white woman know about pleasing a man?"

"I have nowhere to go. And I have no desire to please Wind Rider." Lies! All lies, her mind screamed. She was certain she had pleased Wind Rider, just as he had pleased her.

Spotted Doe smiled complacently. "Just as I thought. It is good he has taken a second wife. I will show him how a real wife acts."

Taking a water bag from where it hung on a tent pole, she thrust it into Hannah's hands. "Get water. Woman's work is hard, and I don't intend to do it all by myself. I will take care of Wind Rider's needs between the blankets and you can do the other chores."

Hannah stared at the water bag, aware that she had gone from slave to wife and back to slave again in a very short time.

Hannah was exhausted at the end of the day. Spotted Doe had given her every difficult task she could devise. She knew so little about Indian culture that she had no idea Spotted Doe had no right to order her about like a slave. But the fact that she was an outsider to the tribe made her vulnerable to the other woman's whims. And Wind Rider had made himself scarce, preferring the company of men to the uneasy atmosphere of his own lodge. He had returned to partake of the evening meal and then disappeared again, joining the warriors who sat around the campfire, exchanging tales of bravery.

When it grew dark Hannah slipped away to bathe in the river. So did Spotted Doe, taking care to choose a location a good distance from where Hannah bathed. Hannah returned to the lodge first and made her bed. Stripping, she climbed beneath the blanket, praying for sleep to come swiftly so she would not have to hear Wind Rider and Spotted Doe coupling. Fate was not kind to her, for she tossed restlessly, painfully aware that the Indian maiden waited for Wind Rider to come to her.

The good-natured teasing of his comrades grated on Wind Rider's nerves until he could stand it no longer. The men offered lewd comments and speculations, none of which Wind Rider found particularly amusing. After listening as long as he could, he rose abruptly and walked away. They let him go, but not before Cut Nose offered a few well-chosen words of advice.

"You are a lucky man, Wind Rider. My sister could have had any warrior she desired. She will please you well. I predict you will soon forget your yen for white flesh. When you tire of your slave I will take her off your hands and teach her how to act like a proper slave."

"I will remember your words, Cut Nose," Wind Rider threw over his shoulder as he walked away, "but I would remind you that Little Sparrow is my first wife." It would be a cold day in hell, he grumbled beneath his breath, before he'd hand Hannah over to a man like Cut Nose.

The tepee glowed with muted light from the dying fire when Wind Rider entered. Adjusting his eyes to the dim interior, he saw Hannah lying farthest from the fire, apparently asleep. He smiled and took a step in her direction. When a hand caught at his leg he looked down, suddenly recalling Spotted Doe. She rested on her elbow, her eyes glowing with dark promise.

"Go to sleep," Wind Rider hissed, shaking free of her grasp.

She smiled up at him. "I am your wife, Wind Rider. This is our wedding night."

Hannah stiffened at the sound of Wind Rider's voice. She had no idea what he said to Spotted Doe, for they spoke in their own language. Whatever it was, the other woman obviously didn't like it. Hannah waited with bated breath for him to join Spotted Doe on her mat, cursing her bad luck at remaining awake when she had no desire to hear Wind Rider making love to his second wife.

"Do not remind me of my duty, Spotted Doe," Wind Rider said sternly. "The truth is, I do not wish to lie with you tonight."

"You go to her!" Spotted Doe spat. "Are you so enamored of her white skin that I am no longer pleasing to you? Are you remembering your own white heritage? Perhaps you should return to the white world."

"Think carefully before you speak again, Spotted Doe." Wind Rider's voice was low with implied menace, bringing Spotted Doe's hurtful words to an abrupt halt. With marked reluctance, she lay down. Wind Rider turned his back on her and continued on to where Hannah lay.

He dropped to his knees, whipped off his breechclout, pulled back the covers, and slid down beside her. When his hand sought her breast Hannah stiffened. Surely he didn't intend to make love to her with Spotted Doe watching, did he? It might be the Indian way, but it wasn't her way.

"Don't!" she hissed when he turned her toward him.

"You are my wife."

"So is Spotted Doe. Go to her."

"I don't want her." His hand slid between her legs.

"Not with Spotted Doe watching!" Her voice sounded frantic, touching something deep inside Wind Rider.

"If that is your wish, we will go where no one can watch us." Scooping her into his arms, he rose, kicked aside the flap, and strode outside. Hannah had sense enough to drag one of the blankets with her as Wind Rider carried her into the woods.

Chapter Nine

The following day the great Sioux chief Red Cloud returned from the council at Fort Laramie, where he and several important Sioux leaders and prominent Cheyenne chiefs had gathered to negotiate terms for use of the Bozeman Trail, which cut directly through much of the buffalo country. But much to Red Cloud's chagrin, there had been no negotiating. The army was prepared only to issue demands. What the chiefs did not find out until the negotiating had reached a stalemate was that as they were parlaying, Colonel Henry Carrington had arrived at the fort on his way to build forts along the Bozeman. When Red Cloud learned of this he fell into a rage and left the fort, which was tantamount to a declaration of war by the Sioux and Cheyenne Nations.

Immediately upon his return to his village, Red Cloud called a council meeting to tell his people what had transpired at Fort Laramie. Wind Rider listened carefully as the great chief described how the army wanted to steal the Bozeman Trail from the Indians while offering cheap gifts to appease them. Wind Rider knew instinctively that nothing short of a miracle, or the demise of the entire Indian nation, could halt the ensuing bloodshed. Mentally, he prepared himself for a long battle that would most likely end with his death.

Hannah felt tension building in the village and was puzzled by it. She had learned a few words of the Sioux language, but not enough to know what Red Cloud's words to his people meant. Spotted Doe consistently refused to speak to Hannah, so Hannah learned nothing from her about the current situation.

Just thinking about what had happened after Wind Rider carried her off into the woods the night before brought color rushing up Hannah's neck. She had tried; Lord knew she had tried to discourage Wind Rider, but he would not listen. Instead, he made love to her until the blood sang through her veins and nothing mattered but the touch of his hands and his mouth on her body, until she begged him to make her one with him.

When Hannah saw Wind Rider striding toward her, his body tense, his mouth compressed into a grim slash across his face, she knew Red Cloud was not the bearer of good news. He stopped inches from her, grasped her arm, and dragged her inside the tepee.

"What is it?" Hannah cried, perturbed by his brusque manner.

"War," Wind Rider said. "The army will not listen to reason. Tonight all the men of the tribe will gather to dance and feast before going to the purification hut. We will remain sequestered in the hut for two days, fasting and praying for the Great Spirit's blessing."

Hannah blanched. "Then what?"

"The War Dog society and the Strong Heart Society will ride out together to raid along the Bozeman Trail, while Red Cloud remains behind to rest and fortify himself before joining us."

"You're leaving." Her voice quivered. "What will happen to me?"

"Nothing. You will remain behind and wait for me to return." Unspoken between them was the possibility that he might not return.

"Coyote will remain behind with the Shield Society to protect the village. I have asked him to provide you and Spotted Doe with meat. If I do not return, he has agreed to take you to the fort."

Hannah sagged, half in relief and half in fear. Without Wind Rider's protection she'd be completely vulnerable to the tribe's whims. They might decide to give her to Cut Nose or another like him. But even more terrifying was the thought of Wind Rider's death. A vicious stab of pain made her gasp and shake her head in vigorous denial.

Wind Rider's expression softened. "Does the thought of my death make you unhappy, Little Sparrow?"

"Of-of course not," she stammered, aware that she was lying. "I fear for my own safety."

"You lie," Wind Rider whispered. His silver eyes glowed hotly as he pulled her against the hard wall of his bare chest. "Last night you were a wild thing in my arms, loving everything I did to you and begging for more."

Long lashes slid down to shutter her green eyes, resting like dark butterfly wings against her pale cheeks. She could not deny Wind Rider's words. "I-I could not help myself."

"Nor I," Wind Rider admitted.

"Spotted Doe is very angry."

"I did not want Spotted Doe. I took her for my second wife to appease her family. I am not required to lie with her. Look at me."

Tilting her chin upward, Wind Rider made it all but impossible for her to look away. Slowly, her lashes swept upward, baring her soul to the hypnotic spell of his silver eyes. What he saw must have pleased him, for he lowered his head and kissed her, drawing her even further into the magnetic power he held over her. His mouth was soft, drugging and addictive. Prodding her lips apart with the hard blade of his tongue, he deepened the kiss, pressing his body against hers, making her fully aware of his blatant state of arousal.

When he slowly bore her down to the mat spread out beneath the smokehole Hannah gasped and fought free from his grasp. "Wind Rider, no! Spotted Doe could come in at any moment."

"She will not return any time soon," Wind Rider said with assurance. "She went with the other women to gather berries and edible roots for the feast tonight." Grasping her shoulders, he lowered her to the pallet. "This is the last time we can be together like this before I leave," he murmured softly against her ear.

Before she could reply his mouth found hers again, his tongue penetrating deeply, unable to get enough of the taste and texture of her. Breaking off the kiss, his lips slid along the slim column of her neck, pausing where the pulse throbbed at the base of her throat before continuing downward to where his fingers had loosened the ties of her tunic. Impatiently, he pulled the opening wider, exposing her to the wet lash of his tongue as he kissed a molten path to her breasts. When even that didn't satisfy him, he worked the tunic down her arms and over her hips and tossed it aside. His breechclout followed.

Desire for her surged, awakening in him a need that almost destroyed him. He hated being so deeply affected by a woman but couldn't help himself. He kissed her again, his sharp teeth nipping at her soft bottom lip, then soothing it with his tongue. His fierce aggression made her tremble with heightened awareness as she willingly surrendered to his passion, kissing him back with wanton fervor.

He was not gentle as his hands possessively gripped her bare back and buttocks, pulling her to him as he vigorously sucked and licked her breasts. She cried out, winding her hands into his hair and pulling him closer. With the detachment of one lost in pleasure, she watched as he released one wet pink-tipped breast and sucked the other deeply into his greedy mouth. Feasting on her as if he'd never get his fill, his hot open lips blazed a burning trail to her bare belly, placing sweet kisses on the copper fleece at the base of her pale thighs.

Trembling violently, Hannah no longer felt in control of her body as molten heat built within her and painful need asserted itself. When his warm fingers stroked the insides of her thighs they parted to allow him total access. In one smooth motion he slid between her parted legs. His hands went beneath her and his strong fingers clasped her rounded buttocks, lifting her to his mouth. His silver eyes glowed with unholy light as he slowly lowered his head. His hot breath seared her. He kissed her as though he was kissing her mouth; his mouth, his teeth, his tongue touching her, caressing her, parting her.

Delight shuddered through her as his tongue boldly invaded her. Hearing her sharp intake of breath, Wind Rider's tongue sought even deeper intimacy as it found the tiny nub of pleasure and stroked, caressed, and nipped until her body was pushed to the very limits of endurance. When he raised his head to look into her eyes Hannah cried out, fearing he would take his dazzling mouth from her and leave her tottering at the edge of madness.

"I won't leave you, Little Sparrow," he vowed raggedly as his lips found her again, this time sending her plummeting beyond mere pleasure to a place that defied description.

Terrified by the height of the rapturous delight she experienced in this man's arms, Hannah suddenly realized that the depth of love she felt for Wind Rider would never be equaled. This white Indian had somehow reached into her heart to banish her fear of all men. Her mind, her body, her soul was his to explore, to arouse, to love at will.

Rushing headlong toward total release, Hannah's body tensed. Heat enveloped her, and she jerked her pelvis into the hot, open center of his mouth. His tongue stroked harder, deeper, lashing her until the first tiny tremors built into a burst of ecstasy so intense, she arched and screamed as molten fire pulsed through her veins. It went on forever. Spiraling through her, upward, outward, down, down . . . wild, wrenching, frightening. Nothing could heal her now but the hot, molten lash of his tongue.

Wind Rider did not leave her, not until he had given her all she needed, despite the urgent clamoring of his own desire. His release was so dangerously close, he knew that all it would take to reach climax was one deep thrust into the slick heat of her. As the last involuntary shudder left her body, he raised his head and smiled at her.

Dragging in deep, ragged breaths, Hannah opened her eyes and saw Wind Rider grinning at her. She knew he hadn't had his own release and felt the crisp hair of his groin and the thick length of his rigid manhood throbbing against her thigh. With trembling fingers she reached between them and grasped him. He groaned as if in agony, his hand closing over hers to guide its motion. When he dropped his hand she continued the caress, her eyes never leaving his face. Her boldness pleased him and his smile told her so.

"Enough, Little Sparrow!" he barked hoarsely, jerking her hand aside.

With their eyes still locked, he gripped himself, inserted the swollen tip into her, and thrust. Hannah sighed with pleasure as his hands moved down her hips to lift her to him, taking him deeply inside her. They moved together in a wild crescendo of fire and passion, give and take, push and pull, their bodies meeting and parting in splendid fury.

Panting and heaving, Wind Rider felt the approach of his climax and tried to delay it, but his passion was too hot, his need too great.

"I cannot wait, Little Sparrow!" His words were wrenched from his lips on a cry of pain/pleasure so intense, he felt himself shattering.

Tilting her pelvis upward to receive the full, heavy length of his violent strokes, Hannah raced to keep up with him. Jerking his hips rhythmically, his deep, driving thrusts brought them both to the brink. The end came quickly and explosively, leaving them emotionally and physically spent.

Later that night, Hannah joined Wind Rider at the feast. When the drums began a wild tattoo he leaped to his feet to join the dancers. She couldn't help but admire the way his sleekly muscled body moved to the primitive music but deliberately refrained from joining him as some of the women did. Spotted Doe was not so reluctant. Her lithe body swayed in sinuous rhythm to the beat of the drum. Her head was thrown back, her long hair flipping wildly about her shoulders as her prancing feet carried her around the campfire. But to his credit, Wind Rider did not seem to notice her.

More than once Hannah caught Red Cloud staring at her in a most curious manner. She was certain he had been told who she was, and though his dark penetrating looks didn't seem particularly threatening, they still disturbed her. Didn't he approve of Wind Rider marrying her? she wondered uneasily.

Before the men were to enter the sweat hut to fast and pray Wind Rider approached her and led her back to their lodge. Spotted Doe was still dancing and hadn't noticed their departure.

"I made arrangements for you to stay with Woman-Who-Waddles," he said when they stood outside the tepee. "I know Spotted Doe will give you trouble once I am gone, and Woman-Who-Waddles is glad for the company. She will see that no harm comes to you." He stared at her lips, remembering their taste, but did not kiss her.

Hannah nodded, grateful that she would not have to share quarters with a woman who hated her. "Thank you." Wind Rider turned to leave. "Wait!" He paused. "Will I see you before you leave?"

"Perhaps. I will return for my weapons and food."

"I will have them ready for you."

Once again he turned to leave.

"Wind Rider!" He whirled and she flew into his arms, holding him tightly, unwilling to let him go, perhaps to his death. "I don't want you to die. Take care; please take care."

Wind Rider's heart swelled with an emotion he'd tried hard to deny. Knowing that Hannah cared for him was a gift he hadn't expected or wanted. There were things he could say to her, but admitting he cared for Hannah was too difficult an emotion to express. Besides, he wasn't certain it was love he felt. Perhaps it was lust. Sometimes it was difficult to distinguish between the two. If love meant needing a person so desperately that the thought of parting from her nearly tore him apart, then he supposed he loved Hannah McLin.

"I will come back, Little Sparrow," Wind Rider vowed. "I will not die." Once again he turned to leave.

"Wind Rider, don't go! I have this terrible premonition of something . . . something . . ." Alarm shuddered through her. "I don't know what. I'm afraid."

"Your fears are no more than what other women feel when they watch their men go off to fight."

Hannah shook her head in denial. "No, this is different. It's not too late to leave the village. You belong to the white world. Your people were white. Find your sister; she will help you. Please, Wind Rider, leave while there is still time."

Wind Rider's expression hardened. "You speak foolish words, Little Sparrow. I cannot leave my people. I must go now to the purification hut."

"Wind Rider . . ." His name drifted away on the breeze. She could think of nothing more to say that would sway him. She squeezed her eyes shut, forcing back the stinging tears. But despite her valiant efforts they slid down her cheeks unchecked. She didn't turn away until he had disappeared into the purification hut.

Two days later Wind Rider and the other warriors emerged from the purification hut. Hannah thought he looked grim and gaunt after his days of fasting and prayer but did not remark on it. She had his weapons ready and handed them to him silently. He stared at her intently and nodded his thanks. Spotted Doe had prepared a parcel of pemmican and parched corn, which he carried in a small parfleche that hung at his waist. He donned his buckskin leggings but not his shirt. While Hannah watched, Spotted Doe painted bold stripes on his torso and face with the black and yellow paint she had prepared.

He seemed distracted, hardly aware of either woman as he prepared for battle. His mind had already detached itself from mundane thoughts of home and family. He felt strong, invincible, ready and able to defeat the enemy. Outside the tepee, his horse pawed the ground in eager anticipation. Warriors from the various societies had already gathered in the center of the village, waiting for the others to arrive so they could ride out to destroy the enemy. Red Cloud, wearing a high-crowned war bonnet made of eagle feathers that trailed nearly to the ground, stood tall and proud outside his lodge as his people clamored for white blood.

Hannah followed mutely as Wind Rider left the tepee. She was waiting for him to say something, anything, as long as he gave some sign that he cared what happened to her. But he said nothing. Spotted Doe seemed to take his silence as perfectly normal behavior; she appeared not at all concerned by his taciturn manner.

He strode toward his horse, still focused on some distant battle. Suddenly he stopped, whirled on his heel, and caught Hannah by the arm. Pulling her hard against him, he kissed her with almost brutal urgency. His teeth bruised her as his lips moved forcefully over hers and his tongue thrust inside her mouth. Though the kiss was of short duration, Hannah was certain she'd never forget it. Into that one kiss he had put all the things he hadn't said, all the feelings he'd held inside him.

Breaking off the kiss, he turned abruptly and leaped onto his pony. With a blood-curdling cry, he thrust his bow high in the air and rode off to join his friends, leading them from the village in a thunder of hooves, war whoops, and victory cries.

A week passed with no word from Wind Rider or the War Dog society. Hannah stayed as close to Woman-Who-Waddles as possible. She learned a good deal from the old woman, including a greater knowledge of the Sioux language. She also learned all the difficult and tedious chores that an Indian woman was expected to perform. Indians had no modern conveniences; the work was endless and time-consuming. Hannah was beginning to understand why Indians took more than one wife, though she'd never forgive Wind Rider for doing so.

One day a man leading a pack of laden mules rode into camp. Though he caused a flurry of excitement, no one stopped him. Red Cloud came out of his lodge to await the man. Women stopped their work to follow the strange-looking caravan.

"It is the trader." Spotted Doe appeared at Hannah's side, startling her. Since Wind Rider had left Spotted Doe had spoken to her only on rare occasions.

"Is he free to come and go as he pleases?"

"Yes, he brings us trade goods. The women are always happy to see him. Sometimes he brings firewater for the men, and guns."

"Guns! That's illegal." Even Hannah knew it was a crime to smuggle guns to the Indians.

Ignoring her, Spotted Doe ran off to join the women who were already pawing through one of the packs the trader had placed on the ground for them to inspect. Hannah walked closer to get a better look and was surprised to see cheap items such as colored beads, mirrors, blankets, and bits of ribbon; there was nothing as valuable as the hides the women were offering for trade. When the trader unwrapped another bundle, placing it before Red Cloud, Hannah gaped at the array of guns lying at the chief's feet. A heated discussion ensued between Red Cloud and the trader.

Hannah regarded the trader with contempt. His long hair was dirty and unkempt, covering his head in a wild disarray of blond tangles. Bits of food clung to his sparse beard, and when he spoke Hannah saw that his rotted teeth were stained with tobacco juice. His buckskin clothing was so filthy it could have stood by itself.

After a lengthy discussion Red Cloud and the trader seemed to reach an agreement. They were about to go inside the tepee to smoke and talk when the man spied Hannah from the corner of his eye. He stopped abruptly, staring at her, his eyes narrowed, his expression thoughtful. Her hair shone like burnished copper in the sunlight, and the whiteness of her pale skin was startling among the dark-skinned Indians. Where had he seen her before? His eyes widened in sudden recognition. He remembered!

"Who is the white woman?" he asked Red Cloud. After years of trading with Indians he was quite fluent in several dialects.

Red Cloud gave Hannah a cursory glance. "She is called Little Sparrow. She belongs to Wind Rider. Why do you ask, Trader?" The man had never offered his name; he was known simply as Trader.

Trader regarded Hannah with open curiosity. "How long has she been with the Sioux? Is she a captive? What is her name?"

Red Cloud frowned. "Do you know the woman?"

"No, but I seen her picture. At Fort Laramie. She's a runaway indentured servant. Some man paid good money for her services and she ran away. He wants her back and has offered a reward. How much do you want for her?"

"She does not belong to me. She is Wind Rider's woman."

"Wind Rider," Trader repeated slowly, memorizing the name. "Ask him if he is willing to sell her."

"He is not here. You are here to trade guns, not women."

Trader knew by the tone of Red Cloud's voice that the subject was not open for discussion. Quelling his excitement over his discovery, he ducked inside the tepee. He knew exactly what he was going to do when he left the village.

A week later Trader, whose real name was Nate Wilton, reached Fort Laramie. He asked to see Lt. Gilmore, and after a short delay was admitted into the man's office. Clutched in his hand was a handbill with a description of one Hannah McLin, runaway indentured servant. He had plucked it from the wall of the outer office where he had been left cooling his heels.

"What can I do for you, Mr. Wilton?" Lt. Gilmore spared a brief glance at the trader, aware of the man's unsavory reputation. He had long been suspected of smuggling guns to the Indians, but so far nothing had been proven.

"You still lookin' for this woman?" Wilton asked, shoving the flyer beneath the lieutenant's nose.

Gilmore stared at the flyer for a moment, recalling that it had come in two weeks before. "Ah, yes, the indentured servant. As if we don't have enough to do without looking for runaway servants. Besides, she disappeared near Denver, not up here in Wyoming. By now she's probably dead, or taken prisoner by Indians—in which case she'd be better off dead. Why do you ask?"

"I seen her."

Gilmore stared at him in disbelief. "You saw her? Where?"

"In Powder River country. In Red Cloud's camp. She's whore to a Cheyenne warrior."

"Good God! What were you doing in Indian territory? Don't you know how dangerous it is? There's a patrol out there right now, looking for Indians."

"The Indians won't hurt me. I'm a trader. I bring geegaws, pots and pans, and useful items for the women."

"What else do you bring them?" Gilmore queried.

"Why, nothin'. That's why they don't bother me. I'm harmless."

"As harmless as a rattlesnake," Gilmore muttered beneath his breath. "What about the woman? If you're on such good terms with the Indians, why didn't you bring the woman back with you?"

"I would have if Red Cloud had allowed it. It's your job to negotiate for captives, ain't it?"

"Are you suggesting I send a patrol out to get her? If you are, I'm afraid you'll have to guide us. We've been hunting for Red Cloud's camp for months, but so far we've had little luck locating him. He's moved frequently to throw us off the trail."

"Hell no! I ain't suggestin' you send a patrol. They'll be slaughtered. There's lookouts posted all over the area. They'd know you was on your way hours in advance of your arrival."

At the end of his patience, Gilmore asked, "Just what *are* you suggesting, Wilton?"

"Just you and me will go in. They know me and won't hurt us. You negotiate for the woman's release and I'll do the translatin', although Red Cloud can speak English well enough. As long as we go alone and they realize there's no patrol with us, they'll not be alarmed. To be safe, don't wear your uniform."

Gilmore sat back in his chair, staring at Wilton over his tented fingers. He imagined young Hannah McLin in the hands of savages and his blood ran cold. "Did she appear well?"

Wilton recalled the radiant beauty who stuck out like a gilded rose in a dark field and answered truthfully. "She looked well enough to me. Evidently, the young buck is treatin' her good. But that ain't no excuse not to rescue her. There's a reward out for her, ain't there?"

Gilmore snorted in disgust. "I should have known there was more to your concern than worry over a servant girl. The reward is yours if I decide to rescue her. But I'll need the colonel's permission first."

Wilton nodded. "I'll be stayin' at the fort for a few days. Look me up when you know for sure."

Lt. Trent Gilmore stared at the handbill describing Hannah after the trader left, and something stirred within him. He knew the woman was probably being abused, but that wasn't the only reason he felt he should negotiate with Red Cloud.

A southerner who had joined the western army after the end of the Civil War, Lt. Gilmore was a man out to regain all that he had lost during the conflict. He was a glory seeker who sought advancement in the army, and he believed that rescuing a woman in jeopardy was a good way to gain the recognition he deserved. Unfortunately, it was not easy to convince Col. Renfro that he should rescue a runaway servant girl.

"We already have a patrol out in Powder River country, Lieutenant," Renfro explained when he heard Gilmore's proposal. "Are you taking the word of a man like Wilton? What if the woman doesn't exist?"

"Oh, she exists all right, Colonel, else Wilton wouldn't be so concerned about earning the reward offered by her owner. We both know for a fact that the trader comes and goes as he pleases inside Indian territory. And though we suspect him of smuggling guns and whiskey, we've never caught him red-handed. Maybe I can kill two birds with one stone. Perhaps I can learn more about his smuggling activities as well as rescue the girl."

"Are you sure you want to do this, Lieutenant? With patrols out, we're short of men right now. Just as soon as we ride to quell one uprising, the Indians strike in another place. We've spread ourselves as thin as we dare. Our men can't seem to find their way to Indian strongholds due to bad maps and inept guides."

"The trader assures me he can find Red Cloud's camp. But we must go alone; otherwise we will not be allowed to enter the camp. Do I have your permission to go after the girl, sir?"

"It's your life, Lieutenant. Since you're so determined, you may go. I will give you a message to carry to Red Cloud. We have prepared a new treaty and need his signature. Tell him that the Plains tribes may keep the Powder River country in return for permission to build forts and roads. I will give you a copy of the treaty for him to sign. Tell him some minor chiefs have already signed. You may also tell him that releasing the woman captive will help cement friendship between our people."

A slow smile curved Gilmore's lips. His mission was to be more important than he originally thought. "You can count on me, sir. I will not return without Miss Hannah McLin. And, hopefully, Red Cloud's signature on the treaty."

Chapter Ten

Fear for her husband's safety plagued Hannah during Wind Rider's prolonged absence. She performed her duties and tried not to anger Spotted Doe during those infrequent times when they met. Coyote appeared regularly with game he had killed, and Woman-Who-Waddles showed her how to skin and cook his catch. She knew nothing of what was happening outside the village, despite the fact that runners arrived frequently with messages for Red Cloud. Obviously, no one thought her important enough to be kept informed of events taking place in the outside world.

Over two weeks had passed since the men of the village had left. Hannah was preparing the noon meal for her and Woman-Who-Waddles when one of the men from the

Shield society rode into camp. He reined in before Red Cloud's tepee and slid from his horse, obviously in a great state of agitation. Red Cloud came out to greet him. An excited exchange of words ensued, accompanied with much gesturing. By now, men, women, and children had crowded around their chief, listening with great interest to the conversation.

Hannah spotted Coyote in the crowd and rushed to join him, since she knew he understood a smattering of English. Using a combination of English, Indian words, and sign language, she asked him what was happening.

"The trader has been spotted traveling toward the village," he said in halting English. "He brings a stranger with him."

"A stranger?"

Coyote nodded. "Howling Wolf wants to know if the Shield society should kill them before they reach the village."

"What does Red Cloud say?"

Coyote withheld his answer until Red Cloud finished speaking and sat down outside his lodge, his legs crossed, his face stoic.

"He told Howling Wolf to let them enter the village. He does not think the trader would bring a stranger if he presented a danger to the village. Red Cloud will listen to what they have to say. Perhaps the stranger bears a message from the Great White Father in Washington, or the commission who makes the treaties."

The people slowly dispersed, whispering among themselves, speculating on the reason for the trader's appearance so soon after his last visit. Hannah was curious herself, wondering what the man with Trader wanted. She thought the stranger a brave man for venturing into an Indian stronghold without a company of soldiers behind him. Or more likely a corrupt one, given what she knew about the trader. Did the stranger also deal in smuggled arms?

Less than an hour passed before the two men rode into the village. Trader had no pack mules with him, which meant there would be no trading taking place. Red Cloud still sat in front of his lodge, waiting patiently. When the two riders approached he rose. His stark features appeared carved in granite, his proud bearing giving mute testimony to his determination to stand fast against the enemy. The people drifted toward Red Cloud's lodge, gathering in small groups as the two men dismounted and greeted their chief.

Trader greeted Red Cloud in the Sioux language, and after Red Cloud returned the greeting Trader began speaking rapidly. Hannah could not follow the conversation. But when Trader gazed out over the crowd, spotted her, and nudged the man standing quietly beside him, panic seized her. They both stared at her, as if they knew her. She wanted to turn and run, but her legs refused to obey the command. When Hannah thought she heard her name mentioned, her heart plummeted to her feet.

"Why have you brought an enemy to my village?" Red Cloud asked Trader.

"This is Lieutenant Gilmore from Fort Laramie. He comes in peace. As you can see, he does not wear his uniform. He brings a message to you from the army."

"You are welcome in peace," Red Cloud replied, turning his piercing gaze on Gilmore. Though he was angry with the army, he still harbored slim hopes of living in peace with the white eyes. If a peace could not be reached, he feared all Plains Indians would be slain or forced to live on reservations. "Tell me about this new treaty."

"Lieutenant Gilmore brings a new peace treaty from the fort. Many great chiefs have already signed it. The commission hopes you will sign it as well."

Red Cloud stared intently at the young man standing before him. With an impatient gesture, he gave Gilmore permission to speak. Gilmore cleared his throat and said, "My superiors strongly advise that you sign the treaty, Red Cloud."

Trader started to translate, but Red Cloud gave the man a withering glance and said, "I understand the white man's tongue. What does the treaty say?" Though Red Cloud was a hostile chief, even he knew it was important to listen to all proposals.

"The treaty gives the Plains Indians full rights to Powder River country in exchange for permission to build forts and roads."

Red Cloud gave a snort of disgust. "Powder River country is already ours. Our people are here in force. We will stay."

"What about the chiefs who have already signed the treaty?"

"Name them," Red Cloud demanded.

Gilmore cleared his throat and named a few chiefs of several small friendly bands. Not one important chief was included in the list.

"I will not touch the pen," Red Cloud declared, "nor will any other important Sioux, Cheyenne, or Arapaho chief. Tell the commission we will fight for the right to live where we please. If they try to build forts they will be destroyed. Travelers through our territory will not be welcomed."

Lt. Gilmore knew that Gen. Carrington had been sent to Fort Laramie with 600 infantrymen to keep the Powder River country safe for white travelers. In order to do so, roads and forts would have to be built through the area.

"Is that your final word?"

"I have spoken."

If Red Cloud expected Gilmore to leave, he was mistaken. The lieutenant merely pocketed the treaty and stood his ground.

"There is another matter Lieutenant Gilmore wishes to discuss with you, Red Cloud," Trader said, trying to defuse a potentially volatile situation. "It has nothing to do with the treaty. I ask that you listen."

191

Red Cloud looked at Gilmore and motioned for him to sit down. Gilmore understood immediately, dropping down to his haunches while Red Cloud lowered himself to the ground, crossing his legs in front of him. "Speak, blue coat. What more do you have to say?"

"It's about . . ." He turned his gaze in Hannah's direction, stared intently at her for a few moments, and then returned it to Red Cloud. "It's about a white captive in your village. A woman."

Red Cloud pretended ignorance. "There are no white captives in the village at this time."

Hannah watched the man with growing dismay. When he singled her out in the crowd she flushed and looked away. But he wasn't the only one staring at her now. People clustered nearby in small bands turned to stare at her. She wanted to turn and run but couldn't make her legs move. She was certain she had never seen the man before. Tall and slim, with brown hair, he appeared to be in his mid-thirties. Suddenly she heard the Indian word for soldier and knew he had come from the fort. But why? And what did he want from her?

Rather than openly calling Red Cloud a liar, Gilmore swiveled his head in Hannah's direction. Then he pointed to her, so that there was no mistaking about whom he was speaking. "What about her? Is she not a white woman?"

Red Cloud frowned. "That is Little Sparrow. She belongs to Wind Rider, a Cheyenne warrior."

"Is she his captive?"

"She is his woman."

Gilmore frowned, aware of what that meant. "May I speak with her?"

Red Cloud considered the request for a moment before giving his answer. "You have my permission, but it will do you little good. She cannot leave the village without Wind Rider's permission. And he is not here."

"Releasing the woman would impress the army and improve relations between our two nations," Gilmore pointed out. "It might even bring more favorable terms in a new peace treaty." Gilmore knew he was speaking out of turn and had no right to make promises, but he felt justified. He had gotten this far; leaving without the woman would be admitting defeat. After the defeat of the South he had vowed never to be a loser again.

"It is not my decision." Gilmore was not fooled by the chief's words. Red Cloud's people would obey him instantly. "Perhaps she does not wish to leave. She seems quite happy with Wind Rider."

"Go talk to the woman," Trader urged, "while I speak with the chief. I know him. If I can convince him that it will help his cause with the commission, he will agree. Go."

Gilmore nodded and lifted himself to his feet. He turned to peruse the crowd, saw Hannah lingering at the edge of the circle, and strode in her direction. The crowd parted to let him pass. Hannah saw him coming and turned to flee.

"Miss McLin, please don't run away! I mean you no harm.

Hannah paused. "Who are you?"

"I'm Lieutenant Trent Gilmore. I'm here to help you."

"How?"

Gilmore gave her a perplexed frown. Was she dense? "By taking you away from here."

Hannah glared at him. "So you can return me to Mr. Harley? No, thank you. I'd rather stay here."

Gilmore blanched. "What have they done to you? Surely you don't mean it."

"Oh, but I do, Lieutenant. Did Red Cloud not tell you I'm married to a Cheyenne warrior?"

"He told me you were the woman of a Cheyenne warrior, but I'm sure it's against your will. Red Cloud said nothing about a marriage. Besides, a heathen marriage, if there was one, isn't legal; you know that."

Hannah gnawed on her bottom lip. "How did you know about me?"

"The trader notified the fort after he saw you in Red Cloud's camp. He saw a flyer describing a runaway indentured servant and recognized you from the description. There's a reward for your return."

"Is that what this is about; the reward?" Her voice held a note of contempt.

"I volunteered to accompany Mr. Wilton because I couldn't bear the thought of a white woman being held captive by Indians." He didn't mention the recognition and promotion it might bring him. "I'll do everything in my power to convince Red Cloud to send you back to your own kind."

Hannah gave an unladylike snort. "If by my own kind you mean Mr. Harley, I prefer to remain with Wind Rider. I want nothing to do with people like him."

A jolt of pity shot through Gilmore. Evidently, Harley had mistreated her; otherwise she wouldn't feel as she did. But what kind of life did she have with the Indians? Did she feel some misplaced loyalty toward the Indian who used her as his whore? Gilmore thought it unlikely that she'd survive an armed confrontation between whites and Indians, which would surely take place, and decided he'd be doing her a favor by rescuing her. Not to mention how it would help his career.

"You don't mean that, Miss McLin. If it will make you feel any better, I'll personally speak with your master when he comes for you and impress upon him the rules governing treatment of indentured servants. I'm sure he will see the light and treat you as you should be treated."

Hannah's face clouded. She couldn't count the times she had begged Wind Rider to release her, but now she couldn't bear the thought of leaving, of existing without him. Holding back the tears, she clapped her hand to her mouth and fled.

Gilmore had no idea what he had said to cause Miss McLin such distress. He knew she had been a captive for several weeks and realized her spirit had probably been broken by her captor. Surely she didn't care for the Indian, did she? The thought was so disgusting, he pushed it from his mind. She was frightened, he told himself, and helpless. She was also beautiful; he had noticed that immediately. She was desperately in need of a protector, and he silently vowed to fight for her release from captivity and to gain her trust. Her beauty was too vibrant to waste on an Indian. He had other plans for her. When Hannah disappeared into her tepee he turned to rejoin Red Cloud and Trader.

"I've just about got Red Cloud convinced," Trader whispered when Gilmore dropped down beside him. What he failed to mention was the promise of another delivery of guns and whiskey if Red Cloud turned the girl over to the lieutenant.

"What did Little Sparrow say?" Red Cloud asked curiously. He gave little thought to Wind Rider's feelings, for he knew the warrior had a second wife to ease his sorrow should he decide to send the white woman back to her people.

"She is confused," Gilmore said carefully. "But I'm certain she will offer no resistance. It can't be easy for her living here in captivity."

Red Cloud merely grunted. After a thoughtful pause he said, "Are you certain that releasing the white woman will please the commission and gain concessions?"

Gilmore replied as truthfully as he knew how. "The commission will be grateful for the release of Miss McLin. As you know, one of the conditions for peace is the release of all white captives. Your gesture will impress the commission, make it anxious to seek a peaceful resolution to the problems facing our nations."

"They will make changes in the terms of the peace treaty?"

Gilmore lowered his eyes. "I cannot promise. But if it were up to me, I would make the terms more favorable to your people. I shall recommend it, in fact. That is all I can promise."

"I will consider it and give you my answer tomorrow. Tonight you will be my guests. My wives will prepare a feast in your honor."

Hannah refused to leave the tepee or join the festivities taking place in the center of the village. Woman-Who-Waddles told her that Red Cloud was considering whether to send her back to her people, and Hannah tried not to think about it. If she left the village now, she would never see Wind Rider again, never experience the magic of his loving, never hear the deep rumble of his voice. God, she couldn't bear it.

*   *   *

Lt. Gilmore had eaten his fill of Indian fare, finding it unusual but tasty. But he was disappointed by Miss McLin's absence. Had she been forbidden to attend? he wondered curiously. When Red Cloud rose, signaling the end of the festivities, Gilmore waited until the chief walked away before making his own departure. He had spread his bedroll nearby in the woods, and now he slowly made his way to his bed. Trader had stayed behind to negotiate with one of the women who was known to sell her favors, but Gilmore wanted nothing to do with Indian women and left to seek his rest.

"Lieutenant! I wish to speak with you."

Gilmore swung around and saw a woman standing behind him. It was dark, so he couldn't make out her features. He hoped she wasn't going to offer herself to him.

"What do you want?"

"I am Spotted Doe." The woman advanced until Gilmore could see her face. She was a dark-eyed beauty with a voluptuous body, and he was almost tempted to accept her offer should she make one. She didn't.

"I am glad you have come for Little Sparrow. She is not happy here."

"How do you know? Why should you care?"

"I am Wind Rider's woman."

Gilmore stared at her, perplexed. "I thought Miss McLin was Wind Rider's woman." Spotted Doe smiled slyly. Obviously, he wasn't acquainted with the Sioux custom of taking more than one wife.

"Little Sparrow is Wind Rider's captive. Do you understand? She is his whore. I am his wife."

"But Red Cloud said . . ."

"Red Cloud does not want you to know the truth. Wind Rider is a cruel man. Little Sparrow fears him. You must be forceful if you wish to take Little Sparrow with you."

Gilmore's eye's narrowed. "Why should you care?"

"I have come to know Little Sparrow very well, and she has expressed her desire many times to return to her own kind," she lied. "Wind Rider beats her, and I am not without feeling for her plight. You must take her and leave before Wind Rider returns."

"I promise I will do my best," Gilmore said through compressed lips. The thought of leaving the helpless young woman in the clutches of a cruel savage like Wind Rider, whoever he might be, was reprehensible.

Suppressing a smile, Spotted Doe nodded and melted into the darkness. But her words left Gilmore more confused than ever. When he had spoken earlier to Miss McLin she had said nothing about being abused by Wind Rider. In fact, she was quite adamant about remaining. Obviously, she was too frightened to speak the truth.

*   *   *

Hannah awoke the next morning in a state of great agitation. She prayed Lt. Gilmore would fail in his efforts to convince Red Cloud to return her to Mr. Harley. She felt certain that if Wind Rider was here he wouldn't allow her to be sent away, but to Red Cloud she was just a useful bargaining tool in his negotiations with the commission. She went to the river to bathe, and when she returned Coyote was waiting for her.

"Red Cloud wishes to speak with you." Hannah stared at him, waiting for him to say something heartening. He knew what she wanted but couldn't comply. Instead, he said, "There is nothing I can do if Red Cloud decides you are to leave with the blue coat. If Wind Rider was here it would be different."

"I know."

Woman-Who-Waddles came out of the tepee, interpreted the look on Hannah's face, and patted her shoulder consolingly. Hannah squeezed the old woman's hand and hurried after Coyote. They found Red Cloud sitting in front of his lodge. Trader and Lt. Gilmore were already there.

Red Cloud spoke slowly, so his words would not be misunderstood. "I have given the matter much thought," he said, addressing Gilmore, "and I have decided not to sign this treaty, but to give the commission one more chance to prepare a peace treaty the Plains Indians can live with. As a gesture of good faith, you may take the woman with you. As you can see, there are no other white captives in the village."

Gilmore tried to conceal his jubilation. "You are wise, Red Cloud. The commission will be impressed by your gesture of good faith."

"Should we not wait for Wind Rider?" Hannah dared to ask.

Red Cloud sent her a quelling look, as if her suggestion carried no weight in the matter. "Wind Rider will do what is best for the People."

"It will be all right, Miss McLin," Gilmore said, eager to leave now that Red Cloud had given his permission. "You've nothing to fear. Wind Rider won't dare defy his chief's orders. He won't be able to hurt you again. I know how you must have suffered."

"No, I . . ." The words froze in her throat. What would the lieutenant say if she told him she loved Wind Rider? That he'd never hurt her?

That he was white.

Unfortunately, she couldn't betray Wind Rider's trust. If he wanted people to know he was white he'd have to tell them himself.

"We'll leave immediately," Gilmore said brusquely. He'd hoped for the opportunity to question the Indians about the trader's illegal activities, but he thought it best to leave before the chief changed his mind. Alone and vulnerable, he could not stop the Indians from taking him captive if he angered them. "Get the horses," he told Trader.

Hannah's eyes grew wild. "I don't wish to leave!"

Ignoring her plea, Red Cloud rose and walked into his lodge, lowering the flap in obvious dismissal.

"We must hurry!" Gilmore urged as he took Hannah's arm and pulled her away from Red Cloud's lodge.

"Don't forget who the reward belongs to," Trader said.

Hannah stopped abruptly, digging in her heels and refusing to budge. "Does the reward mean so much to you? Are you to share in it, Lieutenant?"

"No; that's not my reason for being here," Gilmore said with a hint of impatience. "I couldn't bear the thought of a white woman at the mercy of Indians. The reward will go to Mr. Wilton. I want no part of it." He would gladly accept a promotion if one came his way, but he kept that bit of information to himself.

"And I want no part of Mr. Harley," Hannah returned shortly. "You'd know why if you'd seen how he treated me."

"The law says you must return," Gilmore reminded her, "but if the man isn't treating you kindly, I'll speak with him myself and see to it that the law in Denver is informed of his mistreatment."

Hannah's shoulders sagged in defeat. Obviously, there was nothing she could do or say to change Gilmore's mind or influence Red Cloud. Of one thing she was certain: She'd never see Wind Rider again. He might miss her, but never enough to make him leave his people. She knew he'd be considered a white savage in her world and people wouldn't be far off the mark. Wind Rider's love for her, if indeed he loved her, would have to be strong to lure him from his people. And if he did leave, there was nothing he could do to obtain her freedom. Harley owned her services for seven years; that was the law.

They had reached Woman-Who-Waddles's tepee now, and Hannah saw the old woman standing by the opening, wringing her hands.

"I'll wait outside while you gather your things," Gilmore said. "But don't tarry. I don't trust Red Cloud."

"I have no belongings," Hannah said, "but I would like to say good-bye to Woman-Who-Waddles." Hannah hugged the old woman fiercely, saddened that she would never see her again. A bond had formed between them despite their differences in language and culture.

Just then Trader approached, leading three horses. "I talked the chief into giving us a horse for the woman."

Woman-Who-Waddles ducked into the tepee and emerged a few minutes later with a bundle, which she thrust into Hannah's hands. It contained food, a spare dress that had belonged to her dead daughter, a comb made out of buffalo bone, and soap plant leaves. Then she placed a small bag attached to a rawhide thong around her neck. Hannah fingered the bag, aware that Wind Rider wore one that was almost identical.

"It is a medicine bag," Woman-Who-Waddles said in Sioux, using words Hannah could understand. "It belonged to my daughter and will bring you luck. You must add your own special talisman to make the medicine more potent."

"Thank you," Hannah murmured, wondering what sort of talisman she could add to the contents of the bag. Suddenly, she thought of something. "Wait here for me," she told Trader and Gilmore. "I will be right back."

Running the short distance to Wind Rider's tepee, Hannah ducked inside, grateful that Spotted Doe was absent. Rummaging in a parfleche hanging on a pole, she found what she was looking for. She had come across the object one day when she was searching for something else. It was a tiny miniature of two small children. Engraved on the other side in flowery letters were the names "Abby and Ryder Larson."

Hannah supposed it was a picture of Wind Rider and his sister, and the names were those that had been given to them by their parents. But she had never questioned him about it; the time just never seemed right. She had never seen Wind Rider look at the small painting, and now she thought he'd not miss it. But to Hannah it would be something precious of his that would remind her of their short time together. She slipped it inside the bag hanging around her neck and hurried to join Trader and Gilmore.

"Are you ready, Miss McLin?"

Hannah nodded, too emotionally spent to reply. *Wind Rider*. Her heart called out to him, knowing he would not answer, that he'd never answer. With Spotted Doe to ease any sadness he might feel over her absence, Wind Rider would not miss her for long, she thought disconsolately. Unfortunately, the same did not hold true for her.

Wind Rider . . . Wind Rider . . .

His name whispered from her lips in a silent prayer. The wind swept it away and carried it across the prairie.

Wind Rider stood poised atop a flat butte, facing the east, toward the Badlands and home. For the past two weeks he had ridden hard and fast, striking at army supply wagons, attacking columns of blue coats riding into Powder River country, and generally discouraging travelers through Indian territory. He was weary. Weary of raiding, weary of senseless deaths, and eager to go home to Hannah.

Hannah. Her name moved like a specter across his memory, and his lips stretched in a smile despite his weariness. He recalled how sweetly she had responded to his lovemaking. Her eyes defied the emerald splendor of the dew-kissed prairie grass and her hair challenged the fiery brilliance of the sun. His eyes grew misty as he thought of how bereft she had looked when he'd bid her farewell, perhaps never to see her again if luck deserted him and he did not survive. An ache grew inside him, increasing until his entire body vibrated with it. He missed her so desperately, he imagined he could hear her voice calling to him, wafting to him across the prairie on gentle zephyr wings.

Wind Rider . . . He heard it more clearly now and cocked his ear to the east. *Wind Rider* . . . Was there a note of sadness in her voice? *Wind Rider* . . . The wind ruffled his hair and cooled his flesh but did not quench the fire burning inside him. He stood as if carved in stone, listening, remembering, needing . . .

Suddenly Wind Rider stiffened. He knew. *He knew!* Hannah needed him. It was time to go home.

Chapter Eleven

The War Dog society found the Cheyenne camp by accident. They had not known it was there, for the small band had just recently left Kansas territory for the relative safety of Powder River country. Unfortunately, they hadn't found safety. Several hours before Wind Rider and his companions stumbled upon the camp it had been attacked by Gen. Conner in his sweep of the area. Twenty-four men and boys over twelve years of age had been killed. Most of the women and children had fled into the woods, but they came back later to prepare their dead for burial. Wind Rider was horrified at the destruction wrought by the army. But more than that, he was devastated to find Summer Moon, the maiden who had married his father, weeping over the body of White Feather. He hadn't been aware that White Feather was anywhere in the area.

"Father!" Wind Rider cried, leaping from his horse to kneel beside White Feather's broken body.

Summer Moon turned slowly, her eyes hollow, her face gaunt. The cradleboard strapped to her back held a tiny infant. At first the grief-stricken woman didn't recognize Wind Rider, but when she did she collapsed against his naked chest, shedding tears of fear and anger. "It isn't fair, Wind Rider. Your father was a brave man. He was taking us to Red Cloud's camp. He hoped we would be safe in Powder River country. He wanted a better life for his son."

"I am sorry, Summer Moon." His throat was clogged with unshed tears. "Father will always be remembered as a brave man and a wise chief. I will help you prepare his body for burial."

Those riding with Wind Rider pitched in to help. While some erected platforms to hold the dead, others packed everything of value that the soldiers had not destroyed. Once the dead had been placed on the platforms the survivors would be taken to Red Cloud's camp and integrated into his tribe. They stayed the night to allow the women time to mourn their dead and left the next morning. Wind Rider took Summer Moon and her babe up on his horse before him.

"White Feather knew he was going to die," Summer Moon said softly. "He told me his death had been revealed to him in a vision. That's why he wanted to take me and his son to a safe place. But there is no safe place, is there, Wind Rider?"

"You will be safe with Red Cloud. My wives will take care of you and the babe."

"You're married?" For some reason that surprised Summer Moon. "I don't want to be a burden."

"My father's widow and son are no burden. After your period of mourning there will be many men eager to join with you and raise White Feather's son."

They reached Red Cloud's village the next day. Wind Rider was so eager to see Hannah, he could hardly contain his excitement. He looked for her as he rode through the village, but when he didn't see her a shiver of apprehension slid down his spine. Why hadn't she turned out with the rest of the village to welcome him? Was she still angry at him for taking a second wife?

Red Cloud came out of his lodge to greet them, listening with rising anger as the Cheyenne survivors told of the attack. He was saddened to hear of White Feather's death and offered his condolences to Wind Rider and Summer Moon. Then he welcomed the remnants of the tribe to his village. The cagey chief said nothing to Wind Rider about Hannah's absence.

Wind Rider saw Spotted Doe and placed Summer Moon in her care. He was so anxious to see Hannah that he gave his second wife a few terse directions concerning Summer Moon and led his horse toward the lodge of Woman-Who-Waddles, convinced that he'd find Hannah with the old woman.

Woman-Who-Waddles waited with a heavy heart for Wind Rider to approach. There was no doubt in her mind that Wind Rider would be angry when he learned Little Sparrow had been sent away.

"Where is my wife, old woman?" Wind Rider asked curtly.

"Did Red Cloud not tell you?"

"Tell me what?" There was silence. "Speak! I want to know where to find my wife."

Woman-Who-Waddles's face crumpled. "She did not want to go."

"Go? Go where? Has something happened to Little Sparrow?"

"Do not listen to the old woman. She prattles senseless words." Spotted Doe appeared beside Wind Rider, having already settled the exhausted Summer Moon and laid out a pallet so she could rest. "I will tell you what happened."

Wind Rider whirled on his heel. His expression was so fierce, Spotted Doe stepped backward. "Speak, Spotted Doe. And it had better be the truth."

"A blue coat from the fort came to take Little Sparrow away. Trader had seen her on his last visit, and he told the soldier that she had run away from her master. I do not know how he knew such things, but it must have been the truth."

"Tell me about the blue coat. How is it that Red Cloud let a soldier ride into the village?"

"Trader brought him. He did not wear a uniform, and they traveled alone. Red Cloud decided to hear what the blue coat had to say. The blue coat brought a treaty, which Red Cloud refused to sign. Then the soldier asked about Little Sparrow and told Red Cloud that it would please the treaty commission if he sent her back to her own people."

"Little Sparrow belongs to me, not Red Cloud." He spoke so harshly, Spotted Doe cringed inwardly.

"Red Cloud is chief. After much thought he decided it would please the commission and possibly gain a more favorable peace treaty if he sent Little Sparrow back to her people."

Refusing to believe Spotted Doe, Wind Rider turned to Woman-Who-Waddles. "Does Spotted Doe speak the truth?"

The old woman nodded. A nerve clenched in Wind Rider's jaw, and his expression hardened. "I will speak to Red Cloud myself."

Abruptly, he turned and strode away. Woman-Who-Waddles ducked inside her lodge. She felt as if she had lost a second daughter. Spotted Doe quickly caught up with Wind Rider, pulling on his arm to stop him.

"Wait; there is more. There is something you do not know."

Wind Rider's steps slowed, but he did not stop. "What more is there?"

"I heard Little Sparrow tell the soldier that she was a captive and wanted to leave. She told him that you beat and abused her. She said she didn't like being your whore. She begged him to take her away."

Wind Rider stopped abruptly. He stared at Spotted Doe through narrowed eyes. "You heard this? Why didn't Woman-Who-Waddles tell me?"

"I am the only one who heard. They spoke outside our lodge and didn't know I was inside. I heard everything. Little Sparrow told him you were cruel, that you forced her to become your whore. She said . . ."

"Enough! Go now! See to Summer Moon. I will speak to Red Cloud myself."

"He knows nothing of what I have just told you," Spotted Doe warned. "Forget her, Wind Rider. I am all the woman you need."

Her hands clung to him, and he shook himself free. She stood and watched, a sly smile curving her lips as he strode toward Red Cloud's lodge.

Wind Rider rattled the bones outside the door and waited politely to be invited inside. When the invitation came he ducked beneath the opening and sat cross-legged opposite the great chief.

"I want to know about my woman," he said, not waiting for the chief to speak first, as was the custom. "Why have you sent her away?"

"A soldier from the fort came for her. He said if I let her go, the commission would view it as a gesture of friendship."

"He lied!"

"We shall see," Red Cloud said cryptically. "Future treaties depend upon the release of all white captives."

"Little Sparrow was not a captive; she is my wife. Did she wish to go with the blue coat?"

Red Cloud shrugged. "It did not matter what she wished."

"The blue coat will return with many more of his kind. I saw with my own eyes what they did to the Cheyenne camp. They will do the same to our village."

"The soldiers will not find us. Tomorrow we will move our village to another place, a place deeper in the Badlands, where buffalo have been reported. Go home, Wind Rider. You have no need for a white wife when you have Spotted Doe. She will give you strong sons and daughters."

"Just tell me one thing, Red Cloud. Did Little Sparrow go willingly with the blue coat?"

Being a shrewd man, Red Cloud gave the answer he thought would best serve the People and Wind Rider. He didn't consider it a lie. If Wind Rider thought his wife went willingly, he would not grieve for her, he would turn to Spotted Doe for solace, as it should be. "Little Sparrow seemed most eager to leave. That is all I can tell you." He picked up his pipe, bringing the conversation to an end. Wind Rider had no recourse but to leave. He walked back to his lodge a bitter man.

"I am happy to see you have returned safely. Did you count many coup against the enemy?" Coyote crossed paths with Wind Rider and stopped to speak with him.

"The enemy are more numerous than blades of grass upon the prairie. If we kill one, two more take his place."

"Red Cloud is ready to negotiate a peace treaty if the commission presents one that is fair."

"Ha! That will never happen. My greatest fear is that one day all Plains Indians will be driven to reservations."

"Perhaps I will join the great chiefs in heaven and walk the spirit path before that day arrives," Coyote predicted. "Your father was a great warrior, Wind Rider. I mourn with you."

The village moved the next day. Wind Rider had little time to think about Hannah. But when they reached their destination and the village settled down to normal activities, his mind searched frantically for the truth about Hannah. Had she really wanted to leave badly enough to lie about her treatment? Never had he treated her cruelly or abused her, not even when he had first taken her captive. He cared for her. He'd made her his wife, not his whore. Why would she say such terrible things? Had she also lied about the man she had run away from? No, that much was true; he had seen the result of her master's abuse himself. His confusion had turned from pain to incredible anger after Red Cloud had told him that Little Sparrow seemed most eager to leave.

Summer Moon had been invited to share Woman-Who-Waddles's lodge, and Wind Rider had given permission. She had settled into her new home and seemed to get along well with her Sioux sisters. Mourning rituals demanded that she slash her arms and cut her hair, but the disfiguring wounds she had inflicted upon herself were beginning to heal. Wind Rider also noticed that Coyote was taking an uncommon interest in the young widow.

But Wind Rider was restless. His heart and body dwelt in different places. Try though he might, he could not forget Hannah. He was torn, torn between his Indian upbringing and his white heritage. Part of him wanted to leave the People and find Hannah, and part of him wanted to forget Hannah ever existed and continue to fight the enemy. Matters did not improve when he could summon neither the passion nor the will to make love to Spotted Doe. He did not want her. Spotted Doe grew so angry over his neglect that she threatened to divorce him.

The situation finally reached a head when Spotted Doe forced a confrontation. "I should have joined with Runs-Like-A-Deer," she spat angrily. "He would not become obsessed with a woman who hated him."

Wind Rider stared at her. Was it true? Did Hannah really hate him? "Perhaps it would be best if you did divorce me," he said with a lack of any real interest. "I cannot find comfort in a woman's body right now. You are beautiful and desirable, Spotted Doe, but another man would appreciate you more than I."

Spotted Doe had had about all she could take. After Little Sparrow left she had naturally assumed that Wind Rider would turn to her for comfort, but it had not happened. She searched his face, seeing things she had not noticed before. She had always known he was white, but until now she had never realized just how very much he looked like a white man. He had not one Indian feature or trait. His skin was golden, true, but the color was due entirely to the sun. His eyes were silver, not black or brown, and he was taller than most Indians. It suddenly occurred to her that she didn't want a child who looked white.

"You are right," she said with scathing contempt, "I am sure another man would appreciate me more than you. I was blinded by your handsome features, but I do not want a man who does not want me. You are white. Cut Nose spoke the truth when he said you cannot change the blood flowing through your veins. You fight for the People now, but one day your loyalty will change." Bitterness made her voice harsh. "I divorce you, Wind Rider. I hope Runs-Like-A-Deer still wants me. Go find your white woman, if you must. I wish you joy of her."

Wind Rider said nothing as Spotted Doe gathered her belongings. Once she left his lodge everyone in the village would know she had divorced him. But he did not care. Nothing seemed to matter anymore. The foundation upon which he had built his life lay in shambles. He no longer knew who or what he was: Cheyenne or white, Wind Rider or Ryder Larson. His Indian father was dead. There was only his sister now . . . and Hannah. After White Feather's tragic death he felt his ties to the Indians unraveling. His thoughts were in turmoil, his mind troubled. Never in his adult life had he felt such overwhelming confusion. Not since he had first arrived at White Feather's village as a young boy.

Spotted Doe left the lodge without bidding Wind Rider good-bye. She saw no reason to tell him she had lied about Little Sparrow. Let him go through life thinking the woman he cared for hated him, she thought spitefully.

Wind Rider watched without emotion as Spotted Doe left his lodge. He felt nothing but relief. He had married two women and made them both miserable. Now he was alone. He had always seen himself as a loner, without a wife or children to mourn his passing. He had hinted as much to his sister many moons ago, before he left the Cheyenne village.

Tears Like Rain . . . Abby. How he longed to see his sister. He would have a niece or nephew by now, he realized abruptly. Abby would have liked Hannah, he thought with a touch of sadness. Bitterly, he shoved the notion from his brain. Hannah didn't want him. She hated him. She was as far out of his reach as the moon.

Or was she?

"Something troubles you, my brother." Coyote approached Wind Rider cautiously. Since Wind Rider had returned and found his wife gone he hadn't been the same man. He had seemed more relieved than annoyed that Spotted Doe had divorced him and was now being courted by Runs-Like-A-Deer.

"Many things trouble me," Wind Rider acknowledged.

"You mourn your woman." It was a statement rather than a question.

"I mourn the loss of my identity. I no longer know who I am," Wind Rider admitted with self-derision. "I hear voices calling to me and I know not where they come from. My mind is torn, my soul overburdened."

"She did not want to go," Coyote said.

Wind Rider looked at him sharply. "What!" Was he referring to Little Sparrow? "How do you know this?"

"She told me."

"I find that difficult to believe. Her heart is false. Like most white eyes, she speaks with a forked tongue."

"You must find the answer within yourself," Coyote advised. "Perhaps you should seek a vision. I can see that you are greatly troubled. Only the Great Spirit can guide you. If you wish it, I will go with you to the purification hut to pray and fast. I believe it is the only way."

Coyote was a medicine man, and Wind Rider recognized the wisdom of his words. He had no idea if a vision would reveal something to him, but for his peace of mind he was willing to try.

With difficulty, Wind Rider made his way up the wooded hillside to the crest of the hill overlooking the village. He wore only a brief breechclout and moccasins. His cheeks and chest were slashed with white and red paint. When he reached the top he walked to the edge of a ledge, balancing on the balls of his feet as he thrust his arms high above his head. Fervently he beseeched *Heammawihio* to grant him a vision. Then he prayed for strength, and the courage to follow the sign, should he be fortunate enough to receive one.

From the medicine bag hanging around his neck he removed tobacco, offering a pinch to the Man Above, to Mother Earth, and to the four directions. The wind snatched it from his fingers and flung it aloft. Then he offered his hunger and thirst, for he would neither eat nor drink until his vision appeared. If that did not prove to be enough, he would pierce his skin with his knife and offer his blood. Having done all that was required of him, Wind Rider sat down on the ledge, crossed his legs, and rested his arms on his knees. He chanted and prayed, staring sightlessly into the sun, and when night came he focused his gaze on the moon.

At the end of the second day Wind Rider's lips were dry, his throat parched and his tongue swollen, but he felt neither hunger nor thirst. When no vision came he pulled out his knife and slashed the flesh of his arms, offering his blood as a symbol of his sincerity. But still no sign came from the Great Spirit.

On the third day he was weak and dizzy. Time lost all meaning as he stared fixedly at the sun, chanted, and prayed for a sign from the Great Spirit. He believed deeply in the magic of a medicine dream. He had experienced one years ago, one that had provided him with his name, and he prayed desperately for another.

He thought of Hannah, of how deeply she had hurt him by lying to the blue coat. True, she had been his slave, but he had protected her, not harmed her. He had loved her. . . .

It had cut him to the quick when he heard how eager she had been to leave with the blue coat, and he desperately needed a sign to give his life direction. Should he go after Little Sparrow or remain with the People? His heart was Cheyenne, but he could not deny that he was white by birth. Did the Great Spirit want him to leave the People? How could he do it? He hated white eyes. He should hate Hannah for lying about him. He *did* hate her. If that statement was true, why then was his mind troubled? Why was his heart beset by pain? For the first time in his adult life Wind

Rider felt fear. Meeting Hannah McLin had changed him.

Hunger and thirst carried Wind Rider to the brink of total collapse as he spun in and out of consciousness. He had prayed and fasted for three days and had received no sign, no vision. Perhaps he would die atop the hill, he speculated, and the People would know he had not been worthy enough to receive a vision. He picked up his knife and pierced his flesh, once again offering his blood to the gods. His head dropped to his painted chest. He welcomed the chill of the night air against his flesh. Slowly, he raised his eyes to stare at the moon . . . and a vision appeared before his eyes like magic, gradually sharpening until it was spread out before him in its entirety.

Groggy from lack of food and water, Wind Rider clutched desperately at the vision he had finally been granted. Still seated, trancelike, upon the ledge, Wind Rider saw two paths spreading outward from where he sat, stretching across the dark sky. He saw himself rise and place one foot on either path. Several feet from the ledge the paths curved outward, one to the left and one to the right. A warrior in full battle regalia awaited at the end of the path curving to the right.

A guttural cry slipped past Wind Rider's lips when he recognized White Feather, his foster father. Then he shifted his gaze to the path curving to the left. Two women stood at the end of that path. One was Hannah and the other a woman he was certain he had never seen before. She had sable brown hair that surrounded her head in a riot of curls, white skin, and gray eyes. She was smiling; Wind Rider knew that because he could see the skin crinkle at the corners of her eyes, as if she was accustomed to smiling a great deal. Both White Feather and the women were beckoning to him.

Wind Rider felt keenly the indecision and the physical pain of the man poised with one foot on either path. Then he saw something strange indeed. He noticed that each half of his image was dressed differently, as if his inner self was split into separate beings. His right side was clad in Indian garb and his left side wore white man's clothing. He grasped the implication of the vision immediately.

The path leading to White Feather was the spirit path. If he took it, he would remain with the People and walk the spirit path to death. But if he chose the other path he understood instinctively that he could never return to the People.

On the other hand, Hannah awaited him in the white man's world, Hannah and another woman he didn't recognize. She resembled Abby, yet wasn't Abby. Wind Rider cringed at his choices. Wanting Hannah when she obviously didn't want him was a weakness, a flaw that he attributed to his white blood. Conflicting thoughts and emotions whirled inside his head as his vision began to fade away. But before the shadowy forms disappeared completely he saw his image firmly plant both feet on the left-hand path and walk toward Hannah.

He cried out in dismay as the two paths became nothing more than moonbeams and the people beckoning to him slowly evaporated into the misty heavens. The man walking the path merged with the motionless body sitting on the ledge. And when the vision began to disintegrate into shadows and vapors and his soul returned to his body he slumped to the ground, unconscious.

His mouth was dry, his hunger acute. His swollen tongue flicked out to drag across his cracked lips. The vision was still so clear in his mind, it took several minutes for Wind Rider's body to react to his mind's direction that he rise and leave the mountain.

When he found the strength to return to the village, a promising dawn heralded another day. After Wind Rider had slaked his thirst and appeased his hunger he sat with Coyote inside his lodge and related the details of his vision. The medicine man listened intently, saying nothing until Wind Rider had finished speaking. After the long narration he stared fixedly at Wind Rider for several long minutes, searching the depths of his soul.

"How do you interpret the vision, Coyote?" Wind Rider asked. Though he was more or less certain what it meant, he nevertheless wanted the medicine man's opinion.

"I think you have already guessed that you walk two paths, Wind Rider. You have known for years that the day would come when you would be forced to make a decision."

"I've tried not to think about it," Wind Rider admitted. "My heart is Cheyenne."

"But your skin is white and you love a white woman. The Great Spirit has shown you your choices, and you may choose the warpath if you wish. Only know that if you do, you will meet White Feather in the spirit world very soon."

"And if I follow the path to the white man's world?"

Coyote shrugged. "I do not know what lies in store for you."

"What about Hannah and the other woman?"

Coyote closed his eyes, seeing things not even Wind Rider knew. "Your heart is troubled. You are confused. I understand your dilemma but cannot help you. It is something you must decide for yourself. If you choose the white path, your life will no longer be a simple one. If you want Little Sparrow, you will have many problems to overcome."

"I'm not sure I want her," Wind Rider mumbled beneath his breath.

Coyote smiled knowingly. "If you walk the white path it will be because you want her. As for the other woman, all I can tell you is that she is someone you know."

Wind Rider frowned. "I did not recognize her. I know few white women besides Hannah."

"You will recognize her when you see her."

Weary beyond words, Wind Rider grew introspective, recalling with haunting sweetness how Hannah had taught him to kiss and how wonderfully her body responded to his touch.

Coyote's question jolted him back to the present. "Have you made a decision, Wind Rider?"

"*Heammawihio* has set my feet on the path he wishes me to follow and I will obey, but I know nothing of white men's customs. I have no money; I own nothing of value. How can I survive in a hostile world? And what about Summer Moon and her child? Who will support her if I leave?"

"If you tell Summer Moon her mourning is over, I will join with her. I think she will be agreeable. Her son will become my son."

Wind Rider felt as if a great weight had been lifted from him. Responsibility for Summer Moon had weighed heavily upon him.

"You can sell the furs you trapped during the winter. They are prime and should bring a good price. I will help by giving you ten horses as a bride price for Summer Moon. You can dispose of them at the fort."

"Ten horses! It is far too generous."

Coyote shook his head. "Not generous enough, my friend. Summer Moon is worth the price."

Wind Rider closed his eyes, aware that all the obstacles to pursuing Hannah had slowly disappeared. Clearly *Heammawihio* had set both his feet on the white man's path. His vision had shown him leaving the Indian Nation. He would find Hannah, he decided. But could he face her without anger? He doubted it. Could he face life without her? He doubted that even more. And even if he managed to reach Hannah, how would he gain her freedom from her cruel master?

A shudder rippled through him. He remembered her pitiful condition when he had first seen her and wasn't certain he could keep himself from killing the man who had abused her. The thought of her going back to being an indentured servant made his blood boil. It didn't even matter that she had lied about him to the blue coat; she was his wife. He had joined with her according to Indian custom; she belonged to him.

"I have never known such fear," Wind Rider admitted in a voice he hardly recognized. Cheyenne warriors feared nothing yet here he was, admitting that he feared the future in a world he despised, with people he hated. "But *Heammawihio* has spoken. Visions do not lie. *Heammawihio* has set my feet on a path I would not have consciously chosen for myself. He must have a reason, though I cannot see it now. I will obey."

Chapter Twelve

Wind Rider rode into Fort Laramie, surprised to find no wall or stockade surrounding the outpost. He had never been this far north before and was amazed to discover that the fort had not been attacked in its entire history.

Before he left the village he had taken his knife and cut his hair. It was a symbolic act, and one that caused him a great deal of anguish. As the thick black locks fell to the ground he felt as if he was severing his final link to the Indian Nation. It was a sobering thought that brought him little joy. It was unthinkable that he would desert his people for a white woman, but *Heammawihio* had spoken and he must follow. Yet something deep inside Wind Rider told him that the Great Spirit had looked into his heart before granting him a vision. Self-derision was bitter on his tongue. How could he still desire a woman who wanted nothing to do with him, who had deliberately lied about him?

He wanted to punish Hannah for lying, for leaving him, for destroying his pride, but he wanted something more. Something that only his heart knew.

Leading a string of horses, one carrying the furs he hoped to trade, Wind Rider roused scant curiosity as he rode through the fort. He exuded a restless, forceful energy that was evident in the proud tilt of his head and his watchful, narrowed eyes. He wore buckskins, for he had no other clothing, but that wasn't unusual. Many men wore buckskins in this part of the country. The stark angles of his face were shadowed by the slant of his battered felt hat, given to him by Runs-Like-A-Deer, who had taken it during a raid.

Coyote had contributed a pair of scuffed leather boots that fit well enough but felt strange on his feet. He had contributed the saddle himself, part of the loot he had taken during his months of raiding with the Sioux. He had decided at the last minute that he would raise less suspicion if he used a saddle, though his pony was unshod.

His eyes moved restlessly from left to right, searching, vigilant. He felt uncomfortable amid so many white eyes, but his innate pride did not desert him as he reined in his mount, dismounted, and tossed the reins over a hitching post. Since he had only a rudimentary knowledge of the written language, learned when he was a small lad, he asked directions to the quartermaster, having been told by Coyote that that was where he should take the horses he wished to sell. Coyote, who had had dealings with white eyes in the past, also mentioned the price Wind Rider could expect.

"What can I do for you, mister?" The lieutenant behind the desk eyed Wind Rider curiously.

"I have horses to sell to the army. Are you interested?" His abrupt manner was not unusual. Many mountain men and trappers were stingy with words.

"Depends. Where are they?"

"Outside. There are ten, all healthy. Will you look at them?"

Since the army was always in need of good horses, the lieutenant nodded and followed Wind Rider out the door. When he saw the string of horses his eyes widened, and he ran a hand over the sleek flanks of the nearest pony. "Nice animal." When he lifted up a foot to inspect the hoof, his expression changed and he looked at Wind Rider with renewed interest. "These are Indian ponies."

Wind Rider stared at the lieutenant, neither denying nor confirming his allegation. When the lieutenant finished his inspection he turned to Wind Rider and said, "They are all Indian ponies. Where did you get them?"

Wind Rider merely smiled, refusing to answer.

"If you took them from Indians, you're damn lucky to escape with your scalp intact."

"I am a trader; Indians welcome me to their camps. Do you want the horses?"

"How much do you want for them?"

Wind Rider suggested a price mentioned by Coyote, hoping he sounded knowledgeable. The lieutenant thought about it for a few minutes and named a price somewhat less but still fair. Elated, Wind Rider eagerly accepted.

"What is your packhorse carrying?" the lieutenant asked, eyeing the bulging bundles curiously.

"Furs that I trapped during the winter. I wish to sell them."

"You sure do talk funny, mister. I didn't catch your name."

With a jolt of anguish, Wind Rider realized the moment he had dreaded had arrived. Yet there was no escaping it. In a white man's world he must use a white man's name. For the first time since he was a young child he used the name he had been given by his birth parents. "Ryder. Ryder Larson." He was surprised that speaking his real name had come so easily. He still wasn't comfortable with it, but it didn't sound as strange to his ears as he'd expected.

"Well, Mr. Larson, come inside and I'll pay you for your horses. And if you're looking for a fair price for your furs, Fred Riley over at the trading post is the man to see."

"Thank you, I'll do that."

"Where did you say you're from?" Still curious about the strange young man who had turned up from nowhere, the lieutenant felt compelled to delve more deeply into his background.

"Nowhere in particular. I live in the mountains, trap some, trade some, and roam at will."

"Are you friendly with Indians?"

"You could say that."

Talkative by nature, the lieutenant asked, "In your travels did you ever cross paths with the captive white woman Lieutenant Gilmore brought back from Red Cloud's village? Rumor has it that some heathen savage raped and beat her and forced her to become his whore. Pretty little thing, too. She's a runaway indentured servant. Her master offered a reward for her return."

Wind Rider lowered his eyes, afraid they would give away his rage. Only the nerve jerking along his jaw hinted at the crushing blow Hannah had dealt him. "I haven't been to Red Cloud's camp in a long time. Lieutenant Gilmore is a brave man, going after the woman alone."

The lieutenant's eyes narrowed. "Did I say alone?"

Wind Rider shrugged. "I merely assumed he was alone. Has he sent the woman back to her master?"

"Not yet. She's staying in Captain Coon's

quarters. The captain took his wife to Cheyenne to visit relatives. If you want my opinion, Lieutenant Gilmore is sweet on the woman."

Wind Rider's brow furrowed. "Sweet on her?"

The lieutenant shook his head. "Don't you know anything? It means he wants her." He sent Wind Rider a knowing leer. "You know what I mean. I'm not sure I'd want a woman who's spread her legs for a dirty savage, but there's no accounting for men's tastes."

Wind Rider had to force himself to stand still. If he followed his natural inclination, he would launch himself at the garrulous blue coat and slit his throat. His hands clenched at his sides as he waited for his temper to subside. When he was able to speak again he said, "Does this Lieutenant Gilmore intend to keep the woman here with him?"

"Naw. He can't; it's not legal. He has to return her to her master. He's taking a patrol tomorrow and escorting her to Denver."

Having heard all he needed to know and more than he wanted, as well, Wind Rider took the money the lieutenant counted out for him and left. His next stop was the trading post, where he showed his furs to Fred Riley. Once again Coyote's advice proved invaluable as he dickered with the storekeeper. The lieutenant had been correct; Fred Riley was an honest man who offered a fair price for the furs. The money went into a pouch Wind Rider carried around his waist.

Wind Rider left the trading post and lingered on the wide porch for a few minutes to get his bearings. By now it was growing dark, and men were returning to their homes or mess halls for their supper. His original plan had been to camp a few hundred feet from the fort and leave for Denver the next morning, but upon learning that Hannah was still at Fort Laramie he had altered his plans. On the verge of stepping out of the lengthening shadows, Wind Rider froze, his silver eyes narrowed on a man and woman passing by. Enough daylight remained to recognize the copper sheen of her hair.

Hannah! The intensity and fire of his emotions raged out of control when he saw the blue coat with her lean forward and whisper intimately into her ear. Her tinkling laughter set his blood to boiling. She had never laughed like that with him. Was that Lieutenant Gilmore, he wondered, the man who was "sweet" on her? Did Hannah return his feelings? Obviously, she did. Was everything about her false?

His temper nearly exploded as he watched them walk arm in arm toward a small house, one of many along Officer's Row. He stepped from the porch and followed, keeping to the shadows. He stopped abruptly when they paused at the front door of a small cottage, speaking quietly for a few minutes while Gilmore grasped Hannah's hands and stared into her eyes. Wind Rider did not notice how quickly she removed her hands from his grip, or that she deliberately retreated from the subtle aggressiveness of his body. What he did see were her smile and her flirtatious manner. Did all white women act so shamelessly with strange men? Cheyenne women were shy and highly moral, even more so than Sioux maidens.

He breathed a sigh of relief when Hannah disappeared inside the house and Gilmore returned to his own quarters. If Gilmore had gone inside with Hannah, Wind Rider wouldn't have been responsible for his actions. As it was, he could hardly keep himself from killing the man.

Wind Rider returned for his horse and led the animal across the nearly deserted parade grounds around to the back of the building that he had seen Hannah enter. His conscience told him he was behaving foolishly, that he could get himself killed if he wasn't careful, but his death would be worth it. Just seeing the terrified look on Hannah's face when he confronted her with her lies would go a long way to restore his pride. He wasn't certain what he intended as punishment; he would know that when the time came.

Tethering his horse a short distance behind the house, Wind Rider crept to the back window and peeked inside. It was fully dark now, and he could see a light coming from somewhere inside the house. A satisfied smile stretched his lips when he saw he was looking directly into the bedroom. He tested the window to see if it would open. It did, noiselessly. It never entered his mind to worry about what could happen to him if he was caught as he slipped inside and moved silently into a shadowed corner of the room.

Hannah fixed herself a cold supper, heated a kettle of water for tea, and sat down to eat. Trent Gilmore had been kind enough to provide food for the few days she was to remain at Fort Laramie. He had finally received the colonel's permission to escort her to Denver personally, and they were to leave tomorrow. His excuse for escorting her himself was that he wanted to confront Mr. Harley and inform him that the law frowned upon the mistreatment or abuse of indentured servants, and to let him know that he intended to watch out for Hannah in the future.

Of course, Hannah wasn't so naive that she didn't know Trent was interested in her, despite the knowledge that she had been Wind Rider's woman in every way. Trent appeared to be a kind man, but something about him bothered her. She could love no man but Wind Rider. She'd never forget the piercing brand of his possession, or how eagerly she'd welcomed the thick, heavy thrust of his hardness deep inside her. If only she could have told him good-bye, let him know no one could ever take his place in her heart. But Red Cloud had sent her away and she had gone.

Hannah washed and put away the dishes, grateful to Captain Coon for the loan of his house. Picking up the lamp, she walked the short distance to the bedroom. As she stepped inside the room, Hannah felt the hairs rise at the back of her neck and stopped abruptly just inside the door. The lamp threw a narrow circle of light a few feet wide, but beyond that she could see nothing. Yet her senses were alive; her skin prickled and all her nerve endings were raw with sensation. She held the lamp higher, illuminating all but the far corners of the room. She saw nothing.

"I must be imagining things," she said aloud as she set the lamp down on the nightstand. She moved to the washstand, poured water from the pitcher, and washed her hands and face. Then slowly, with great difficulty, she tried to unfasten the back of her dress. The first two buttons came out of the holes easily, but unfastening the lower buttons was more difficult.

Wind Rider watched Hannah struggle with her dress, admiring her in the fetching calico creation that hugged her curves. His lips curled into a sneer when he realized that Gilmore had bought her the clothing she wore. Two silent strides brought him directly behind her. Shoving her hands aside, he released the remaining buttons.

"Oh!" Hannah whirled, her knees buckling when she saw Wind Rider. He grasped her by the shoulders, holding her upright. "Wind Rider! What are you doing here? Did Red Cloud tell you what happened?"

Wind Rider's lips compressed. "He told me. Why did you lie, Little Sparrow? Why did you tell the blue coat I raped and abused you?"

Hannah's mouth gaped open. "I what? Who told you that? I would never tell such terrible lies about you."

"Your tongue is false." His gray eyes glittered in splendid fury and his hands tightened on her shoulders, wringing a cry of pain from her lips. "Why? Did you hate me so much?"

"No, I didn't want to leave. Ask Red Cloud; he'll tell you the truth. I-I don't hate you at all."

"I have already spoken to Red Cloud."

Relief surged through Hannah. "Then you know I didn't leave willingly." His fierce expression frightened her.

"I know no such thing."

"But Red Cloud . . ."

" . . . Told me that you wished to leave."

"If you believe that, why are you here?"

There was no weakness in his face, no sign at all of softness. There was strength and determination and harshness. And deep in the heated center of his silver eyes, she saw the need to punish, to lash out, to repay her for what he perceived as her falseness.

He stared at her, unable to give an answer that would satisfy her. To Hannah, he looked like a caged animal, dangerous if angered, predatory if aroused. As if to prove her assessment, he grasped the sleeves of her dress and pulled them past her shoulders and down her arms.

"What are you doing?"

"Taking what is mine by right. I do not think your lieutenant will mind too much if we share you."

Hannah gasped, staring at him as if he'd just lost his mind. "What are you talking about? There is nothing between me and Trent. He is a kind man who has treated me decently despite what every man and woman here on the post thinks about me."

One more yank brought the dress pooling around Hannah's feet. Wind Rider lifted her up and kicked the garment aside. Then he stood back and stared at her. "White women torture themselves with too many clothes." Whirling her around, he fumbled with the ties of her corset. When they refused to give he took his knife and neatly slit the strings. He pulled the steel-boned garment from her body and held it aloft, looking at it curiously. "What is this?"

"It's a corset. All decent women wear them. It molds their bodies into a pleasing shape."

Raising his knife he slashed it in two and tossed it after the dress. Hannah cried out in dismay. "You do not need such a contraption. Your body is pleasing enough for me."

Hannah flushed, wishing she wasn't so pleased by his backhanded compliment. Obviously, he wanted to punish her and nothing she could say would sway him. She could not imagine why Red Cloud had lied, or who had told Wind Rider untruths about her conversation with Trent, but she had a sneaking suspicion Spotted Doe had had a hand in it.

Wind Rider's silver gaze slid over Hannah with scathing contempt. After he had removed her dress and corset she still wore a chemise, drawers, stockings, and shoes. He ripped apart the chemise and tossed it after the dress. Then he reached out to untie the strings holding up the drawers. Her hands grasped his wrists to stop him.

"Don't do this; we need to talk."

"We have talked enough."

"You're punishing me falsely. Can't you trust me a little?"

"You're white."

"So are you."

He growled out something she couldn't understand and shoved her hands aside. His eyes refused to meet hers as he pulled the string and the drawers slid down her hips. He sucked in his breath, fixing his gaze on the fiery triangle between her legs. He stared a long time, then lifted his eyes to look into her face. His fierce expression chilled her blood and filled her with a nameless horror. She made an unconscious move toward the door.

"Running outside naked isn't a good idea." She stopped in her tracks, staring at him. "I should beat you, you know. Or at the least cut out your tongue so you can tell no more lies."

"This isn't going to settle anything," Hannah cried when he scooped her off her feet and tossed her on the bed. Then he slowly, methodically, began peeling off his clothes, his eyes never leaving the lush curves of her nude body.

"It doesn't have to be this way, Wind Rider." He seemed intent upon hurting her.

He fell to his knees beside her, placing his palm on her breast, measuring the throbbing heartbeat with his callused hand, feeling it become violent in seconds. "You cannot imagine how much I looked forward to returning to you, to finding you waiting for me in our lodge. I knew I had angered you by taking Spotted Doe as a second wife, but I hoped to make it up to you. When I learned you were gone I was beside myself with grief. I thought you were forced to leave, until I questioned Red Cloud and he told me otherwise. I wanted to kill you when I learned that you told the blue coat I raped and beat you."

Hannah swallowed convulsively, imagining how deeply Wind Rider had been hurt. Why had he been lied to? "Is that why you're here, to kill me?"

Wind Rider stared at her. "No. I did consider it, but that action no longer appeals to me."

She slid her tongue across her lips to moisten them. Wind Rider seemed mesmerized by the simple act. He moved his hands over her breasts, refamiliarizing himself with them. He thumbed her nipples, watching her green eyes darken.

Hannah realized Wind Rider meant to humiliate her, but she couldn't control the way her body responded to his touch. With satisfaction she noted that his body was not immune to hers. His sex was large, impossibly large. She could see it pulsing to life, its head wet and throbbing as it rose thick and hard from his groin. It was a formidable weapon, but one she did not fear.

"I'm surprised you came to the fort. Don't you know it's dangerous for you here?" She knew she was prattling, but she needed time to defuse Wind Rider's anger.

"I'm a white man; have you forgotten?"

"No, but I thought you had. Unless . . ." Her words faltered. It seemed highly unlikely that Wind Rider intended to leave the People forever and live as a white man, but the notion brought a glimmer of hope. "Do you intend to take me back to Red Cloud's camp? If so, it would be unwise. The army would only search for me again and bring trouble to your people." Her eyes narrowed in speculation. "Why did you leave Red Cloud's camp? Didn't you consider my being returned to Mr. Harley sufficient punishment?"

Wind Rider's hands moved idly over her flesh, considering her question. He decided to answer truthfully. "I went on a vision quest. I sought an answer to my dilemma. The Great Spirit set my feet on the path to the white world. At first I could not believe he meant for me to do this, but Coyote said it is so and I have obeyed."

"You have left for good?" Hannah asked, a resurgence of hope rising in her breast. "What about me? What about us?"

"I do not want a woman who does not want me. I will try living as a white man, but it will be on my own terms."

"I want you, Wind Rider. I've never stopped wanting you."

Wind Rider scowled. "Is this another lie, Hannah McLin?"

"It is the truth. Will you take me with you?"

"We will talk about it later." He was annoyed at how easily his anger had dissipated, how desperately he wanted to believe her words.

His hands slid over her belly and lower still, his gaze intense, his breathing labored. A moment later he was molding his hands against the most intimate part of her. His thumbs separated and explored, his fingers thrusting into the deep cleft he found there. Hannah cried out, undulating her hips to match the rhythm of his fingers. Then he was kissing her, his mouth open and wet, his tongue matching the thrusting of his fingers below. Hannah whimpered, desperately needing to feel his thick manhood against her softness. It had been so long—so very long . . .

Wind Rider felt a dam burst inside him as his control shattered. He had dreamed about taking Hannah like this for so long that it had become a constant ache deep inside him. When he thought he'd never see her again something inside him had died. At first he had wanted to punish her for leaving him, for lying, but all he could think of now was thrusting inside her and filling her with himself. It had been so long—so damn long . . .

He tore his mouth abruptly from hers and stared at her. Hannah met his gaze. She felt swollen, close to exploding. He climbed atop her and she arched upward to meet him. He slid down her body and lowered his head. Wind Rider's glance met hers for the space of a heartbeat, and then she felt his breath touch her. Fierce pleasure radiated inside her. His thumbs held her open and his mouth ravished her. The wet sweep of his tongue brought wave after wave of rapturous spasms. They continued unabated as his tongue continued to circle her relentlessly, endlessly. If this was Wind Rider's idea of punishment, Hannah thought dimly, then she would suffer it gladly, ecstatically. She cried out again and surrendered to another wave of potent, heady pleasure.

The spiraling, throbbing splendor had not yet receded when Wind Rider rose to his knees, spread her legs and thrust his engorged sex into her, dropping frenzied kisses over her face, her breasts, and finally on her mouth. He could have climaxed instantly but forced himself to control the hot blood thundering through his veins. It was too soon . . . too soon . . .

Unaware of the battle Wind Rider was waging as he strained over her, Hannah jerked her hips up to meet his frantic strokes. Wind Rider cried out, calling upon the Spirit Above to calm him. Desperate to contain the wild thrusting of her hips, he anchored them to the bed with his hard hands. But Hannah was beyond the point of no return as she cried out and hurtled toward a second climax fully as dramatic as the one she had just experienced. Wind Rider felt his own control slipping and kissed her hard, thrusting his tongue into her mouth. Then he removed his hands from her hips and let her have her way.

He pumped himself into her, deep, hard, huge. Hannah felt fierce joy in his violent penetration, pulsing inside her so hot, so deep, as she contracted around him. They came together. This time the pleasure was so intense, tears streamed down Hannah's cheeks. Moments later he collapsed atop her.

Wind Rider rolled over and stared at the ceiling. Nothing had turned out as he meant it to. Instead of punishing Hannah as he'd intended, he'd ended up giving her pleasure and receiving pleasure in return. He wanted to believe Hannah, but Red Cloud had had no reason to lie about her eagerness to leave him. Spotted Doe was another story entirely. Wind Rider knew that his second wife was jealous of Hannah, and lying would have come easily to her.

"Wind Rider." The words whispered past her lips on a breathless sigh.

He turned to look at her. Her face was flushed, her eyes a luminous green, and her lips were swollen from his kisses. He thought her the most beautiful woman he had ever seen. "What is it, Little Sparrow?"

"I don't want to return to Mr. Harley. Will you take me with you?"

"Will you return with me to Red Cloud's village?"

"You want to go back?"

"I don't know."

"No," she said slowly. "I don't want you to return to the Indian way of life and I won't go with you." They were the most difficult words she'd ever uttered. "I'm afraid. I don't want you to die, and that's what will happen if you return to Red Cloud's village. You'll go on the warpath again, and maybe the next time you won't return. Please, Wind Rider, don't go back."

"Would you prefer to return to Mr. Harley?"

"I'll be free in less than seven years. And maybe," she said hopefully, "he'd be willing to sell my indenture and I'd be free sooner."

"I have no money."

"You can work. It's the way of society. Men work and earn money."

"So I can buy your indenture?"

She stared at him. "I didn't say that. I'll go away with you, anywhere you say, but not back to Red Cloud. You don't belong there. You're white, not Indian."

He turned toward her, placing a finger beneath her chin and tilting it upward. "Look at me. I don't know if it's possible to live my life as a white man. I'm twenty-five years old. I'm so thoroughly Indian, my own culture is strange to me. I can just barely remember my own mother and father."

"Your sister returned," she reminded him.

"Not without a fight." Wind Rider smiled in recollection. "She fought Zach every step of the way. She left him on more than one occasion to return to White Feather and the People."

"I'd like to meet her," Hannah said wistfully.

"Perhaps one day you will."

"Do you believe me when I say that I didn't tell Trent that you raped and abused me?"

"Perhaps," he allowed. "You call him Trent. I didn't know you were on such intimate terms with him." He scowled, remembering how he had seen them speaking together, heads bent toward one another, almost like lovers. "Have you lain with him?"

Hannah gasped. "Wind Rider! I would never do such a thing and you know it." She turned away, disappointment bitter on her tongue.

"No, don't turn away." He grabbed her roughly and pulled her back to face him.

She felt his heat press against her, breast to breast, thigh to thigh, and knew he wanted her again. His sex was hard, heavy, probing into the softness between her legs. He lowered his head, finding her mouth, his own mouth open and wet. He kissed her hard, bruising her lips. Hannah whimpered, feeling his urgency, his need, his confusion, his utter desperation. His life was changing and he didn't want to accept it. Nothing would ever be the same for him, and her heart went out to him.

"I want you, Hannah. I'll never stop wanting you. You have bewitched me." A shudder swept through him.

A scant moment later he was driving himself into her. She gasped, trying to adjust to his hard, quick strokes as he slid into her and pumped violently. She could not bear it. She clasped him tightly around the neck and moved against him. It was too wild to last long, too sweet to prolong. The moment he heard her cry out and felt her contract around him, he shouted and spilled himself into her.

"Yes," he said, the moment his breathing slowed to a steady pounding.

"Yes, what?"

"Yes, I'll take you with me. We'll go where no one knows us. I'll even find work and try to get along with the white eyes."

Hannah couldn't recall when she'd felt such incredible joy. "You won't be sorry, Wind

247

Rider. I'll be a good wife to you. But we must hurry; Trent is escorting me to Denver tomorrow."

"There is still time. It's best to leave in the dead of night, while the fort is sleeping. That's still several hours away. Sleep, Little Sparrow. I will awaken you when it is time."

Trusting Wind Rider completely, Hannah fell into an exhausted sleep. Then the unthinkable happened. Tired from his long ride to the fort and his vigorous lovemaking, Wind Rider slipped into a deep slumber. He didn't awaken until he heard pounding on the front door, and he realized it was full daylight.

Chapter Thirteen

Through a mist of sleep, Wind Rider heard the commotion at the door and jerked awake, horrified to see daylight streaming through the window. He groaned in dismay and jumped out of bed. Hannah awoke nearly at the same time.

"Oh, my God, what happened? It's daylight." She leaped from bed, too distraught to care that she was naked. When she turned to Wind Rider she saw that he was already struggling into his clothes.

"I do not know how it happened," Wind Rider gritted out harshly.

"Hannah, are you in there? Answer me, please. We leave in fifteen minutes."

"It's Trent! How could we have overslept? What should I do?"

The lieutenant's voice carried easily through the small house. "Hannah! Are you there?" The doorknob rattled.

"Answer him!" Wind Rider whispered harshly. "Tell him you overslept, but that you'll be ready in time."

Suddenly realizing that she stood as naked as the day she was born, Hannah grabbed a blanket from the bed, wrapped it around herself, and approached the front door. "I'm awake, Trent. I overslept, but I'll be ready in fifteen minutes."

"Are you all right, Hannah? Your voice sounds funny."

"I—I'm fine, just groggy from sleep."

"We'll be waiting for you in front of headquarters. I've got a surprise for you."

When his footsteps faded away Hannah returned to Wind Rider, who was fully dressed now and had one leg through the back window. "It will only take me a few minutes to dress; then we can leave together through the window."

Wind Rider sent her a bleak look. "That's no longer possible, Little Sparrow. It's daylight. You will be seen leaving. There is no way now that we can leave together."

Hannah stared at him. "You want me to go with Trent and the patrol?" A shudder swept through her. "How can you leave me behind after last night? I can't go back to Mr. Harley."

Grasping her shoulders, Wind Rider pulled her against him and kissed her hard. "Be reasonable. We can't leave together, not now. You have to go with the blue coats. I will follow and strike when they least expect it. It will take many days to reach Denver. Be prepared at all times, for I will be following behind you."

"I'm afraid. What if they see you?"

He gave her a cocky grin. "Have you forgotten that I was raised by Indians? They taught me well."

Before she could offer further protest Wind Rider kissed her again and slipped through the window. He walked nonchalantly to the place where he had left his horse, and by the time Hannah stepped from the house to join Lieutenant Gilmore, he was lounging in the shadowed doorway of a building only a few feet away—close enough to hear what was being said.

"There you are," Gilmore greeted her cheerily. "You look flushed; I hope I didn't rush you too much. I'd hoped to get an early start."

Hannah shook her head in a negative motion. "I'm fine. I'm sorry I overslept. How long will it take to reach Denver?"

"I thought you'd be more comfortable riding at a leisurely pace in a wagon, and that will stretch our time to at least ten days."

Since she was a poor rider, Hannah thought his reasoning sensible. And if they didn't ride too fast, she thought Wind Rider would have less difficulty following them.

"I haven't told you my good news yet," Gilmore said, beaming. "I hope you'll be as pleased by my surprise as I am."

251

"Surprise?" Hannah had a sneaking suspicion she wasn't going to like his "surprise."

He placed an arm around her shoulders, giving her an intimate hug. Hannah stiffened but said nothing.

"You've probably wondered why you've remained at Fort Laramie so long instead of being taken to Denver immediately." Hannah stared at him, waiting for him to continue. She had been curious, but had assumed it had something to do with an escort not being available. "It's taken this long for me to get myself transferred to the Colorado militia in Denver. The captain just received word that my request for transfer has been granted. And I hope a promotion will follow. Do you know what that means, Hannah? It means I'll be able to keep an eye on you. With me nearby, Mr. Harley will be less likely to mistreat you. And maybe," he hinted, "with enough pressure, he'll sell your indenture. We'll deal well together, Hannah; you need someone to protect you."

He hugged her closer, ignoring the men who were staring at them. Hannah felt heat rise to her cheeks. Why was Trent doing this? What did he want from her? His brazen behavior confused and humiliated her. Did he think she was a whore? Did he think less of her because she had been Wind Rider's woman? What role did he expect her to play in his life? She tried to pull away; the greedy look in his eyes sent chills down her spine.

"It's a long way to Denver," he murmured, for her ears alone. "We can get to know one another better." He placed his hands around her waist to lift her onto the wagon seat.

Wind Rider's teeth were clenched so tightly, he felt the pain clear up to his temples. When the lieutenant placed his arm around Hannah's shoulders he wanted to leap the distance between them and tear him away. And when the lieutenant's hands circled her waist Wind Rider pushed himself away from the doorway, his face contorted with rage. Glancing over Gilmore's shoulder, Hannah saw Wind Rider moving resolutely toward her, and she gasped out his name. If there had been anything she could have done to stop him, she would have done it, but he didn't even glance at her. His furious silver gaze was focused entirely on the hapless lieutenant.

"Wind Rider, no!"

Gilmore heard Hannah, and his hands dropped from her waist. He whirled to confront the enraged man storming toward him, his hand on his weapon. Wind Rider recognized the rashness of his act, but by then it was too late. He didn't stop until they stood toe to toe. His eyes were hard, unpredictable, dangerous.

"Take your hands off my woman." The quiet menace in his voice was unmistakable.

Gilmore stared at him, astounded. "Wind Rider? You're Wind Rider, the Indian who raped Miss McLin? Damn! You're not even an Indian!

If you're not full-blooded white I'll resign my commission." He slanted an accusatory glance at Hannah. "Why didn't you tell me Wind Rider was a white Indian?"

Hannah's lips trembled. Wind Rider had gone and done it now. Though he was white, they would still call him a savage and treat him accordingly. "I-I didn't think it was important," she stammered. "Besides, Wind Rider didn't . . ."

"Don't try to deny it, Hannah," Gilmore said sternly. "I can see how frightened you are of the man. Don't worry; I won't let him hurt you again."

"No, you don't understand."

"I understand only too well. Rumors have been flying for a long time about a white Indian, but the army put no stock in them. What do you want, Wind Rider? Do you have a white name?"

"My name is Larson, Ryder Larson. I want my woman."

Gilmore laughed harshly. "I'm taking her back to Denver, to her master. You do know she's an indentured servant, don't you?"

"Hannah is my wife."

"Your whore, you mean." Hannah cried out in dismay at Trent's harsh assessment of her. "You must know that even if you did marry her in some heathen ceremony, it isn't legal."

"Go away, Wind Rider. Can't you see you're only making matters worse?" Hannah's voice was shrill with fear. "I am ready to go with you,

Trent." She placed a hand on his arm, trying to draw his attention from Wind Rider. She'd do anything to keep Wind Rider safe.

Wind Rider saw Hannah's gesture, heard her place herself in Gilmore's protection, and his temper exploded. "You will go with no man but me." He grasped her arm, intending to pull her away, but Gilmore reacted swiftly.

"Sergeant MacGregor, arrest that man!"

Immediately, a burly man advanced toward Wind Rider, brandishing his weapon. When it looked as if Wind Rider would resist Gilmore said, "Privates Pilcher and Mickley, help Mac-Gregor."

In growing horror Hannah saw the three men surround Wind Rider, cutting off all avenues of escape. A sob lodged in her throat. What would they do to him?

Wind Rider stood very still. His uncontrollable temper had thrust him into a dangerous situation. What had happened to the restraint he had learned at the knee of his Cheyenne father? he wondered dimly. In the end, his white blood had prevailed over his Indian upbringing, and he grieved for the loss of that part of himself he considered Indian. Calmly, almost too calmly, he considered his chances for escape and found them severely limited. He sent Hannah a look so filled with venom, it nearly broke her heart. Did he really think she wanted to go with Trent?

"What should we do with the man, Lieutenant?" Sergeant MacGregor asked once they had Wind Rider subdued.

"Put him in chains and throw him in the stockade, Sergeant. Tell the sergeant of the guard not to release him under any circumstances."

"What are the charges, sir? Captain Purdue will want to know."

"Rape, for one thing. I'll get a deposition from Miss McLin to verify the charges. And his activities with the Indians will need further investigation. Tell Captain Purdue I'll conduct the investigation from Denver and wire him the results. Meanwhile, let him rot in the stockade." He turned to Hannah and smiled. "Didn't I tell you I'd protect you from the savage? He'll not harm you again."

A choking sensation rose up to steal Hannah's breath as Sergeant MacGregor poked Wind Rider forward with his gun. He paused once to glare at her over his shoulder. He raised his clenched fist, then quickly lowered it. But it was all the sign Hannah needed. She knew by that brief gesture that he would find her somehow, to punish her for this perceived wrong.

"Are you ready to leave, Hannah?" Gilmore asked, pleased with the way he had handled the situation.

"What will happen to Wind Rider?"

"That's for the army to decide. Rape is a serious charge. There is also the matter of his going on the warpath with the Indians. I can't believe he's actually a white Indian. What do you know about him?"

"Not much," Hannah lied. "I think he was raised by the Cheyenne. But he didn't rape me. We were married according to Indian rites."

Gilmore frowned. "Don't defend him, Hannah. I know you were forced. There's no court in the country that will fail to convict him if he's brought to trial. Forget him; he'll never hurt you again. Concentrate on the future. I've transferred to Denver just so I could take care of you."

"You don't care that I've been Wind Rider's woman?"

"Oh, I care. I'd like to kill the bastard." He leered at her. "Still, he must have taught you something while you were his woman."

Hannah gasped in dismay. The longer she was with Trent Gilmore, the more she distrusted him.

What Gilmore didn't say was that while she wasn't exactly the kind of woman he'd bring home to his mother, he was no longer living in the South. Western standards were different. Women were scarce, and Hannah McLin was beautiful enough to forgive her lapse as long as she was repentant. She was far lovelier than any woman he'd seen here so far. He doubted he'd ever marry her, given her unsavory history, but he certainly hadn't anything against being her protector and lover.

Gilmore was the product of the aristocratic South, where taking a mistress was perfectly acceptable behavior. Rescuing Hannah had appealed to his sense of honor and had earned him a certain amount of glory, but offering marriage was taking his infatuation a step too far.

Gilmore lifted Hannah onto the wagon seat and climbed up beside her. Grasping the reins with one hand, he signaled the patrol forward. As they left Fort Laramie behind, Hannah knew a terrible fear. The man she loved was in the stockade and would likely be sent to prison. If Trent proved that Wind Rider had participated in Indian raids, he might even hang. If she hadn't insisted that he leave the Sioux, or refused to return to Red Cloud's camp with him, he wouldn't be in this mess. It was all her fault, and now she might never see Wind Rider again. Would he ever forgive her?

Wind Rider paced the cell like a caged animal. The chains on his arms and legs reminded him of his lowly position among white eyes. He pounded on the door and earned nothing for his trouble but a harsh warning from the sergeant of the guard. Over a week had passed since he'd been locked behind bars, and he'd cursed his impetuous nature many times since that day. If he'd bided his time and waited, he could have used his cunning to spirit Hannah away from the blue coats. But the moment he had witnessed the lieutenant's proprietary manner toward Hannah, caution had deserted him.

* * *

After being denied his freedom for two weeks Wind Rider felt himself teetering on the brink of insanity. Accustomed to open spaces, to going where he willed, he found confinement the worst kind of torture imaginable. He was seriously thinking of wrapping his chains around the guard's neck when he brought the next meal and squeezing the life from him, regardless of the fact that it would mean his death. Desperate as he was, he would welcome death; living like an animal did not appeal to him.

Zach Mercer drove the freight wagon into Fort Laramie, cursing his incredibly bad luck. Three of his most experienced drivers were incapacitated, leaving him shorthanded and forcing him at the last minute to drive one of his Denver-based company's freight wagons to Fort Laramie to fulfill the contract he had negotiated with the army. It was a lucrative deal; otherwise he would have delayed the shipment until a driver was available. Leaving Abby and their new son was one of the most difficult things he'd ever done.

Even though he had left Abby well protected by a small army of hired men, most of them proficient with guns, he worried about them in these unsettled times. Just thinking about Abby and their small son brought a smile to his lips. Little Trey was a perfect child, a delight, and there would never be another woman for him but Abby. He loved her to distraction despite their unconventional meeting. When they had first met she was known as Tears Like Rain. She had claimed him for her slave and by so doing had saved his life.

Zach drove the lead wagon of the four-wagon convoy to the supply depot, where it and the others would be unloaded. First thing in the morning, he and the other drivers would drive the empty wagons back to Denver.

"Mr. Mercer, your wagons are right on time. What brings you to Fort Laramie?" the officer in charge of the supply depot asked. It was a rare occasion that brought the owner of Mercer Freighting to Fort Laramie.

"Necessity, Lieutenant Coppersmith, pure necessity. Two of my drivers are laid up because of accidents, and one was involved in a gunfight. All three are recuperating, but I didn't have time to hire and train another driver. What's new in this part of the country, Lieutenant?"

"Same as in your part of the country, I reckon. Indians are still on the warpath. General Conner took three columns into Powder River country, but word is, they've encountered few Indians. A short time ago he sent word that he had wiped out a Cheyenne camp and an Arapaho camp. The deputy commander is in charge of the fort during his absence."

Zach's attention sharpened. "A Cheyenne camp, you say? Do you happen to know the name of the tribe's chief?"

The lieutenant scratched his head, trying to recall the rumors he'd heard. "Yeah, now that you mention it, I do recall hearing the chief's name. Rumor has it that Chief White Feather was killed in the attack."

Zach went still. White Feather. Abby would be devastated. He had no idea how to tell her that her foster father had been slain by the army during an attack on his camp. "What about the women and children?"

"Most of them ran away. Conner let them go. He didn't want it referred to as another Sand Creek."

Zach was thankful that Summer Moon was still alive. He wondered about the child he knew she had been expecting. "I'll report to the quartermaster," Zach said, eager to receive payment for the shipment and be on his way. He feared Abby would hear the news from someone other than himself. Perhaps he'd leave tonight if the wagons were unloaded by then.

Zach had received payment for the shipment and was on his way out the door when a chance remark stopped him in his tracks. Two enlisted men who had just entered the office were discussing a man being held in the stockade. The words Zach heard were "white Indian."

Zach whirled, smiling at the men in a friendly manner. "What did you say, Corporal? I just arrived at the fort and haven't heard the latest news. Did you say the white Indian was being held in the stockade? Is he truly white? Or is he merely a half-breed?"

"He's white, all right," the corporal smirked. "His skin is tan from the sun, but his eyes are a strange silver-gray. He hasn't denied he's white. Says his name is Ryder Larson, but Lieutenant Gilmore said he's called Wind Rider."

Zach tried to suppress his shock. "What are the charges against him?"

"Rape," the corporal offered. "And Lieutenant Gilmore suspects him of raiding with the Sioux."

"Rape," Zach repeated dully. That certainly didn't sound like the Wind Rider he knew. For Abby's sake, he had to find some way to help her beloved brother. "Who did he rape?"

The corporal leered knowingly. "A pretty little piece he captured. Turns out she was a runaway indentured servant. Lieutenant Gilmore rescued her and escorted her to Denver. Word is, the lieutenant has a hankering for her."

Pretending to lose interest in the subject, Zach excused himself and went on his way, all thought of leaving that night forgotten. His mind was in a turmoil as he walked slowly across the parade grounds.

"Zach! Zach Mercer! What in tarnation are you doing at Fort Laramie?"

Zach's face lit up when he recognized Captain Frank Purdue, a friend of long-standing. They had served together in the Federal Army during the War Between the States. They were both from Boston, and their families were close friends. "Frank, what are you doing in the West? I thought you'd left the army after the war."

"I found I liked the life and reenlisted to serve on the Western frontier. I've been Deputy Post Commander at Fort Laramie for six months. What about you?"

"I've left the army," Zach revealed. "Mercer Freighting is now serving the West. I'm also married and have a son. We live near Denver."

"Well, I'll be damned," Purdue said, pumping Zach's hand. "A son. Congratulations. I imagine those are your freight wagons that just arrived."

As they spoke of old times, an idea began to form in Zach's mind. When Purdue asked Zach to join him in his office for a drink Zach accepted eagerly.

Seated in a comfortable leather chair in Purdue's office, Zach sipped his whiskey and planned his strategy. When Purdue asked about his wife's family Zach was as truthful as he could be.

"My God, that's an incredible story," Purdue said after Zach told him about Abby and her brother having been raised by the Cheyenne. "Thank God Abby saved your life. Whatever happened to her brother? You can't help feeling sorry for him."

Zach had awaited just such an opening. "Wind Rider is being held in your stockade."

"What?" Incredulous, Purdue leaned forward. "You mean that white Indian in the stockade is your wife's brother?"

"I haven't seen him, but I have every reason to suspect that he is. And Wind Rider would never rape a woman. If you knew the Cheyenne at all, you'd know that they do not rape. Has the woman accused him? If so, I'd like to question her myself."

Purdue grew thoughtful. "As far as I know, formal charges have yet to be filed against Mr. Larson. He claims he and the woman were married in an Indian ceremony. Lieutenant Gilmore denies that any kind of ceremony took place. He is to investigate the claims and wire his findings to us."

"I'm inclined to believe Wind Rider," Zach said. "I know the man. My wife dotes on him. During all those years with the Indians, he watched over and protected her. He's not a savage, Frank."

Purdue rubbed his chin thoughtfully. "Perhaps we should talk to the man. Lieutenant Gilmore might have been overzealous in his duty. I've heard rumors that Gilmore is quite taken with Miss McLin. That's the woman's name—Hannah McLin."

"I'd appreciate anything you could do, Frank," Zach said gratefully. "If you saw fit to release him into my custody I'd see that he causes the army no more trouble. If he's identified himself as Ryder Larson, I seriously doubt he intends to return to Powder River country and the Sioux."

Purdue strode to the door, opened it, and called out, "Corporal Finnigan, have the prisoner in the stockade brought here."

"You mean the white Indian, sir?"

"That's right, Corporal."

* * *

With growing alarm, Wind Rider listened to the murmur of voices outside his door. It wasn't mealtime yet; he wondered if they had decided to execute him without a trial. He knew little about military justice or white man's laws, and he wouldn't put anything past them. He thought briefly about trying to escape and taking his chances on getting killed. That might be preferable to being executed. When the door opened the sergeant of the guard stood aside, allowing another soldier to enter his cell. Wind Rider noted that the man was young and looked inexperienced, and his hopes soared. Maybe escape wasn't impossible after all.

"The captain wants to see you, Larson," the corporal said. He stood well back from the dangerous-looking man. "I'm to take you to him." He drew his weapon and pointed it at Wind Rider.

Wind Rider held out his arms. "Remove the chains."

Corporal Finnigan shook his head. "I'm not crazy. Move, Larson; Captain Purdue doesn't like to be kept waiting."

Sending the man a black scowl, Wind Rider shuffled from the austere room, his stride limited by the length of the chains. When Finnigan prodded him cruelly he swung around and snarled, pleased when the corporal's face whitened and he retreated in haste.

It seemed to take forever to reach post head-quarters, but Wind Rider was in no hurry to hear his death sentence. His one regret was leaving Hannah in the hands of men like Harley and Gilmore.

Finnigan held open the door so Wind Rider could enter the captain's office, then stationed himself just inside the door in case of trouble. His face impassive, Wind Rider directed his gaze at the man sitting behind the desk. He did not see Zach, seated off to one side.

Zach leaped to his feet, angered to see the fiercely proud Wind Rider chained like an animal. "I say, Captain, was it necessary to place the man in chains?"

Purdue shrugged. "It was Gilmore's order. With the General gone, and the entire fort to run, I've had little time to devote to the prisoner."

Wind Rider's eyes widened in shock. Zach Mercer was the last person he expected to see at Fort Laramie. What was Abby's husband doing here? he wondered. Not that he wasn't glad to see him. He hoped Tears Like Rain was with him; he longed to set eyes on her one last time before he walked the spirit path.

"This man is my brother-in-law, Captain. The charges against him are totally false. Where is his accuser?"

"I understand that Miss McLin has been returned to the man who purchased her indenture. And Lieutenant Gilmore has been temporarily attached to the Colorado militia in

Denver. He is supposed to get a deposition from the woman and question some men who have seen the prisoner riding with Indian raiders."

"If the woman didn't admit to being raped before she left the fort, I doubt she'll do so any time in the future," Zach said with such firm conviction, the captain took another look at Wind Rider.

"I suspect it's too embarrassing for the woman to talk about," Purdue reasoned. "She must have admitted it to Lieutenant Gilmore or he wouldn't have made those charges."

Zach took two long strides until he stood beside Wind Rider. He placed a hand on his shoulder. "That's pretty flimsy evidence. I suggest you turn him loose. I'll personally accept responsibility for his behavior."

Wind Rider started violently. At one time he had hated Zach Mercer, but now he couldn't ask for a better friend. He turned to the captain and said, "Hannah McLin is my wife. I would never harm her." That was almost true. Her lies had hurt him deeply, and he remembered how she had clung to the lieutenant after telling Wind Rider she'd go anywhere he chose so they could be together. She spoke with a forked tongue. When he saw her again, if he ever did, he wouldn't be responsible for his actions.

"Harumph." The captain cleared his throat. "An Indian ceremony, if one actually took place, isn't legal. In the eyes of the civilized world, Miss McLin is not your wife."

"Civilized men do not kill innocent women and children," Wind Rider spat, his eyes blazing. "Are you forgetting Sand Creek?"

"I'm not going to argue with you, Larson. Unfortunate atrocities have taken place on both sides. But having a man like Zach Mercer speaking on your behalf is good enough for me."

"Then you'll let him go?" Zach pressed determinedly.

Purdue rested his chin on his tented fingers, staring at Wind Rider, still undecided. "Where do you intend to go if I free you, Mr. Larson? If it's back to Red Cloud's village, I fear releasing you is out of the question."

Zach flashed Wind Rider a warning glance. "I will go to Denver with Zach," Wind Rider said. "I wish to see my sister and new niece or nephew."

"Nephew," Zach said, grinning proudly.

"I suppose the militia can find you easily enough if you make trouble in Denver. But I'll hold your brother-in-law responsible if you break the law."

Wind Rider flashed Zach a grateful look. "I will not break the law."

"And meanwhile, if Lieutenant Gilmore finds proof that you rode the warpath with your Indian friends, the army will come looking for you. Do you understand?"

Wind Rider nodded, though he seriously doubted anyone could be found who had seen him riding with the Sioux.

"Remove the chains," Zach said crisply.

Purdue called to the corporal standing just inside the door, ordering him to remove Wind Rider's chains. He approached Wind Rider gingerly and quickly unlocked the fetters. They fell away, and Wind Rider kicked them aside, massaging the raw spots they had left on his wrists.

"We'll be leaving immediately, Frank," Zach said. "I sincerely thank you for what you've done for my family. I won't forget it."

"I hope neither of us will regret this," Purdue mumbled as he stared into the silver depths of Wind Rider's eyes. He hoped he hadn't made a mistake. The man looked dangerous and untrustworthy. If he didn't respect Zach Mercer, he'd never have let the white Indian go, though God knew it wasn't Larson's fault he and his sister had been captured and raised by Indians.

"Let's go home," Zach said, slapping Wind Rider on the shoulder. "We've got a lot of catching up to do."

"There is something I must do first," Wind Rider said once they stood outside headquarters. "I go to find my wife."

Chapter Fourteen

Hannah had to admit that life as an indentured servant was less difficult with Trent Gilmore making Mr. Harley abide by the rules. The drab brown dress she now wore was much like the one she had worn when she'd run away all those months before, but at least this one was clean and not so ragged. And since Mr. Harley hadn't suggested that she sell herself to his customers, she no longer tried to make herself as unattractive as possible.

During her long absence Harley's frail wife had died, and now the man was looking at Hannah with renewed interest. His assessing glances worried her, and she was grateful that Trent visited the inn several times a week to check on her.

"Quit daydreaming, girl," Harley grumbled as he caught Hannah staring off into space. "The reward I paid for your return has to be repaid, and you can't do it by woolgathering. Get into the kitchen and help Conchita prepare tonight's meal. If it wasn't for that damn lieutenant, you'd be earning extra money on your back. Spreading your legs for my customers can't be any worse than spreading them for Injuns."

Color flooded Hannah's cheeks. She might regret many things, but becoming a woman in Wind Rider's arms wasn't one of them. It took very little effort to recall Wind Rider, and even less effort to remember the way he made her feel. He was an incredible mass of sinewed strength—a powerful, imposing creature, who had been taught to survive by Indians. Just thinking about him made the blood rush to her head and her stomach flutter. Until she met Wind Rider, she hadn't known the meaning of pleasure. Unfortunately, she would never know that pleasure again.

Hannah hurried into the kitchen to help Conchita, welcoming the opportunity to escape Mr. Harley's notice. She hated the way he'd been ogling her lately. Something was festering in his mind, something she didn't dare think about.

Wind Rider entered the inn shortly after Hannah had disappeared into the kitchen. Since it was the time of day when most men were engaged in work, the common room was nearly deserted, but for a few unemployed miners and drifters passing through town. He took a table in a far corner, pulled his hat low over his eyes, and sat down to wait.

He had come directly to Denver, not even stopping off at the farm to see Abby and his nephew first, though he'd promised Zach he'd be by in a day or two. Finding Hannah was a driving force within him, and he couldn't ignore it, no matter how dearly he loved his sister or longed to see his new nephew.

"You new in town, mister?"

Wind Rider glanced from beneath his hat brim. He recognized Harley immediately from that one encounter several months ago, when he had seen the man abusing Hannah. He wanted to leap at Harley and pound him into the ground, but he managed, with admirable restraint, to remain seated. It was extremely difficult when he thought of Hannah's pitiful condition the day he'd found her cowering in the woods.

"You could say that," Wind Rider replied.

"What are you drinking, mister?"

"Whiskey." Wind Rider pulled a silver dollar from his money pouch and tossed it on the table. During their trip from Fort Laramie to Denver Zach had explained many things to him, including how to count money and make change.

Harley left and returned a few minutes later with a bottle and a glass. He seemed in no hurry to leave. "What did you say your name was, mister?"

"I didn't. But it's Larson. Ryder Larson." By now the name had begun to feel comfortable.

"You gonna be in town long, Mr. Larson? I've got a nice room for rent upstairs. Business is slow lately."

"I don't need a place to stay." He sipped his whiskey, pointedly ignoring the innkeeper. Harley took the hint, ambling off toward the bar.

Ryder sipped and waited, his mind roaming absently. For a breathless moment he recalled Hannah's hair reflecting the colors of the sunset, her eyes defying the emerald splendor of the dew-kissed grass. Loving her had been easy, but thinking she might care for him was a mistake. When they had made love he could have sworn there was some feeling between them. Was she leading Lieutenant Gilmore on the same way she had led him on? he wondered harshly. Never would he forget how sweetly they had loved at Fort Laramie, or how quickly she had turned to Gilmore after they had parted.

The shadows deepened and the level in the bottle of whiskey dropped. People began to drift into the bar on their way home from work. The light barely reached the corner where Ryder was seated, which was the reason he had chosen it. He wanted to be aware of Hannah before she saw him so he could observe her reaction. It annoyed him to think that he had no idea what was going to happen or what he intended to do when he did see her. He had promised Zach he wouldn't make trouble, but it seemed trouble always came looking for him.

Then trouble walked through the door in the guise of Lieutenant Gilmore. He selected a table in a well-lit area, close to the bar. Harley went to take his order, and Wind Rider watched closely as the two men engaged in heated conversation, wishing he was close enough to hear what was being said. After a few minutes a frowning Harley stormed off into the kitchen. He must have gone to summon Hannah, for she appeared almost immediately, carrying a tray of food, which she placed before Gilmore. They chatted for a short time and when she turned to leave Gilmore placed a hand on her arm to stop her. Though Ryder strained his ears, he heard only the low murmur of voices.

"Is Harley treating you well, Hannah?" Gilmore asked. He rested his hand on her arm in a possessive manner.

"Yes, thanks to you. I appreciate your friendship and help, Trent."

"I want to be more than a friend to you, Hannah, and you know it. Why are you making this difficult for both of us? I thought we would become close on the trip down from Fort Laramie, but you resisted me at every turn. I want to protect you."

Hannah licked her suddenly dry lips. She knew exactly what Trent wanted; he'd often alluded to their becoming lovers during the tedious journey to Denver. "Have you forgotten? I'm not free to make choices."

"I've been negotiating with Harley to buy your papers, but so far he's resisting. No doubt he'll be most agreeable when we reach a mutually satisfying price. Meanwhile, I've convinced him to give you some time off. Even indentured servants deserve a day off now and then. I'll pick you up at ten o'clock tomorrow morning. I'll bring a buggy and we'll take a ride around the city."

A slow smile curved Hannah's lips. "How in the world did you get Mr. Harley to agree to that?" Trent really could be charming when he wanted to, Hannah decided. But she had no intention of taking a lover. Wind Rider was the only man she wanted. All others paled in comparison.

"That's my secret. There's something I want to show you tomorrow. I hope you'll like it."

"I have to go, Trent. The room is getting crowded, and there are people wanting food and drink." Her gaze took a turn around the room, coming to rest on a man slouched in a chair in a dark corner, his hat pulled down over his eyes. There was something about the set of his shoulders . . .

Ryder lifted his head and his gaze collided with the startling green of Hannah's eyes. He saw her gasp and raise her hand to her mouth to stifle the sound. At that moment there might have been only two people in the room, so intently did they stare at each other. The tension was so thick, it clung to them like dense fog, blocking out all but these two people. Hannah whispered his name.

Gilmore heard and leaped to his feet. "Where!" But he didn't need to ask, for Ryder had already risen and was glaring at him in a threatening manner. "What in the hell is he doing out of the stockade? Heads will roll for this blunder."

Hannah was beyond speech; she could only stand and stare.

"Hannah, listen to me. You're not to communicate with him in any way. Stay here while I speak to him."

Hannah wanted to rush to Wind Rider, to throw herself into his arms, to beg him not to leave her, but she did none of those things. The closed look on his face was warning enough. She merely nodded when Gilmore issued his order.

Ryder saw Gilmore approach and waited, his fists clenched at his sides. He dare not look at Hannah for fear of what he'd read in her expression. Did she love the blue coat?

"How did you escape from the stockade, Larson?" Though nearly as tall as Ryder, Gilmore still didn't measure up to Ryder's magnificent physique as they stood toe to toe, glaring at one another in open challenge.

"I didn't escape, Lieutenant. I was set free."

"Like hell! Who would dare disobey my orders?"

"Captain Purdue."

"The deputy commander? Why would he do such a thing? I have enough evidence to put you behind bars for the rest of your life."

"You'll have to ask the captain. I suspect you're lying about evidence. I doubt there is enough to convict me." Ryder's impassive features gave away nothing.

"We'll see about that. Have you forgotten about the rape charges? What are you doing in Denver? Why didn't you hightail it back to Powder River country?"

"I've come for my wife." No matter what she had done, she still belonged to him.

"Your wife, pah! You made her your whore."

Wind Rider's hand reached for the knife in his belt. Despite his promise to Zach, he was damn close to slitting Gilmore's throat and hang the consequences. "Hannah might be your whore, but she was never mine."

Gilmore's face turned fiery red. "You're not to talk to Hannah, is that clear? If you were to ask her, she'd tell you the same thing. We've become lovers," he lied. "She wants nothing more to do with you."

Ryder's face drained of all color. The thought of Hannah and Gilmore together sickened him. "I make no promises, Gilmore."

"I'm going to get to the bottom of your precipitous release and have you back in the stockade so fast your head will spin. If you're wise, you'll leave town while there's still time."

Turning abruptly, Gilmore strode back to where Hannah stood. Grasping her arm roughly, he dragged her with him into the storeroom behind the bar. Ryder had to force himself not to follow, knowing that he must bide his time. When he spoke to Hannah—and he would speak to her—it would be without Gilmore's interference.

"Trent, you're hurting me." Hannah shrugged free of Gilmore's bruising grip and whirled to face him. "What is the meaning of this? What is Wind Rider doing here? How did he get out of the stockade?"

"I wish I knew," Trent said tightly. "But you can damn well bet I'm going to find out. I've got enough witnesses to convict the man of raiding and killing with the Sioux. And as soon as you sign the deposition, rape will be added to the charges."

Hannah's chin rose defiantly. "I've refused to sign those papers and will do so again."

"If you don't, I'll assume you became his whore willingly."

"I wasn't . . ."

"No! Tell me no lies. I meant what I said, Hannah. You're to have nothing to do with that white savage. I'm giving you ample warning. If you disobey me, I'll make certain he's returned to the stockade and kept there until he rots." He gave her a calculating look. "On the other hand, if you do as I say, I might be persuaded to drop the charges. By your own words you've admitted to being the savage's whore. Therefore, I am no longer obliged to protect your virtue, such as it is." He laughed harshly. "I want you, Hannah. We will become lovers. If you agree, I will conveniently bury the evidence against Wind Rider."

With a force he'd never used before, he hauled her up against his chest, tilted her face, and slammed his mouth down on hers. Hannah whimpered in protest. When he grasped her hand and placed it on his erection she managed to fight free.

"Don't! Don't do that!"

"I don't want to hurt you, Hannah. You'll find I can be quite generous, but as your lover I'll demand loyalty. Put that savage out of your mind."

"You're mad! I can't become your lover. I'm Wind Rider's wife. And if I were free, I'd still not agree to your proposal."

"Do you want to see him rotting behind bars for the rest of his life?"

Hannah shook her head. It would kill Wind Rider to be imprisoned in a tiny, airless room without the sun on his back and the wind in his face.

"Then you'll do as I say. No communication, understand? Or else I'll put the information I've gathered to good use. And don't worry about your freedom; I'm working on that."

No matter how desperately she wanted to be with Wind Rider, she could not hurt him. Trent wasn't one to make idle threats. For his own sake she had to avoid Wind Rider at all cost.

Gilmore did not wait for Hannah's reply. He kissed her once more, hard, thrusting his tongue into her mouth. Then, releasing her abruptly, he stalked from the room, leaving Hannah thoroughly shaken. She didn't want Trent; just the thought of making love with him sickened her. Head bowed, shoulders bent, she left the room and returned to work. When she dared to glance in the dark corner where Wind Rider had been seated she found that he was gone.

Wind Rider crouched behind the inn until all the lights were doused. Peering through a rear window, he saw Hannah take a lamp and light her way up the stairs. She was the last to retire. He glanced upward, elated when he saw a light appear a few minutes later in a third-floor window. He was pleased at how easily he had located Hannah's room. Now all he had to do was find an unlocked window. The need to confront Hannah was a raw ache deep inside him. He had to know exactly what the blue coat meant to her and if they were truly lovers.

The storeroom window slid open without a sound. Ryder climbed through the opening and crouched low until he was certain no one had heard him. After a short interval he entered the common room and noiselessly ascended the two flights of stairs to the single room on the third floor. He turned the knob and a curse slipped past his lips when he found it locked. Now he had two choices: He could either call out to Hannah and take his chances that she'd open the door, or he could leave as quietly as he'd come. The choice was taken from him when the door suddenly opened. He slipped quietly into the shadows.

The breath slammed from his chest when he saw Hannah standing in the doorway, holding a lamp aloft. The flickering light made her thin shift transparent, outlining every luscious curve, every shadowed valley. He stood mesmerized as she stepped from the room and started down the stairs. Had she forgotten something? he wondered. Was she going off to meet her lover? Assuming she'd have to return eventually, he slipped into the room to await her.

Hannah's stomach growled hungrily. She'd been so upset over the confrontation between Wind Rider and Trent that she'd had no stomach for food. But now that the grueling day was over she found her appetite returning. Now, after she washed and made ready for bed, she went in search of something to eat. In the kitchen she found cold lamb, leftover biscuits, and fresh berries. Pouring herself a glass of cold milk, she sat at the table and devoured every morsel. She returned to her room thirty minutes later, carefully locking the door behind her.

Sighing wearily, she slid into bed and blew out the lamp. The moon was full, leaving a bright splash of light on the floor below the solitary window. She closed her eyes, trying not to think about Wind Rider and the cold contempt with which he had regarded her. She sighed again, realizing how futile her efforts were. Her thoughts always returned to Wind Rider.

"Are you sighing for your lover? Have you just come from his arms? Did he satisfy you in so short a time? It always took me much longer." He stepped from the shadows, looming over her like an avenging angel.

"Wind Rider." His name whispered past her lips on a note of fear. She sat up and the blanket fell away, revealing the pert tilt of her breasts beneath the flimsy material of her shift. "How . . ." She knew better than to ask how he had gotten in, for he had a knack for appearing in the most unlikely places without being seen or heard. Suddenly she recalled Trent's threats and she grew pale. "You must leave before someone sees or hears you."

"No one will see or hear me. Unless you're expecting your lover tonight."

"My lover?"

"Did you think Gilmore wouldn't brag about his conquest? Did you find you couldn't do without a man between your legs on the long trip from Fort Laramie to Denver?"

"Oh, god, how can you say that after all we've been to one another? Have you forgotten so soon those nights in Red Cloud's village? Or that night at Fort Laramie? Have you forgotten that I begged you to take me with you?"

"I have forgotten nothing, but apparently you have. Gilmore tells me you want nothing more to do with me. Is that true?"

283

Trent's threatening words came back to haunt her. She closed her eyes and said in a voice so low, Wind Rider had to strain to hear, "Yes, it's true. Trent and I are lovers." Oh, God, how it hurt to say those words, but she did it to save him. "Go away. Forget I ever existed." Didn't he know that her love could destroy him?

His face was stark with a nameless emotion. "I thought I knew you, Hannah McLin. Since you are a whore you shouldn't mind taking another man to your bed. At least I will be a familiar man, one who knows what you like and need."

He dropped to his knees beside her on the bed. His reaction was instinctive, primal, uncontrollable. He could no more leave her untouched than he could stop breathing. Whore or not, he had been the first to love her. She had attained womanhood in his arms, and now the need to punish pushed him too far to back down. His hands reached down to drag her hand between his thighs, curving her fingers around the powerful thrust of his erection. Involuntarily, her fingers tightened, squeezing him, feeling the throbbing heat pulsing through him. He cursed, flinging her hand aside. His mocking laughter pelted her.

"You are an eager whore, Little Sparrow. I hope your lovers appreciate you." His voice was bitter with resentment.

Hannah bit her tongue to keep from crying out that there were no lovers, that she wanted no one but him.

He lay down beside her. He was so hot for her, he was shaking with desire. He had meant to teach her a lesson, to show his contempt by taking her callously, but nothing was working out as he had planned.

Hannah felt the warmth of his breath, sensed the heat and tension in him, felt his muscles contract, and knew a moment of panic. It was clear to her that she could not resist him, despite Trent's threats. He was her life, her love, the reason for her breathing. Yet she must forget him to keep him safe. Knowing Trent as she did, if she disobeyed him, he'd carry out his threat without a hint of remorse. Wind Rider would be back in the stockade, this time for good.

"Please go away, Wind Rider. Don't you understand? We can't be together like this."

"Wind Rider no longer exists. My name is Ryder Larson. Say it, Hannah. Speak my name."

"Ryder."

The moon rose higher in the sky, its light spreading to the bed, falling across Ryder's face and body. There was something about him—something so brutally compelling that she couldn't look away. His sharp, relentless eyes held her captive within their silver depths.

Ryder met her gaze squarely, unflinchingly. His gaze moved over her face to her lips, full and temptingly lush. Kissing those sweet lips was a white custom he'd learned to enjoy. "Speak my name again."

"Ryder."

He watched her lips form the words, his mouth hovering inches from hers. Then his lips molded to hers, claiming them completely, giving fire and heat and passion and demanding it in return. He kissed her wildly, deeply, thrusting his tongue into the sweet warmth of her mouth. He groaned, losing control of his senses as he pushed her backward onto the bed and slid his leg on top of her to hold her in place.

Hannah barely had time to adjust to the loss of his mouth on hers when she felt the delicious sweep of his tongue over her sensitive nipples. She jerked violently and cried out, lost to sensations she'd thought never to feel again.

"Do you still want me to leave, Little Sparrow?"

Her heart utterly denied the words that came from her mouth. "Yes, you must! For your own good, you must."

"For my own good?" he repeated with grim amusement. He lowered his head again, scattering tender love bites along her stomach and lower still, his breath hot against the swollen flesh of her womanhood. "This is for my own good."

She rolled her head from side to side, unable to deny the pleasure this magnificent man was capable of giving her. With a will of their own, her hips tipped up, inviting a deeper caress. He raised his eyes and regarded her with such fierce possession, she felt a shattering deep inside her. Then he spread her legs and lowered his head.

She buried her fingers in his thick black hair and felt the shocking pressure of his tongue. She arched her back as he found her hot center, his fingers exploring the moist folds of her most sensitive being.

Hannah cried out, all conscious thought centered upon that wet, throbbing place where his tongue played most provocatively. Incredible heat and rapture rose to consume her; her climax was swift and explosive. While her aroused body shuddered in rapture, Ryder quickly divested himself of his clothing. Then, in a frenzy of need only this woman could assuage, he lifted her hips, wrapped her legs around his waist, and thrust into her.

His breath was hot and desperate against her lips as she rode upon his hardness, wanting it now, needing it as much as he. His hands gripped her bottom as he thrust inside her like a man possessed, fast, hard, relentless, until her mind and body and senses were centered upon that throbbing place where they were joined. Her whimpers and cries of ecstasy were silenced by his kiss as he thrust into her deeply, once, then again . . . and again, his whole body shuddering with the ferocity of his passion. He tore his mouth from hers as his seed, hot and pulsing, spewed from his flesh. She pressed upward against him and felt the shattering jolt of her own climax.

"Ryder." His name drifted past her lips on a sigh of contentment.

"Did I please you?"

She paused for a breathless moment, then said, "You know you did."

"More than your lieutenant?"

Hannah went still. "Why did you have to go and ruin everything? This is likely to be our last time together."

Ryder went still. "Last time together? You're my wife."

Panic seized Hannah. "No, we can't be together! Our marriage isn't legal. Why can't you understand? Trent won't like it." She had no idea how damning that sounded.

Ryder raised up on his elbow to stare at her, his face hard, his eyes glacial. "I do understand, 'wife.' Only too well. Of course you must obey your lover."

"If I don't, he'll . . ."

"He'll what?"

"He has evidence that can send you to prison."

Ryder's eyes narrowed. "Did he threaten you?"

"N-no, of course not." Knowing how hot-headed Ryder was, she feared telling him the truth. It would likely destroy his pride if he knew she was protecting him.

"Let Gilmore do his worst; I'm not afraid of him. Get dressed. I've decided to take you with me." His words should have surprised him but they didn't. When he'd learned that Hannah and Gilmore were lovers he'd wanted to punish her. But once he'd taken her into his arms his intentions fell by the wayside. It was quite laughable, really, for deep in his heart he'd always known the only reason he'd left his former life was to take back what was his. And Hannah was his, no matter how many men she'd bedded.

Hannah's lips were stubborn. "I won't go."

"Do you love Gilmore?"

"No! No! Never!" *I love you,* her heart silently cried.

Ryder regarded her through narrowed eyes. Then he grasped her arms and hauled her out of bed. "Get dressed!"

Hannah's protest died in her throat when a knock sounded at the door. "Hannah! Are you all right? I thought I heard voices."

"Mr. Harley," Hannah hissed, sending Ryder a startled look.

"Hannah? Can you hear me?" The knob rattled, and Ryder was grateful that Hannah had thought to lock the door.

"Answer him."

"I-I'm fine, Mr. Harley. I was having a bad dream."

The doorknob rattled again. "Let me in, Hannah." His voice was softly wheedling. "Let me comfort you. I've been thinking about you a lot since my good wife died. We can give each other comfort."

"The bastard," Ryder snarled beneath his breath. "Is he another of your lovers?" He took a step toward the door.

"Ryder, no! You'll hang for sure if you do anything foolish. I'll get rid of him."

Suddenly her key fell to the floor as Harley inserted a spare key in the lock on the other side of the door. The panel was flung open and Harley held a lamp aloft, illuminating the room and its two occupants. He took one look at the nude couple, his expression registering total shock.

"You little slut! How dare you entertain customers behind my back? Did you intend to keep all the money for yourself? From now on I get my cut. And," he added crudely, "I get to sample the wares." He turned to Ryder. "Get dressed and get the hell out of here. Next time deal directly with me if you want to bed the little doxy. And I'll collect now, if you don't mind." He held out his hand.

Red dots of rage burst behind Ryder's eyes. Not only did he hate Harley for mistreating Hannah, but also for assuming she was his for the taking. Flinging himself across the bed, he leaped for the man. Harley blanched, knowing he was no match for his powerful opponent. Not the bravest of men, he decided retreat was the wisest choice. Whirling on his heel, Harley ran. When coal oil splashed from the lamp he was holding onto his hand he dropped it. It smashed on the landing, setting fire to the frayed carpet. Turning the momentary diversion to his advantage, he fled down the stairs.

Harley's leg, still stiff from having been broken previously, refused to do his bidding, twisting beneath him. He fell forward, grabbing for air, and bounced down the stairs. He clung for a brief moment to the second-floor landing before spiraling downward. At the bottom of the stairs his head slammed into the brass railing of the bar.

"Oh, my God!" Hannah stood, frozen, while Ryder beat out the fire with a blanket.

"Stay here," Ryder growled once the fire was out. Then he descended the stairs. A long silence ensued before Hannah heard him returning.

"What happened?"

"He's dead," he said without remorse. "Serves the bastard right. Get dressed and let's get out of here."

But it was not to be. A commotion at the front door sent them scurrying into their clothes. A voice drifted up to them.

"What's the ruckus in there? Open the door, Harley. It's Sheriff Douglas. I was making my rounds and heard a commotion inside."

"Go," Hannah cried, giving Ryder a shove. "Go out the back. I'll take care of things here."

"You're coming with me."

"No. Don't you see? If I leave, they'll think I killed him. Go, please go, Ryder. Leave Denver. Go back to Red Cloud."

Leaving Hannah to her lover was the last thing he wanted to do, but white laws confused him. He pulled her hard against him and slammed his mouth down on hers. "Your lover will not have you. I will kill him first." His kiss was fast and hard and brutal. Then he turned and fled down the stairs.

Hannah watched him disappear into the darkness. Then she followed, avoiding Harley's body at the foot of the stairs. Composing her face, she opened the door. "I'm glad you're here, Sheriff. I was on my way out to find you."

Chapter Fifteen

The inn was quiet, having been closed by order of the sheriff. Dawn was breaking over the city. Sheriff Douglas had questioned Hannah for two solid hours, and when he left shortly before dawn he seemed satisfied that Harley's death had been the result of an unfortunate accident. None of the rooms abovestairs had been rented, so there were no witnesses and, lacking evidence of foul play, the sheriff had accepted Hannah's version of what had transpired.

Deliberately vague, Hannah had told Sheriff Douglas that she had been sleeping when she heard Harley tumble down the stairs. She had expressed no opinion on how he might have tripped or what he was doing roaming around so late at night. Douglas had ordered the body carted off to the undertaker and told Hannah to get some rest, saying he'd return in the morning to take a look around.

Hannah had moved quickly after that. She had no idea what would happen to her now that Harley was dead. Would they sell her indenture to someone else, or would she be free to live her life as she pleased? The longer she thought about those indenture papers, the more frightened she became that Trent would manage somehow to purchase them. When an outrageous idea occurred to her she acted without reservation or conscious thought of wrongdoing.

Desperation drove Hannah as she made her way to Harley's room. She opened the door and hesitated. But when she thought of being sold again she marshaled her courage and moved resolutely to the desk, where she assumed he kept all his important documents. She knew instinctively that she'd find her papers in the one drawer she found locked, and she began a methodical search of the room for the key. Twenty minutes later she located it in the pocket of one of Harley's vests, hanging from a hook on the wall.

The drawer slid open noiselessly and Hannah's hands shook as she drew forth her indenture papers. Her one fear had been that Harley had already sold them to Trent, who had told her that they had nearly reached an agreement. Thank God the sale hadn't been finalized. She tucked the document in her bodice and returned everything exactly the way she had found it. Afraid to hide the document, lest the sheriff find it in his search of the inn, she decided to carry the papers on her person until she had time to think more clearly.

Promptly at eight o'clock the next morning, Sheriff Douglas returned with two deputies and Trent Gilmore. "Hannah, I just heard. Are you all right? How terrible it must have been for you." Trent was effusive in his sympathy.

"I'm fine, Trent. Actually, I was sleeping when it happened."

"The sheriff has returned this morning to make a thorough search of the place. It's customary, you know. He has to notify the next of kin. Do you know if Harley had any relatives?"

"I'm not sure. I think he might have had someone back East; a cousin or something."

"He'll have to be notified so he can let us know what to do about the inn and whatever else of value Harley left behind." Hannah knew Trent was alluding to her articles of indenture.

"Take us to his room, Miss McLin," Sheriff Douglas directed. "That's as good a place to start as any."

Hannah stood silently by as the men began a methodical search of Harley's belongings. They found a cashbox under his bed with a substantial amount of cash. Douglas was impressed with Hannah's honesty; she could have taken the money and run.

"At least there's money to pay for his burial," Douglas muttered as he handed the cashbox to one of his deputies. Then he concentrated on the locked drawer he found in the desk. Not bothering to look for the key, he broke the lock with the butt of his gun. "Ah, here's the address of a Percival Harley. Must be some kind of relative. I'll send a wire immediately."

"What else did you find, Sheriff?" Trent asked sharply. He was more than a little surprised that Hannah's indenture papers weren't found in the locked drawer.

Douglas rummaged around for several minutes longer. "Ah, a sealed will, some bank statements, a bank book, a few bills; nothing of value."

Trent gave Hannah a searching look. "I understood Miss McLin was an indentured servant. Are there no indenture documents in any of the drawers?"

"Look for yourself, Lieutenant," Douglas said shortly. He didn't appreciate Gilmore's intrusion into something that he could handle quite adequately without the army. "There is no mystery here. It's an accidental death, pure and simple."

"I'm not arguing that fact, Sheriff. I'm merely curious as to the disposal of Miss McLin's articles of indenture."

To humor Gilmore, Douglas directed his next question to Hannah. "Did you know that your articles of indenture were missing, Miss McLin?"

Hannah's mouth went dry. She was never able to lie convincingly, but this time she must. "Just tonight Mr. Harley told me he'd sold them." She didn't dare look at Trent, but she heard his shout of denial.

"Did he say who bought them?" Douglas asked, ignoring Gilmore's obvious shock. Hannah shook her head. "I imagine we'll know soon enough," Douglas continued. "The man is bound to show up soon to claim his property. Meanwhile, the inn will remain closed, but you're free to stay on until your new owner shows up."

Hannah touched her bodice, where the papers rested against her breast. "Thank you, Sheriff."

"I'll be on my way, Miss McLin. I find nothing to suggest that Harley's death wasn't accidental. I'll be keeping an eye out for your new owner. If you need me for anything, you know where to find me."

After the sheriff and his deputies had left Gilmore remained behind. Hannah could tell by the simmering anger in his eyes that he was upset at the turn of events.

"I don't understand, Hannah. Harley promised he'd sell your articles of indenture to me. Are you sure you don't know who purchased them?"

"I-no, he didn't tell me."

"I had plans for us, Hannah. I rented a house on a quiet street, and I meant for us to live there. You wouldn't have to work hard, as you're doing now. All you'd be required to do is please me. I really am quite fond of you, my dear. Perhaps even fond enough to marry you, should you prove fertile and give me an heir."

"I'm sorry," Hannah said, trying to sound

contrite while in truth she was elated. "If you don't mind, Trent, I'd like to rest now. I was up all night, answering Sheriff Douglas's questions."

"And I must return to duty. There's talk of the militia riding out soon on a search-and-destroy mission. The Sioux and Cheyenne are getting bolder. They're striking more frequently. Denver is virtually cut off from eastern travel. I'll try to stop by frequently until your new owner arrives. I'm most anxious to learn who purchased your articles of indenture. I shall offer to buy them myself."

Staring at the dingy ceiling gave Hannah little comfort. Despite her weariness, sleep would not come. She had hoped and prayed that Ryder would come for her, but he had not appeared. She knew she had hurt him by saying that she and Trent were lovers, but it had been for his own good. She had advised him to go back to Red Cloud's village, and now she wondered if he had done as she'd suggested. God, what a muddle her life had become. When she'd left Ireland it had all seemed so simple: serve her seven years indenture to pay for her passage and then send for one or two of her siblings after she found a paying job and saved some money.

She hadn't counted on complications like Mr. Harley, or Wind Rider, or Lieutenant Gilmore. How innocent and naive she must have been. And to further complicate matters, she had stolen her articles of indenture. Worse yet, she didn't know what to do with them. The sheriff would become suspicious when no one showed up to claim her, and he might even reverse his thinking about Harley's death and charge her with robbery and murder. Yet out of it all had come the one pure emotion she might never have experienced if she hadn't ventured to America. She might never have known love—not the kind of love she'd found in Ryder's strong arms. And she wasn't sorry, not one tiny bit.

Hannah fell asleep recalling hungry kisses devouring her, the hard, solid weight of flesh, bone, and muscle pressing against her . . . wild, desperate embraces, moans, sighs . . . and the sweetest, most tormenting rapture she had ever known.

She awakened the following morning feeling as if she hadn't slept. Dark circles marred the delicate skin around her eyes, and her stomach felt raw and unsettled. An eerie, unnatural silence prevailed in the inn, for normally it was a place of loud voices and raucous laughter. Sickened by the thought of food, she made a cup of tea and sipped it, wondering what was to become of her. Later, she forced herself to perform a few simple chores, mainly to keep from thinking about Ryder and wondering if he hated her for telling him that she and Trent were lovers.

Lunch consisted of dry bread, cold meat, and water, which Hannah was barely able to keep down, so unsettled was her stomach. The events of the past few days had taken a toll on her, she decided, although if she was truthful, she'd admit that her stomach had been upset often since she had left Fort Laramie. Lost in her morose thoughts, Hannah didn't hear the door open or see the tall, broad-shouldered man enter.

"Hello! Is anyone here?"

Hannah started violently. Rousing herself from her reverie, she left the kitchen, wondering if Sheriff Douglas had returned. Or Lieutenant Gilmore. She didn't recognize the powerfully attractive man standing in the center of the common room. He was looking about the deserted inn curiously. He heard her enter the room and spun on his heel to face her. Hannah drew in a sharp breath, stunned by the magnetic intensity of his vivid blue eyes.

"What happened here? The place is deserted. Are you Hannah McLin?"

"Yes. Who are you?"

"Zach. Zach Mercer. I'm looking for my brother-in-law. He promised to come out to the farm to visit his sister and we haven't seen him. Abby was worried and insisted I come to Denver to look for him."

"You're the man who married Ryder's sister! He spoke often of you and Abby."

"Do you know where he is? I'd hoped I'd find him with you."

"I'm sorry. I don't know where he is."

"What happened here? Something is wrong; I can sense it."

"There's been an accident. Mr. Harley is dead."

"Good God! Did Ryder . . ."

"No! Ryder had nothing to do with it. It was an accident."

"Where is Ryder?"

"I-we argued, and he left. I haven't seen him since."

Zach regarded her with obvious skepticism. "That doesn't sound like Ryder. He wouldn't run away from trouble. More likely, he caused it."

Hannah flushed and looked away. "I'm sorry; that's all I can tell you."

Zach still had questions . . . and doubts. But they were left unspoken when Lieutenant Gilmore walked through the door. For the space of a heartbeat Hannah panicked; then her green eyes widened in sudden inspiration. Plunging her hand inside her bodice, she withdrew her indenture document and shoved it into Zach's hand.

"Take this," she hissed, trying to convey her urgent message in the short amount of time allotted to her. The dimly lit room served her well. She knew Gilmore couldn't see what she had done, for her back was to him and he was still halfway across the room.

"What the . . ." Zach stared at the paper in his hand and then at Hannah.

"Don't argue, please. Just take it and follow my lead. If you want to help Ryder, it's imperative that you do exactly as I say."

Zach had no idea what was going on, but he decided to go along with the woman Ryder loved. There was more here than met the eye, and he intended to get to the bottom of it. He placed the document in his vest pocket.

"Are you all right, Hannah? I had some spare time and thought I'd drop by and check on you." He sent Zach a piercing look. "Is this your new owner?"

"Yes, yes it is," Hannah said quickly. "Zach Mercer, this is Lieutenant Trent Gilmore."

Zach extended a hand, immediately recognizing the name. Ryder had told him it was Gilmore who had taken Hannah from Red Cloud's camp and ordered Ryder imprisoned.

"Zach Mercer," Gilmore repeated thoughtfully. "Funny; I don't recall Harley mentioning your name before. In fact, I'm surprised he sold Hannah's articles of indenture at all. He seemed reluctant to discuss it when I approached him."

"*You* wanted to buy Miss McLin's articles of indenture?" Zach said, arching a thick blond brow.

Suddenly Gilmore realized how that sounded, since he was an unmarried man. "Well, yes, but only in order to free her of her obligation, you understand. Hannah and I have an . . . um . . . understanding. I'd hoped to make her my wife."

Hannah started violently. Wife? Trent had made it clear that she was to be his mistress. "That's not possible, Trent. I told you I was married to Ryder."

"That heathen ceremony wasn't legal,

Hannah. But all that aside, I'd like to see Hannah's articles of indenture, Mr. Mercer, if you have them."

"Of course," Zach murmured, removing the document from his vest pocket, and realizing now what Hannah was about. It didn't even matter to him that Hannah had stolen the document. He spread it out for Gilmore to peruse.

"When did this sale take place? Why haven't I seen you in the inn? Lord knows I've been here often enough. Do you have a bill of sale?"

Zach's mind worked furiously. "I purchased them over a month ago, when Harley learned that Hannah was safe at Fort Laramie and would be brought back when an escort became available. I'd been looking for a hired girl to help my wife with our new baby and learned of Miss McLin one day when I stopped by the inn to confer with Mr. Harley about a freighting contract. I asked him then if he'd consider selling her articles of indenture to me. He was reluctant at first, but his business had fallen off lately and he was strapped for cash. When I offered to pay the reward for Miss McLin's safe return as well as purchase her indenture he agreed."

Gilmore eyed him narrowly. "You waited long enough to claim your property."

"Yes, well, Harley asked me to wait until he found someone to take her place." Lord, he hoped it sounded plausible.

"Assuming you have one, you still haven't shown me the bill of sale."

Hannah groaned inwardly. She hadn't considered a bill of sale. She'd thought that merely having her articles of indenture in his possession would be proof enough of Zach Mercer's ownership.

Zach cleared his throat, silently cursing his brother-in-law for getting him into this kind of predicament. Not only had he lied, but if he was found out he could be charged with stealing. How in the hell was he going to come up with a bill of sale?

"What's this about a bill of sale?" Sheriff Douglas strode through the door in time to hear Gilmore ask for one. His face broke into a grin when he saw Zach. "Zach Mercer; well, I'll be damned! You're the last person in the world I'd expect to buy an indentured servant. That is, I assume you're Miss McLin's new owner."

"You know this man, Sheriff?" Gilmore asked. He still wasn't convinced of the legality of the deal.

"Of course, Lieutenant. Surely you've heard of Mercer Freighting." Gilmore had. "Mercer's wagons carry just about all the goods reaching Denver from the East these days."

"Hello, Sheriff Douglas. Good to see you again. As you've just heard, I've come to claim my property. Too bad about Harley. Nasty accident."

"Accidents do happen." He spied the indenture document. "I see you have Miss McLin's articles of indenture in your possession."

"He has the document but no bill of sale," Gilmore said. He was still highly doubtful that a deal had taken place.

"It was a gentleman's agreement. I required no bill of sale," Zach said.

"Sounds phony to me," Gilmore returned shortly. His anger was barely contained.

"The word of Zach Mercer is good enough for me," Douglas said, sending Gilmore a censuring glance. "He has the document in his possession; that's all the proof I need."

"I still think . . ."

"Lieutenant Gilmore," Douglas began, in a tone that clearly displayed his annoyance. "Civil law is my jurisdiction. Please confine yourself to military matters. I'm sure there are plenty of Indians for you to chase without involving yourself in something that is none of your business."

Douglas's speech stole the wind out of Gilmore's sails. Without making a nuisance of himself, there was nothing more he could do, no matter how suspicious he was of a fictitious sale to Zach Mercer. Something smelled fishy, and one way or other he'd learn what it was.

"Of course, Sheriff. I certainly don't want to interfere in your jurisdiction."

Douglas nodded and turned to Zach. "You and Miss McLin are free to leave any time you wish."

"Thank you, Sheriff. Abby will be grateful for Miss McLin's help. We've been needing a hired girl around the place for a long time."

Both Gilmore and Douglas took their leave. They had no sooner closed the door behind them than Hannah's knees buckled. Zach caught her and helped her to a chair. She sat down gratefully.

"Now, will you please tell me what in blazes that was all about?"

Hannah nodded, waiting for the furious beating of her heart to slow to a normal cadence. "I was afraid Lieutenant Gilmore would purchase my articles of indenture, so I stole them. I had no idea what I was going to do with them until you walked through the door. Trent Gilmore had been negotiating with Mr. Harley since we arrived in Denver, or so he led me to believe. He wanted to install me in a house he had rented and . . ." Her face turned fiery red, unable to continue. But Zach got the picture.

"A few minutes ago he said he wanted to marry you."

"He was lying. He wanted me to sign a deposition accusing Ryder of rape. When I refused he said I wasn't good enough to become his wife."

"The bastard," Zach hissed from between clenched teeth. "Tell me about Harley. How did he really die? Was Ryder involved?"

"Indirectly. Harley found us together in my room. He made some remarks that enraged Ryder. Ryder lunged at Harley, and the coward turned to flee down the stairs. He tripped and fell the entire length. When Ryder went to check on him Harley was dead. A few minutes later the sheriff arrived, having heard a commotion while he was making his nightly rounds."

"So Ryder fled," Zach surmised. "Why in blazes didn't he take you with him?"

Hannah's lashes lowered, unable to look Zach in the eye. How could she tell him that Ryder believed she and Trent were lovers? Despite the fact that she'd deliberately lied to Ryder to save him from being sent to prison, it wasn't something she was proud of.

"I insisted that Ryder leave without me. I told him I'd be blamed for killing Harley if I ran away."

Zach sent her a searching look. "Are you sure that's all there is to it? It just doesn't sound like something Ryder would do. Leaving you alone to face the consequences isn't his style. I know he cares for you."

Hannah flushed. "Yes, but we argued. Please don't ask me what about."

"You have no idea where Ryder is now?" Zach queried.

Hannah shook her head, her eyes sad. "None. I expected him to return, but . . ."

"Don't worry," Zach said, patting her shoulder awkwardly. "Pack your things. I'll take you to the farm. Abby is looking forward to meeting you."

Hannah looked down at the drab brown dress she wore and wrinkled her nose. "There's nothing to pack. Except for one or two personal items I brought from Ireland, everything I own is on my back."

"Get them," Zach directed. "We'll stop by the

general store and buy you something decent to wear; then we'll be on our way."

"Mr. Mercer . . ."

"Zach."

"Zach, I don't know how to thank you."

Zach's expression softened, and Hannah thought him almost as handsome as Ryder. No wonder Ryder's sister had fallen in love with him. "You owe me nothing. You don't remember, but I witnessed firsthand how Harley abused you. Neither Abby nor I have forgotten that day. What I am about to do gives me great pleasure."

Hannah watched in stunned silence as Zach found a sulfur match in his pocket, struck it against the rough surface of a nearby table, and set fire to the indenture document. He held it between two fingers as it burned down to a tiny square of paper. Then he let it flutter to the floor to burn itself out.

"As of this moment, you're free, Hannah McLin. But I hope you'll be our guest at the farm until you decide what you want to do with your life."

Too grateful to speak, Hannah burst into tears.

Stripped to breechclout and moccasins, Ryder knelt on a ledge near the crest of a tree-covered hill, facing east. He had been fasting, praying, and chanting for three days, ever since he had left Hannah at the inn. His life no longer

as simple as it once had been, he had gone into
seclusion, hoping for a sign from the Great Spirit. He had offered tobacco and pollen. He had
offered his blood three times, but still no sign
came. Was it because the Great Spirit wanted
him to find the answers within his own heart?
he wondered despondently. Should he go back
to the People where he had been happy, as
Hannah had suggested? Or should he try to
fashion himself after the whites he'd always
held in contempt? Should he go back and fight
for Hannah's love? Or leave her to her lover?
He'd never run from anything in his life; should
he do so now?

His mind wandered from his chanting and
he found himself repeating one word over and
over. *Hannah. Hannah. Hannah.* Was she all
right? Was she with her lover now? Was that
why she'd wanted him to leave? It wasn't difficult to imagine why Hannah preferred the
blue coat to him. The blue coat could give
her things he could not. The blue coat knew
who he was, while he, Ryder, couldn't decide
whether he was white or Indian. He was both
and he was neither. He was a curiosity to be
pitied. He had tried to be white, but his own
kind had rejected him. They had confined him
in a room with bars and would have left him
there for the remainder of his days.

Raising his eyes to the brilliant sun, Ryder
stared at the blazing ball until a blinding white
light exploded in his brain. And he waited for a
sign. "Tell me, *Heammawihio*," he cried aloud,

nearly desperate now for a vision, "tell me what to do."

Silence. Thick and portentous.

Suddenly the sun seemed to rip apart, sending fiery balls flying to earth. Girding himself, Ryder did not evade the blazing onslaught. His senses told him that something of great importance was about to be revealed to him. When one of the fiery balls hurtled directly toward him he stared unflinchingly into the luminous white-hot center. As it hovered before his eyes, a vision took shape within its core.

Hannah. She was standing slightly to the right. He stared intently as a faint image began to form behind her. Lieutenant Gilmore. As Gilmore stepped forward to stand beside her, she recoiled in terror. Ryder didn't understand. Why was Hannah so frightened of her lover? Slowly the image faded, replaced by the faces of Abby and her husband Zach. Abby seemed to be looking directly at him, her expression one of strong disapproval. Even Zach appeared annoyed with him.

"Why are you displeased?" Ryder cried out.

The vision receded. The fireballs danced away to merge with the sun. Ryder closed his eyes. When he opened them he could not see. Staring into the sun so long had blinded him.

Chapter Sixteen

Hannah liked Abby from the moment of their first meeting. Except for her blond hair, she was like Ryder in many ways. They both had those distinctive silver-gray eyes that looked deeply into one's soul. Obviously Abby and Zach were devoted to one another, and their five-month-old son was an adorable replica of his father. Both Abby and Zach made her welcome, treating her as if she were truly Ryder's beloved wife. They had given her a pleasant room in the sprawling home that had once been a small cabin.

In the two days she'd been with the Mercers Hannah had tried to be as helpful as possible. She was greatly appreciative of Zach's kindness toward her. He didn't have to get involved in her life, but he had done so willingly. He had even destroyed her articles of indenture, giving her the freedom she'd only dreamed about since her arrival in America.

"What can I do to help?" Hannah asked as she walked into the large kitchen where Abby was preparing the evening meal.

Abby turned and smiled at her, and once again Hannah was struck by the serene beauty of Ryder's sister. According to Ryder, Abby hadn't always been so serene. She and Zach had been at odds a great deal of the time before they realized they loved one another. If only she could look forward to the same happy life Abby and Zach now shared. But Hannah knew she'd probably never enjoy that kind of happiness with Ryder. More than likely, she'd never see Ryder again.

"You can peel potatoes and carrots, if you'd like," Abby replied. "Zach wants to hire a cook, but I really don't mind cooking. Although with a baby to care for, it is becoming a chore to have meals on the table on time."

"As long as I'm here, I'll be glad to help in any way I can," Hannah offered. "But I can't impose on you forever." Suddenly, an idea occurred to her, one that solved both their problems. "I'd be glad to hire on as your cook, or work in any capacity you'd like. In addition to room and board, I'd only require a small salary. I'm hoping to save enough money to send for some of my brothers and sisters."

Abby stared at her, aghast. "But Hannah, you're my sister-in-law and our guest. I couldn't ask you to become a servant to the family."

"You know as well as I that my marriage to Ryder isn't legal in white society. Besides, by now Ryder is with Red Cloud. I doubt I'll ever see him again."

"That's not true, Hannah. Ryder promised Zach he'd come to see me and his nephew, and I refuse to believe he'd lie about something so important to me. I am disappointed in him for staying away so long, but I truly believe he'll show up one day soon. I know Ryder. He thinks of himself as Cheyenne. When he joined with you it was for life. And, according to Zach, Ryder cares for you deeply."

"He might have once," Hannah admitted sadly. "But I killed those feelings when I told him Lieutenant Gilmore and I were lovers."

Abby looked startled.

"I had to, Abby!" Hannah cried. "It was for his own good."

"It's not true, is it?"

"No! Of course not. Trent has evidence against Ryder. He threatened to return Ryder to prison if I didn't . . . didn't . . ."

"I see," Abby said, wishing she could get her hands on the despicable Gilmore. "I'm sure Ryder realizes the truth."

"If he did, he would be here now, instead of God-only-knows where. Now he'll never know the truth."

After her talk with Hannah Abby turned to Zach for help. "I know something terrible has happened to Ryder. Please, Zach, find him for me. You know how close we are. My heart tells me that something is desperately wrong."

"Perhaps you're right, sweetheart," Zach concurred. "I don't think Ryder would return to Powder River country without coming first to see you and our son. But I don't think I'll find him in Denver. He's unaccustomed to cities. I might have to travel to the Black Hills to find him, but rest assured I'll do my best to bring him home."

The only way Ryder could tell in which direction he rode was by the warmth of the sun on his face. He rode west; he was of no use to the People now that he was blind, and could not return to them. He had no idea if his affliction was permanent, but he sincerely believed that the Great Spirit had struck him blind for abandoning Hannah when she needed him.

Perhaps the blue coat was her lover and perhaps he wasn't, but Hannah was still his wife, and he had left her unprotected. Pride had made him insensitive to her feelings, and against his better judgment he'd believed that nonsense about her being Gilmore's lover. In his vision he had seen her anguish and felt the bitter weight of his sister's disappointment.

As long as he was blind, he was no good to anyone. Hannah was better off with the blue coat, he decided. After making peace with his family he'd travel by himself deep into the mountains and commune with the earth and the sun and the heavens until the Great

Spirit saw fit to lift the burden of blindness from him. His sense of direction, even though he was blind, was acute. He was aware as never before of his surroundings. Each sound told a story all its own. Attuned as he was to Mother Earth, Grandfather Sun, and the sky above, Ryder felt at one with the elements. He felt confident the Great Spirit would guide him.

Zach rode east toward the Black Hills. He hadn't realized the almost impossible task he'd set for himself until the immense prairie stretched out before him. After two days of steady riding he missed Abby and his son terribly and almost turned back. Only his promise to Abby, and the fragile hope visible in Hannah's green eyes, kept him going. He was riding along a ridge now, where he could look down into the valley below. He was so stunned to see another rider crossing the desolate valley that he stopped and stared hard at the tiny dot gradually growing larger at it approached.

Squinting against the brilliant glare of the sun bouncing off the hills, Zach grew more and more convinced that the rider was his brother-in-law. What puzzled Zach was the dejected droop of Ryder's shoulders, the way his head remained bowed, as if Ryder was unaware or uncaring of where he was going. Zach knew Ryder to be an alert, watchful man, yet nothing in his manner gave the slightest indication of alertness. Snapping the reins, Zach guided his mount down the hill to intercept the man whom he now felt certain was Ryder.

Ryder's keen ears picked up the sound of Zach's horse and he stiffened, his hand resting on his knife. He might not be able to see, but he was fully capable of defending himself if the need arose. His body tense, he reined in his pony and waited for the rider to approach.

Zach felt a surge of relief when he noted that Ryder appeared healthy and unharmed. It also pleased him that Ryder was riding west, toward the farm. He halted beside Ryder. "Thank God I found you."

"Who is it?"

Zach sent Ryder a curious look. "It's Zach; are you blind? Abby was worried about you and . . ." Suddenly he saw the blank look in Ryder's eyes and the way he looked past him as if . . . His heart thundered against his chest as he realized the horrible truth. "My God, you are . . ."

"Blind," Ryder supplied. "I cannot see, Zach."

"My God! How did it happen?"

"The Great Spirit took my sight as punishment for . . ."

"Punishment for what? I don't understand."

Ryder clamped his teeth together. "I cannot say." Ryder couldn't talk about it. He had lost Hannah and failed miserably in his effort to conform to white ways. He had left his people for a white woman and she had chosen another because he had failed her. And now the Great Spirit had struck him blind, making him unfit for any woman.

"I'm taking you home, Ryder, where you can rest and recuperate. This affliction can't be permanent. I'll get the best doctors in this part of the country to treat you. And if they fail, I'll send to Boston for a specialist. You may not know this, but I am a wealthy man."

"Wealth is found in Mother Earth, in Grandfather Sun, and in the sky above, not in shiny metal," Ryder replied.

"In the white world money is important," Zach defended. "I am happy to be able to give your sister all she deserves in life."

Ryder offered Zach a knowing smile. "Tears Like Rain needs nothing more than you and her son to be happy. Indians have no need of money."

"But white men do. Once you get settled in at the farm I have a proposition that might interest you. You'll need a way to earn a living."

Hannah had vomited upon arising for the third day in a row, and she had too many brothers and sisters not to know that she was pregnant. So far she had kept her condition from Abby. But she knew that sooner or later her astute sister-in-law would find out; already she had missed her woman's time twice. Ryder's baby. The idea thrilled her. If only Ryder was here to share her happiness.

Just then, little Trey awoke and let out a loud wail. Hannah knew that Abby was out in the barn, so she went into the baby's room, changed him, and carried him out into the parlor. Sitting down in the rocker before the hearth, Hannah rocked back and forth, hoping to appease him until his mother returned to feed him. The motion was so soothing, the baby fell back to sleep, and she closed her eyes and drifted into a light doze. She didn't hear the commotion in the yard a few minutes later.

Abby heard riders approaching and ran out of the barn into the yard, knowing instinctively that Zach had returned. And if she knew her husband, Ryder was with him. Squealing in delight, she threw herself into Zach's arms the moment he dismounted. She gave him a quick hug, then turned to Ryder, her throat clogged with tears. It had been so long since she'd seen her brother, and she'd been so afraid for him since the army had been given orders to wipe out all Indian males over the age of twelve. In some case the soldiers paid little heed to age or gender. She had seen firsthand what happened at Sand Creek.

"Wind Rider!" It was difficult to call him by his white name. "I'm so happy Zach found you. Where have you been?"

At the sound of her voice Ryder turned in her direction. He held out his arms and she rushed into them. "Tears Like Rain." When he'd left her a year ago he'd thought he'd never see her again. He recalled how close they had been when they had first arrived at White Feather's camp, two children who had only each other to cling to. They had remained close throughout the years, relying on one another for their emotional needs, until they had learned to think and act like true Cheyenne.

"Ryder was riding this way when I found him," Zach said, waiting for Abby to discover that her brother was blind.

"Come inside, Ryder. I want you to meet your new nephew," Abby gushed as she pulled him inside the house. "You should see him, Ryder; he looks just like Zach."

Hannah heard the voices and footsteps on the porch and came fully awake. Seeing that the baby was still asleep, she placed him in his crib and walked toward the front door to investigate. The door flew open and Hannah grasped a nearby table for support when she saw Abby walk into the room, dragging Ryder behind her. Zach followed close on their heels.

Abby saw Hannah and grinned, waiting for Ryder to notice his wife. She hoped he'd be pleased to find her here. She watched him expectantly, but there was no change in his expression. In fact, his eyes were blank, as if he saw nothing at all.

"Ryder, aren't you going to say anything to Hannah?"

"Hannah? What about Hannah?"

Abby stared at him as if he had lost his mind. "Ryder, what is wrong with you? Hannah is right here, standing in front of you."

Hannah made a strangled sound deep in her throat. Pain lashed through her, more pain than she'd ever known in her life. Ryder hated her.

Hated her so much that he refused to acknowledge her presence. Why had she ever told him that terrible lie? Didn't he realize she'd rather die than let any man but Ryder touch her? Stifling a sob, she turned and ran from the room.

"Ryder! What is wrong with you?" Abby's voice was taut with displeasure. Ryder had never heard that tone before.

"He can't see, sweetheart." Zach's words brought Abby spinning around to confront him.

"What did you say?"

"It is true, Tears Like Rain. I cannot see," Ryder concurred, forestalling Zach's reply.

"When did this terrible thing happen to you? *How* did it happen?"

"I went on a vision quest. It happened while I was staring into the sun. The Great Spirit is angry with me. He took my sight. Where is Hannah?"

"She ran out of the room. She does not know that you're . . . blind. I'm sure she thought that you were angry with her and deliberately ignored her. Go to her; tell her what happened. I'm sure she'll understand."

"Why isn't she with her lover?"

"Perhaps there is no lover," Abby hinted, unwilling to divulge something Hannah had told her in confidence. "I don't know what happened between you and Hannah, but you must let her explain. She is a free woman now. No one owns her services. Go to her and let her tell you what happened."

Ryder shook his head. At times pride was a most difficult cross to bear. "Without eyes I am fit for no woman. Hannah is better off without me."

"We will find the best doctors to treat you," Abby assured him. "Perhaps the condition is a temporary one. I'm just so glad you're here, I don't care whether you can see or not. Wait here; I'll go get Trey. He's anxious to meet his uncle."

"She's right, you know," Zach contended once Abby had left the room. "Your condition is probably temporary. You've got to think about Hannah now. She's your wife; you can't just abandon her."

"She abandoned me, Zach. She's better off with the blue coat."

"Here he is, Ryder. This is your nephew, Trey Mercer." Abby placed the baby in Ryder's arms, watching his expression change to pure delight. The baby cooed up at him and Ryder's sightless eyes lit up. With a gentle fingertip he traced the baby's features.

"You say he looks like Zach?"

"The spitting image." Abby took the baby back, snuggling him to her breast. "I'm sorry to take him away so soon, but it's feeding time, Ryder."

"I'll come with you, sweetheart," Zach said. "I need to become reacquainted with my son. But first I'll take Ryder to his room." He wagged his eyebrows at Abby, took Ryder's arm, and guided him toward the bedroom. "Rest until suppertime. I know you must be exhausted. You'll find water for bathing in a pitcher. Do you need me to help you?"

Fierce pride demanded that Ryder face this affliction alone, asking for and accepting no help. If he was to live the rest of his life in the world of shadows, then he had to learn to adjust to his circumstances. "I can manage." The door opened and he walked inside.

Hannah lay across the bed, where she had thrown herself after Ryder had refused to acknowledge her presence. Did he still distrust her? She heard the door open and close and was shocked to see Ryder standing just inside the room. She scooted to her knees, watching him warily. Alarm shuddered through her. She saw him take two faltering steps into the room, then stop abruptly, still refusing to acknowledge her.

Ryder knew he wasn't alone after he'd been inside the room ten seconds. His nostrils quivered with the heady scent of woman. His eyes might not see her, but his keen perception told him that she was here. He recalled with fierce longing the fiery brilliance of her hair, the pert tilt of her breasts, the tiny waist, and that soft woman's place where he'd found the kind of rapture he'd never known existed.

"Ryder?" Her voice quivered with nervous anticipation. He heard and turned in the direction of her voice. Hannah sucked in a ragged breath. He appeared to be looking right through her, his expression blank and unreadable.

"Hannah. I didn't know this was your room. Zach must have made a mistake." Knowing Zach, he suspected his brother-in-law knew exactly what he was doing.

With slow precision Ryder walked toward Hannah, guided by the sound of her voice. When his knees hit the side of the bed he stopped and perched gingerly on the edge.

"Where have you been, Ryder?"

"On a vision quest."

"I expected you to come back. Weren't you interested in what happened to me?"

Ryder seemed to look beyond her. "You made it quite obvious that you wanted nothing more to do with me."

"I don't blame you for leaving. At the time it was what I wanted, what needed to be done, but I had a reason."

"I know the reason," Ryder said with bitter emphasis. What if he was wrong? What if Hannah really did have a reason? Was *Heammawihio* punishing him for his inflexible pride? Unfortunately, he couldn't stop the bitter accusations dripping from his tongue. "The blue coat could give you more than I could and you took him for your lover. Deny it all you want, Little Sparrow, but you were mine first and will always be mine, even if . . ."

"Even if what?"

Refusing to look into her eyes, Ryder merely shook his head.

"Why won't you look at me, Ryder? Do you hate me so much? I can explain." For her sake and that of their child, she had to make him understand that she had lied for a reason.

"It's too late. All the explanations in the world won't help us now."

Angered by his refusal to look at her, Hannah seized his face and turned it toward her. His silver eyes, usually so expressive, were blank, and a hint of something dark and sinister shuddered through her. She began to understand and prayed she was wrong. Her voice grew panicky. "Look at me, Ryder. Please look at me."

"I cannot. I am blind."

"No! It can't be. How did it happen? Tell me it's not true."

Ryder turned away. "I do not wish to speak of it. Tell me instead what happened after the sheriff arrived the night Harley was killed."

Needing the time to compose her thoughts and become accustomed to the shocking notion that Ryder was blind, Hannah told him everything that had transpired up to the time Zach had walked into the inn and inadvertently become involved in her problems.

"I do not understand. Why didn't you want Gilmore to buy your articles of indenture? Since he is already your lover I see no reason for involving Zach in all this."

Tears turned Hannah's green eyes into shimmering pools. Now that the two of them were safely ensconced in the bosom of Ryder's family, she no longer saw a need to lie. Trent Gilmore was in Denver; what could he do to Ryder now?

"Lieutenant Gilmore was never my lover, Ryder. I lied. I did it to keep him from arresting you and sending you to prison. He said he had irrefutable proof that you rode with Sioux renegades. He wanted to become my lover, but thank God it never came to that. I told you we were lovers so he would leave you alone."

"Perhaps you *should* have taken him for a lover." Hannah stared at him. He no longer sounded like the Ryder she knew. This Ryder seemed to have no heart, no spirit.

"You are the only man I want. We can be together now." She reached out to place a palm against his bronzed chest. She felt the erratic beat of his heart, felt the ripple of his corded muscles beneath his flesh, felt the heat and strength of his body, and longed to experience once again the depth of his passion.

Ryder sucked in a ragged breath, recoiling from her touch. He closed his eyes and moaned, feeling the violent surge of his manhood beneath his breechclout and knowing that he was being tested. He had lost the right to take Hannah as he ached to do. He should have realized she had lied about loving the blue coat. He didn't deserve Hannah's love. Without eyes he wasn't a whole man. Not until *Heammawihio* gave him back his sight would he touch her. It was his punishment for failing the woman he loved. He had no idea what the Great Spirit wanted of him, but he would know when the time came.

"Ryder, don't pull away from me. Don't you understand? I love you. I want no one but you. There is nothing now to keep us apart."

"You are wrong, Little Sparrow. I am not worthy of your love. I should have known you would not be false to me, but my pride blinded me. This is *Heammawihio's* way of telling me that pride is a good thing, but love and trust are more important. I failed you."

"Just tell me you love me, Ryder, and nothing else matters. I will be your eyes."

Ryder shook his head sadly. "It is not the right time."

Hannah's Irish temper flared. "When is the right time?"

"I will know when it arrives."

"What if I'm not here when you decide it's time for us to be together? Perhaps I won't wait for that day to arrive."

"I will find you."

"Ryder, this is ridiculous." She could tell by the stubborn set of his jaw that her words did not influence him. His belief in Indian superstition and lore was too strong. He thought he was being punished, and nothing would change his mind. Because he was blind he considered himself unworthy of her love.

What about their baby? she wondered dimly. How could she burden him with a child while his mood was so negative? She couldn't. Telling him he was going to be a father would drive him even further into depression. She'd just have to wait, and hope, and pray.

"What are you going to do? What am I going to do?"

Ryder turned his face in her direction. "You will remain here with Zach and Abby. I will return to the Black Hills."

"You will join Red Cloud?"

"I am of no use to the People as I am. I will remain in the hills until I learn what it is *Heammawihio* wants of me."

"No! You can't leave, not when we have found each other again. I won't let you go."

She threw her arms around his neck, pulling him close, until his arms opened to bring her tightly against his chest. She pressed her lips to his and opened her mouth, inviting his tongue. She felt the hard rise of his manhood against her stomach and tilted her hips until he fit snugly against her soft, aching core.

Ryder groaned, grasping her face between his palms and thrusting his tongue into her mouth. She tasted sweet, sweeter than honey. His hips jerked forward, and his solid length slid effortlessly into the heated hollow between her thighs. Moaning her need into his mouth, Hannah pulled him atop her, bending her knees to cradle his hips between her thighs. Her dress slid upward around her waist, giving him ample access to her secret treasure. She waited breathlessly for the hot thrust of his manhood inside her.

Lost in a haze of need, Ryder nearly forgot all the values he'd been taught by his Cheyenne father. He had practiced restraint for many years before the Great Spirit brought Hannah McLin into his life, and he could do so again. With an effort that nearly cost him his sanity, he pulled from her embrace, panting to gain control of his senses.

Disappointment surged through Hannah. Had she lost Ryder forever? What if he never regained his sight? What would happen to her and their baby if he left and never came back? "Don't leave me, Ryder, please. I want you." How could he reject her after she'd bared her soul to him?

"I have no right to touch you. Not until I know *Heammawihio's* plan for me."

"Why do you think your God is angry with you?" She was growing angry now.

"He took away my sight."

"Then go! Do what you must; I won't stop you." She flung away from him. Why must he be so damn stubborn?

Flouncing from the bed, Hannah left the room, slamming the door behind her.

"I love you, Little Sparrow." His words echoed hollowly in the empty room.

Chapter Seventeen

"I really need your help, Ryder," Zach said earnestly as he and Ryder walked toward the barn. "I want to take Abby and the baby back East to meet my family, and I need someone to look after things on the farm. I have a good man in the freighting office in Denver, but no one to keep an eye on the farm and the several hundred head of cattle I run on my land. In addition to the original homestead, I bought several parcels of land adjoining mine when they became available."

"I cannot keep an eye on things if I do not have two good eyes," Ryder reminded him.

"You and Hannah will do just fine here in our absence. I know you will. In payment I'll deed to you several hundred acres fronting the river that I don't use. One day you and Hannah can build your own home on the land. I haven't been home for a visit in years."

They had reached the barn now, and Zach placed a hand on Ryder's shoulder, guiding him through the door. "What you ask is impossible, Zach. You need a man who is whole to oversee your interests. I will not be staying on with you and Abby."

"What! What about Hannah? For God's sake, man, she loves you. I don't know what it is with you two, but I'm sure it can be worked out. You remind me of Abby and me not too long ago. How foolish we were to battle each other when all the time we loved one another desperately." He shook his head. "So much time wasted. Learn from me, my friend."

Ryder sensed that Zach had stopped walking and halted beside him. Ryder's keen sense of smell told him they were inside the barn. His nostrils twitched with the pungent odor of horse and straw and leather. He heard Zach moving around behind him and turned his head in Zach's direction. Shock shuddered through him when he found himself staring at a bright light.

"I just lit the lantern, Ryder," Zach explained when he saw Ryder swivel in his direction. "It's pretty murky in here."

Unable to speak, Ryder watched in growing excitement as the light wavered back and forth. He heard the crunch of Zach's footsteps and realized that he was moving away, carrying the light with him. And then, miracle of miracles, he made out a shadow; nothing definite, but it had been more than he'd been able to see in days. Unfortunately, this miracle was of short duration. A black mist slowly drifted before his eyes, bringing darkness with it.

"No!" The single word was a harsh cry of anguish, raw and wretched.

"Ryder, what is it?"

Ryder heard Zach hurrying to rejoin him and he strained forward, searching for the light, but it did not reappear. Ryder was left wallowing in a black void. What did it mean? Was *Heammawihio* trying to convey a message to him?

"Nothing. It is nothing." Ryder thought it made little sense to tell Zach about something that he might have imagined.

"I heard you cry out."

"It is nothing, I tell you."

Shrugging his shoulders, Zach didn't try to pry further into Ryder's secret thoughts. Obviously, Ryder preferred not to talk about the demons driving him. "Come on; let's get out of here. You need to get on a horse and ride until the cobwebs clear from your head. And while we're riding, I want you to think seriously about staying on here while I take Abby and the baby back East."

"I will think about it, but I will not change my mind. Soon I will leave and go into the hills. I hope you will provide Hannah with a home for as long as she wants one."

"Do you think that's fair to Hannah?"

"What is fair? Is it fair for her to tie herself to a blind man? Is it fair that Indians are being driven to reservations? Is it fair that whites despise me because I was raised by the Cheyenne? No, brother-in-law, nothing in life is fair. I am thinking of Hannah and what is best for her. If the Great Spirit restores my sight one day, I will return."

If there were answers to Ryder's questions, Zach did not have them.

Hannah paused in the yard as she watched Ryder and Zach mount their horses and ride away. She knew Zach was trying his best to help Ryder and she appreciated his efforts, but her heart told her that Ryder's problems were vast and complex. She'd lived with the Indians long enough to understand their deep-rooted, mystical belief in spiritual signs and visions. If Ryder believed he was being punished, nothing short of a miracle would dissuade him. The simple explanation that he had stared too long into the sun was not acceptable to him. Like Zach and Abby, Hannah believed Ryder's sight would return in time, but convincing him of that was impossible. And now he was dead set on leaving.

Hannah had no idea where Ryder had slept these past few nights; she only knew it wasn't with her. Didn't he know she needed him? Her body ached with the need to feel his arms around her, his mouth on hers, his body claiming hers in all the wonderful ways he had taught her. Their baby needed him. Hannah's hand flew protectively to her stomach, wondering what would become of her and her child if Ryder left them. Sighing regretfully, Hannah turned back toward the house. Before she reached the back door she had arrived at a decision. For the sake of her child, she had to try one last time to change Ryder's mind about leaving.

Later that day, while talking with Abby, Hannah learned that Ryder had been sleeping in the barn. Abby knew that Ryder intended to leave very soon, and she was both saddened and angered. Why did her brother have to be so stubborn? She had no idea how to heal the rift between Hannah and Ryder, but she did know that they loved one another desperately.

"Sometimes a woman must take matters into her own hands," Abby hinted sagely. "Sometimes men are so obstinate, they fail to see what is right before their faces. And in Ryder's case he cannot see at all, so it is up to you to tell him."

Hannah stared at her consideringly. "Ryder already knows I love him."

Abby smiled. "I'm sure he does, but it's always good to remind him. If you let him go away without trying to convince him to stay, you may live to regret it."

"I want Ryder to remain because he loves me. He thinks because he's blind he's no good for me. His damn Indian pride is coming between us."

"It's up to you to convince him otherwise, Hannah, but I'd think carefully about letting him walk out of my life. We're about the same age, and I think of you as my own sister. If Sierra is still alive, I'd give the same advice to her."

"Ryder spoke of his little sister. Do you know what happened to her?"

Abby's silver eyes dimmed. "Zach checked the army records and learned that Sierra was picked up by a family and taken West. Until that time I had no idea that Sierra had survived the Crow attack."

"Do you know the family's name?"

"The records were fifteen years old and the writing was faded and difficult to read, but we think the name was either Alden or Adler. Zach has hired a man to check into it, but so far he's been unable to locate Sierra."

"I'm sorry."

"Don't be. I have a feeling Sierra is happy wherever she is. Meanwhile, concentrate on Ryder and what you must do to stay together."

That night Hannah mulled over Abby's words. The house was quiet. Everyone had retired for the evening, and Hannah hoped they were sleeping. The longer she thought about Ryder riding away, perhaps never to return, the more she realized she couldn't let him do it. The Irish in her made her just stubborn enough to fight for what she wanted.

Hannah left her bed and tiptoed to the door. She heard nothing but chirping crickets and night birds singing their sad songs. The door swung open on silent hinges, and she stepped out into the hallway. Dressed in a thin shift, Hannah's bare feet moved silently down the hallway and out of the house. A full moon lit the path to the barn. The door was open. It was pitch black inside. Since she had no idea where to find Ryder in the cavernous interior of the barn, she called his name softly.

Ryder was caught in the midst of a vividly carnal dream. In his dream his eyes were no longer sightless and he was making tender love to Hannah. At the height of her pleasure he heard her whisper his name and groaned wordlessly in reply. Hannah heard and moved unerringly in the direction of his voice. Slowly and carefully, she made her way through the dark barn. When Ryder groaned a second time Hannah, her eyes having adjusted to the darkness, found him lying on a bed of fragrant straw. A half smile curved her lips as she pulled off her shift and lay down beside him. Instantly, his arms came around her.

"Oh, Ryder," she whispered against his ear. "I've missed you so. Love me. Please love me."

Ryder turned to cover Hannah's mouth with his. If he couldn't have Hannah in the flesh, he could at least have her in his dreams. In his dreams he was not blind. He was whole, and strong, and hungry to taste Hannah's sweetness again. Blood swelled his manhood, bringing it to full erection. When Hannah's mouth opened beneath his he thrust his tongue inside, the

sweet taste of her driving him into a passion-
ate frenzy. He wanted to push himself into
her immediately, feel her tight heat surround
him, but he restrained himself, unwilling to
bring his dream to an abrupt end. Instead,
he slipped his hand between her legs, his
fingers seeking her slick, wet heat. He was
rewarded by Hannah's sharp inhalation of
breath.

He deepened the kiss, his fingers teasing
the tender bud hidden between her thighs.
He felt it swell beneath his fingertips and
rejoiced that he could bring the woman of
his dreams pleasure. The searing ache in his
loins built to such intensity that his face
contorted in pain. From a far-off distance
he heard her cries of rapture, and his fingers delved deeper inside her. She whimpered and began tossing beneath him, her
hips thrusting upward, impaling herself more
deeply.

"Ryder, please."

Ryder almost laughed aloud as he felt her
incredibly tight, searing heat gripping his fingers, and her body stiffen. He felt her climax
wash over her in wave after wave of rapture
as his fingers continued the rhythm and his
mouth pulled at her nipples, until she had no
more to give. Then he rose above her, desperately eager to join their bodies. This was
one dream that would not elude him. Flexing
his hips, he thrust into her, driving himself so
deep, Hannah gasped and clung to his neck.

The breath jammed in his chest as pure sensation overwhelmed him. No dream had ever felt so real.

Pumping his hips furiously, panting, groaning, Ryder wasn't certain when he realized that he wasn't dreaming, that he held a flesh-and-blood woman in his arms. A woman hot for him, needing him, whimpering and panting as loudly as he was. He felt her muscles contract around him, heard her call out his name, felt the scorching heat of her body, and spewed forth his passion into her receptive body. Drained, he lay like one dead; indeed, he had experienced a kind of death in Hannah's arms. But after a few minutes he began to stir, rolling over and carrying her with him until she was lying on top of him, their bodies still fused, his erection still potent despite his violent climax.

"I love you, Ryder," Hannah said once she had caught her breath. "I swear if you leave me now, I'll never forgive you."

"You made me break my vow, Little Sparrow. You knew how I felt. Why did you come to me? Why do you torment me?"

"You could have sent me away instead of making love to me."

"I did not think you were real. Night and day you are in my mind. If I couldn't have you in person, I would have you in my dreams."

"Since you've already broken your vow, there is no need for you to leave," Hannah said smugly.

If it hadn't been so dark in the barn, Hannah would have seen Ryder's face contort into a grimace of pain. "Hannah, we've already had this discussion."

Hannah wasn't willing to accept his answer. Still joined, she moved her hips experimentally, reassured when she felt him throbbing against the walls of her tight passage, growing larger inside her. "If you are so sure about your decision, I dare you to leave my body, to tell me you don't want me again." She sat up and straddled him, sliding her thighs down hard on his. His strangled groan was all the answer she needed.

"You are a witch," Ryder gasped as he grasped her buttocks and moved her up and down the length of his erection. "And I have no will where you are concerned. It would take a stronger man than I to leave you right now. I will gladly suffer *Heammawihio's* wrath for this moment with you."

Her ripe breasts dangled within his reach and he raised his head to suckle the tender fruits, certain that paradise had never tasted so sweet. She rode him wildly, gripping him with her knees, fearing he'd leave her if she relaxed her hold. Then her thoughts left her head as rapture exploded inside her, consuming her body with wracking shudders. Ryder gave a great shout and followed her down pleasure's path.

Collapsing atop his powerful chest, Hannah allowed herself to drift peacefully for a time, forgetting everything but the man she loved and his child, carried safe inside her. She offered token protest when Ryder lifted her from him and nestled her in the curve of his body, curling himself around her.

"So much for my resolve," he said in self-derision.

Hannah smiled inwardly. "You didn't have much of a chance. I was pretty determined, you know. I love you, Ryder." She briefly considered telling him about the baby, but she decided she wanted him to remain for her sake, not because of their child.

Ryder went still. Then his arms slackened and he turned away from her. Wrenching pain shot through Hannah. She felt as if she'd been punched in the stomach. Her arms went protectively around her middle, her head rolled from side to side, and she moaned. The terrible ache of rejection nearly tore her apart. Ryder didn't want her. A sob gathered in her throat and pushed past her lips. Ryder heard and turned back to gather her into his arms.

"Why now, Little Sparrow? Why has the Great Spirit stolen my sight so that I cannot take care of you properly? I am no longer a whole man. My sight is gone; I am helpless without eyes."

"You are a brave man who fears no one. You are a fearless warrior. Nothing else matters."

"It matters to me."

"Are you saying you don't want me?"

She felt his muscles tense and was heartened. "No, Little Sparrow, I will always want you. I want to see your face when I make love to you. I want to see Grandfather Sun rise in the morning and set at night. I want to hunt the bounty provided by Mother Earth. Is that asking too much?"

Tears gathered in Hannah's eyes. "You will have all of those things, Ryder. You'll have your sight again. You *will!*" She said it with such fierce conviction, such resolute assurance, that Ryder wanted to believe her. If she had so much faith, how could he doubt?

"If my sight never returns, I will be fortunate to have been loved by you."

"Then you won't leave?"

"I must. I will go into the hills and pray to *Heammawihio* to restore my sight. If it is restored to me, I will return."

Hannah dared to breathe again. She truly felt his sight would return. But the one thing she wanted to hear from Ryder still remained locked within his heart. He hadn't said he loved her.

"You must be exhausted. Go back to the house, Hannah. I will see you in the morning."

"No. I hate lying in that bed alone. I'd much rather share this bed of straw with you."

"Then sleep, Little Sparrow. I will hold you all night so you do not get cold. Until I leave, we will share the same bed. I'm sure my meddling sister and brother-in-law will be pleased."

"I'm sure they will," Hannah concurred, hiding a smile. Abby had been right in advising her to go to Ryder. Soon his sight would return—she was certain of it—and then she would tell him about the baby. They'd be a real family. She knew Zach had offered Ryder a job and land, and her dream of living in peace with Ryder in their own house was within her grasp.

Hannah fell asleep thinking happy thoughts while Ryder dwelled on his dark future. A future without eyes, without the means to support a wife or family, without a notion in which world he truly belonged.

Hannah stretched luxuriously, aware of warmth and happiness and contentment. The straw beneath her crackled and, abruptly, she recalled where she was and why. She had swallowed her pride and gone to Ryder last night. They had made love more than once, and afterward they had slept entwined in each other's arms.

"It's about time you woke up."

"Ryder." She gave him a foolish grin, but it faded the moment she realized he couldn't see her. "Is it morning already?"

"I can't really see it, but I sense daylight. My senses have grown keener since I lost my sight."

Snuggling into the warmth of his body, Hannah was loathe to rise. But she knew she must before Zach came to the barn to start the chores. Sunshine pierced through the open door, bathing them in blazing light, and

Hannah stifled a giggle when she thought of what Zach would think if he stumbled upon them lying naked upon the straw.

Lost in their own happiness, they didn't hear riders enter the yard. And since the barn was set some distance back from the house, they didn't see Zach arguing with his early-morning visitors in an effort to convince them to leave.

"I tell you he's not in the house," Zach insisted.

"Where is he? You might as well tell me; I'll find him sooner or later anyway."

Unaware that they had visitors, Abby came into the room, carrying a howling baby who demanded his breakfast most boisterously. "Is that Ryder you're talking to, Zach? Has he come in from the barn already? Breakfast will be ready just as soon as I feed your son." The words died in her throat and her smile faded when she saw Lieutenant Gilmore standing in the doorway, talking to Zach.

"Thank you, Mrs. Mercer," Gilmore said, tipping his hat. "To the barn, men."

Abby clutched Zach's arm. "What is it, Zach? What do they want?"

A nerve twitched in Zach's jaw. "They want Ryder."

"Dear God! Why?"

"I don't know yet, but I aim to find out." He took off for the barn at a run.

"Wait for me!" Clutching the baby to her breast, Abby followed close on his heels.

* * *

"I'd better go up to the house and help Abby with breakfast," Hannah said with marked reluctance. She touched Ryder's face and bent down to kiss him.

"Now isn't that a pretty sight."

Hannah froze, her gaze swiveling upward. She saw Trent Gilmore looking down at her and jerked upright, her hands flying up to cover her bare breasts. "Oh, no!"

Ryder sprang to his knees, rummaging in the straw for his knife. He gave a feral snarl, crouching low and swinging the blade from side to side.

"Take him, men. Be careful of the knife. You know how vicious animals can be when cornered."

Instantly, six men jumped on Ryder. It took all six to wrestle him to the ground and bind his hands.

"Leave him alone," Hannah cried, too distraught to care that the men were leering at her.

Suddenly Zach and Abby burst into the barn. It took Abby a moment to recover from the shock of finding Hannah and Ryder both naked; then she rushed forward to shield Hannah from view. "Zach, don't let them do this!"

"What is this all about, Lieutenant? You're invading my home."

"I know who you are now, Mercer," Gilmore said. "A courier arrived yesterday from Fort Laramie with an answer to my dispatch.

You're Wind Rider's brother-in-law. You used your influence to have him released from the stockade. But Captain Purdue didn't have the authority to set him free. When I presented my evidence to Colonel Chivington he signed an order for Wind Rider's arrest."

"What are the charges?"

"Murder. There are witnesses who will swear they saw a white savage riding with Indians and taking part in raids that resulted in the deaths of soldiers and civilians."

"That's going to be difficult to prove," Zach charged.

"Nevertheless, Chivington has ordered Wind Rider held in jail until his trial."

"Get him on his feet, men." The six members of the Colorado militia wrestled Ryder to his feet.

"For God's sake, let him dress first," Zach said. He spied Ryder's clothes lying nearby and picked them up.

"He can put on his pants, but I'm not untying his hands until he's behind bars."

Hidden behind Abby's skirts, Hannah scrambled for her shift and pulled it over her head. When she peeked up at Ryder and saw the closed look on his face her heart went out to him. Speechless, she watched as Zach helped Ryder step into his pants. When the troopers led him out the door she sprang from behind Abby and grasped Gilmore's arm.

"You can't take him," she cried beseechingly. "Please, what can I say that will stop you?"

Gilmore stopped abruptly and stared at Hannah, her disheveled beauty stunning him. "We'll talk about this later." His voice was pitched low, so that only she could hear.

"You can't take him. He's blind. He can't see."

Gilmore stared at her in disbelief. "Blind? What do you take me for, a fool?"

"It's true. Why would I lie about something like that?"

"Why, indeed?" Gilmore stepped close to Ryder and passed his hand before Ryder's face. There was no reaction. Ryder's eyes were blank, expressionless. But Gilmore still was not convinced. "Mount him up, men." Then he turned back to Hannah. "I'm not taking your word on this. I'll have a doctor check him out. But I warn you, it will make little difference. Chivington wants to find Red Cloud's camp real bad, and Wind Rider knows where it is."

"You don't understand," Hannah cried, shaking with anger.

"Hannah, don't."

Ryder's strident voice carried a silent message that Hannah recognized immediately. Having a woman plead on his behalf shamed him. Reminding Trent of his blindness would embarrass Ryder and make him bitter, Hannah thought as she clamped her lips tightly together. One way or another, she silently vowed, she'd help Ryder. She watched miserably as Gilmore's men dragged Ryder through the yard to where the horses were tethered. A small cry escaped her lips when she saw him stumble to his knees. He was pulled roughly to his feet and hoisted onto his horse.

"Where are you taking him?" Hannah asked. "What will happen to him?"

Gilmore sent her a searching look, grasped her arm, and pulled her away from Zach and Abby, where he could speak to her privately. When both Zach and Abby moved to follow Hannah shook her head, warning them away.

Gilmore's voice lowered to a whisper. "What happens to your lover depends on you."

"Me?"

He sent her a meaningful glance. "Come to town tomorrow and we'll talk about it." He turned his head in Zach's direction. "Don't bring your guard with you."

"I'll come to town now," Hannah said. "Why wait until tomorrow?"

Gilmore was adamant. "Tomorrow, Hannah. Colonel Chivington wants to question him first."

Chapter Eighteen

Hannah stared with growing horror into the small windowless cell where Ryder had been imprisoned. For the past two days she'd been trying to gain permission to visit him, but to her chagrin, Lieutenant Gilmore did not have the authority to grant visitation rights. Zach had found her a room at a boardinghouse shortly after they had arrived in Denver, and together they had sought permission to visit Ryder. When their request was denied Zach had gone straight to the governor, but thus far he'd been unable to gain the man's ear. Zach had been kept cooling his heels in the governor's outer office with promises of an audience.

Meanwhile, Trent had managed to cut through the red tape, and when Hannah had presented herself at his office early on the morning of the third day to argue her case she had been gratified to learn that he had pulled some strings and gotten her a visitor's pass, allowing her a brief visit with Ryder. But he had warned her that his generosity carried a heavy price. Too excited at the time to inquire about the cost, Hannah had accompanied Trent to the dank cell where Ryder was imprisoned. Unfortunately, there hadn't been time to inform Zach so he could join her.

To Hannah's horror, she realized Trent hadn't warned her about what she was likely to find.

"Oh, my God! What have you done to him?"

A single candle provided the only light in the room. Ryder lay sprawled on the floor, his face turned away from her. His hands and legs were shackled and the chains were attached to the wall, preventing free movement. He was so still, Hannah feared he was dead. Rushing into the room, she dropped to her knees beside him.

Ryder heard her voice and tried to tell her to go away, but his split and bloodied lips were too swollen to work properly. He didn't want her to see him like this, beaten and bruised beyond recognition. In an incredibly short time he had gone from proud Cheyenne warrior to lowly prisoner. They could beat him all they wanted, he silently vowed, but he'd never tell them where to find Red Cloud's camp.

Hannah reached out and gently turned his face toward her. What she saw sent the breath rushing from her lungs. "Ryder, dear God, they've beaten you!" Her head whirled around to glare accusingly at Gilmore. "Why did you let them do this to him? Look at him: He's been severely beaten. Get me some water, quickly."

She didn't waste precious time wondering if Gilmore would do as she bid. Instead, she ripped the hem from her petticoat to use as a cloth. When he reappeared at her elbow with a bucket of water she merely grunted, too enraged by Ryder's condition to speak coherently. Dipping the cloth into the water, she tenderly cleansed his face of blood and gore. Both his cheekbones were discolored, and the swollen flesh around his eyes had turned an ugly shade of purple. There was a deep cut above one eyebrow and another at the corner of his mouth.

Gilmore sent Hannah a censuring look. "I didn't order the beatings. Once I turned Wind Rider over to Colonel Chivington and the Colorado militia it was taken out of my hands. Chivington wants information badly, and he believes Wind Rider can give it to him."

By now Hannah had finished bathing Ryder's face and was turning her attention to his torso, still bare from the waist up. When she ran the cloth over his ribs he groaned.

"His ribs are broken," Hannah accused. "How could they do this to a helpless man?"

"I told you, Hannah, I had nothing to do with it. I understand Wind Rider has been questioned daily since his capture. He was also examined by a doctor, who confirmed that he is blind. This isn't my doing; I had no idea Chivington's men would be so brutal."

Tears streamed down Hannah's pale cheeks. "You could have stopped them! You must have known what would happen."

Placing his hands on Hannah's quaking shoulders, Gilmore tried to lift her to her feet. "It's out of my hands, Hannah."

Hannah shrugged his hands aside. "You can do something, Trent; I know you can. Please, help him."

Gilmore gazed down at Hannah, thinking her more beautiful than any woman he'd ever known. He wanted her as much now as he had the first time he'd set eyes on her in that Indian camp. "Perhaps there *is* something I could do," he allowed cautiously.

"Hannah, don't. Don't believe anything he tells you." Bordering on the edge of consciousness, Ryder struggled to make himself understood. "Don't worry about me. Go back to the farm."

"Tell them what they want to know, Ryder, please. I can't stand to see you like this."

Ryder tried to rise to his elbow, grimaced, and fell back down. "I will not betray the People."

"Think of yourself for a change. Think of me!" She almost said, "Think of our child," but now was not the time to let Ryder know he was going to be a father.

"Come away, Hannah. There is nothing more you can do for him. He can escape these beatings if he tells us what we want to know."

"He'll never do that. You don't know Ryder as I do."

The words had scarcely left her lips when two enlisted men entered the cell. Surprised to see visitors with the prisoner, they stared at Hannah before recalling protocol and saluting Lieutenant Gilmore.

"We're here to interrogate the prisoner again, Lieutenant," the senior enlisted man said. "We didn't expect to find anyone here."

Gilmore returned the salute. "Sergeant Collins, Corporal Holmes. We were just leaving."

Hannah leaped to her feet. "No! You can't beat him again. Can't you see he can't stand anymore? You'll kill him."

The sergeant, a husky man with meaty fists and a thick neck, gave her a leering grin. "Well, now, ma'am, that's just too bad, ain't it? Our orders come from Colonel Chivington, and we're only doing our duty. Are you this here white Injun's squaw?"

Before Hannah could answer Gilmore said, "No, she's not his squaw. We'll leave now so you can get on with your duty. Come along, Hannah; we can't interfere with justice." He tried to drag her from the room. Hannah dug in her heels, but her strength was no match for Gilmore's.

"Trent, no! You've got to do something."

"Go, Hannah!" Ryder's deep voice cut into the

confusion. His head was turned in her direction, but Hannah knew he couldn't see her. "They won't kill me; they need the information I hold. Soon they will learn it will do no good to beat me."

"You heard him, Hannah. Let's get out of here." Gilmore grasped her around the waist and literally dragged her from the cell.

The door banged shut behind her and she let out a strangled sob. "He can't survive too many more beatings, Trent. You said you can do something. For God's sake, tell me."

The soft thudding noises and muffled groans emanating from behind the closed door gave Hannah the kind of desperation she'd never experienced before. She'd do anything, anything at all to save Ryder from further beatings. "Tell me what you want of me."

Gilmore glanced down the dim corridor and saw that they were alone. Grasping her arms, he pulled her hard against him. "I want *you*, Hannah McLin. I think you know that by now."

Hannah swallowed convulsively and looked away. She knew what was coming and dreaded it.

"I've asked for a transfer back to Fort Laramie. Duty with the Colorado militia isn't what I thought it would be. I'll be leaving in a day or two. I want you to come with me. If you agree, I'll arrange an escape for your white Indian."

"You want me to be your whore?"

Gilmore shook his head. "No, it would never

do. Once we arrive at Fort Laramie we'll be married by the chaplain and assigned a house on Officer's Row. It's the only way we can live together in assigned quarters without causing a scandal."

"Marriage?" Hannah's voice shook. She said she'd do anything to save Ryder, but marriage? She'd thought she was already married, but obviously an Indian ceremony had no standing in the white community. And what about her child? If she told Trent about the baby she was expecting, he'd no doubt withdraw his offer to help Ryder. She was caught in a vicious trap.

"I've decided marriage is the only way," Gilmore continued smugly. "The white community at Fort Laramie is small but rigid in its morals. I realize my parents wouldn't approve of you, but times have changed since the war. The West is a world apart from the South, and I want you enough to forget your past."

Hannah tried not to think about the baby now, or what Trent would do when he discovered she was carrying Ryder's child. By the time he learned about it Ryder would be free, in Powder River country, and Trent could take his vengeance out on her.

"What do you say, Hannah? Will you go with me?"

"How do I know you aren't lying about helping Ryder? How do I know you won't go back on your word once I leave with you?"

"You'll just have to trust me."

Hannah was far from convinced. "No. I have

to know for certain that Ryder is free before I'll go with you."

Gilmore's mind worked furiously. He wasn't certain how he intended to set Ryder free, but somehow he had to convince Hannah of his sincerity. Once he took her away she'd have no way of knowing what happened to the white Injun. He could even arrange to have Wind Rider recaptured and returned to his cell before his absence was noticed.

"Give me a day to arrange it. You can watch him walk free yourself if you won't take my word for it. Once he walks away a free man you must agree to come with me immediately, without speaking or communicating with him in any way."

To see Ryder free with her own eyes was all Hannah wanted. If Trent could arrange that, she would be forever grateful. "I agree."

Hannah waited for Zach at the boarding-house. Somehow she had to convince Ryder's brother-in-law that leaving with Trent was her decision. It wasn't going to be easy. It was fortunate that neither he nor Abby knew about the baby.

It was late afternoon when Zach knocked on Hannah's door. His mood was jubilant. "I've seen the governor! He listened to my story and said he'd consider Ryder's case. I tell you, Hannah, it's the most encouragement I've had in days. I even submitted a plan that I'm hoping Governor Evans will endorse."

"What kind of plan?"

"I don't want to get your hopes up, Hannah, so I think I'll keep it to myself until Ryder is released. I'm to see the governor tomorrow for his answer. If amnesty is granted, Ryder will never have to worry about being a fugitive again."

"Tomorrow might be too late."

Zach searched her face. "What do you mean?"

"I saw Ryder today. He's been beaten. He could barely speak, his face is unrecognizable, and I'm sure he has cracked ribs. I was told the beatings will continue until he reveals the location of Red Cloud's camp."

"Good God! He'll never give them that kind of information. How in the world did you manage to get in to see him?"

Hannah flushed. "I went to see Trent. He obtained a visitor's pass for me."

"Hannah, I told you to leave this to me. I don't want you begging Gilmore for anything. I'm sure the governor . . ."

Hannah looked away. "You can't be sure, Zach; that's the problem. I've decided to handle it in my own way. I've agreed to accompany Trent to Fort Laramie. We're going to be married."

Zach stared at her, stunned. "What in the hell are you talking about?"

"It's true. Ryder and I are from different worlds. There is no future for us. You heard him; he wants to return to the Indian Nation.

He believes it's what the Great Spirit wants. I'll not stand in his way."

"I don't know where in the hell you're coming from, Hannah, but I don't buy it. Why are you really doing this? What did Gilmore promise you? Did he offer to release Ryder if you went with him? Surely you don't trust him, do you?"

Hannah refused to meet his eyes. "No, it's nothing like that. It's just that I see no future for Ryder and me." God, please let Zach believe me, she silently prayed.

"Dammit, Hannah, you're being foolish. Promise me you won't do anything rash until I see the governor tomorrow. I'm sure he'll order Ryder's release once he understands the situation."

"I wish Ryder the best, but it no longer concerns me." Each word was like a knife wound to her heart.

Zach stared at Hannah as if he were seeing her for the first time. Hotheaded as ever, he jumped to the wrong conclusion. "Why, you coldhearted little bitch! I thought you loved Ryder, but I see now I was mistaken. Go, then. Ryder will be better off without you. But rest assured that neither Abby nor I will desert him. I'll see him free if it's the last thing I do." Spinning on his heel, he stormed from the room, slamming the door behind him.

Hannah sank down on the bed, too upset to cry. She hoped that Ryder and his relatives would understand and forgive her one day, but all that mattered now was freeing Ryder before he was beaten to death. If Trent could do that, then it was well-worth her sacrifice.

Trent Gilmore had little difficulty arranging Rider's release once he offered Sergeant Collins sufficient monetary reward to win his compliance. Since Ryder's release was to be temporary, Collins agreed to the deception, though he understood none of it. According to Gilmore's plans, Collins was to set Ryder free, have a horse waiting for him, and allow him to ride away. Then he and Private Holmes were to follow and recapture him after Hannah saw him ride away a free man. Gilmore suspected the savage would offer little resistance. Since his arrest three days ago he'd been ruthlessly beaten and could scarcely stand on his own two feet.

What mattered was that Hannah would think him responsible for the savage's release and be most appropriately grateful. Marrying Hannah hadn't been part of his original plan, but he'd come late to the realization that marriage was the only way he could have her. She would make him a suitable frontier wife. He admired the way she had traveled alone from Ireland, indentured herself to pay for her passage, and survived numerous hardships. She had spunk, he'd give her that much, and he'd do anything to have her in his bed. Once she was his wife he'd make her forget the white savage she fancied herself in love with.

On the morning Trent had arranged for Ryder's "escape" he arrived bright and early at Hannah's boardinghouse. Zach had already left for the governor's office. Today Governor Evans was to decide if amnesty was to be granted in Ryder's case, but Hannah held out little hope for help from that quarter. She met Gilmore in the formal parlor of the boardinghouse.

Gilmore took Hannah's hands in his and stared earnestly into her eyes. "It's all arranged, Hannah."

Hannah's green eyes, lusterless from lack of sleep and constant worry, lit up. "Ryder will be set free? How in the world did you manage it?"

"Anything is possible with enough money. I've saved my pay. There's little to spend it on out here."

Hannah was so grateful to Trent that she threw her arms around him and hugged him tightly. "Thank you, Trent. You don't know how grateful I am."

"You'll have your chance to prove it soon enough. I've arranged for Wind Rider to be released at noon today. If you don't trust me, you can watch him ride away yourself from a window on the upper floor of the building where he's being held. Does that meet with your approval?"

Hannah nodded eagerly.

"Pack your clothes. I'll come back for you shortly before noon. After Wind Rider is released we'll meet the patrol that will escort us to Fort Laramie. We'll be happy there, Hannah; you'll see."

Hannah lowered her eyes, unable to meet his gaze. She was unaccustomed to lying and she feared Trent would know. But she could never marry him, no matter that he had arranged Ryder's freedom. She was carrying Ryder's child and someday, somehow, they would be together again.

"I'll be ready, Trent."

Ryder had no idea how long he'd been imprisoned in the dark, dank room. If the frequency of his beatings, which were administered regularly by the meaty-fisted sergeant and his cohort, were any indication, he assumed that at least four days had passed since he'd been tossed in jail. Always the questions were the same. Where was Red Cloud's camp located? How many Indians were living in the Badlands? What were Red Cloud's plans for taking up arms against the whites? And always Ryder met their questions with silence.

Then came the beatings. When he passed out he was doused with water, revived, and beaten again. The two sadistic soldiers were masters at their craft, Ryder thought bitterly, for they knew just when to stop. Evidently, Chivington didn't want him dead. Not until he'd divulged the information the army wanted, anyway.

Ryder tried to sit up and groaned as raw pain surged through him. He had no idea how many of his ribs were cracked, but judging by the violent pain, it had to be more than one. His lips were so swollen, he could barely speak, and his eyes and face felt like raw meat. Ryder knew he couldn't last much longer under these conditions, but that no longer mattered. Seeing Hannah had made him realize that he had no business loving her. She deserved much better than what he could offer. He didn't even know who he was or where he belonged. And furthermore, his blindness made him totally useless as a husband. Besides, he was likely to die from the constant beatings if they continued.

When footsteps sounded in the passageway Ryder cocked his head and turned his sightless eyes toward the door. He went rigid when the door opened. He'd already been beaten once today and doubted if he could survive another brutal attack. Then something happened that made Ryder forget all about his split lips and battered body. The fuzzy veil lifted from his eyes and he saw the flickering light of a candle and the shadowy figures of two men. As they moved farther into the room, the mists clouding his eyes miraculously parted, allowing him a glimpse of the men's features.

Since Ryder had never seen Sergeant Collins before, he identified him by his voice. He sounded grumpy and somewhat disgruntled. "Someone to see you, Injun. If you want my opinion, you got more luck than you deserve. I sure as hell don't know how he did it, but evidently your brother-in-law's got friends in high places." Collins thought about the money

Lieutenant Gilmore had paid him to release and then recapture the prisoner and shrugged. He couldn't help it if orders came from higher places. Besides, Gilmore was leaving today for Fort Laramie, and it shouldn't matter to him what happened to the prisoner.

"Ryder, it's Zach. I've come to take you home."

Slowly, Ryder turned his head in Zach's direction. He blinked, realizing he could see Zach as clearly as he had before he'd lost his sight. Instinct as well as shock convinced him to keep the information to himself for the time being.

"Did you hear, Ryder? The governor has granted you amnesty. You're free. I'll tell you about it after we leave this disgusting place."

"Free?" Confusion registered on Ryder's swollen face. How could it be? One minute he was enduring brutal beatings and the next he was free to leave. Never would he understand the workings of white society.

"Yes, free. Just as soon as Sergeant Collins removes your shackles, I'll get you out of here. Can you walk?"

The chains fell away as Collins bent and unlocked them. "It's against my better judgment to do this. Colonel Chivington ain't going to like it one damn bit."

Ryder groaned and tried to rise, but his legs buckled beneath him. Zach sent Collins a poisonous glare and assisted Ryder to his feet. "You sure as hell didn't need to be so damn brutal. The man can hardly walk."

Collins shrugged. "Chivington wanted information. All he had to do was tell us what we wanted to know and we would have left him alone."

"Bastard," Zach gritted from between clenched teeth.

"I can walk, Zach," Ryder said, declining Zach's help. He wanted to walk out of this place on his own two feet.

About the time Ryder was leaving his cell, Hannah and Gilmore entered the building and ascended the stairs to the second floor. They entered an office facing the street, and Gilmore led Hannah over to the window. "It's almost noon, Hannah. Wind Rider should be making an appearance any moment now. I'd venture to say one of those horses tethered to the hitching post outside will carry him away from Denver."

Hannah's intent gaze did not stray from the street below. She had no idea how Trent had managed this, but she still didn't trust him.

Ryder paused in the doorway, blinded by the sun. It had been many weeks since he'd lost his sight. Darkness had become a way of life. Hannah had been right; his blindness had only been temporary. He didn't have time right now to analyze what all this meant, but he felt certain Heammawihio would reveal it to him in his own good time. Dimly, he wondered why Hannah hadn't accompanied Zach. He was eternally glad she hadn't, for he didn't want her to see him in the state he was in. Pity wasn't what he wanted from her.

"The horses are right outside," Zach said as he paused behind Ryder. "Wait here. I'll help you mount after I give your clearance papers to Sergeant Collins."

"I do not need your help," Ryder said, looking directly into Zach's eyes. "I can do this by myself."

Zach sent him a stunned look. "Ryder! Dammit, man, you can see! When . . . how . . . ?"

"Finish your business. I will explain later."

Zach searched Ryder's face, nodded, then lingered behind to confer with Sergeant Collins. Ryder took a shaky step forward and nearly fell flat on his face. Steadying himself against the doorjamb, he mustered his strength and ventured another step. He was encouraged when his legs moved on command. Gritting his teeth, he made it all the way to his horse. Mounting took considerable effort, but he accomplished it on his second try. He had no idea Hannah was watching his every move.

"He's alone! He can't see!" Hannah cried, growing panicky. "I should have asked Zach to meet him. How will he find his way out of the city?"

Gilmore was considering his answer when suddenly Zach strode out of the building and joined Ryder.

"Oh, there's Zach! Did you contact him, Trent? You must have known Ryder wouldn't be able to manage without help, didn't you?"

"What?" Gilmore couldn't believe his eyes. How in the hell had Zach Mercer gotten involved in this? But it was too late now to worry about it, he reasoned as he searched his mind for an answer to Hannah's questions.

"Yes, that's it. I knew you'd worry if someone wasn't on hand to help him." This really complicates matters, Gilmore thought, stunned by the turn of events. If his superiors learned what he had planned, his army career was over. Something he wasn't aware of had occurred, and he needed to find out about it before Hannah did.

"You've kept your promise, Trent," Hannah said, ignorant of the elaborate plans he had laid for Ryder's release and recapture. "I'm very grateful."

Gilmore sent her a sly smile. "Show me, Hannah. Show me just how grateful you are."

He pulled her into his arms, his desire making him forget that they were standing before a window where anyone could see them. When his lips slanted across hers she stiffened but did not resist. She supposed she owed him this much. Once Ryder was safe she'd let him know that she didn't intend to stay with him.

Stiffening his spine against the stabbing pain, Ryder rode away from the place where he had been imprisoned and tortured. But a nagging demon inside him prompted him to look back one last time. What he saw brought a vicious snarl to his lips. Framed in the window, her bright hair catching the noonday sun, Hannah was being soundly kissed by Lieutenant Gilmore. His brief glance had revealed her pliant body pressed hard against the bluecoat's virile length. Nothing in her stance led him to believe she was unwilling.

Zach heard Ryder's outcry and turned his head in the direction of Ryder's gaze. He saw the same intimate scene Ryder was witnessing and let out a curse. "Damn little bitch. I was wrong about her, Ryder. Forget her; she isn't worth your time."

Once they turned the corner, Ryder brought his mount to a halt. "All right, Zach, out with it. What happened between Hannah and Gilmore? I cannot believe she could change so in such a short time. I misjudged her once; I refuse to do so again until I know the truth."

"You saw yourself what happened," Zach muttered darkly. "Hannah decided Gilmore would give her a better life than you could. She's going with him to Fort Laramie. They're going to be married."

"Married!" Ryder started to rein his horse around in the direction from which he had just come, but Zach grabbed the reins and refused to let go.

"You're in no condition to confront anyone, Ryder. Look at yourself. You're having a difficult enough time just keeping your seat on your horse. It took some fancy talking to get the governor to sign your amnesty papers, and I'll not let you jeopardize your freedom." Even if Zach thought Hannah was lying about her reasons for abandoning Ryder—and it was very possible she was—he wasn't going to allow Ryder to return.

Ryder's head spun dizzily and his cracked ribs made breathing painful. He couldn't have defied Zach if he'd wanted to. But leaving Hannah to Gilmore was abhorrent to him. Something was wrong, desperately wrong. If only he could think clearly, he'd figure it out. But Zach, aware that Ryder needed immediate medical attention, wasn't allowing him time to think as he slapped the rump of Ryder's horse, sending him on his way. Zach followed close on his heels as they left Denver behind them.

Meanwhile, finding the kiss much to his liking, Gilmore couldn't wait to get Hannah away from Denver and all to himself. He left her alone in the room briefly while he went to confer with Sergeant Collins. What he learned stunned him. The governor had granted Wind Rider amnesty and set him free. Once Hannah was told he knew she would refuse to honor her part of their bargain. She would leave him and go back to her white savage. He couldn't allow that to happen. Haste was important. He must take Hannah away from Denver as soon as possible.

Fortunately, that wouldn't be difficult since he'd already made arrangements to leave immediately after Hannah had viewed Ryder's release. A small contingent of Colorado militia was waiting to escort them to the fort. Once

Hannah was his he'd make damn certain he was the only man in her life. As for his own complicity in the "release and recapture" of the prisoner, the money he'd paid Sergeant Collins would keep the aborted affair from public disclosure.

Hannah felt a wrenching grief as she left the city. Would Ryder ever forgive her for leaving so abruptly without an explanation? she wondered despondently. Would he realize that she had done it for his sake? Or would he return to his People and forget all about her? She pressed her hand lightly to the place where Ryder's child grew beneath her heart and felt a crushing sadness. How she wished she had told Ryder about the baby.

As she rode away from Denver, Hannah begged God to let Ryder understand and forgive her. To let him be pleased when he learned about their child. And to bring them together as a family. It didn't matter if Ryder never regained his sight. Her love was too solid to let his blindness make a difference.

Chapter Nineteen

Three days of bed rest was all Ryder would tolerate. Abby had wrapped his ribs tightly and tried to get him to remain in bed longer, but he was adamantly opposed to doing nothing while each day took Hannah and Gilmore farther away from him. His emotions had run the gamut from outright disbelief that she had gone willingly with Lieutenant Gilmore to outrage and anger. Though she had told Zach she had gone with the blue coat of her own free will, Ryder was not convinced. He needed to hear from her own lips that Gilmore was the man she wanted before he'd believe it.

To his dismay, Ryder could not make himself believe that Hannah didn't love him. He harbored a glimmer of hope that Hannah had gone with Gilmore for reasons that had nothing to do with her wanting the blue coat as a lover. But even that small hope seemed farfetched; the governor had already granted him amnesty, and she'd had no reason to sacrifice herself. The more he thought about the abrupt way in which she had left, without a word or a proper good-bye, the angrier and more confused he became. And the more determined he was to go after her.

After three days under Abby's tender care Ryder was able to move around freely, but not without considerable pain, which he ignored. On the fourth day Zach found him in the barn saddling his horse.

"Good God, Ryder, you can't go anywhere in your condition."

"I am well enough to ride." Actually, Ryder wasn't at all certain he could sit his horse.

"I suppose you're going after Hannah."

"I must."

His great anguish was clearly visible in the darkening of his silver eyes.

Zach searched frantically for a way to keep Ryder on the farm until he was fully healed. "Are you forgetting your commitment to the governor? One of the conditions of your release is that you work for the government."

Zach had revealed to Ryder, once they had reached the safety of the farm, that the only way the governor would grant amnesty was if Ryder agreed to put his expertise to work as an Indian agent to the Sioux and Cheyenne nations. He hoped to put Ryder's vast knowledge of Indians to good use.

"As Indian agent you'll be able to work closely with the People to bring about a lasting peace," Zach continued. "Have you forgotten that you are to confer with the governor as soon as you're well enough to travel to Denver?"

"I have not forgotten," Ryder said. "And had I known beforehand about the conditions attached to my amnesty, I might not have accepted. The white eyes want no honorable peace. They wish to annihilate the People. At the very least they want them confined to reservations where living conditions are dismal."

"Now you will have the opportunity to improve those conditions," Zach reminded him. "You know yourself the day is approaching when all Indians will be living on reservations, or be killed resisting. If you want to help your adopted people, you must accept the governor's terms."

"For the sake of the People I will accept the position, but I will not compromise my honor like some of these men who hold the same position. I will see that the People have warm blankets and food for their bellies. I will fight for what is right."

Zach slapped him on the back. "I expected no less from you. When the day arrives there is always a place for you with Mercer Freighting Company. And a piece of land waiting for you down by the river. Rest a few days longer, and when you are fully recuperated we will go together to call on the governor."

Ryder's face hardened. "I will see your governor, but in my own good time. First I must find Hannah. If you give me the supplies I need for a journey to Fort Laramie, I will bid my sister good-bye and go."

Zach shook his head. Never had he seen a more stubborn brother and sister. "Go if you must, Ryder, but I have to know if you really intend to return. It would hurt Abby if you rejected amnesty and returned to Powder River country."

Ryder sent him a disgruntled glare. "I will return, Zach Mercer. With or without Hannah, I will return to honor my promise to your governor. No one but my sister, who has experienced the same fears, knows the anguish and confusion I suffer because my skin is white and my heart is Cheyenne. We have both felt the despair of not knowing in which world we belong. But with your help she has bridged the gap and seems happy. I may not like it, but I will strive for the same kind of understanding. But first I must find Hannah and learn if she truly wants that blue coat."

"Take what supplies you need, Ryder. They are yours for the asking. And I hope you find the answer you seek. If Hannah had a reason for leaving, I know you will find it. But don't let your emotions blind you to the truth."

Ryder tried to keep Zach's admonition in mind when he rode away from the farm a full four days behind Hannah and Lieutenant Gilmore. But no matter how hard he tried to find an excuse for Hannah's behavior, the rage was still there. If only he could make sense of her abrupt departure. Was something escaping him? Had he failed her again by questioning her loyalty? No matter how hard he tried to find answers, it all came down to the inescapable fact that Hannah didn't love him. She really didn't love him. The difference in their upbringing was obviously too vast to allow true love to flourish.

Trent Gilmore sent Hannah a sidelong glance, thinking that it wouldn't be long before he'd have her in his bed. He'd fantasized about it for so long, he didn't know how much longer he could control his desire. For propriety's sake he'd not tried to bed her these past few nights on the trail. He intended to make her his wife and didn't want the men gossiping about their intimacy before marriage. "We'll stop overnight in Cheyenne," he said to Hannah when they were within a few miles of the city. "I imagine a hot bath and a bed will be welcome after the discomfort of the trail."

Hannah barely heard him. Discomfort was hardly the word she'd use to describe the trip from Denver thus far; hell was more like it. Being pregnant didn't help matters any. Or the stifling heat. At the end of the day she was so tired, she could barely eat her supper, and she was asleep minutes after crawling into her bedroll. The uneven motion of her horse kept her stomach in a constant state of turmoil.

"Did you hear me, Hannah? Does a bed and bath tempt you at all?"

This time Hannah concentrated on his words and answered accordingly. "It sounds wonderful, Trent. There's nothing I'd like better."

Gilmore sidled his horse closer to Hannah's mare. "Perhaps we'll have the privacy in Cheyenne that we lack on the trail." His voice was husky with desire as he placed a hand on her knee and smiled into her eyes. "The men will be billeted with the militia, but I can stay wherever I like. I'll arrange a room for us at the best hotel in town."

Hannah stiffened. The thought of sleeping with Gilmore was abhorrent to her. Unfortunately, it was too soon to tell him that she didn't intend to honor her promise. She had to make sure Ryder was safe before she did that, and she wasn't certain Ryder had had enough time yet to reach safety. His injuries were severe enough to keep him in bed for at least a couple of weeks.

"I-I don't think that's wise, Trent. I'd prefer to wait until we're married. It wouldn't be right."

A flush of anger crept across Gilmore's face. "Right? How can you question my right when you've slept with that white Indian? Was that right?"

Hannah glared at him. "Ryder and I were married at Red Cloud's camp." When he opened his mouth to protest she added, "I know the marriage isn't considered legal in white society, but while I was in the Indian camp I lived according to Indian law, and in Red Cloud's camp I was Ryder's wife."

Gilmore fought to control his temper. Just thinking about Hannah spread beneath the white savage, taking him into her body, made him burn with jealousy. He hated it that the white savage had been the first with her. Swallowing his anger, he tried to answer her reasonably, without earning her hostility. Giving offense at this point was definitely not in his best interest.

"You can't help what you were forced to do, Hannah, but I'd prefer that you didn't act as if you were the man's legal wife. I am trying to forget what happened to you and I want you to forget it too. You're going to be my wife. You're never to speak about or think of Wind Rider again."

Hannah bowed her head. She knew her face would reveal the rage she felt over Trent's words. Forget Ryder? Never! How could she when his child rested beneath her heart? The moment they reached Fort Laramie, she fully intended to tell Trent that she could not marry him; then she'd find passage back to Denver. If she was fortunate, she'd be able to convince Ryder she had left with Gilmore for his sake. She prayed he would believe her.

Hannah was dirty, tired, and hungry when they finally reached Cheyenne. The sun was just setting and the town was teeming with people. Some had come to work on the railroad, some were cowboys coming into town after a hard day's work, and others were drifters. She and Gilmore parted company with the patrol at militia headquarters after Gilmore made arrangements to meet them the next morning to continue their journey. Then they continued on to the hotel, where Gilmore engaged rooms for them.

"I paid for two rooms, Hannah, to save you embarrassment, but I intend for us to use only one," he told her as he carried her bag up to her room. "I have to report to Major Delaney at headquarters, but I'll not be late. I've ordered a bath for you." His eyes glowed hotly. "Rest while you can and I'll join you as soon as possible. We'll have dinner together and then . . ." His words fell off, leaving no doubt about how he intended to spend the night.

Before Hannah could offer a word of protest, Gilmore kissed her hard and left.

When her bath came she hurried through it, fearing Gilmore would return before she finished. Her mind worked feverishly, searching for a way to keep Trent from claiming her in the most basic way. She feared that when she told Trent she didn't intend to marry him, he would wire Denver and have Ryder seized and confined. Then all that she had sacrificed for Ryder's sake would have been for nothing.

Hannah dressed hurriedly. She had just finished buttoning the front of her gown when Gilmore burst into the room, cursing loudly.

"Trent, what is it?"

"Damn army brass. Major Delaney invited me to spend the night in his home and there's no polite way I could refuse. Believe me, I had other plans for tonight. He's eager to discuss Indian activity in the area and what the army is doing to defuse the situation. Thank God for our escort. I wouldn't relish traveling the country between Cheyenne and Fort Laramie without one."

Hannah nearly collapsed in relief.

"We'll still leave at dawn tomorrow. That hasn't changed," Gilmore continued. "I'm sorry, Hannah; you'll have to eat alone. The major has invited me to share dinner with him and his wife."

It was all Hannah could do to keep from shouting. Once again God had heard her and given her the reprieve she'd so desperately prayed for. Afraid to trust her voice, she merely nodded.

"I'll return for you at dawn," Gilmore informed her. "Get a good night's rest. We've still got a long way to go to reach the fort."

The hours Hannah spent in the saddle those next days were among the most miserable she'd ever experienced. Not only was the traveling difficult, but Hannah sensed Trent's unease. To Hannah's relief, they hadn't crossed Indian tracks, and she felt fortunate to be traveling with an armed patrol.

As if reading her mind, Gilmore rode up beside her and said, "I know you're worried about Indians, but since we are within a day or two of the fort I anticipate no trouble. If there were Indians in the area, they would have attacked by now."

"I'm sure we'll be safe," Hannah said, not at all as certain as she sounded.

The afternoon sun blazed down on her with relentless fury, and Hannah swayed in the saddle. Her mouth was dry, her face and clothing coated with dust. Despite her wide-brimmed bonnet, she felt her fair skin reddening. She hated to think about making the return trip to Denver, but she'd brave anything to be reunited with Ryder. She fervently hoped she would be able to make the trip before her belly got in the way of her traveling. Taking off her bonnet and fanning her flushed face, she let her mind wander back to the last time she and Ryder had been together in the barn on the Mercer farm.

Though inexperienced, she knew of no man who could make her tingle and burn in her most private places the way Ryder did. She recalled the way he touched her, as if he knew just how much pressure to apply to certain areas to bring her the most pleasure. His hands were firm but gentle, his mouth hot and wet. When he thrust into her she had welcomed him eagerly, her receptive body taking all of him and demanding more. There was nothing in her vocabulary to describe the climax she attained in his arms.

Immersed in her erotic daydreams, Hannah failed to notice the flurry of activity within the ranks of the patrol. It wasn't until Gilmore rode up and grasped her reins that she finally realized something out of the ordinary was happening. Then she looked into Gilmore's taut features and knew. Her gaze shifted upward, scanning the wooded ridges surrounding them.

Then she saw them. A large war party of braves crested the hill in front of them. Even from a distance she could see the garish stripes slashing their bodies. In growing horror, Hannah watched as they spread out in attack formation, their feathered lances raised high in the air. Their ringing war cries echoed across the prairie, freezing the blood in her veins. Her hat fluttered to the ground, and Hannah clung to the pummel as Gilmore raced her horse to a sheltered place behind a rock.

"Stay here!" he shouted as he wheeled his horse around to rejoin his men, "and pray they haven't seen you."

Hannah knew better than to believe she hadn't been seen; Indians had keen eyesight. Her one salvation lay in the possibility that Trent and his patrol would drive off the war party. But the way things were going, it didn't look as if that was going to happen.

The battle was fierce. Trent was in the midst of it, his skill doing him little good against the vast number of renegades. Before long Hannah knew it was a losing battle. One by one the soldiers fell beneath the fierce attack. The Indians were inspired by revenge. Their mistreatment by whites made them burn to avenge all the terrible wrongs done to them throughout the years. Hannah watched helplessly as the ranks of the patrol thinned drastically. She prayed she hadn't been seen and squeezed her eyes shut to blot out the bloody slaughter. All of the fallen men were good men, even Trent, in his own way, and she couldn't bear to see them cut down in the prime of life.

Had Hannah kept her eyes open she would have realized that she had, indeed, been noticed. One of the painted braves scooped up her bonnet and rode into the hills, circling behind her. She didn't know she was being stalked until she heard the horse crashing through the underbrush toward her. Just before she was snatched from the saddle, she opened her eyes and looked up into the grotesquely painted face and glittering black eyes of a fierce warrior. Suddenly it all became too much for her. The stress of the past few weeks, the hardships of traveling while pregnant, and now the Indian attack, all combined to force the breath from her lungs. With a gasping sigh, she fainted.

She did not feel the warrior scoop her from the saddle and set her before him on his pony, or see him place a hand upon her bright head, or notice that he did not rejoin his party, but grasped the reins of her horse and rode east toward the Badlands.

* * *

Hannah came awake slowly, aware of the bouncing rhythm of the horse beneath her. She felt warm flesh at her back and saw brown arms surrounding her, holding her in place in the saddle. A small cry escaped her lips when she looked up into the Indian's painted face. His body glistened with the sweat of battle, and she could feel his heart pounding against her back. The flesh on one of his arms had been mangled by a saber and his upper thigh had been pierced by a bullet and was bleeding.

Sheer black fright swept over Hannah. What did the Indian intend to do with her? Without Ryder to speak in her defense, would they torture and kill her? Or would they use her vilely and then kill her? Her body began to shake uncontrollably and she shielded her stomach with her hands. She wanted to live. She wanted Ryder's child to live.

"Do not be frightened, Little Sparrow. I will not harm the woman of my brother."

Shock shuddered through Hannah as she swiveled her head to take another look at the fierce warrior. Beneath the paint, beneath the blood and grime, the bold face looked vaguely familiar. It wasn't until the warrior smiled that she recognized him.

"Coyote!" She nearly wept with relief. "Thank God."

"Where is Wind Rider?" Coyote asked curiously. "Where is your husband? Why are you not with him?"

Hannah sighed hugely. "It's a long story, Coyote, and I'm not sure you will understand."

"When we reach the camp of Red Cloud I will listen and judge for myself."

"You're taking me to Red Cloud's camp? What about the soldiers? Some of them may be wounded. I must help them."

Coyote gave her a startled glance. "No one can help them now."

Hannah stared at him. When she realized he meant that they were all dead she sucked in her breath sharply. "Oh, God. So many lives lost." She began to weep softly, praying that her child would be spared these violent times.

"Do not cry, Little Sparrow. What we did is right. The blue coats attacked a small Sioux camp consisting mainly of women and children. The white eyes must be taught that they cannot kill our people without reprisal."

No matter what Coyote said to justify the killing, Hannah could not help feeling pity for those poor soldiers who had just lost their lives in battle. She continued to sob softly.

"You are weary, Little Sparrow. I will carry you upon my horse while you rest. Later, you can ride your own mount. It is a long way to the Badlands."

Ryder saw the vultures circling long before he came upon the battle scene. The bodies were several days old and the stench was overpowering. Dismounting, he studied the signs, examined the arrows protruding from the bodies, and determined that both Sioux and Cheyenne had participated in the attack. One by one, he turned the bodies over, recognizing no one until he stared down into the sightless eyes of Lieutenant Trent Gilmore. A cry of dismay escaped his lips; Hannah had been with Gilmore. Mindless with fear, he went from body to body, looking for a feminine form amid the sea of blue uniforms.

Relief shuddered through him when he realized that Hannah wasn't among the dead. His greatest fear now was that she had been taken captive by hostile Indians. He gazed toward the east, his face bleak. It was almost as if *Heammawihio* wished him to return to the People. Resolutely, Ryder turned his horse in an easterly direction and rode away. The Indians had taken the blue coats' horses and all their gear. Without a shovel, he could not bury the dead. The best he could hope for was that another patrol would pass this way soon and find the bodies. When the patrol failed to arrive at Fort Laramie Ryder knew a search party would be sent out to find them.

Hannah was pleased but embarrassed by the hearty welcome she received at Red Cloud's camp. Woman-Who-Waddles was ecstatic to see Hannah again, and within a few hours all the Indian words she had learned previously came back to her. She hadn't yet revealed to Coyote her reason for traveling without Ryder, for he had fallen ill with a fever due to his wounds. His wife, Summer Moon, was at his side constantly. Woman-Who-Waddles had explained that Summer Moon was the widow of White Feather, Wind Rider's adoptive father, and that Coyote had joined with her after her period of mourning and was raising White Feather's son.

Hannah thought Summer Moon looked awfully young to have been married to Ryder's father, but she said nothing; obviously, the young girl was now devoted to Coyote. Hannah was also surprised to learn that Spotted Doe had joined with Runs-Like-A-Deer and seemed quite content.

When she'd arrived at Red Cloud's camp Hannah had slept almost constantly for three days. Her total exhaustion did not escape Woman-Who-Waddles, who shrewdly guessed that Hannah was pregnant. When the old woman made mention of her condition Hannah could not deny that she carried Ryder's child. When she asked for Woman-Who-Waddles's confidence in the matter, the old woman agreed. Hannah also told Woman-Who-Waddles why she had been traveling with blue coats instead of with her husband.

Woman-Who-Waddles clucked sympathetically over Hannah's plight and assured her that Wind Rider would understand when he learned the truth.

"He cannot learn the truth if he cannot find me," Hannah lamented sadly. "If he is not here, then he is still with Zach and Abby at the farm. I must go to him."

"It is not safe to travel," Woman-Who-Waddles warned. "What if you had been captured by Crow warriors? Or someone who didn't know you? You must remain with us until Wind Rider comes for you."

"He will not come." Hannah's voice carried the heavy weight of rejection.

"He will come. You carry his child."

Hannah saw no reason to explain that Ryder didn't know about their child.

During the following days Hannah pitched in to help Woman-Who-Waddles with the mundane chores that were a part of every Indian woman's life. Summer Moon told her that Coyote was recovering and would soon be well. When she was allowed to speak with him she hoped the Cheyenne warrior would be as sympathetic as Woman-Who-Waddles had been.

Since her arrival at the Indian village Hannah had occupied the same tepee that she and Ryder had shared when they were together. She was grateful for the privacy and believed that as long as she and Ryder were considered husband and wife, no one would bother her.

Hannah had been in Red Cloud's camp nearly two weeks before she saw Cut Nose. He had been out raiding with a war party and had just returned, victorious and crowing about his brave feats. When he saw that Hannah was alone and learned of the circumstances under which she had returned to them he made sly plans to claim her for himself.

Hannah was more exhausted than usual that night. She ate dinner with Woman-Who-Waddles and retired to her own tepee shortly afterward. Because of the heat, which had built up inside the tepee during the hot summer day, she left the flap open. Stripping to her chemise, she lay down on her pallet and fell asleep almost immediately. The camp had just settled down for the night when a lone figure slipped into her tepee and carefully closed the flap behind him.

Cut Nose stood over Hannah, his body taut with the need to pound himself into this woman. If she resisted, he would have his way with her and then kill her so she could not accuse him afterward. Dropping to his knees, he stared into her sleeping face. Illuminated by the dappled moonlight finding its way through the smokehole at the top of the tepee, her hair reminded him of the shiny coat of a fox, neither red nor brown but a vibrant mixture of the two.

Hannah was sleeping so soundly, she did not feel Cut Nose lift a lock of hair that had fallen across her shoulder. Nor did she see the gleam in his dark eyes as he slid them along the length of her thinly clad body. The night was warm and she had kicked off the blanket. Her shift had ridden up, revealing a slim white leg and shapely thigh.

Cut Nose's mouth watered and his hardened staff prodded against the apron of his breechclout. Untying the thongs, he tore it off and flung it aside. Dropping to his knees, he placed a hand over Hannah's mouth.

Hannah awoke with a start, frightened and disoriented. She sensed immediately a menacing presence and opened her mouth to scream, but a pressure against her lips prevented the sound from escaping. Her eyes widened with terror when she saw the hulking form bending over her. Cut Nose! She could see the feral gleam in his black eyes and smell his arousal. Shaking her head from side to side, she attempted to convey her unwillingness, her revulsion. But Cut Nose had never cared what Hannah wanted or didn't want. He only knew what he wanted.

"Do not resist, Little Sparrow," he hissed. "Your man is not here and you left your tepee flap open in invitation. I will pleasure you in Wind Rider's absence. Perhaps you will find that you prefer me between your sweet thighs."

Hannah shook her head in vigorous denial, trying to bite his hand so she could scream. The pressure on her mouth increased and Hannah tasted blood as her teeth cut into the tender flesh of her lower lip.

Rising over her, Cut Nose spread her legs and flexed his hips, preparing to thrust into her, but at the last minute he hesitated. Despite his raging lust, the sounds of shouting and raised voices drifting to him on the night wind finally registered in his brain. At first he was too sexually aroused to pay them heed, but as the voices became louder and more excited, he could no longer ignore what was happening.

Cut Nose uttered a harsh, guttural cry, then leaned down and whispered something in Hannah's ear that stunned her. "Tell no one that I was here, Little Sparrow. If you do, I will kill Wind Rider." Then, abruptly, the pressure was gone from her mouth. Before Hannah had time to think about his threat and what it meant, Cut Nose pulled aside the tepee flap and slipped into the darkness.

Hannah lay in stunned silence, wondering what had happened to frighten him away and thanking God for the diversion. A shudder rippled through her as she recalled Cut Nose's words. How could he harm Wind Rider when he wasn't even here? Then she, too, became aware of the excited voices and shouts of the villagers. Though she had gained a good understanding of the Sioux language, she still couldn't make out what the excitement was about. Was the village under attack? She didn't think so, else she would hear battle sounds.

While she was still contemplating Cut Nose's strange behavior and hasty exit, Hannah became aware of the sudden silence that had fallen over the village. The abrupt lack of noise was more startling than the babbling she'd heard earlier. She sat up, intending to go out and learn for herself what was going on, but before she could rise the tent flap was thrust aside and someone entered.

Hannah drew in a ragged gasp, fearing that Cut Nose had returned. She let her breath out slowly when she realized that the figure was much too tall and muscular to be Cut Nose, who was short and squat. The man's face was hidden in darkness, but his torso and lower body were clearly outlined in the moonlight poking through the smokehole.

Her eyes traveled from his ankles upward, over muscular calves, corded thighs, and slim hips, pausing briefly where his breechclout provided scant protection for the bold thrust of his manhood. Her eyes lifted from that dangerous part of him to settle on the broad expanse of his chest. The moment she saw the fading bruises she knew.

Ryder! He had come for her.

Squatting down on his haunches, Ryder's silver gaze met the startling green of Hannah's eyes. Involuntarily, Hannah shuddered, chilled by the coldness she saw there. Errant moonbeams cast the planes of his face in demonic lines. Hannah wanted to fling herself into his arms, but fear held her back.

"Did you think I would not find you, Little Sparrow? I was on my way to Fort Laramie when I came across the dead blue coats. Finding you with the People is a gift I did not expect. I cannot say I am sorry that your lover has been slain."

Hannah went still. Was he still under the misconception that Trent was her lover? Would she never be free of his suspicions and accusations?

Chapter Twenty

Suddenly Hannah realized that Ryder couldn't have known about Trent unless he had seen him with his own eyes. Then she was aware that he was looking at her, *really* looking at her. His eyes were keen and sharply penetrating. Her breasts rose and fell with each breath as she realized what that meant.

"You can see! Oh, Ryder, you have your sight back!"

"Is that why you left me, Hannah, because I could not see? Did your lover offer more than I could give you? You almost had me convinced that you loved me. I decided not to go away for your sake, because you pleaded with me to stay with you."

"I do love you. Everything I've done has been for you."

Ryder laughed harshly, but there was no mirth visible in the silver depths of his eyes.

"You took a lover for my sake?" He grasped her shoulders, pulling her so close she could feel the heat of his body searing her through her thin chemise. His eyes glittered like shards of glass. "Explain yourself."

"Trent promised to arrange your release if I accompanied him to Fort Laramie. He-he wanted to marry me. I let him think I was agreeable. He even let me watch when you left the jail, to prove that he had kept his word. I was grateful that he had notified Zach so that he could accompany you home. I didn't know that you had regained your sight."

Ryder's mouth thinned in derision. "Good, but not good enough. Gilmore had nothing to do with my release. Zach persuaded the governor to grant me amnesty. It seems the governor was impressed by the fact that I had no Indian blood and had been a captive of the Cheyenne." He gave a derisive laugh. "Little did he know that I loved my Indian family, fully embraced the Indian way of life, and scorned white society. Until . . ." He was going to add, "Until I met you," but he thought better of it.

"Until what?" Hannah prompted.

"It no longer matters."

"I'm your wife, Ryder. You can tell me anything."

"My *faithless* wife." He hurled the words at her like stones. She flinched and shook her head in vigorous denial.

"There was never anything between me and Trent. I truly believed you had been freed because of his efforts. I did not know the governor had granted you amnesty. I can't believe Trent lied to me."

Ryder sent her a hard look. "Men will say anything to get what they want. But I do not believe for a minute that you really thought he could help me."

Hannah inhaled sharply. Was there nothing she could say to convince him? "What *do* you believe, Ryder?"

Ryder stared at her, his fingers pressing so hard into her shoulders, his knuckles turned white. "I believe you saw me in jail and realized I am not like other white men."

"That's the reason I love you, because you are different from most men. I did what I thought right to keep you safe."

Ryder sent her a skeptical glance. "Did you really believe Gilmore had the authority to free me? I did not think you were so naive. He lied, Hannah. He was using you for his own selfish purposes. Did you sleep with him? Did you allow him to make love to you? Did you take him into your body and cry out in the same way you did when I made love to you?"

She cringed inwardly. "No! I would never have allowed him to touch me. I never meant to honor my promise to Trent. How could I marry him when it's you I love? But I feared telling him the truth too soon. Then he might have wired Denver and had you taken into custody again. I went along with him and would have told him the truth once I knew you were safe. I feared for your life, Ryder. I had to do something, anything. You couldn't have taken many more beatings. The next one might have killed you."

"Why didn't you tell Zach the truth?"

"I couldn't; don't you understand? If you thought I was sacrificing myself for your sake, you would have come after me and endangered your life. I wanted you to think that I went willingly with Trent, that I truly intended to marry him. Later, after I told Trent the truth, I would have returned to Denver and confessed everything."

Ryder searched her face. "Do you expect me to believe that you went with Gilmore for my sake, that you didn't let him make love to you on those nights you were alone with him on the trail? Do you think me a fool?"

"No, no fool," Hannah said softly, "but the man I love." Suddenly a thought occurred to her. "How did you know where to find me?"

"I stumbled across the bodies of the patrol. Signs revealed that the patrol had been attacked by a war party of Sioux and Cheyenne. I recognized Gilmore among the dead and knew that you were traveling with him. When I searched through the bodies and did not find you I feared you had been captured by men who would take great pleasure in hurting you. Few of the People outside of Red Cloud's camp know who you are. In these times white women are fair game.

"Shortly afterward I crossed paths with the war party led by Runs-Like-A-Deer. I learned that Coyote had taken you to Red Cloud's camp. I was relieved to know you were safe."

Hannah stared into the heated depths of his eyes, stirred by the emotion she saw there. Relief? Was that all he felt? "Why did you come after me if you thought I'd betrayed you? Wouldn't it have been much easier just to forget me? Even in this dim light I can see that you're still not fully healed. Your ribs must pain you terribly. It amazes me that you can even sit your horse."

Ryder smiled thinly. Early in life he had learned that pain was a state of mind. He had tried to put himself above it. It was the only way he could bear the excruciating agony of endless days in the saddle on rugged mountain trails.

"At first I wanted to hear from your lips that you'd gone with Gilmore of your own free will. But as my anger grew I wanted to punish you. Now I know I wanted to find you for my own peace of mind. I fell in love with you, Little Sparrow. Against my will I learned to trust someone white. For the first time since I was a small child you made me feel that perhaps I actually did have a life with the white eyes. You have no idea how it feels to be a man without roots, to never know where you belong, to feel the confusion and utter desolation of trying to find kinship with people who think of you as a savage. With you by my side I thought it might be possible to bridge the gap between the society I grew up in and the one to which I belong. My sister made the adjustment, but it is easier for a woman. I am a warrior. I know no other life."

Hannah stared at him, stunned. It was the first time he had bared his soul to her. She knew now how deeply she had hurt him and wondered if she could ever repair the damage she had done. Would he ever trust her again? Would he ever trust anyone with white skin?

"I don't care what you are, Ryder. I love you. You are the man I want above all others; that's all I care about. At the time I had no way of knowing you had already been granted amnesty. If Trent knew, he did not tell me."

His grip on her shoulders tightened and she winced, willing to accept the pain if it helped convince him she loved him. Their bodies were almost touching now, breast to breast, thigh to thigh, their lips inches apart. She could feel the searing warmth of his breath fan her cheeks and she swayed against him. He groaned and dropped his hands to her buttocks, lifting her against him.

The air left his lungs in a harsh expulsion of breath. "I must be crazy to want you. You have destroyed my dream of finding a woman who would love me for what I am."

Hannah's mouth went dry. "Do you still want to punish me?"

"My mind wants to punish you, but my body wants to thrust inside you until no other man exists for you but me. It nearly destroyed me, thinking about that blue coat making love to you, filling you with his seed."

"I want no man's children but yours." Hannah nearly blurted out that she already carried Ryder's child but deliberately withheld the information. She wanted Ryder to believe her, to trust her, before telling him. Otherwise she'd never know if he wanted her for herself or for their child.

His hand came up and sifted through her hair, then tightened reflexively, grasping the lustrous strands and pulling her head back so he could stare down into her face. She saw uncertainty in his eyes, and something else, something deep and disturbing. What would it take to convince him that she loved him?

The hard lines of Ryder's face did not soften as he gazed into Hannah's eyes. Could he trust her? Did he want to fall under her spell again? It would be so easy . . . so damn easy. He didn't want to go through life never knowing who or what he was or where he belonged. He wanted to be loved. He wanted a home and children. Was that asking too much from life? Since he'd met Hannah his life had been nothing but confusion and upheaval. If he was smart, he'd steer clear of Denver and say to hell with his promise to become an Indian agent. If he was wise, he'd remain with the People and champion their cause, as he had done in the past. But since meeting Hannah things were no longer clear in his mind. His life and thinking had changed in subtle ways.

Ryder hesitated, then slowly slanted his mouth down over hers. His lips were hard, but under the hardness Hannah felt the underlying warmth and rejoiced. Parting her lips beneath his, she eagerly accepted the stabbing heat of his tongue as she slid her arms around his neck. She tasted the maleness of him, experienced the strength of his corded muscles as his arms tightened around her, and felt the hardness of his erection, pressing against her softness. When her hands slid over his ribs he groaned and flinched, unable to conceal his pain.

"Ryder, oh, Ryder. You're still not healed. You should allow yourself more time to rest before . . . before we . . ." Her words belied her feelings. This was what she had yearned for, dreamed about, wanted . . . needed.

"You have strong medicine, Little Sparrow," Ryder moaned against her mouth. He released her lips to press kisses along her jaw and down her throat to her shoulders. "Wanting you is a sickness inside me. Heal my pain with the heat of your sweet body." He shoved her chemise down her arms and filled his hands with her breasts, recalling how scrawny she had been the first time he'd seen her and thinking that she was now as voluptuous as any woman he'd ever seen. Her breasts were even larger than he remembered.

"You are more beautiful than I remember." His hands found her swollen nipples, lifting them to his mouth, tasting, licking, pebbling the crests to hard, throbbing peaks. When he suckled them like an infant the pleasure was so great, Hannah cried out.

His hands traveled the length of her body, stroking her buttocks, molding her tightly against him. When her chemise proved too much of a barrier between them he stripped it over her head and tossed it aside. Then he kissed her again. She kissed him back, probing his mouth with the hot tip of her tongue, her hands roaming freely over his chest, testing the sinew and muscles, needing desperately to feel the hot thrust of his body inside her. Growing bolder, her hands roamed lower, to the rawhide string of his breechclout. With a flick of the wrist she released it, glorying in the size and strength of his desire for her.

"Ryder."

At the sound of his name he laid her back against the sleeping mat, gazing deeply into her eyes. "Tomorrow I may regret this, but tonight you are mine."

"You will never regret loving me, Ryder. I won't let you. Love me now. I need to feel you inside me."

Ryder cupped her face in his hands, then kissed her long and deep. This time his lips were soft and supple, all traces of anger gone as he settled himself in the cradle of her thighs. Hannah spread her legs wider and reached for him, her fingers closing around his thick shaft. Undulating currents shuddered through Ryder, her touch more jolting than a bolt of lightning. When Hannah tried to guide him inside her he pushed her hands aside and seared her mouth with his kisses, leaving her weak and trembling.

"Ryder, please."

Breaking off the kiss, Ryder sent her a sardonic look and slid down the length of her body, spreading nipping kisses along the way. Hannah moaned and dug her fingers into his shoulders. His lips and hands left a trail of fire that led directly to the juncture of her thighs. He looked deeply into her eyes, then lowered his head, at the same time sliding his hands beneath her and raising her buttocks up to meet his mouth. Hannah screamed as the torrid heat of his mouth found that throbbing place between her legs that begged for his attention.

Rapture shuddered through her in bright waves as she laced her fingers in his hair and held him tightly against her. Her heart pounded wildly; his mouth tormented her, his tongue drove her into a frenzy as it probed and teased. She felt his fingers ease inside her and she jerked violently. Then she exploded, bucking, arching against him until the last tremor left her body. When she opened her eyes she found him staring at her.

"What-what is wrong?"

"You have put on weight. I do not remember your breasts so heavy." His gaze slid down to her stomach; then he placed a large hand over the slight rise that hadn't been there three months ago.

Hannah flushed. "I am eating well. Would you prefer me the way I looked when you first saw me?"

Ryder grinned. "You looked like a little brown sparrow. I thought you were quite plain. But even then my mind must have known you were the little bird from my vision. I prefer you plump, unless you get too fat."

Hannah opened her mouth, then clamped it shut. She was bound to get fatter, but only temporarily. Before she could form an answer that would satisfy Ryder, he placed his hands around her waist and lifted her astride him.

"Ride me, Little Sparrow. Take me into your body."

Taking him in her hand, she lifted slightly and then impaled herself. Ryder shuddered and sighed as he pushed deeply inside her. He felt her stretch and squeeze around him, felt the heat of her, and struggled to keep from climaxing.

"It's too soon, too soon," he groaned as he went still beneath her. "Bend down so I can taste you."

Hannah leaned over, offering him her breasts. Greedily he accepted her offering, suckling her until she could no longer remain motionless. When she began to move slowly up and down, Ryder encouraged her by grasping her buttocks and guiding her rhythm. Soon his rigid staff was thrusting in and out, plunging into her until the blood in her veins thickened and congealed. She was writhing against him, moaning, clutching his shoulders while he gripped her buttocks with almost bruising force, pounding into her again and again.

In minutes she was reaching for the stars, soaring to a greater height than she'd ever attained. Then she was careening into space, watching the stars explode as she dissolved into shimmering rapture.

Ryder pumped into her furiously, spilling his seed in a great gush of wet heat as he plunged over the edge.

Hannah felt like crying but resisted the urge. Surely Ryder couldn't make love to her with such fire if he didn't love her, could he? She prayed that she hadn't killed his love. Would he welcome their child? Unable to cope with the terrifying thoughts whirling inside her head, Hannah escaped into the sheltering arms of slumber.

"Wake up!" His voice was harsh, harsher than she'd ever heard it before.

His fierce growl nudged Hannah from a sound sleep. She opened her eyes slowly, turning her head to escape the slice of sunlight stabbing against her eyes. Was it morning already? It seemed only moments ago that Ryder was making love to her. After the first time he had awakened her twice more to make love to her. Gray dawn had arrived before he'd been sated.

"Ryder, what is . . ." Her words came to an abrupt halt as the mist before her eyes cleared and she saw Ryder glaring down at her, his silver eyes as cold as ice. Even his stance was menacing as he frowned down at her. What had she done now? Then she saw that he held something in his hands and her brow furrowed.

"What are you holding?"

Ryder extended a scrap of cloth, dangling it between his fingers as if it were a snake. "Do you recognize this?"

She saw now that it was a breechclout. Was there something about the breechclout that made Ryder angry? "It's a breechclout. Is there something special about it?"

"It is not mine. Who does it belong to? It was lying beside your sleeping mat. Which of my friends have you taken as a lover?"

"What!" Hannah couldn't believe her ears. "Damn you, Ryder, your false accusations are driving me mad. It was bad enough when you accused me of taking Trent as a lover, but this is ridiculous. You've no need to be jealous." Hannah hoped she sounded believable, for if she told Ryder that the breechclout belonged to Cut Nose, there would surely be a fight, and Ryder was still in no shape to defend himself properly.

Ryder's face darkened. "Jealous? I am not jealous." The words stuck in his throat. He knew he was acting like a fool, but he couldn't help it. The thought of another man touching Hannah made his blood boil. "I want to know who the breechclout belongs to and why it was lying beside your sleeping mat."

"I don't know. Why are you being so unreasonable?" She threw off the blanket that Ryder had placed over her during the night and rose to her feet. Her body was rosy and flushed from sleep and Ryder's mouth went dry.

"Is it unreasonable to want to know why an article of man's clothing was found in my wife's sleeping mat?"

Hannah licked her suddenly dry lips, recalling with vivid clarity how Cut Nose had whipped off the breechclout when he'd tried to rape her. "Perhaps it was left here by mistake."

"And perhaps it wasn't." Abruptly he whirled on his heel.

"Where are you going?"

"I can tell by your eyes that you're lying. I'm going to find out who left his breechclout in your lodge and why."

"Ryder, wait!"

Her plea had little impact upon Ryder as he threw aside the flap and stepped out into the sunshine. Something just didn't ring true. After last night he could no longer doubt that Hannah loved him. In his heart he'd known she'd told him the truth about Gilmore, and when he awakened this morning he had intended to tell her what was in his heart, to admit that he trusted her, that he realized she had sacrificed herself for him. Until he had found the breechclout. But he wasn't satisfied with her answers to his pointed questions, nor the evasive way her eyes refused to meet his.

Hannah dressed quickly. She had to head off
Ryder before he learned that Cut Nose had
barged into her lodge last night and tried to
assault her. She had no idea how Indians challenged one another, but she knew that Ryder
was still too weak to fight. Despite his passion
last night he had winced and groaned more
than once when she'd touched him in a tender spot.

Hannah hurried outside, thought briefly
about starting their morning meal, but decided
to go after Ryder instead. Eating could come
later. She found him talking to Coyote outside
his lodge. She was glad to see that Coyote had
recuperated from his wounds, though you'd
never know it from the way Summer Moon
hovered over him. Then, from the corner of
her eye, Hannah saw Cut Nose heading directly toward Ryder. She started running but was
too late to head him off. They arrived at the
same time.

"Welcome home, Wind Rider." Though Cut
Nose addressed Ryder, his eyes lingered on
Hannah. "I wondered when you were coming
to join your woman."

Ryder sent him a searching glance. "Did you
think I would not?"

Cut Nose shrugged. "It occurred to me. When
Little Sparrow left your lodge I assumed she
had divorced you."

Ryder's eyes narrowed. "You would have
liked that, Cut Nose. You wanted Little Sparrow once."

Cut Nose grinned. "She is very beautiful. Her hair is like fire and her skin is as white as snow." Suddenly his gaze rested on the breechclout Ryder held in his hands. "Ah, I see you found my breechclout." His dark eyes raked Hannah suggestively before turning back to Ryder. "I had forgotten where I left it."

Hannah groaned. Cut Nose was deliberately goading Ryder into a fight.

Ryder's face hardened. "Did you? I think you know exactly where you left it. I found it in my lodge, lying beside my woman's sleeping mat."

Cut Nose sent Hannah a sheepish look, as if to apologize for his oversight. He didn't fool Hannah for a minute. She knew he was waiting to see what she would say. When she remained silent, Ryder gave her a hard look, his hands clenched tightly at his sides.

"Perhaps I am mistaken and the breechclout isn't mine after all," Cut Nose offered. The sly gleam in his black eyes suggested otherwise.

"What were you doing in my woman's lodge?" Ryder demanded.

Cut Nose smiled at Hannah. "Ask your woman. I do not go where I am not invited."

Hannah gasped, left speechless by his damning words. Surely Ryder didn't believe Cut Nose, did he? Once he thought she'd taken Trent as a lover. Did he also think she'd invite Cut Nose into her bed? When Ryder turned to her, his face a glowering mask of fury, Hannah knew that was exactly what he thought. She was caught in the web of Cut Nose's lies.

Ryder could not adequately suppress the outrage he felt at Cut Nose's words. He did not believe for a minute that Hannah had invited the man into her bed. He'd been an utter fool to think she'd taken Gilmore as a lover. He knew better now. No woman could lie with such conviction and at the same time make love so sweetly. He should have accepted her explanation immediately and trusted her reasons for leaving Denver with Gilmore. She had done it for him, pure and simple, and he'd been a fool to believe otherwise. Jealousy did crazy things to a man, and no matter what their differences, he could no longer deny the love he felt for Hannah McLin.

Hannah realized Ryder was staring at her, his expression grim and unreadable, and she stepped toward him, holding her hands out in supplication. "Cut Nose lied, Ryder. He did come into my lodge last night, but it wasn't at my invitation. He fled in fear when you arrived in camp. If you hadn't come when you did, he would have . . ." She sent Ryder a bleak look. "He would have raped me."

"False words from a white whore," Cut Nose said with scathing contempt.

Summer Moon, who had been listening, paled, and Coyote, who was also present, waited to see what direction Ryder's wrath would take. He didn't have long to wait. With a feral cry, Ryder grabbed the knife at his waist and lunged at Cut Nose. Cut Nose, expecting retaliation, ducked and found his own knife. Crouching low, the two men circled one another, each looking for an opening to sink his blade into the other.

"Come on, white eyes," Cut Nose goaded. "You've convinced the People of your loyalty, but the color of your skin does not lie. I know what you are. A Sioux warrior is stronger and braver than any white man."

Ryder lunged at Cut Nose, and once again Cut Nose dodged. Then Cut Nose struck out. Ryder neatly sidestepped while Hannah looked on in horror. Then, suddenly, Coyote was standing between them, separating them by the length of his arms.

"Stop! You both know tribal law. There will be no killing. If Cut Nose tried to rape your woman, it is for the council to decide what will be done with him."

"Do you think the council will believe a white whore?" Cut Nose laughed. "This must be settled between me and Wind Rider."

"Cut Nose is right," Ryder concurred. "We will fight here and now. Innocence or guilt will be decided in hand-to-hand combat."

"No!" Hannah screamed. She feared that Ryder wasn't sufficiently healed from his ordeal with the militia to fight Cut Nose. She'd seen and felt firsthand the result of the beatings he had received. "Let the council decide. If it is the law, Ryder, you must abide by it."

"Your woman is wise," Coyote observed. "Listen to her. I will call for a council meeting so you and Cut Nose can resolve your difference. If punishment is due, let the council decide."

Ryder was coiled like a spring. How could he walk away from the man who had tried to rape his wife? Yet the People must obey tribal law. If he disobeyed that law, it would aid Cut Nose's claim that he wasn't Cheyenne. At this moment his instincts were white: He wanted to kill Cut Nose and to hell with the council and tribal law. But in the end good sense prevailed. That, and the stricken expression on Hannah's face, convinced him to heed Coyote's words. With great effort he forced his body to relax, and his grip on the knife eased.

"Call your council meeting, Coyote, but if Cut Nose goes unpunished I will kill him." He turned and walked away rapidly, grasping Hannah's hand and pulling her along with him. He didn't stop until he had pushed Hannah inside the lodge and entered behind her.

"You did the right thing, Ryder," Hannah said softly. "You are in no condition to engage in a fight with a man like Cut Nose."

"Why didn't you tell me?" Ryder growled. "You should have told me immediately that Cut Nose tried to rape you last night."

Hannah flushed and looked away. "Cut Nose threatened to kill you if I spoke of it."

"And you believed him? Don't you know by now I can take care of myself?"

"You aren't healed yet from the beatings you took in jail!" Hannah exclaimed. "I couldn't live without you. I love you, Ryder."

Ryder shook his head, marveling at the emotion that made people lose their sense, their will, even their pride. He wondered if he would survive it. He had been ready to kill for Hannah, and he still would if anyone dared to touch her again. "I have known a sister's love, parental love, but never have I known a woman's love. When I left the Cheyenne nation to fight with the Sioux I assumed I wouldn't live long enough to find a woman to love, let alone take a wife. I envied the love Tears Like Rain felt for Zach, for I knew I would never attain that kind of happiness. And now . . ."

"And now?" Hannah prompted. She held her breath, waiting for the words she'd waited so long to hear.

"And now I have a woman to love."

"Are you saying you love me, Ryder?"

Not one for flowery words, Ryder said, "Is that not what I just said? Did I not follow you when you left me? Did I not leave the People for your sake?"

Hannah nodded solemnly, her gaze intent upon his face. And still she waited for something more. If he couldn't say the words, how could she believe he meant them?

Ryder sighed, then flashed her a disarming smile, aware of what she wanted. "I love you, Little Sparrow. I have always loved you. Even when you looked like a scrawny bundle of rags with matted hair and dirty face. With your help maybe I can learn to trust men with white skins and live with them in peace."

410

"Oh, Ryder!" She threw her arms around his neck, raining kisses on his face, his chin, his nose, wherever her lips could reach. "I've always loved you, too. And if you want to live in Red Cloud's camp, I won't complain. As long as we're together, I'll be happy."

Ryder hugged her close, realizing how precious she had become to him and amazed that he would be so willing to sacrifice a way of life he was comfortable with for her.

"I must find my way in the white world, Hannah. No matter how much I admire the Indians, no matter how deeply I feel about the injustice done to them, I can no longer live with them. Your life is too precious to me to place it at risk. Life in the Badlands is too uncertain. The whites are too plentiful. One day all Indians will be forced to live on reservations, and that is not what I want for you.

"I will still help my people. But I will help them in ways that don't involve killing. The governor granted me amnesty, but I have given something in return. I have agreed to act as Indian agent to the Sioux and Cheyenne. I will deal honestly and fairly with them. They will have food and blankets to see them through the winter, and a champion to argue their cause."

Hannah's eyes sparkled brightly. "Your child will be proud of you."

Chapter Twenty-one

Ryder stared at Hannah for so long, she felt a slow heat creep up her neck. Had she misjudged Ryder? Didn't he want their child? It was a subject they hadn't previously discussed.

"You're carrying my child?" His voice was thick with emotion. His next words set her back on her heels. "You went with Gilmore knowing you carried my baby in your belly?"

Hannah's mouth went dry. "I never would have endangered your child, Ryder. I never would have allowed Trent to touch me. Don't you understand? I did it for your sake. How many times do I have to repeat it before you believe me?"

"I do believe you, Little Sparrow. I was a jealous fool for not realizing you'd never go off with Gilmore without a good reason. I shudder to think what might have happened to you and my child."

"Trent had many faults, but I'm convinced he would never have hurt me. He would have been angry, but I truly believe he cared for me in his own way. I never wished for his death, or the death of any of those men escorting us to Fort Laramie. Will this senseless slaughter never end?"

She began to sob softly, and Ryder gathered her into his arms, content for the time being to have her resting against his heart. "I do not know how all this will end, but I intend to use my authority as Indian agent to help the People. We will leave Red Cloud's camp soon. The governor is waiting for me to take up my new position. I hope you won't mind living with Abby and Zach until our own home can be built."

"I won't mind as long as we're together."

Ryder's hand strayed down to her stomach, coming to rest on the barely discernible rise. A look of pure delight spread across his features. "I never expected this. Not long ago I was certain I would die fighting white eyes. Then I met you and began to dream of a different life, one that included a wife and children. Not just any wife, but one with bright hair and green eyes. Now, through you, my personal talisman, my dreams have become reality. I love you, Hannah, and I'll love our child."

Ryder's words forced the tenseness from her body. Hannah hadn't realized just how tightly she had been coiled while awaiting Ryder's reaction to her pregnancy. Finally she was able to relax. Ryder wanted the baby! He loved her. Nothing else mattered.

He kissed her then, with so much tenderness she wanted to weep with joy. He kissed her so long and so thoroughly, tasting her with such obvious relish, that the blood flowed thick and heated through her veins. When he broke off the kiss and set her aside a soft cry of protest slipped past her lips.

"I want to make love to you, my love, but I cannot until this thing between me and Cut Nose is settled. By now Coyote has summoned the council members and I must go."

"I don't like this, Ryder. Cut Nose is cunning. He will lie about his reason for entering my lodge. He will say that I invited him. You looked so fierce when he hinted that I welcomed him into my lodge that I-I feared you would believe him."

"Never! I know you too well. By that time I had begun to realize how great a fool I was for not believing you about Gilmore. What made me angry was the fact that Cut Nose dared to suggest that you invited him to share your mat. No one in the council will believe him."

"Go then," Hannah said. Her reluctant sigh hinted at just how loathe she was to part from him. "I will pray for the council to make the right decision."

Hannah was cooking supper over a fire outside the lodge when Ryder returned. His expression was grim, but she saw no signs of aggravation or displeasure. Without a word he sat down beside the fire, and Hannah handed him a bowl of venison stew that had been simmering on the fire. He must have been starved for he was halfway through the bowl before he spoke.

"Cut Nose has been banished from the tribe. He will never bother you again."

Hannah went still. "The council ruled against him? Even though he is Indian and you are white?"

"My skin is white, but these are my people, Hannah, just as they are Cut Nose's people. They listened to us equally, then based their judgment on our testimony and that of Coyote, who had witnessed the confrontation between you and Cut Nose this morning."

Hannah sank to her knees beside Ryder. "Cut Nose must have been angry."

Ryder chewed thoughtfully. "Very angry. He gathered his belongings and left immediately. When he rode away the People turned their backs on him. Even his parents. Rape is a serious crime among the Sioux and the Cheyenne."

"What will he do now?"

Ryder swallowed the last morsel of stew. "Perhaps join a band of renegades. It is unlikely he will be welcomed into another tribe. Word travels fast from tribe to tribe, and soon all will know of his banishment."

"I wish it didn't have to be like this," Hannah said sincerely. "There was no trouble until you brought me to Red Cloud's camp."

"Do not blame yourself, Hannah. Cut Nose never liked the idea of my white skin. He would have found another excuse to make trouble for me."

Hannah digested that bit of information. "Then we are free to leave?"

"I have already spoken to Red Cloud. He agrees that I can do much good for the People in my capacity as Indian agent. If I can make a substantial difference in this way, then I will try my best to adjust to the white world." Pulling her close, he planted a kiss on her forehead. "Of course we will have to marry again in order to satisfy white society. I want no doubt concerning the legitimacy of my child."

Hannah grinned happily. "I couldn't feel any more married than I do now, but I'll be most happy to repeat our vows before a priest. It would please my family to know that we are married in the eyes of the church."

"I know nothing of such things, but I'm sure you will explain it to me. Let us seek our sleeping mat. It is a tiring journey to Denver." The twinkle in his silver eyes suggested that he had more on his mind than sleep. He rose and pulled her to her feet. Then he picked her up and carried her inside the lodge. He laid her on the sleeping mat and stretched out beside her. When he would have kissed her Hannah placed a restraining hand on his chest.

"Ryder, wait. There is something I wish to discuss with you."

"You want to talk?" His strained voice told her talk was the last thing he wanted.

"Yes. It's about Woman-Who-Waddles. I want to take her with us. She has no living relatives and has to rely on the charity of others for her food and sustenance. I don't think Abby will object, and she will be a great help to me when the baby comes."

Ryder was stunned that Hannah cared enough about the old woman's welfare to want to bring her to live with them. "What does Woman-Who-Waddles say about this? Does she wish to leave the People?"

"Woman-Who-Waddles lost her husband, her son, and her only daughter, and she is alone. I've come to care a great deal about her and am concerned about her welfare. We have spoken and she is agreeable. She is healthy and not as old as she looks, so I am certain she is capable of riding the distance to Denver. She looks forward with relish to the day our baby is born."

"It will be as you wish. After our house is built I am certain you will be happy to have an extra pair of hands to help."

"Thank you, Ryder," Hannah said, pulling his head down so she could reach his lips. He kissed her slowly, thoroughly, with all the passion rampant in his rapidly beating heart.

His tongue searched out the sweetness of her mouth as his hands undressed her. Then the moist heat of his kisses followed the path of his hands, over her breasts, her stomach, her thighs, and the succulent flesh between. Within minutes Hannah's body took on the rosy glow of arousal, but this time she wasn't content to lie back and let Ryder have his way. He frowned when she pushed him down and rose slightly above him so she could look down into the shimmering depths of his eyes.

"I want to do the same things to you that you do to me," she whispered shyly, though shyness was the least of what she was feeling.

Ryder grinned, lying back so she could have her way. And she did, tasting him thoroughly and finding him delicious. Her small tongue examined his flat male nipples and her teeth nipped a trail of fire along his stomach and thighs. When the exquisite torture rendered him nearly senseless, she found him with her mouth and tasted his male essence. Ryder cried out, jerking violently beneath the searing heat of her mouth. After several agonizing minutes he reared up and shoved her down on her back. Then he paid her back in kind. When she was nearly mindless with rapture, he reared back and plunged into her.

A slice of moonlight slanting through the open smokehole was the sole witness to the writhing bodies, the whispered words of passion, and the sharp, guttural cries of pleasure. And as the night wore on, the moonlight paled in comparison to the luminous glow of love that filled the lodge.

*   *   *

Hannah shifted uncomfortably in the saddle, aware that her pregnancy was making travel more difficult than normal. The day was scorching hot and a searing wind blew down from the Black Hills. Solicitous of her health, Ryder made certain they rested frequently during their journey, stopping wherever they found shade and water. Woman-Who-Waddles traveled with them, apparently happy to be of use to someone and no longer a burden to the People.

At night they usually sought shelter by water, allowing Hannah the opportunity to bathe away the dirt and grime accumulated during the day. They were near the Colorado border and camped on a branch of the Platte River when Hannah set off by herself to walk the short distance to the river, eager for a bath. Woman-Who-Waddles was engaged in building a fire and Ryder had gone off to hunt game for their supper. It was growing dark, but Hannah felt no urgency to hurry.

They had experienced no trouble thus far in their journey, and she had forgotten that Ryder had cautioned her not to stray too far from their camp. He had seemed more watchful than usual the last two days, but his demeanor indicated nothing out of the ordinary. Besides, she could see the campsite from the river, and what could happen with Ryder nearby?

Stripping to her shift, Hannah stepped into the water. It was dark and muddy but nevertheless refreshing after a day in the saddle. The hot, dry summer sun and lack of rain had literally dried up the river in many places, and Hannah was pleased to note that at the center of the river the water was waist deep. She splashed happily, unaware of a pair of dark eyes greedily devouring her. It wasn't until she was ready to leave the water that she sensed a threatening presence. She could feel the hair rising at the back of her neck and whirled about to scan the dark shoreline.

She saw nothing, chiding herself for being fanciful. Then, abruptly, she recalled Ryder's words when they had made camp tonight, telling her to remain close to their campsite, that he would hunt nearby in case there was trouble. She even recalled how he had scouted ahead several times during the day and picked their campsite with special care. She was so anxious to bathe, she had foolishly disregarded his orders and wandered off by herself. The last remnants of daylight slid into darkness as she waded to shore.

Hannah did not see the hand that reached from behind her to cover her mouth, or the arm that wrapped around her waist to drag her behind a nearby bush. But she felt the strength and heat of the massive body as she was pulled toward a waiting horse. When the hand was taken from her mouth she did not have time to cry out before a fist came flying out of the darkness at her jaw. With a moan of pain, she spiraled downward into a deep, dark void.

Ryder returned to camp with a plump rabbit

he had shot with an arrow. He'd deliberately refrained from using his rifle for fear of inviting unwanted attention. For the past two days he'd been aware that they were being followed, but he'd kept the news from Hannah so as not to distress her. If they were being trailed, it wasn't by a large war party; that much he was sure of. In fact, he was convinced that only one or two men were keeping a close watch on their progress. Whoever it was was smart, he'd give them that much. He'd caught no more than a fleeting glimpse of a rider. But at least he'd had the foresight to warn Hannah to stay close to camp, he thought as he stepped into the circle of light provided by the fire Woman-Who-Waddles had kindled.

Ryder noticed Hannah's absence immediately. He felt a spurt of fear.

"Where is Hannah?"

"She went to bathe," Woman-Who-Waddles told him.

He looked toward the river where a dark ribbon of water was barely visible in the evening gloom. "How long ago did she leave?"

Woman-Who-Waddles frowned and cocked an eye at the rising moon. "The moon had not yet risen when she left. I heard her splashing in the water just moments ago."

Ryder picked up his gun. "Put the rabbit in the pot to cook. I will go after her. She should not have gone off on her own. Perhaps I did not stress strongly enough the danger that exists in this territory."

Woman-Who-Waddles stared at him, suddenly aware that Ryder was more worried than the situation seemed to warrant. "Are we in danger?"

"I will explain later," Ryder called over his shoulder as he sprinted toward the river.

Ryder moaned in dismay when his search failed to locate Hannah. He called her name several times but received no answer. Sweat broke out on his forehead and his gut clenched painfully. Examining the shore, he found moccasin prints in the soft mud. Dropping to his knees, he studied the signs, cringing inwardly when he noted that a struggle had ensued and someone had been dragged along the shore. The prints led to a bush, and Ryder quickly followed them. Whoever had been there was gone. Pursuing a trail of trampled grass and brush, Ryder came to a place where a horse had been tethered. The horse's trail led north.

Ryder realized immediately that Hannah had been taken prisoner by an Indian. Obviously, only one man had participated in the kidnapping; he saw nothing to indicate that others were nearby. Then a sudden, wrenching thought came to him.

Cut Nose! Cut Nose had taken Hannah!

Supported by muscular brown arms, Hannah came awake slowly. Still groggy from the vicious blow to her jaw, she shook her head to clear the cobwebs from her brain. She had no idea how long she'd been unconscious, but the sky had turned from black to mauve, indicating that many hours had passed since she'd gone to bathe in the river. Her jaw felt as if it was on fire, and when she tried to move pain shot up her cheekbone to her head. She moaned, and the arm holding her tightened.

"I did not think I hit you so hard, Little Sparrow."

That voice! Cut Nose. She smelled his musky scent and bitter gall rose up in her throat. "Why have you done this?" Hannah cried out desperately. "What do you hope to gain?"

"Wind Rider will come for you. He will challenge me and we will fight as we should have before Coyote interfered. I will kill him and take you for my woman. Then I will slake my lust on your white body and hear you cry out my name when I bring you to pleasure. Then we will see who is the better man."

Hannah's head spun with the implication of Cut Nose's words. Was Ryder strong enough to fight Cut Nose and win? Was there nothing she could do to stop them from killing one another? Briefly she considered telling Cut Nose that she carried Ryder's child, but quickly discarded the notion. That knowledge might anger Cut Nose to the point of harming her or the child she carried.

"Where are you taking me?"

"Not far. I wish to settle this matter between us soon so I can plant my seed inside your body."

"You cannot win against Ryder."

"I have already won. I have you, don't I?"

"Not for long," Hannah goaded. "Only a cowardly dog would act as you have, stealing me away in the dark of night."

Cut Nose's lips curled in resentment. Until Hannah came into their midst he had never committed a dishonorable deed. It was her fault, he reflected, blaming Hannah for inciting his lust to the point of making him lose control of his senses. Being banished from the tribe had been so humiliating, he'd vowed to punish those responsible. He had watched the camp until Hannah and Ryder left and had followed stealthily, intending to seek vengeance in his own way in his own good time. Finding Hannah alone had been a stroke of luck he hadn't anticipated.

Being called a cowardly dog sent him into a rage, and he struck Hannah viciously. Once again Hannah went spinning into blessed oblivion, unaware that Cut Nose had deliberately slowed his horse and that the trail he left could have been followed by a child.

Ryder rode like the wind, his sturdy Indian pony obedient to the slightest pressure of his knees and hands. With the onset of daylight it was a simple task to follow the trail left by Cut Nose. It was almost as if Cut Nose wanted to be found. Ryder's fists clenched on the reins and he urged his horse to a faster gait. If Cut Nose hurt Hannah, he'd tear him apart with his bare hands.

Ryder plunged without hesitation into the narrow passage between two flat bluffs, aware that this was the spot Cut Nose had chosen for their confrontation. He had stripped down to breechclout and moccasins, to be unhampered by clothing during the battle. The vivid discoloration across his ribs bore mute testimony to the beatings he had endured just a short time ago. But he ignored his pain, focusing instead on Hannah and his unborn child.

Halfway through the narrow passage, Ryder halted and scanned the collection of rocks and boulders he considered large enough to offer protection to Cut Nose and Hannah. He realized he provided a large target for Cut Nose, but his gut told him that Cut Nose would challenge him openly rather than use cowardly methods of attack. And so he stood fully exposed and waited.

Hannah groaned as pain exploded in her brain. She had no idea where she was, but the hard ground beneath her and the relentless sun in her eyes told her that she was lying on her back, shielded from view by a large boulder and helplessly tied hand and foot.

"If you cry out, I will stuff my breechclout in your mouth," Cut Nose threatened her ominously.

Hannah realized immediately that she was still Cut Nose's prisoner. "Where are we?"

"At a place I know well. Wind Rider approaches. Soon you will be mine, and to celebrate my victory I will take you here on the ground while vultures pick his bones."

Hannah paled. "Ryder is here?"

As if in answer to her question, a deep voice boomed out. "Cut Nose. I am here. Show yourself. If you release my woman without harming her, I will spare your life."

"Ryder!" Hannah's shrill cry sounded like sweet music to Ryder's ears.

"Little Sparrow! Be brave. You will soon be free."

"Call out again and I will silence you," Cut Nose hissed. He glared at her, promising swift retribution if she disobeyed.

"What is it you want of me?" Ryder inquired. He knew from the direction of their voices that Cut Nose and Hannah were sheltered behind a large boulder about fifty yards ahead and to the left.

"We will settle this matter between us the Indian way. We will fight to the death with knives. The woman will be the prize. Once I have Little Sparrow impaled upon my mighty sword she will forget all about you."

Red dots of rage exploded in Ryder's brain. The thought of Hannah spread beneath Cut Nose's body, submitting to his crude fumbling, left him with a sick feeling in the pit of his stomach. He would never allow it to happen. "I accept your challenge, Cut Nose. Show yourself."

Hannah watched in trepidation as Cut Nose stepped out from behind the boulder. Struggling to her knees, she propped herself against the boulder and peered around the edge. The breath caught in her throat when she saw Ryder dismount and walk slowly toward Cut Nose. She saw that his rifle was still in the saddle boot and offered a fervent prayer that Cut Nose wouldn't seize the opportunity to shoot Ryder. He didn't. The Sioux warrior waited stoically for Ryder. When they faced one another Cut Nose whipped his knife from its sheath and crouched low.

Ryder reacted swiftly, whipping out his own knife and circling Cut Nose warily.

"You are a fool if you think you can win." Cut Nose laughed harshly. The sound sent a shiver up Hannah's spine.

"You are a fool if you think I will lose," Ryder shot back.

Cut Nose lunged. Ryder stepped back and sucked in his breath. The blade missed him by a scant inch.

Hannah nearly cried out when she saw how close Cut Nose had come to disemboweling Ryder, but she fought for control. The last thing Ryder needed was distraction.

Ryder struck back, but Cut Nose neatly side-stepped. Then, unexpectedly, Cut Nose kicked out with his foot, hitting Ryder squarely in the ribs. Ryder cried out and staggered, pain searing through him like a burning brand. But when he saw Cut Nose moving in for the kill he rallied and easily deflected the thrust. Once again they circled one another, each looking for an opening to bring home the victory. Ryder was still hurting from the vicious kick to his ribs, but it had served to make him more wary of Cut Nose's sly tricks.

"Come on, white eyes," Cut Nose goaded as he jabbed unsuccessfully at Ryder's gut. "I cannot wait to kill you. I have already had your woman and long for another taste of her white flesh."

Ryder knew he was being goaded and almost succumbed to his rage. It took every bit of his self-control not to lose his head, for he knew it was exactly what Cut Nose wanted. An enraged man was an uncautious one, prone to errors, and Ryder couldn't afford to make mistakes. The life of Hannah and his child were at stake. He hoped Cut Nose's claim wasn't true, but if he had raped Hannah he'd make sure the villain suffered a painful death.

Somehow Hannah managed to roll from behind the boulder and sit up, where she could see more clearly. Both men were bleeding from several small cuts, none of them serious. But the fight was becoming more intense, more fiercely combative as both men lashed out viciously at one another. It worried her that Ryder seemed to be favoring his right side, where the bruises on his ribs were the most prominent. Cut Nose also became aware of Ryder's weakness and took advantage of it by striking most often at the injured ribs. That was when Hannah's Irish temper drove her over the edge. It was up to her to help the man she loved.

Her wrists were tied behind her but with great effort she maneuvered around, bringing her legs through the loop of her arms until her arms were stretched in front of her. Then she struggled with the rope binding her ankles until the knots came free. But that still left her wrists tightly bound together. Searching frantically for a way to free herself, Hannah spied a jagged rock lying on the ground near the boulder. Stretching her wrists over the jagged edge of the rock, she sawed them back and forth, ignoring the pain. But after several frustrating minutes she realized that her efforts were getting her nowhere. The tough rawhide rope refused to part.

Glancing toward the combatants, Hannah could see that Ryder was tiring. Cut Nose wasn't in any better shape. Both were bleeding from numerous wounds, both still determined to win. She cried out in dismay when Ryder stepped backward to escape a brutal frontal attack and stumbled into a gopher hole. Taking advantage of Ryder's momentary confusion, Cut Nose lunged, sending Ryder crashing to the dusty ground. Before Ryder could gain his feet, Cut Nose fell on top of him, the point of his knife pressed to Ryder's throat.

Hannah did not waste precious time bemoaning Ryder's wretched bad luck; she acted instead. Grasping the jagged rock in her bound hands, she levered herself to her feet. Despite her numb legs, she raced toward Ryder, reaching him just as Cut Nose's blade pierced the flesh of Ryder's neck. A thin line of blood trickled down his chest.

"Noooo!" Hannah's anguished cry momentarily distracted Cut Nose as he poised himself for a fatal thrust. Shock registered on his face when he saw Hannah looming over him, preparing to crush his skull with a jagged rock.

The brief lapse was all Ryder needed to marshal his strength and toss Cut Nose backward off of him. Cut Nose flew through the air and landed on his stomach. He grunted and went still.

"Get out of the way, Hannah!" Ryder cried as he flung himself atop Cut Nose. He knew Cut Nose was sly and often resorted to trickery. Hannah stepped back, still ready to come to Ryder's defense.

When nothing happened Ryder grasped Cut Nose by the hair and pulled his head back. When he received no response he levered himself off Cut Nose and turned him over.

"Be careful," Hannah called out as Ryder bent over the wily Indian. "I don't trust him."

"He's dead." Ryder's voice was devoid of emotion. "He fell on his knife. It pierced his heart and he died instantly."

The rock Hannah still held in her hands hit the ground with a thud. "Thank God." It wasn't so much that she wished for a man's death but that she wanted Ryder alive.

Ryder heard the exhaustion in her voice, sensed her profound relief, and went to her immediately. "Are you all right, Little Sparrow?

Did Cut Nose harm you?" His hand splayed across her stomach. "Is our child safe?"

Hannah allowed Ryder to support her as she collapsed against him, dragging in long steadying draughts of air. "I am tired but otherwise unharmed, and our child rests easily beneath my heart. Your son or daughter is strong, Ryder."

"No, Hannah, you're the strong one. Here, hold out your hands so I can untie them." When he saw the bruises on Hannah's wrists and face he was so enraged he was sorry he hadn't killed Cut Nose with his own hands.

"I was so frightened for you," she breathed shakily.

"Even though you were bound hand and foot you managed to come to my aid. If you hadn't distracted Cut Nose, he would have slain me. I owe you my life."

"You've saved my life many times," Hannah returned softly. "It is only right that I should save yours."

He kissed her then, moving his mouth over hers in a long, slow affirmation of love. Hannah felt his love flowing over her, felt his strength absorbing her, and knew a peace she'd never expected in this life. When he broke off the kiss he lifted her into his arms and carried her to his pony.

"It is time to go home, my love. Woman-Who-Waddles is waiting for us at our last campsite."

"Home," Hannah sighed wistfully. "It's been

so long since I've had a real home."

"It may be a while before our own home is built, but Abby and Zach's home will be ours while they are visiting Boston. Zach wants Abby to meet his family. I've promised to keep an eye on the farm until their return next year."

"We'll be a real family," Hannah said happily, recalling with fondness the large family she had left behind in Ireland.

Ryder's face assumed a faraway look. "A real family," he repeated. "The only thing that would make me happier is to learn that my sister Sierra is alive and well. I often think of her, you know. She was the sweetest little thing, with hair the rich color of Mother Earth and eyes as silver as mine and Abby's. I pray that she is happy wherever she is."

Suddenly his reminiscence came to an end and he smiled that heartstopping smile Hannah loved so well. "I may never know Sierra's fate, but as long as I have you, I am content. You're everything to me, Hannah. Will you be my wife?"

"I am already your wife, Ryder, and I love you beyond reason. Even if you don't find Sierra, she will live in your heart. Let's go home. I need you to make love to me."

Suddenly his face grew reflective. "The Great Spirit always meant for us to be together. That is why he placed the small bird on my shoulder in my vision. You are truly my personal talisman. Your medicine was strong enough to give my life meaning. If not for you, I would have walked the Spirit Path. I shall always need you. Forever," he added on a sigh of happiness.

"Forever," Hannah repeated, melting into his arms.

Epilogue

May 1866

As far as houses went, this one wasn't large, but Hannah thought it quite grand. Facing the river and sheltered from winter winds by a bluff, the house, built entirely of logs, was finally ready for occupancy. And just in time, too. Abby and Zach were due to return from Boston this month.

After she and Ryder had returned from Red Cloud's camp they had found a church and a priest in Denver and had their marriage blessed. Both Abby and Zach had witnessed the brief ceremony before they left for the East with their son. During the exceptionally cold fall Ryder had argued and fought for adequate quantities of food and warm blankets for the

Indians who had moved to reservations for the winter.

When Ryder heard that the army was going ahead with the building of Fort Phil Kearney on a branch of the Powder River he feared more bloodshed and worked tirelessly to see that peaceful Indians were not cheated by unscrupulous agents. By careful planning he'd managed to be home when their daughter Lacy was born. The tiny bundle of joy had come into the world during a fierce snowstorm, squalling like a banshee. Already she had her father wound around her little finger.

Hannah smiled in pleasure at the wildflowers blooming on the hillside outside the window. In her estimation the homesite Zach had given them as a wedding gift was the choicest spot in the entire valley. They owed a lot to Abby and Zach, a debt that Ryder had repaid by keeping watch on the farm during their absence. Fortunately, Zach had hired an excellent overseer who needed little supervision.

"Daydreaming, Little Sparrow?"

Hannah turned and grinned at Ryder. After all this time he still preferred the Indian name he had given her so long ago. There were even times when she called him Wind Rider.

"I was just thinking how very fortunate I am to have found you."

"If I recall correctly, I was the one who found you. At the time I thought you quite plain. If I hadn't been in pain, I would have seen your beauty through all that dirt and grime. You

436

have to admit, though, that you were a skinny little thing, all bones and angles."

"And you were an arrogant bully who wanted to make me his slave."

"Instead you made me yours."

He moved up behind her, wrapping his arms around her waist.

"Having a wife and family is something I never expected to experience. You've changed the course of my entire life, Hannah. Never in my wildest dreams did I imagine I'd be living and working with white eyes."

Hannah turned in his arms, gazing intently into the silver depths of his eyes. "Are you sorry?"

Sliding her arms about his neck, she pulled his head down and stood on tiptoe so she could reach his lips. The attraction she felt for this special man would never wane. He was her life, her love, her very existence. And part of that attraction was what he was. It didn't matter whether he considered himself Indian or white, he was uniquely himself, a product of two cultures.

Ryder needed no special invitation to taste his wife's sweetness as he covered her lips with his in a lingering kiss that expressed all the words he was too tongue-tied to say.

"Sorry that I have you and a wonderful daughter?" he answered after he broke off the kiss. "Never! What bothers me is that I'm still having difficulty discovering myself. It's impossible not to hate whites after being raised by Indians and experiencing firsthand the injustices done to them. I loved White Feather and Gray Dove. I wanted no other life until you came along. My greatest fear is that you will regret having married me."

"Do I act like I'm sorry?" Hannah asked impudently as she rubbed herself against him in a most suggestive manner.

"No, thank God. Is Lacy sleeping?" He looked pointedly toward their bedroom. He never knowingly passed up an opportunity to make love to his wife.

Hannah laughed. "Unfortunately, the little imp will be wanting her dinner soon."

Ryder sighed in pained resignation. "Well, if there's no hope of having you to myself for a little while, I might as well tell you my news."

"News?" She grew excited. "You've learned something about Sierra!" Hannah was aware that Ryder and Abby had hired a detective to find their younger sister.

"We've learned the name of the family who picked up Sierra after our wagon was attacked by Crow raiders. Holly and Lester Alden were passing by on their way to California. They stayed in Denver only a short time while they made their report to the authorities before traveling on."

"California; that's a very large territory."

Undaunted, Ryder nodded. "I'm convinced we'll find each other one day. Meanwhile, how long do you think we'd have before our daughter demands her dinner? An hour perhaps?"

The gleam in his eyes hinted at a languorous hour of splendid pleasure, lying in his arms, sharing his passion.

"At least an hour," Hannah replied with a twinkle. He had already ignited a flame within her that would need at least that long to burn itself out.

Having overheard the exchange between Hannah and Ryder, Woman-Who-Waddles, who was bringing Lacy to her mother to be fed, turned and walked back into the kitchen, chuckling to herself.

"Come, little one, I will give you a sugar teat to satisfy your hunger while your parents satisfy theirs."

Gurgling happily, the dimpled darling seemed quite unperturbed, accustomed by now to her thoroughly unconventional parents.

Author's Note

Wind Rider is the second book of my *Trails West* trilogy. *Tears Like Rain* was the first. I hope you enjoyed both of them. I tried to keep the events in order chronologically, but you may find I have changed some of the dates of specific battles to fit the story.

Sierra is the title I've given the third book of the trilogy. The series concludes with the story of the youngest sister, Sierra, and the trials and tribulations she encounters as she searches for her siblings. Besides the incorrigible, spoiled darling of rich adoptive parents, you will also meet Ramsey Hunter, the reluctant hero who accompanies Sierra on her journey from California to Colorado. Handsome and outrageously arrogant, Ram Hunter is a man with a secret past. I hope you enjoy my fast-paced, rip-roaring tales of the Old West.

I enjoy hearing from readers. For a news-letter and autographed bookmark, write to me in care of my publisher at the address printed in the front of this book. For a prompt reply please include a long, self-addressed stamped envelope.

All My Romantic Best,
Connie Mason

Connie Mason
Bestselling Author of *A Promise Of Thunder*

"Connie Mason tempts her readers with thrilling action and sizzling sensuality!"

—*Romantic Times*

When he sees Cassie Fenmore sneaking down the stairs of a fancy house, Cody Carter thinks her a tasty confection he can have for the asking—and ask he shall.

When she meets Carter on the Dodge City train, Cassie believes him a despicable blackguard capable of anything—like denying the two adorable urchins who claim to be his children.

When Cody and Cassie learn they are to share the inheritance of the Rocking C Ranch, they have no doubt trouble is brewing. But neither can guess that, when the dust has settled, all their assumptions will be gone with the wind—replaced by a love more precious than gold.

_3539-1 $4.99 US/$5.99 CAN

**Winner of the *Romantic Times*
Storyteller of the Year Award!**

Cool as a cucumber, and totally dedicated to her career as a newspaper woman, Maggie Afton is just the kind of challenge brash Chase McGarrett enjoys. But he is exactly the kind of man she despises. Cold and hot, reserved and brazen, Maggie and Chase are a study in opposites. But when they join forces during the Klondike gold rush, the fiery sparks of their searing desire burn brighter than the northern lights.

_3376-3 $4.99 US/$5.99 CAN

Winner of the *Romantic Times* Storyteller of the Year Award!

Storm Kennedy can't believe her bad luck! With six million acres of fertile territory open to settlers in the Oklahoma Territory, she loses her land claim to Grady Stryker, the virile Cheyenne half-breed she holds responsible for her young husband's death. And the only way to get it back is by agreeing to marry the arrogant Stryker and raise his motherless son. But while she accepts his proposal, Storm is determined to deny him access to her last asset—the lush body Grady thinks is his for the taking.

_3444-1 $4.99 US/$5.99 CAN